WOLF ROTTEN

WOLF ROTTEN

ASTERIA GONZALEZ

White Hart Press

WOLF ROTTEN

Published by White Hart Press, LLC

Library of Congress Control Number: 2025925098

ISBN (hardcover): 978-1-969610-00-4
ISBN (paperback): 978-1-969610-01-1
ISBN (ebook): 978-1-969610-02-8

First Edition: March 2026.

For the lost and the dreamers.

Empire of Atassia, Khtonyx

She the sidereal harbinger is the end. She who drinks deep of pain and decay, crushing the writhing, withering worms of the world below Her trod. The highest authority of the astral undying hunters, those whose hearts no longer pulse with mortal threads—the darkest depth, the brightest of teeth in the night. She shall descend again. When the prey is nigh and the wind sings, She will call forth from beyond, and you shall heed Her call.

— PASSAGE FROM OF DESPISED RYODIN

Chapter One
Hadrien

It was the night of a full moon, and so the hunt was on.

The silver face of Argento was round and perfect in the cloud-shrouded sky, casting its cold light down upon the forests of Atassia. Here, a beast born of an eclipse prowled; it stalked through the trees upon nimble paws, its curved talons leaving behind furrows that hopeful hunters tracked like glittering feathers from a golden goose.

The hunters wanted what anyone who entered these forests did: a chance at reaping a reward so magnificent they'd never need to work a day again. Most thought they wouldn't die out here. Their odds were good, they'd say. Odds were as good as the next hunter's. All they needed was an iron-tipped arrow and a strong bow.

Hadrien had seen the reports, late at night when he was meant to be planning his own next hunt. The Wild Moon Wolf was untouchable, but that didn't stop him from tracking its appearances. There were smaller, easier prey that Hadrien went after when he was assigned to, little glories. But the Wild Moon Wolf was a beast he dreamt of hunting one night.

Tonight wasn't that night.

Tonight wasn't even a night that Hadrien was hunting a beast of legend and lore. His prey was a different sort: the Blade of Dreams. Currently safe and secure in the possession of Lady Chiara, it was displayed within glass and gold in the hearth-lit drawing room of her villa outside Ferrugo. The crystalline blade was kept honed and polished to a brilliant shine.

Perched in the shadows atop the roof, Hadrien could see the sword through the grand windows. If he twisted and looked over his shoulder, he could peer into the dark of the forest where the Wild Moon Wolf might be roaming, if it was out tonight. A glimmer of a thrill flitted along his spine. What if the beast was in this forest tonight?

He both prayed it wasn't and hoped it was.

The Wild Moon Wolf had lurked around Atassia for a few years, as far as the reports said, and its reputation of fearsomeness preceded it. As of late, no full moon had gone without blood shed by its claws or fangs.

What a story that would be to tell the other Shadows, Hadrien thought.

Shifting his weight, he propped his chin on his hands and watched through the windows. The drawing room was still alight with warm amber firelight, the residents and guests, all clad in brocade-rich clothes, chatting away the hours of the night. Wine shone ruby-red inside decanters, clear crystal and elaborately faceted.

His mouth watered; he drew a flask from his jacket and tossed back a burning sip. The sun had sunk three hours ago, and yet the party inside wore on. It was for a birthday, given what he'd overheard earlier. His own birthday was tomorrow, and he doubted he would garner a party like this, let alone a well wish.

Nineteen.

The thought alone felt like an ocean pressing down on him. Hadrien withdrew the flask again, eyes on the party. A woman was laughing at something a man had said, hand flung to her chest. What was so funny, he wondered and then grimaced as something in his wrist pinched.

Brow furrowing, he rolled out his wrist. By all the holy bones, that tumble he took last hunt was still troubling him. Maybe he should have told the Arch Shadow so he could see the healer about it. But that would've meant admitting that he had lost the prey—a golden-coated unicorn that would've fetched a high price. Instead, he had claimed he'd never found it and had treated his injury himself.

Hadrien, rubbing at the joint of his wrist now, swore softly. The climbing he'd done to reach this roof had aggravated whatever injury was there. He could steal a few extra coins while he was in the house, then visit a healer before he returned to the House of Shadows. It sounded like a decent plan.

But as with many plans Hadrien made, it didn't turn out well.

The party inside the villa wore on for many hours. Hadrien fought to keep himself awake, jabbing his elbow into his thigh when his eyes slipped shut. It was barely enough to keep him from dozing and falling off the roof.

At long last, the view through the windows showed the guests sprawled out among the drawing room in various states of undress, all asleep. Given the myriad of empty bottles strewn about, they wouldn't wake for a while. Usually, that made for a perfect time to sneak in. But the sun was rising, and without the cover of darkness, Hadrien's job was going to be much harder.

He couldn't wait for night again. The Arch Shadow had a strict schedule she expected all the Shadows to keep to, whether they were hunting beasts or fetching items. Hadrien had to venture into the villa now, much as he disliked it.

Huffing out a sigh, he clambered down from the roof. The gentle light of morning dogged his steps as he slunk into the villa through an unlocked window. He crept through the halls past the ornate gilded frames of grand paintings and the elegant lines of sculptures carved like gods and monsters of old. Quickly, he made his way to the drawing room where the Blade of Dreams awaited.

Holding his breath, he tiptoed around the sleeping bodies. A floorboard creaked underfoot as Hadrien stopped before the display case. He winced, glanced about. No one stirred.

Hadrien slipped his fingertips under the lip of the lid and tested it. No lock. The hinges were blessedly silent. Holding the lid up with one hand, he reached in and eased the sword out. At his touch, the blade began to glow with the ever-shifting palette of galaxies.

The monumental branches of a maple tree, leaves vibrant with the bite of fall. Lights glimmered like fallen stars throughout the branches. Wind whispered among the leaves, and it sounded like the haunting music of faeries in a night-cloaked glade.

Hadrien jolted back, swearing viciously.

Someone groaned.

Hadrien grabbed the blade, ignoring the visions it pushed into his mind, and ran. He passed the empty frame of an Ianis Frame on a wall and faltered for a heartbeat. But no, Ianis Frames could be tracked, and the Arch Shadow would have his hide if Hadrien led Lady Chiara right to the House of Shadows.

Keeping the Blade of Dreams close, Hadrien burst out of the villa and sprinted for the edge of the grounds. A flurry of hounds cried behind him. His head swum; a headache pounded at his temples.

He checked the sky. The triple moons were nowhere in sight. A soft, pink blossom-blush tinted the eastern horizon. The forest should be safe for now from the jaws of the Wild Moon Wolf. Hadrien could flee through the trees without fear of the beast haunting his steps. Other beasts might be around, but it was a chance he'd take.

The hounds barked like glass shattering. His heart afire, Hadrien sprinted into the forest. The lingering darkness enveloped him. The trees here were ancient, towering and full of voluminous branches. The forest muffled his footsteps and the pursuing hounds.

He kept running.

And then he heard the tolling of bells.

He skidded to a stop, leaves kicking up. A stream burbled before him, so tranquil and normal, even as the sound of bells came again. These were no bells belonging to a church or to traveling priests; these were the bells of the hunt.

He needed to hide.

The peal of a bell rang out again.

Then silence.

And in the silence, he heard the rasp of breathing.

His eyes traveled to the forest across the stream. Three golden eyes glowed in the dark. A glimmer of moonlight shone off the curl of silver horns. His breath shot out.

The Wild Moon Wolf stepped out, branches and undergrowth rustling against its broad shoulders, liquid shadows dripping off the fur like wisps of blood in water. Hadrien could barely breathe. The golden eyes were upon him. He was going to die here. The bells tolled softly. The Arch Shadow would be so disappointed.

A hound howled nearby. The beast's hackles raised, and a growl like thunder rumbled in its furred throat. Before Hadrien could think to move, the beast leapt overhead in a single, effortless bound.

Paws alighted behind him, the ground trembled, bells resounded, and then the Wild Moon Wolf was disappearing into the forest.

His knees failed him; Hadrien dropped to the ground, his shoulders shuddering. But he had to rise, had to move before the beast returned. A distant, short-lived shriek prompted him. He pushed himself up, his palms gritty with dirt. The forest was holding its breath, the bells were ringing.

Hadrien fled the forest and vowed he would one day hunt the beast.

Chapter Two
Nox

I had been warned to never go near Isla Tower.

From the shore, the forested island appeared as tranquil as the moonlight-lined waters around it. But faeries were rumored to inhabit the island and the tower erected upon it. Some were little mischief creatures, prone to knotting hair and cursing shoes to always pinch. Others were more formidable, liable to glamour you and enchant you into dancing the days away until your feet bled and you wore your very bone away. The latter kind was what I had heard of.

Yet here I was, lurking on the shores across from the island.

I was about to break so many rules.

But I was prey again, and rules did not matter to prey.

I slung my pack over my shoulder, wincing as the movement pulled at the shoddy stitches on my arm. It had been a small wound received a few days ago in a scuffle with a hunter. But it wasn't healing. I checked the bandage—stained a hundred million different shades of red. Damn, it was *still* bleeding.

Whatever that hunter had tipped the blade in, it was something nasty.

With a glance around for the hunter, I slunk out from the cover of the undergrowth. Lights glimmered silver and gold on the island, spiraled high where they wrapped around the Isla Tower itself. I would need a way to cross the waters of the lake.

Despite the fact that the pact made it technically illegal to step foot on the island without prior permissions from the current ruler, I spotted a small dock with unguarded boats. I stole onto the dock, weathered wood creaking underfoot, and untied the glittering thread tethering a boat of curling filigree. I settled in the boat on a delicate bench and shoved the boat away from the dock with a massive leaf and twig bound in gilt.

The boat glided seamlessly over the waters, bringing me closer and closer to the island. I tried to think of what exactly I would say to the Exalted Queen of the Isle—if I could make it to her—but my mind came up blank. Merely a simple bargain, I told myself.

The scrape of the shore against the boat drew me out of my mind. I sprang out and dragged the boat further up the sand, eyes darting around for the watchful gazes of faeries. The shore here, past the small shelf of sand, was thick with lush, verdant undergrowth and ancient trees.

I left the boat secure on the shore and ventured into the forest. The island, I had heard, was more expansive than it appeared, but the tower was in the heart of it. As long as I walked a sure path, I would find it.

A breeze, soft and warm with spring's lingering heat,

swept by me. It stirred the leaves and my hair; it brought with it the scent of sunflowers and ripe, bursting plums and the lilting sound of distant flutes. My steps angled off the path I'd been taking, drawn to the sound like a moth to a flame, damnation or not.

I felt far from my bones.

So when the faerie melted out of the forest and took my hand in hers, I followed her as if she was the light I'd been waiting for my whole life.

Past trees older than empires and mushroom rings and herds of lilac-coated deer with illuminated bones, the faerie held my hand in a grip I couldn't break out of if I had wanted to. I didn't look around. I simply looked at her. She glanced back at me every so often; her features were hidden by a jeweled mask, but her eyes, brilliant and blue, gleamed from behind the mask.

The faerie took me to the center of the island, where the tower was. Faeries were gathered around the structure, sipping from goblets and spotted eggshells. A faerie, tall and tawny and tailed, offered an eggshell to the faerie leading me and then another eggshell to me.

I looked into the depths of the shell. The inside was coated in gold, filled with a honey-thick, ruby-red liquid. Syrup? I raised the eggshell-cup and sniffed it: sharp and bitter, definitely not syrup.

"Drink it," a faerie said.

All the faeries were looking at me.

"You desire to see the Exalted Queen, do you not?"

They knew.

"Drink it."

I tipped back the contents of the eggshell. It was hot at first, like any strong alcohol. Then it turned ice-cold in my throat. Something crunched in my hand. Shivering against the chill creeping over my whole body, I opened my clenched fingers; the eggshell was a shattered mess in my hand, glistening with red.

"Now," the faerie said, and I couldn't tell which said it, "you may see the Exalted Queen."

Brushing my hands against each other to clean them, I stepped towards the tower. The faeries parted before me, their smiles like knives under the masks and veils.

"Shadow," they hissed. "Killer of our kin."

Not a Shadow anymore, I wanted to tell them.

The other thing, I couldn't wash my hands of as easily.

I entered the tower, and behind me, the faeries began to dance to music that pulled at my veins like threads spinning out.

One step up the spiraling staircase, and my vision went sideways. I found slick surfaces under my palms, smooth and cool like the inside of a seashell. I ran my fingers over the whorls in the surface, the hundred million nautiluses forged into these stairs.

Distantly, I wondered what the faeries had given me.

I pushed myself up and started up the staircase again, more carefully this time. My hand on the golden horn railing—it curled like an everlasting, never-ending horn harvested from some great bighorn sheep—I wound around and around and around. Climbing in a circle that would go on forever.

Then the circle stopped, and with it, the staircase. I stood at the end of the staircase, blinking and trying to clear my spinning, spinning, spinning head. I knew what I was here for. The Exalted Queen.

I pushed my way through air full of sparkling motes that tickled as they brushed past my skin. The open door led into an empty room with only a window. Silhouetted before the window was a faerie with a crown shining upon her head.

The Exalted Queen turned, her eyes betraying no surprise to see me there. The crystals dangling from her gilded antlers quivered. Gold-painted lips opened, and in a mellifluous voice, she said, "You seek a bargain."

I nodded.

"It has been many moons since I granted a bargain. As you do not hold permission to walk upon this land, you will first complete a task for me."

I should have seen that coming. "What is it?"

The Exalted Queen held out her hand. From her fingers dangled the fine links of an amulet's chain. "Bear this to the cursed at the top of Domhan Arbre."

Domhan Arbre. I could find that and make my way there. "Easy enough." I reached for the amulet, but she didn't let go. I looked up, met her gaze. "Do I have to say a specific phrase?"

Her eyes were narrowed, focused, so wholly intent I wasn't sure she'd even registered my words. Finally, her fingers uncurled and released the amulet; I stepped back, coiling the amulet into my hands.

"I will know when you do as I have asked," the Exalted Queen said. She reached out her empty hand to me. "I will mark your hand so that you have safe passage through the fair lands across the world. They will know you are a ward of the Exalted Queen of the Isle."

When her fingertip touched the back of my hand, it was a lightning strike of pain.

I leapt back, clutching my hand to my chest. "What did you do?"

The Exalted Queen turned her back on me. "Return, and we will discuss your bargain then."

"But—"

She had returned to the pose she had been in when I entered: staring out the window at the forest below. The dismissal was clear.

Holding the amulet tightly in my fist, I hurried down the stairs and left the tower. The sharp light of dawn was slipping through the trees, and the faeries were nowhere to be seen. I supposed they were in homes somewhere on the island.

My pace quick, I headed towards where I'd left the boat. Domhan Arbre was in Brumais, right? It *sounded* like it was Brumesian. I would need to check a map and then cobble together funds to leave Atassia and set sail for Brumais—and quickly, too.

I shoved the boat into the waters and hopped in. It didn't take long to reach the dock. I tethered the boat to the dock and walked away, opening my fist to look at the amulet. It was astonishingly simple with a rose etched into silver, surely there was more—

Searing pain shot up my leg.

I froze, a pained cry faltering on my lips. A glance down told me what I had feared. I had stepped right into a trap. It hadn't been there before, I knew that much. Meant to capture a faerie or an animal, but I'd fallen for it.

Breathing quick through my nose, I knelt—the shift of my weight sent agony tearing through my ankle—and braced my hands against the ground. *Shit.* My vision was rapidly turning fuzzy.

The *pain*—I couldn't—I scrabbled at the jaws of the trap—there had to be a latch to get me out—something clicked—iron sunk further into my ankle—I screamed.

It didn't matter that the wound on my arm wasn't healing and would fester soon. This trap would keep me here until I died.

A branch cracked, and I knew my end was near.

My fingers caught on a slender pin. I yanked it free; the trap's jaws went slack. Whimpering, biting down on my lip, I pulled the jaws apart. Blood shone bright on the iron teeth.

Teeth gritted, I rose shakily. My vision swooped in and out, and the ground seemed oh so welcome. A tread, a whisper of cloth against undergrowth; my gaze snapped over to the hunter stepping out from the trees. The one who had been tracking me.

Fear bolted up my spine.

I leaned on my injured ankle, crumpled like a leaf under a boot. Bone-jarring, stomach-flipping pain shot through me. But I closed my hand around the trap. Blood had slicked it.

The hunter sauntered up. Boots crossed into my vision. "You," he said, "have been very troublesome."

I lashed out with the trap, swinging the teeth into the hunter's leg. He cried out, I lurched up and fell upon him. Beating, bashing the trap against limbs and joints.

Panting, I smashed the edge of the trap against his skull one more time. The hunter stirred. I hopped on one leg, a wounded animal, towards the dock. I could tumble into a boat and—

The hunter tackled me, shoulder colliding with my legs. A scream ripped from someone's throat—mine? I snapped my boot against the hunter, shoved and clawed away. Dug my fingers into the dirt and wood and pulled myself along. I could taste the blood on every breath, knew that I was leaving a trail behind my dragging leg.

A long groan and a scraping of stone. "She said you were trouble," the hunter muttered, "but the Three Mothers only know." A boot landed square on the wound, and I spat out a curse. "Stop *fucking* moving."

The cold bite of a blade settled against the back of my neck.

I fought to throw my head back because no, no, Mothers Three no, I was not going back there, and the hunter clucked his tongue, moved away the last chance I had to escape. "You can't die just yet." He reached down, jerked my arms behind my back, and bound them. "You have plenty to pay for. Death is too easy for you."

It was over.

I let my head thud against the dock.

"It's time for you to come home, Nox."

Chapter Three
Hadrien

His flask was empty.

Hadrien stared into the depths of the flask, tipping it this way and that. He could have sworn he filled it before the last time he slept. A frown tipped his mouth down. When *had* he last slept?

Before he stole the Blade of Dreams, that was certain. Which had been multiple days ago. Hadrien pressed his fingers into his temples. That explained why his eyes had been aching and straining to pick out details for the past twelve miles.

At least, he thought, staring unseeingly at the door knocker crafted into a grinning gargoyle, *I'm back at the House of Shadows.*

Hadrien opened the door and crossed the threshold. The dimness of the entry soothed the ache of his eyes. If he was lucky, he could take a long nap before he had to report to the Arch Shadow.

But luck had never been with Hadrien.

The Arch Shadow was waiting in the hall that led to

her office, her face unreadable. "Heir," she said, "you're late."

He was late? He really wished his flask wasn't empty now. "I brought it." Shrugging the sheath that held the Blade of Dreams off his back, he held it out to the Arch Shadow. "Here it is. No one saw me take it."

The Arch Shadow accepted the sheathed sword. "You're two days late."

"I…" Hadrien trailed off. Struggled to pick the right response. "I'll send word next time."

"There won't be a next time."

He was glass, about to shatter.

His mouth opened. Closed. He couldn't think of words to say, to convince the Arch Shadow to let him keep his position as the Heir. This was all he had; he was nothing without this. He choked out, "I'll do better."

"Better? Better like when you failed to face the Chimera of Chalybos and cost me more than you can ever repay?"

Words failed him.

"Go to your room," the Arch Shadow said, like Hadrien was twelve and a pouting child.

Hadrien was left staring agape at where the Arch Shadow had stood, the door to her office now closed off to him. His fact hot, he looked around. No one had seen that, right?

Two other Shadows were in the drawing room just down the hall, frozen, their eyes on him. Their dropped jaws indicated they had heard everything. They were sure to tell all the other Shadows that the Heir had been scolded by the Arch Shadow and was about to be kicked out. They would say what a failure he was.

Tension built between his gritted teeth. Hadrien ducked his head and walked fast to the stairs. His boots pounded against each step. He burst onto the landing for the third floor and stalked down the hallway, scuffing the back of his gloved hand against his brow. He was nothing but a damn failure. He'd lost track of time. He had been late. He wasn't good enough.

"Hadrien!"

He faltered to a stop.

Xenna stood on the stairs, her fine brows drawn together. As always, she looked suitable for an audience with the emperor, wearing white that set her dark skin to glowing. Her hazel eyes held a bright gleam, turned nearly gold by the lantern light like her beaded bracelets and the makeup lining her eyes.

Xenna ascended one more step. "Where were you?"

"I had a job near Ferrugo." He indicated the book Xenna held, darkened leather with gilt flowers sprawling across the cover. "What's with the book?"

"Oh, something for Rook. It's her birthday today. She said she likes poetry from Mallina, so I found this." Xenna gave the book a doubtful look. "I'm not too keen on poetry myself, but I suppose it's fine."

He wondered if Xenna even know that his birthday had come and gone. The girl, a year or two older than him, had been quick to introduce herself to Hadrien and take on the title of friend—tentative as it was, still—when he joined the Shadow Guild, but it wasn't as if he had been here long. So he said nothing except, "Tell her I wished her a happy day."

Xenna lingered on the stairs. "Some of us are taking

Rook to the tavern tonight, if you'd like to join." She said it like she already knew the answer.

Hadrien offered his friend a small smile that weighed a thousand pounds. The answer was there. Xenna just shook her head, her own smile rueful.

"See you around, Hadrien."

Hadrien stared long at where Xenna had stood before turning and continuing towards his rooms. There was a sour taste in his mouth. Xenna had known that Hadrien wouldn't agree to go with the others to the tavern. Was he that predictable? Was he that much of a recluse? If he was kicked out of the Guild, would anyone even notice he was gone?

Too many thoughts plagued him as he unlocked the door to his rooms. A note fluttered on the door. Tally marks were lined up below a question. *Odds that the Wild Hunt killed the Heir?* There were far more tallies below the Wild Hunt, imaginary though they were, than his name. He was certain Xenna hadn't seen this; she would have torn it down.

Crumpling it in his fist, he shoved the door open and guided it shut behind him. His eyes drifted up, settled on the initials carved in the doorframe. *NV.*

The Shadow who had been the Heir before Hadrien. His mouth twisted. Whoever they had been, they wouldn't have left such a trail of missteps in their wake. Their own Guild wouldn't have bet on a children's tale against them.

Then again, they had tried to kill the Arch Shadow, so perhaps they were not such a great example of a pinnacle Heir after all was said and done.

Despite his shortcomings, Hadrien had not made egregious mistakes akin to that.

Hadrien leaned his forehead against the door, wanting nothing more than to sleep for a week or until the exhaustion fled his bones.

A bleary voice said, "Who are you?"

Hadrien whirled, eyes flying wide. There was someone here. A girl, around his age. Sitting in one of the four chairs that Hadrien had arranged in the drawing room. Bleeding all over one of those chairs, staining the leather irrevocably.

"You're getting blood on my chairs," Hadrien managed.

"Your chairs?" She tipped her head to the side, cobalt eyes not quite focusing on him. Sunlight gleamed off a silver ring in the top of her left ear, half-hidden by dirty onyx-hued hair. "These are my chairs."

"Your chairs?" Hadrien realized he had mimicked the stranger, and he quickly added, "I'm the Heir of the Shadow. These are my rooms, this is my drawing room, and those are *my* chairs."

The stranger laughed once—then bared her teeth in a grimace. "You don't get it, do you?"

Wondering how this stranger had gotten in his rooms with the door locked, he shook his head. "I don't know you."

"Oh, but you know of me."

"No, I don't."

The stranger frowned. "They don't tell tales of my horrible, horrible misdeeds? Consider me disappointed."

Hadrien dared to move away from the door. A bottle of Brumesian cognac waited for him in his bedroom, and he needed a glass of that and a nap. This stranger was between him and that.

"Then why don't you tell me who you are? And why you're in *my* rooms?"

"Isn't it obvious?" She tilted her chin up, gaze sharpening to be steady and cutting. "You're the current Heir of the Shadow. I—" There was the slightest upturn to her mouth, like she was finding amusement in the situation. Crooked smile, crooked nose. "I'm the former Heir of the Shadow. What better place to keep me until my death than in the place I once lived?"

His pulse tripped. Beat faster. He swallowed hard. "Nox," he got out in a strangled voice. "You're Nox."

"Smart boy."

"You tried to kill the Arch Shadow."

"Well, they do tell tales of me after all." Nox pointed at Hadrien in a wondering way. "You, though, you I have never heard tales of. You're new. You weren't part of the Shadow Guild when I was. So you *must* be new. What is it —six months? Four months? A week? How long have you been a Shadow, and *how* did you get the title of Heir so quickly?"

Hadrien didn't know how to respond.

"Little new Shadow," Nox mused, "taking on a title."

She's delirious, isn't she? She's bleeding all over the chair and floor. He ventured closer but kept a chair as a shield between him and the former Heir. From here, he could see that she was resting one foot gingerly on the floor, and the ankle looked like it had been chomped on by some large beast.

"What happened to you?"

Nox blinked slowly. Then her brows drew together in

a scowl that didn't quite function as a scowl. "Have you ever stepped in a bear trap?"

A shake of his head.

"I have. I don't recommend it."

What a strange girl. As Nox gazed at the wall where a map of Brumais hung, Hadrien gripped the back of the chair, trying to push aside the cold unease. He got the feeling Nox wasn't seeing the map. Maybe Nox was seeing what she had once hung on that wall.

The former Heir of the Shadow was here. In Hadrien's rooms. Injured and bleeding and out of her mind.

This was a nightmare.

Hadrien strode into his bedroom, retrieved the bottle of cognac, and poured a slosh of it into a tumbler. He held out the tumbler to Nox.

"Fancy," Nox muttered.

But she took the tumbler and sniffed at the amber liquor inside. Her nose wrinkled. The scar running over her right eye scrunched, too. Shutting her eyes, she knocked back the drink.

Hadrien drank straight from the bottle while Nox wasn't looking. The necklace resting against Nox's sternum had seized his attention. It was strange, as strange as her, a large jawbone that was most decidedly lupine with silver etchings flowing across the bone. She had one finger resting on it, like it was a pulse point.

Finally, Nox opened her eyes again, and they settled on Hadrien. "You know, you should see a healer."

A flicker of anger. He grabbed onto it and held tight. "No, *you* should." Hadrien shoved the cork back into the bottle. "I'm not the one bleeding all over everything. You need to leave."

"I have my own orders from the Arch Shadow. Stay here and wait." Nox considered her ankle. "Maybe I'll be dead before she remembers I'm here."

What was he supposed to do? Leave? Drag Nox outside? Ask the Arch Shadow what was going on? No, Hadrien couldn't do that. He couldn't give the Arch Shadow any other reason to kick him out.

Cursing this entire day, Hadrien thumped down in the chair. "Fine. Stay here. But you need to wrap that wound up before you get blood elsewhere."

As if to spite him, Nox flicked her wrist, and he watched in horror as blood splattered on the floor.

He fetched bandages from the washroom and dumped them unceremoniously in her lap. "You're cleaning up all the blood."

Nox held up a roll of bandage and considered her wounded ankle. "You expect me," she said slowly, her deep cobalt eyes pinning Hadrien in place, "to wrap an injury caused by a bear trap. According to you, a little cloth is going to fix this. *This*. I have broken *bone* bits stuck in my flesh."

A shudder rolled through his shoulders—*That's disgusting*—and Hadrien held up his hands. "Spare me the details. I'll get the healer."

If he was lucky, the former Heir would be dead before he returned.

Chapter Four
Nox

The moment the Heir fled, I leapt out of the chair.

Leapt was entirely wrong.

I fell in a heap. The movement jarred my injury; fresh blood bloomed hot. Cursing, casting a furtive glance at the door, I wrapped my ankle in a length of bandage to soak up the blood.

Most of the drawing room, I had noticed, was the same as I had left it. This new Heir hadn't made these rooms his, had he? I was hinging on that.

I shuffled along the floor into the bedroom. The more I saw of the quarters, the more hope fluttered like a trapped bird in my chest. The lavender sprigs in a violet ceramic vase that I had made as a child by the window, the deep navy blankets on the bed with an ouroboros embroidered in golden thread, the blue Ianis Frame with gilt flowers at each corner, those were all *mine*.

I reached the bookshelves near the window and paused, panting. A scoff rasped out of me. These books. Even these were mine, though I noticed one shelf was full of books that weren't mine. Why had this new Heir not rid the quarters of my belongings?

Running my fingers along the floorboards, I found the small notch. *Please be there.* I wedged my finger into it and worked a cut-out of the board free. My breath whooshed out in relief. In the small alcove revealed, there was a bundle wrapped in leather, nestled among the velvet lining. I withdrew the bundle and swept back the leather; my knives were still there, glittering in the sunlight.

I traced the hilts. Thank the Mothers Three these were still here.

I selected one knife and slid it into a sheath strapped around my wrist. After smoothing my sleeve, bloody and muddy, over the sheath, I replaced the other knives and the floorboard, hiding the alcove.

I turned and found myself face to face with a leggy wolf. I froze, fully aware of how vulnerable I was with my wound. The wolf was like none I'd ever seen in my nineteen years: a coat of russet red with inky black climbing the long legs, huge ears, watchful amber eyes. This wasn't a usual wolf of Atassia.

"You're fine," I said quietly, "I'm not here to hurt you."

The wolf sniffed the air, one ear flicking back as if hearing something in the hall. The Heir. Shit. I needed to get by the wolf and back to the chair.

I pushed myself up slowly, gritting my teeth against how my leg quaked. The wolf's lip curled, a silent snarl. It wasn't far to the door. I shoved off of my good leg. Collided with the doorframe. Whirled around to see the wolf sitting and watching me.

Keeping my eyes on the wolf, I returned to my chair.

The injury from the bear trap was throbbing with my elevated pulse. A sigh heaved out, and I dropped my head into my hands.

"Stay over there," I told the wolf, peeking at her between my fingers.

Of course, the wolf didn't.

The wolf padded out and investigated the tip of my boot. I watched her warily. Surely, her shoulders alone would come up to my hip if I stood by her.

The door opened, and the Heir stepped in. "Zira," he said, "leave her alone."

I tipped my head back and considered the Heir.

His voice had been what I first noticed when he entered the room earlier.

He had a low, quiet voice that sounded like it would be perfect for soft, whispered words at midnight. I should not be thinking that. I certainly should not be thinking that I wanted to hear his voice again, and I wanted to hear him say my name, if only to hear how he would utter it.

But now, with my head a little clearer, I saw the rest of him.

My attention went to his eyes first. He had dark paint around his eyes like warpaint, smudged and faded around the edges. It was a darker shade of blue-grey than his irises, and in the darkness of the warpaint, his eyes glittered like my knives had. But it didn't quite hide the scars that surrounded his eyes like starbursts.

I realized I was staring.

I narrowed my eyes and raked my gaze up and down him. Tall. Taller than me, built more like a statue in the gardens of Sidero, all languid and long lines, than a hunter like I was. Olive skin, light though it was, signaling that his family was from here. His hair, a deep brown and gilded with sunlight, was tied back from his face in front but the rest left loose to brush the nape of his neck, a traditional style for men around here. He held one wrist in a possessive manner, his gloved fingers wrapped around it. It was injured. Just as injured as that look in his eyes.

He wasn't the Heir.

He couldn't be.

"What?" the Heir snapped, but his voice lacked much bite. "Why are you staring at me?"

"Because your beauty is that the poets speak of."

A flush stained his cheeks faster than I could blink. He turned his face down and buried his fingers in the ruff of the wolf. "The healer will be here soon."

"What's with the wolf?"

The Heir ruffled the wolf's ears. "Zira. She's a maned wolf I rescued from some carrion birds in Borrasca when she was a pup."

That was… sickeningly sweet. How was this boy a Shadow, let alone the Heir of the Shadow? If he couldn't walk by an abandoned pup, how could he kill a beast of legend?

The Heir glanced at me for the barest flicker of a heartbeat. He vigorously scratched his maned wolf's long shoulder; strands of russet fur floated into the air. "What's with the jawbone?"

Out of reflex, I closed my hand around the jawbone hanging against my sternum. The teeth dimpled my palm. "It's mine."

"I assumed so," the Heir replied. "Why do you wear it?"

Wish, o dreamer mine.

Hush, Lupakaria. "I—" A knock on the door interrupted me. "Looks like your healer is here," I said, thankful for the distraction. *Lupakaria, I owe you nothing for that.*

Fine, she groused. *But you do owe me cheese later.*

The Heir opened the door and let the healer in, a short figure in voluminous black robes. Black to hide the blood, like Xenna used to say with a grin.

"Take care of her first," the Heir said, pointing to me.

I raised my gaze to the endless void that was within the healer's hood. No discernible face was within. "It's the ankle. Stepped in a bear trap. Then there's a cut that won't heal on my arm. I think the hunter poisoned the blade."

The healer motioned to the Heir and said something too low for me to catch. The Heir hesitated, then approached. "While the healer prepares things, I'm to take your boot off."

My mouth went dry. By the Mothers Three, I needed to get a hold of myself. The Heir was just a boy, a boy who had replaced me. It was the blood loss clouding my focus.

His fingers were slow on the buckles of my boot. "This didn't stop that trap at all." Before I could protest, he flicked a knife out and cut the leather. "It was ruined already."

He wasn't wrong, but that didn't stop me from leveling a hot glare at the top of his head as he worked the boot off. I hissed when the leather pulled away from the wound.

The Heir paused, staring at the damage the boot had

been hiding. I heard him swallow. He set the boot aside before saying, "I'm supposed to cut away the pants, too. And the sock, I guess."

The sock was blood-soaked and disgusting. I almost felt bad that he had to ease it off. That quickly vanished as the Heir slid his knife under the cuff of my pants. I shivered. Gritting my teeth, I forced myself to watch him in case he decided to take the opportunity and slice a tendon. The back of the knife scraped softly against my skin with each saw of the blade.

The Heir paused again. "Don't kick me."

"I make no prom—you *ass!*"

The Heir, in one swift motion, had ripped away the cut pant leg. Blood welled up instantly in the parts where the threads had been woven into the wound. I touched my lip gingerly; scarlet dotted my fingertip. I'd bitten it.

"A little more warning next time," I muttered.

"I hope there's never another time." The Heir rocked to his feet and walked away, taking the ruined and bloodied materials with him. He returned with a basin and towel and then retreated into his bedroom, door shut.

Zira remained in the drawing room, eyes on me.

The healer knelt by my ankle and ran careful fingers around the edges of the wound. I said nothing, and the healer said nothing, and so it was in silence that the healer began the slow, painful process of cleaning up the wound. I was glad the Heir wasn't here to witness how I screwed my eyes shut and dug my teeth into my lip. Or how my hands gripped the chair arms in tight, white-knuckled claws. My heart hammered in my chest like a rabbit running from a wolf.

At some point, I passed out.

When I woke, the healer had tied a neat bandage around my entire lower leg with splints for support. I hadn't broken it completely, had I? The healer shoved a small glass bottle into my hands. I recognized the smell instantly. Grace Breath, meant to expedite the healing of severe wounds. That explained the bandage and splints then; there was only so much Grace Breath could do immediately. It would likely be at least a full day before I could walk without lingering pain.

I worked the cork out and downed the Grace Breath. It fizzled in my mouth and tasted of blackberries. I ran my tongue over my teeth. The last time I'd had this, it had tasted like strawberries and peaches.

The healer checked the wound on my arm, then began to clean up the supplies. I twisted my arm and ran my fingers over the skin through the slice in my sleeve. Healed, smooth, and like it had never been damaged.

"What did the hunter use on the blade?" I asked.

"Badger's Blood," the healer said in a whisper.

"Thank you."

I wondered if it would've been better had the wounds drawn me into death, however slow it might have been.

The healer knocked on the door to the Heir's bedroom. When it eased open, the healer entered, and I was left alone with the Heir's maned wolf pet. I glanced at Zira, and she climbed to her paws. She sniffed at the bandages on my leg; her lip curled back.

"It's not going to smell good," I told her. "Stop sniffing it."

She nudged at my hand, once and then again, more insistently. Closing my fingers around the item she'd dropped into my hand, disconcertingly damp, I scratched the top of the maned wolf's head. Zira shifted around and leaned her whole body against the side of the chair, her skull pressing into my fingers. Was she supposed to be any sort of vicious?

I stayed there, scratching the maned wolf as she seemed to like it, until the Heir and the healer appeared again. The Heir no longer gingerly held his wrist. He was busy tugging at the cuff of his left sleeve, pulling it down to cover—I tipped my head to the side—the telltale black ink of tattoos sweeping across his forearm. Then his sleeve was down, and I couldn't see what the design was.

Absently, I rubbed at my own tattoo: a draconic ouroboros encircling my right wrist. Then I stood, only to promptly stumble when Zira leaned her full weight against my leg. I had been right; she was a towering beast, and her shoulders rose above the height of my hip. When Zira padded over to the Heir, I realized the truth of the height difference between us. Zira's shoulders were level with the Heir's hips. The Heir had to be at least half a foot taller than me.

My eyes narrowed. I did not like that.

Still.

If it came to a fight, I bet I could take him.

The Mothers Three knew that the Heir was taller, but height wasn't everything. Even if it did allow him to reach more shelves, I thought sullenly as I watched him pluck a coin purse off the top of a bookshelf without any trouble.

With payment in hand, the healer left, and the Heir considered me. "At least you won't bleed to death on my chair now."

"Don't put it past me," I muttered. Pain was filtering up my leg; I lowered myself into the chair again. The

Grace Breath needed to kick in fast. "Run along now," I told him, biting my words out, "tell the Arch Shadow I am still alive." *Tell my mother—no, right, not my mother.*

Nostrils flared. Then the Heir turned on his boot heel and strode out of the room. The door was wide open, and I gazed at the familiar sight of the hall for a minute.

I didn't have long.

I uncurled my fingers from around the item Zira had given me. The amulet from Isla Tower. My eyes slid over to the maned wolf. "Why were you carrying this?"

And the Mothers Three strike me down, Zira replied, "The Exalted Queen bade me."

"You *talk?*"

"Why would I not?"

A million reasons but: "Are you a faerie?"

Sitting and kicking one massive paw against her neck, Zira said, "Why would I be?"

"I'm hallucinating," I said. I closed my fingers over the amulet. Resting my head on the back of the chair, I shut my eyes and mumbled, "Grace Breath normally doesn't do this."

It struck me then that the Heir might have paid the healer off to add a hallucinogen into the potion. Maybe he had. Or I had finally, truly lost my mind.

I wouldn't wait for the Heir to return.

I walked out of the Heir's quarters, not even noticing the limp dragging at my steps or Zira's barked warning. I felt so far from my body, far enough that I didn't feel so much as a flicker of fear when I approached the door to the Arch Shadow's office. I paid no heed to the stares and whispers of the Shadows, they were no more than flitting birds to me.

My hand on the door. Light spilling into the room, cutting across the night-born blade on the wall. Eyes gold and cold alighting upon me.

Before she could say a word, before the Heir could tell me to leave, I spoke.

"Hello, Skota," I replied, and the flicker, the falter, in her expression was worth the hell I had been through. My mouth turned up in something sharp and clever, as sharp and clever as she had taught me to be. "Didn't expect to see me again, did you?"

Then she smiled, and her smile was far worse than mine had been, was, could ever be. "Hello, dear Nox." Gesturing for me to approach, she added, "How lovely it is to see you whole and hale again."

What was fear but this?

"I'm pleased to welcome you back to the House of Shadows."

I couldn't draw in a breath. I raised my hands and wrapped my fingers around the Jaws of Lupakaria. The bones hummed gently under my hands. Like in a dream, I crossed the threshold into the room, and the door eased shut behind me.

A bleak little room with no windows. The sole source of light was a pair of lanterns affixed to the walls, casting light upon the sleek surface of the desk and the bitter edge of the sword displayed upon the wall behind her chair.

The Heir shuffled a few steps away, his hands twisted behind his back.

The Arch Shadow's eyes locked on the Jaws. But a haze glossed over her eyes, and she looked away without a remark. She poured tea into a cup carved from a unicorn horn. "Sit, both of you."

Reality was filtering back into my mind. I sat, folded my hands across my lap like I didn't care. A pretense to hide the trembling in my fingers. My mind was sharpening again, the Grace Breath taking the blur of pain off.

I was Nox Vis, former Heir to the Shadow.

I knew how to play this game.

Chapter Five
Hadrien

The room was stifling.

Hadrien could have cut the tension with a butter knife. The Arch Shadow was looking at Nox like she could kill the girl with a look alone. Nox, for her part, was leaning back in the chair, her gaze unerringly on the Arch Shadow—unerringly, except for a quick flicker up to the displayed sword.

The Arch Shadow caught it. "Such a well-crafted Amaranthic blade. I found it abandoned in the catacombs of the Caerulei Apici mountains. It's a shame that its owner didn't take better care. Blades like that are meant to be treasured." The words were pointed like the sword itself but held no meaning for Hadrien.

"Perhaps the owner didn't mean to lose it," Nox replied.

"Perhaps," the Arch Shadow said, her voice the chill of winter's bite. "You grievously injured one of my best Shadows."

"Did I now?"

Hadrien was nothing more than an observer to this conversation. He was a bird on a windowsill, eyes bright and head cocked. His wrist itched. He covertly rubbed his thumb against it.

The Arch Shadow drank long from her tea. "I gave you everything, and you repaid me with a blade in my back."

Nox said nothing.

"I suppose it is fortuitous that my Shadow finally was able to bring you home. As you can see, I appointed Hadrien my Heir in the aftermath of your horrid betrayal. However, he is not quite adept at being my Heir."

Before Hadrien even had a moment to realize exactly what the Arch Shadow had said, the leader of the Shadow Guild was continuing, "So. I propose a challenge."

She flicked a paper onto the desk; it skidded across to Hadrien and Nox. Splashed across the page were words written in thick black strokes and edged in gilt. At the bottom was the looping, languid signature of the emperor and the imperial signet stamped in sapphire blue wax.

Neither Hadrien nor Nox reached for it.

"The Emperor of Atassia is holding an official hunt for the Wild Moon Wolf, as it has scared away too many hunters in recent months with its repeated killings. These hunters would otherwise bring in revenue from common beasts like griffins and jackalopes. Once, hunters traveled from afar to try their hand at felling the beast; now it only serves to empty his coffers of coin. Hunters must register as a pair for this Wild Moon Hunt. You two will sign up, and whoever brings me the head and heart of the Wild Moon Wolf will be named my Heir."

One last hunt, Hadrien thought. The Wild Moon Hunt, in fact.

He had been thinking of what it would be like to hunt the Wild Moon Wolf, to track its prints and stalk it through shadowy forests, just the other day at the villa. And now, he was hearing that he would hunt the beast alongside the former Heir of the Shadow.

Could he keep the title, after all?

Could he erase every misstep and falter with the death of one beast?

His thoughts awhirl, he barely listened to the rest of what the Arch Shadow said. A sanctioned hunt, a race between different pairs, a single month to win it. While the winning purse would diminish with each passing full moon, the absolute minimum purse was still enough for a lavish year of life.

"Remember, there are some who would consider this *beast* sacred, blessed by the Moonsworn. They may try to stop you. Don't let them fool you. This is nothing more than an unholy monster. And I will have its head upon my wall and its heart in my grasp."

The Arch Shadow dismissed them, and Hadrien took the paper with the imperial words on it. The door to the office closing behind him, he ran his thumb over the ridges of the signet. Nox pinched the top of the paper and slowly wiggled it out of his hand. She ran her eyes over it, the cobalt of her irises a more brilliant blue than the wax.

Hadrien frowned. Nox had said such a strange thing earlier. A trace of heat blossomed across his face as he remembered it. The former Heir must have said it with the intent to embarrass him because there was no other reason for her to have. Rude. The Arch Shadow had never taught Hadrien such an underhand tactic like *flirting* for setting his opponent off-kilter.

He could try the same tactic. He opened his mouth to say something, but Nox happened to glance up and meet his gaze, and he rushed out, "Your eyes are imperial."

Nox arched one eyebrow. "My eyes… are imperial?"

This was not going to plan. "B-blue."

"Blue." Nox considered Hadrien for a long moment, unblinking. "You aren't very good with your words, are you?"

Hadrien grabbed back the paper and started for the stairs. His face was afire. He was *never* trying that again, and he swore to disregard everything the former Heir said for the rest of time.

And then he heard something that made him freeze, one boot planted firmly on the first stair. Xenna, asking, "Who are you?"

Hadrien whirled and watched Xenna walk over to Nox, who had pulled a hood over her face. Before he could think better of it, he called, "She's new. I'm supposed to be training her."

"Well, tell your new apprentice that she needs a Shadow medallion." Xenna tugged at her own. "Someone might kick her out of the House otherwise."

"I'll be sure to do that." As soon as Xenna was out of sight, Hadrien motioned to Nox and hissed, "Hurry up."

The former Heir kept her hood up until they were on the third floor. Then Nox slipped it back, revealing her tired face, and said, "I have a medallion already."

He glanced at where the medallion would rest, if it was there. "I don't see it."

"If I had my knapsack back, I'd have it."

He fumbled in his pocket for his key. Where was it? He found it in the other pocket—strange, he never put it there—and unlocked the door to his rooms. "You can have that back before we leave. We need to sign up for the hunt."

"We also need a plan." Nox brushed past him, sprawling across a chair.

"Wait for the next full moon. Find the Wild Moon Wolf. Trap it. Kill it. Done." Even as Hadrien said the words, something cold and slick slunk through his stomach. But no. The Wild Moon Wolf was just another beast to hunt and bring down.

"That's not a plan. That's a set of objectives. Besides, the next full moon is tomorrow night, and the hunt doesn't officially start until the beginning of the new month."

He brought out his flask, remembered too late it was empty, and sighed. "I'll figure it out." Heading towards his bedroom, he tossed over his shoulder, "Don't leave."

Maybe he should lock the door, but it wouldn't make a difference to someone trained by the Arch Shadow like Nox had been. Maybe he should—No, that wouldn't work either. Short of binding their wrists together by cuffs, Hadrien didn't see a way to keep the girl there. For now, he'd have to assume that the threat of whatever the Arch Shadow held over Nox would be enough.

Hadrien grabbed the bottle of Brumesian cognac and didn't bother with a tumbler. Three deep sips burned down. He pinched the bridge of his nose, massaged his temples. What a day it had been.

Sprawling out on the chair by the bookshelves, he unbuckled his boots and vambraces. It was the safety of his room; he rolled his sleeves up to his elbows. On the inside of his left forearm was the latest addition to the tattoos on his whole arm. On the inside of the right, scars.

He tugged his sleeves back down. No one needed to see any of that, not even himself, and certainly not the former Heir sitting in the other room. His steps softened by socks, Hadrien padded to the door, cracked it open a hair, and peeked through the sliver.

Cobalt eyes stared back.

He yelped a curse and startled back.

Nox only barked out a laugh, though it was clear as day that there was no mirth in her. The girl had a chipped canine tooth on the left and a scar arced over her lips there. She held out one hand, palm flat and open. "Give me the paper."

Opening the door more, Hadrien tried to adopt a relaxed pose and leaned his elbow against the doorframe. "I'm still reading it."

"I was the Heir of the Shadow longer than you've even been a Shadow, boy. How many hunts have you gone on and succeeded in?"

His moment of hesitation was too long.

"You've see those trophies downstairs, I trust. The Three-Headed Sun-Lion of Kryzia, the Manticore of Bone and Flesh, the Skallya of the Southern Sea, those and more were my doing. I have hunted among these forests and hills for years, and my name is known to the beasts themselves. They tremble and quake when I am near, for they know I never lose my prey." Nox jabbed a finger at her chest, pointing back at herself. "I am the one who will craft the plan to trap the Wild Moon Wolf."

"If you're so good, then you don't need the paper."

In hindsight, maybe it wasn't the best idea to antagonize the former Heir of the Shadow.

Nox snarled like a wolf, scars rippling, and slammed her palms into Hadrien's shoulders; he stumbled back, nearly lost his balance. Steadying himself, fists flying up, he struck back at the former Heir. But he didn't account for their height difference.

She ducked easily. Lunged forward.

Hadrien hit the floor hard. "Shit," he gasped out. Nox was sitting on his ribs, one hand planted in the middle of his sternum, the other drawn back in a fist. "Get off me, you lug, I can't breathe."

"You don't understand," Nox said lowly. "This is not a game. Do you know what you hunt?"

"Beasts." Simple.

"Beasts. And cursed souls."

Hadrien frowned. "What?"

"Did you ever look at what lay under their skin once you had trapped them, slain them? The ones with the strange eyes and the impossibility of their appearance?" Her eyes glimmered bright. "They were something else once."

Nox paused, then said, "Humans. Faeries. Others. Cursed souls."

Memories slammed into his mind like a lightning strike. His stomach flipped suddenly, bile slicked the back of his throat. "Get off me."

Nox didn't move, and Hadrien bucked his hips up. The former Heir lurched forward, off-balance, and he latched onto her wrist and rolled. Now Nox was under him, and Hadrien had his weight pinning her. Her arm was still in his grasp, in a twisting, pinching hold.

"You got something wrong, *Nox*," Hadrien said with as much venom as he could draw from his heart, "and it's that I don't fucking care what's under the Wild Moon Wolf's pelt. Beast, human, faerie, or other, I don't care. The Wild Moon Wolf will fall at my hand, one way or another."

Then he climbed off the former Heir and pointed to the door. "Pack your things. We leave at first light."

Moving at the pace of a glacier, Nox stood. She was favoring her injured leg again. Hadrien winced inwardly. Of course the injury had been aggravated by this scuffle. Stupid, it was all so stupid.

Nox didn't leave yet. "You forget I don't have my things anymore. I'll need some if I'm to be your partner for this hunt."

His heart seized. It was with bitter cold in his voice that he replied, "You aren't my partner, and you never will be."

This time, Nox left.

Hadrien woke in the night.

His heart hammering like a thousand drums of war, he sat up and kicked away the blankets twisted around his legs. He put a hand to his neck, felt his pulse thrumming against his palm. His breath swept out.

It had only been nightmares.

Hadrien, careful not to move fast, leaned over the edge of the bed. Zira was curled up in front of the door, where she had been when he fell asleep. As for the former Heir… the spot between the bed and the wall was empty.

He leapt out of bed and lunged for the door.

"Shh."

A shameful squeak slipped past his teeth.

"You'll wake the wolf," Nox whispered.

"Why," Hadrien asked, keeping his voice quiet, "are you not sleeping?"

"Can't sleep."

It was so honest, so plainly spoken that it drew him up short.

Not being able to sleep was something he knew all too well. He settled on the edge of his bed, adjusting the long sleeves of his nightshirt. A rusty patch marked an old bloodstain. He shifted it out of sight.

Nox was in the chair by the bookshelves. Moonlight, mostly golden from the near-full Little Sun, cut across the book open on the girl's lap. Not long ago, Hadrien had stood guard while Nox washed and dressed in clean clothes, mostly because he didn't want the former Heir getting dirt and blood over the furniture anymore. She was still in those clothes, like she was ready to leave at any moment.

"So you're reading instead of sleeping," he said.

"And you're waking from nightmares."

"We all have things in the shadows we'd rather not speak of."

Nox considered him with eyes struck gold by the light of Little Sun. "Perhaps," she replied, and she sounded so much like the Arch Shadow that it sent a shiver down his spine. And it reminded him who exactly he was talking to. "You should try to not have nightmares while we are on the hunt."

Hadrien scoffed. "You say that like it's easy."

Nox's smile was a glint in the dark.

In the silence that followed, he saw flashes of the nightmare again. He shuddered and disguised the involuntary reaction by crawling back under the blankets. "Go to sleep."

But sleep eluded him, and Nox never did sleep either.

Chapter Six
Nox

I TRIED to stifle my yawn as I waited for the Heir of the Shadow to leave his bedroom. The night had passed in agonizingly slow minutes, marked by the turning of pages. I had found my copy of *The Dragon Knight*, a tale about a spellsword who traveled with her dragon familiar to rescue rare beasts of legend, and reread it through the night.

It was the sort of book the Arch Shadow would've thrown out had she ever found it—for who could ever befriend a dragon? Those were targets of the hunt. Why the current Heir had not tossed it aside was beyond my wondering.

A Shadow had brought my knapsack by earlier. Nothing was missing, and I had slipped all my knives, retrieved from the hidden niche in the dead of night, into the pack.

The Heir opened the door and said without preamble, "You have some leather armour pieces here in the wardrobe: vambraces, vest, boots. Take them. Do you know how to use a bow?"

"Not my style."

"I'll carry a bow, then." The Heir paused in reaching for something out of view. "Where did you get that sword?" His voice was low with dread.

I glanced at the sword strapped around my hips. "It was always mine."

"That's the sword you… you used when you tried to kill the Arch Shadow."

"Eclipse."

The Heir flattened his lips. "Hand it over. You can have your armour but no weapons."

I held his gaze. "What, pray tell, do you think will happen when we encounter a beast? You will guard me as though you are some knight and I a lady in distress? I'm no lady, and you are no knight."

"Thanks," the Heir muttered, "I'm so glad to know that's how you see me." He shook his head. "Fine. You get your weapons but only once we are out of the city. Get your armour now."

I brushed past him into the bedroom and pretended like he wasn't there while I brought out my armour. It was dusty and stiff, the extra set I'd commissioned when I was the Heir. I buckled the vest on over my shirt, let my fingers drift over the scales patterned into the vermillion-dyed leather. It had taken me three golden unicorn horns to pay for all the armour, not to count the young dragon I'd slain for the leather. Well worth it.

"Interesting armour," the Heir said when I turned towards him. His brow furrowed slightly, and he appeared deep in thought, but he didn't add anything.

"It's dragon," I replied.

The Heir smoothed his gloved hand over his own leather vest. His was dark brown, but lacked any patterning aside from the stitched nightshade flowers along the edges. Where the shirt under his vest was cream-colored, mine was the color of thunderclouds. He'd been wearing a jacket similar to his vest earlier, but now it was draped over his knapsack. "You must have hunted it yourself, didn't you?"

"Indeed I did." I stilled. "Someone is at the door."

"Don't talk."

"You can't hide me forever."

The Heir shot me a withering look before he left the bedroom. His steps strode to the door. "Xenna."

"Hadrien," my oldest friend replied, and I edged closer to the open door, keeping out of sight. "I heard you're taking your new apprentice on a hunt."

The Heir's sigh was audible. "The Arch Shadow has ordered it. I'll be gone a while."

Xenna's steps wandered closer. "Are you taking Zira?"

"I... I haven't decided yet." The door to the hall closed softly. The Heir walked around, moving further into the drawing room. "She should probably stay."

"Where's your apprentice? I haven't officially met her yet."

Disregarding what the Heir had said, I stepped out of the bedroom and tossed Xenna a grin. "It's a lovely day, isn't it, Xenna?"

There was a moment of stillness, and then she was crossing the space in quick strides. I tensed a heartbeat before she embraced me. But no, this was Xenna, Xenna who would never slide a blade between my ribs. I wrapped my arms around her and closed my eyes.

"I knew she lied." The words were quiet, treasonous. Dangerous words to utter in the presence of the Heir.

I pulled back. "Xenna."

"I knew you weren't dead." She gripped my shoulders, looking into my eyes like she could see the past and the truth of it. Her eyes were bright with tears. "While—while you were... away—"

"Rogus died," the Heir said suddenly, the words rupturing forth from him like a hawk's talons sinking into a rabbit. "He died on a hunt."

I looked to Xenna to deny this, but she only nodded, her chin quivering. I slipped out of her grip. This was too much. My hands clutched at the Jaws.

You can have him back, you know. Lupakaria's purr wrapped around my ears, slunk through my mind, sinuous. *You only need say the words.*

Stop it. I forced my hands off the bone and down to my sides. I lifted my chin. "Well, Heir of the Shadow, shall we leave?"

"Nox," Xenna started.

I didn't want to hear more. "Just tell me where he was buried."

There was a small pause; I didn't look at anyone.

Then Xenna said, "The body was never recovered."

My inhale was long, slow, and agonizing. Rogus was dead. He'd never had funeral rites. He was dead. I didn't know when he had died. My fingers twitched.

"Nox," Xenna said, and this time it was a word of warning.

It was the Arch Shadow's doing.

I knew it was.

She had sent him on a hunt too dangerous for anyone, and he'd been sent alone. Sent to his death at her order.

"Nox."

I snapped my head over to Xenna. Her expression was soft, the trails left by tears shining on her skin. She stepped closer and placed her hands on my shoulders again. She said nothing this time. She couldn't. The Heir was standing right there.

I forced my lungs to expel the air I'd been holding captive.

Xenna nodded and mouthed, *"Good."* Then she stepped back, scuffed her hand over her face, and laughed weakly at the streaks of golden, glittering kohl smeared across the back of her hand. With a smile that rang as false as the so-called dragon skulls sold in the day market, she added, "Travel safe, you two."

My eyes cut over to the Heir.

"Nox, stop sizing him up like you're going to start a fight. Play nice."

It was easier to hide behind a veil of aggression. "I never play nice."

Xenna rolled her eyes. "I expect both of you to return from this hunt." She crossed the room to embrace the Heir, and I noticed that she handed a small box to him. The Heir looked at it like he had never seen a box before.

Curiosity seized me. I wanted to know what was in that box. Was Xenna sweet on the Heir? That could be a possibility. But last I'd been around, Xenna had been exchanging playful smiles with a quick-witted traveler from Skogia.

The Heir stashed the box into his knapsack and gave Xenna a nod before walking out of the room. I followed silently. Behind me, I heard the door close. I glanced back; Xenna wasn't there, so she must be in the Heir's quarters. Maybe there *was* something between them.

I passed a Shadow on the stairs. Thoughts of the Heir and Xenna swirled away, replaced by thoughts of Rogus. I would never see him on these stairs again. I quickened my steps, catching up to the Heir and nearly pushing past him.

"In a hurry?" he asked, glancing down at me.

Mothers Three, I hated how much taller he was. "Yes," I replied and opened the door leading out of the House of Shadows. Bright sunlight beamed against my eyes, and I squinted. "Do the Shadows still keep their horses at the old stables?"

The Heir nodded.

A thought crossed my mind. Just a dash, a flicker. But it was enough to spark the hope that the Arch Shadow had brought back my horse after she left me for dead.

"You are walking very fast," the Heir muttered. His strides lengthened. "And I only now realized I will have to find you a horse. The Arch Shadow has a few extras. I'll have you take one of those for this hunt, but you have to return them after."

The closer we drew to the stables, the faster I walked. The sounds of horses drifted out from the stables, nickers and snorts and the stamp of hooves. I crossed into the first aisle and began checking the horses in each stall. Some pricked their ears at me, others swished their tails in irritation, but none were Embra.

"The extras are this way," the Heir said. "Where *are* you going?"

I darted into the second aisle. The Heir huffed and

followed, mumbling things to himself. I passed more and more stalls, faster and faster, but then there she was, a coal-coated horse with fire-toned eyes. Embra. I hurried to her and let her sniff my palm before running my hands over her head.

The Heir slowed down. "That's the Arch Shadow's horse. You can't take her."

My blood felt suddenly afire. "She's *my* horse."

"Yours?" The Heir looked at Embra, his brow furrowed. "No, she's the Arch Shadow's new horse, one of those revered ones from Ostitha. The Arch Shadow got her six…" He trailed off, and I could see the realization strike him. "Months ago. Oh."

"This is Embra," I told the Heir.

"I'm sorry, but you can't take her." The Heir shifted his weight. "Take one of the others for now. Maybe you can have Embra back after the hunt if we're successful."

Maybe it would be better if Embra was here in case the hunt went wrong. I forced my head to move in a nod. "I'll—" I fell silent at the approaching footsteps.

The Heir eyed the Shadow walking up. "What is it?"

"The Arch Shadow said for you to take Ikarus and Embra for your hunt."

"Message received."

The Shadow jogged off, and the Heir turned to me. "Well," he said, "I suppose you are taking your mare. Her tack is in the tackroom. I expect you know where it is. Tack up and meet outside. Be quick about it."

I slid back the latch on Embra's stall. Embra shuffled back a step, and I moved in. My gaze raked over her, searching for signs her health was poor. But her coat was gleaming, and in the shifting rays of sunlight, dapples of health shone in the black. Her eyes were bright and like the embers I'd named her after. Despite everything, the Arch Shadow had been taking good care of her—or some lackey had.

Embra pushed her nose against my chest, and I couldn't stop the smile that broke across my face. The world was solid under my boots again. I had Eclipse and Embra back, I had seen Xenna, and she was alive and well, and Rogus was—

The smile dropped.

"He's dead," I told Embra quietly.

Then I left and retrieved her grooming kit and tack. I tried to fall into the familiar routine of brushing her coat and picking her hooves. But my thoughts were on Rogus. On how he would smile so broadly and easily. On how he was gentle and kind, even when dealing the last blow on a hunt. Death was a mercy at his hands.

My fingers stilled on the last buckle of Embra's bridle. I couldn't see. Breathing out a shaky sigh, I wiped at the tears. It was time to leave, and it was time I packed thoughts of Rogus away.

"You're late," the Heir said when I joined him.

"Barely," I replied.

"Enough." He climbed into the saddle of his gelding, a buckskin with a star and a snip. "This is Ikarus. Watch out, he kicks."

Ikarus whisked his tail, the strands snapping.

"Just keep him away from her." I clambered atop a mounting block and settled into the saddle. "We can reach Sidero by midday tomorrow."

The Heir clicked his tongue at Ikarus, and he set off in a long walk, ears pricked. Embra raised her head, muscles tensing under me. I pressed my heels against her; she walked after Ikarus and the Heir like fire was under her hooves.

"When was the last time you were out?" I muttered.

Embra calmed by the time we reached the road that we would follow up to the turnoff before the town of Chalybos. The Heir glanced back at me, then motioned for me to go in front. Likely so he could keep an easier eye on me.

Giving Ikarus a wide berth, I sent Embra into a trot and led the way through the cypress-lined road. We passed farms and villas of various sizes, groves of olive trees and citrus trees, fields of lavender and wheat. A gentle breeze swept over us as we crested a soft hill; clouds scuttled along through the bright blue sky. It was a picturesque, sun-soaked day in southern Atassia.

I hated that I was spending it under the Arch Shadow's thumb again.

The Heir let out a sigh.

I looked at him before I could stop myself.

"It's pretty," was all he said.

And we continued.

The sun was high in the sky when we passed through a small town. The Heir called up to me to stop, and I guided Embra off the main road.

"We need to decide where we're stopping for the night," he said. Ikarus pinned his ears and snapped at the air. "Stop it, you temperamental ass." He checked the reins, backed the gelding up a step further from Embra.

"We should stop near the turnoff." I flicked my gaze around the town. "Too busy here." I wasn't sure how many people believed I was dead and how many still held grudges. "The horses are fine. Let's move on."

With care, I brought Embra back onto the main road and started for the opposite end of the town. It was as if everyone had decided to clog the road at once. I patted Embra's shoulder, whispering soothing words as a group of riders trotted past.

I heard the Heir swear and then snap, *"Hey!"*

I twisted in time to see Ikarus, ears flat against his skull, kick out at a passing horse. The Heir cursed soundly at the other riders; Ikarus danced and tossed his head. Squealing, the other horse skittered away, tail tucked tight.

With no warning, Embra jolted into a choppy canter. I slid the reins between my fingers, tightening them, and angled her away from the cluster of horses and travelers. I half-halted her, small pulses on the reins, until Embra slowed with a tremendous snort.

I halted Embra fully. "Was that necessary?"

Turning in the saddle, I searched for the Heir and Ikarus. They weren't far behind me. Travelers, on foot and horseback alike, had moved to the other side of the road. Everyone was skirting around the Heir of the Shadow and his buckskin gelding. His scowl was visible from here.

The Heir caught my eye and urged Ikarus forward. "Son of bitch," he muttered, "getting so close to us." He sighed and lifted one hand from the reins to rub at his temple. "I should have tied the red ribbon around his tail before entering the town. Ikarus despises other horses crowding him."

With that display, I would've never guessed. I left the dry remark unspoken. "If he's fine, then let's move on."

The sunset was casting red and gold stains across the hills and trees when the Heir decided we should stop for the night. He picked the top of a hill with a broad beech tree at its crest. There was a farmhouse not half a mile back, but the Heir hadn't wanted to ask for lodging for the night.

I cast a quick glance at him; he was setting out hay for the horses. He straightened up and backed away from them, then he swept his fingers through the air. A wolf shimmered into being. I startled, and the wolf turned silver eyes on me.

"You have an Ink," I said.

"Her name is Astre Noir," the Heir replied, watching the wolf with her impossible coat of midnight blue bound away. "She will scout for danger in the surrounding area."

How convenient for him and inconvenient for me. I began to set out my bedroll. "I never had one."

The Heir frowned. "Danger?"

I blinked. Was he serious? "No, an Ink." I situated my knapsack at the top of my bedroll and rummaged around for the smaller pack of food within. "I don't have an Ink. Wasn't born with one, and unless the Moonsworn herself decides to grant me one, I'll die without one."

The Heir stared at his knapsack. Then he held out a wedge of wrapped food. "Cheese?"

I couldn't say no to cheese. The Heir sat down cross-legged near me and laid out food on a plaid blanket. A sharp orange cheese highlighted by chives, a small loaf of crusty bread, an apple with a shining red exterior, and an assortment of dried fruits. I added another apple and a bundle of round grapes.

It was nearly laughable. This was like a picnic. But instead of a pleasant picnic, it was one with the boy who had replaced me and had been chosen by the woman I thought was my mother.

I took a slice of cheese and nibbled on it.

"I'll keep watch," the Heir said, sawing off a hunk of bread.

"You can't stay awake forever," I replied. I considered throwing a grape at him but ate it instead. "Just how are you going to ensure I stay here while you sleep?"

"I could hobble your mare, tie your hands, or have Astre Noir keep watch."

"Inks only stay active an hour."

"Then I'll only sleep for an hour."

"That will end in disaster."

The Heir pointed the dull knife at me. "You got a better plan?"

I carefully laid slices of cheese and apple atop a piece of bread. "The Arch Shadow will hunt me down if I do not comply. She has already proven her Shadows can find me. If she wants, she will use Xenna against me. Friends are leverage—weakness—in her eyes."

"She wouldn't kill Xenna. Xenna's one of the best Shadows."

There was so little he knew. So little he understood.

I ate my cheese and apple sandwich slowly. Different responses swirled in my head, each worse than the last. Finally, I told him, "Believe me when I say that I'm not going to let the Arch Shadow harm my friend. I'll be here in the morning."

The Heir considered me. "If I wake up and you're gone, you will regret it."

"Consider me warned."

"And I will bind your hands."

"Whatever helps you sleep better at night, princeling."

He scowled. "Don't call me that."

I'd hit something sensitive. I couldn't tell yet what it was. Stowing that information aside for later, I said, "Get to it then. I'm ready to sleep."

The Heir stifled a yawn.

I made a show of settling into my bedroll and closing my eyes. I heard Astre Noir return on quiet paws and the Heir dismiss her. The Heir then laid out in his own bedroll, grumbling to himself. He stopped moving soon after. *Beginner's mistake,* I thought.

I counted down the minutes.

With a glance to make sure the Heir was asleep, I slipped out of my bonds and into the darkening evening.

CHAPTER SEVEN
HADRIEN

HE WOKE to the tolling of bells.

His eyes shot to where Nox had been asleep. Empty. She was gone. *Again.* The bells were close. Hadrien snatched up his bow and quiver. He'd find her later.

For now, the Wild Moon Wolf was near.

Ikarus snorted and tossed his head, but Hadrien jogged right past the gelding. He descended the hill in a rush. Furrows in the dirt had caught his eye. Kneeling, he touched his fingers to them and breathed out a quiet word of wonder. Claw marks from the Wild Moon Wolf.

With a quick flick of his fingers, he summoned Astre Noir into being. The starlight wolf peered up at him. "Track this," Hadrien said in a low tone and pointed to the claw marks.

Astre Noir sniffed at the marks, then shook out her coat and loped off. Hadrien gripped his bow and ran after, his strides light and springy. This, this was what he had been waiting for. A chance to hunt the beast of highest legend in Atassia and to prove himself.

He *was* the Heir of the Shadow.

Astre Noir circled back, her eyes glowing silver in the night. Her pricked ears meant she'd found something. With ground-eating strides, she led Hadrien across the hills and stopped at the banks of Fluvius Argentus. The river swept by with white-capped currents. Hadrien knew if he fell in, he would drown.

His eyes skimmed the surface of the river. The Wild Moon Wolf's tracks led into the mud at the bank on this side but didn't reappear on the other. The beast was far too large to be carried away by the current.

Golden moonlight bounced off the waves. Hadrien eased closer. He crouched in the mud and dipped his fingers into the water. The current hissed and foamed around rocks in the middle. If the tracks ended here, at the bank, and Astre Noir was staring intently at the river...

The curve of ram's horns broke the surface.

By the Three Mothers.

This was his chance to win. Now. Before the hunt truly began.

Hadrien struggled to notch an arrow on his bow, his fingers trembling. A single bell tolled, resounding in his bones. The arrow fell, tumbled to the mud.

Water and shadow cascaded off the Wild Moon Wolf as it stood. Moonlight streamed over its shoulders, turned the fur, black as spilled ink, into gilded oil. The three eyes fixed upon Hadrien, and a snarl pulled at the beast's lips. It was missing a canine tooth, but the three remaining were more than enough to rip his throat out.

Astre Noir growled.

Hadrien ran.

Pure, primal fear flooded his veins, lent fleetness to his legs. Behind him, the Wild Moon Wolf let out a howl that shook the very moons. Sounds of scuffling and snapping teeth chased after Hadrien.

Where could he hide?

The full, damning golden face of Little Sun was still high in the sky. Too many hours of night left to run from the beast. Astre Noir couldn't fight the beast forever either.

He charged up a hill and paused at the top. Panting, he scanned the night-doused landscape. There was a farmhouse about a half mile back from the campsite, but he'd never make it. He needed something closer.

His eyes snagged on the straight lines of a wall.

Something like that.

He skittered and slid down the hill and tumbled through the grass at the bottom. Scrambling up, he found his hands empty. Where was his bow? Shit, the bells were tolling again; the beast was on the move.

Hadrien dashed for the wall. Through the dark, a roof became visible. His heart soared. A roof meant a building, meant shelter, meant safety from the Wild Moon Wolf.

The bells rang closer.

His whole body turned cold.

Breathing hard, he skidded around the corner and into the open space. His eyes darted about. One wall—two, three. Three walls wouldn't keep out the beast.

His eyes settled on the statues, one at each wall. Three women carved from polished olivewood, all the same height and build.

One with a simple iron band round her head, one

with gilded laurel leaves crowning her brow, one with thorns and berries ringing her head.

One held a pair of scales and a spool of thread, one was forever extending her hands to the believer, one bore aloft a spear in one hand and a sickle in the other.

One with a mask divided between smooth youth and wrinkled age, one without eyes and smiling benevolently, one with a silver skull beneath a veil of lace.

Mother Fair.

Mother Grace.

Mother Death.

The Three Mothers.

This was a temple.

His breath slipped out. Hadrien startled at a tolling bell and hurried to hide behind Mother Grace. His boots creaked as he crouched. He fought to still his breathing. His eyes fixed on the ground, his hand gripping the hilt of a dagger.

The bells tolled closer, the thudding steps of the Wild Moon Wolf slunk nearer. Hadrien dared a peek around the statue, and in the gloom, the hulking form of the beast approached. Shadows and mist coalesced around it; its three golden eyes, glowing like focused lantern-light, were fixed upon the small temple.

The Wild Moon Wolf halted at the threshold. It swung its head low and sniffed at the ground. Then its eyes fell unerringly upon the statue of Mother Grace.

It knows I'm here.

This was no mere beast. His body shook, and he was relieved no one was here to see the terror that overtook him. For the Wild Moon Wolf, there was a reason it had evaded capture and death. It was smart. There was nothing mindless about it.

The Wild Moon Wolf raised one paw, sniffed again at the threshold of the temple, and backed up a step. Hadrien furrowed his brow. It wasn't the height of the structure preventing the beast from entering; it was… it was the nature of the structure itself.

An unholy beast could never cross into a holy space.

With a sigh like the heavens breaking, the Wild Moon Wolf settled on the ground outside and rested its head upon its death-bringing paws. It was going nowhere for now.

Hadrien gripped his dagger tighter and slumped against the wall. His eyes stayed on the beast, took in the details of it that he could make out in the dark.

The Wild Moon Wolf gazed back.

A shiver went cold down his spine. There was something truly haunting and terrifying about seeing the Wild Moon Wolf's eyes looking back at him. The fabled beast of the woods and night, right there.

Hadrien stood.

His legs threatened to give way with each step.

The Wild Moon Wolf raised its head, ears swiveling forward.

He stopped in the middle of the structure, one hand empty, one hand twisted behind his back with a dagger hidden. Surrounded by the statues of his deities, Hadrien faced the Wild Moon Wolf.

The beast let out a low snarl.

His boldness fled in a single stuttering heartbeat, and he cowered behind the statue of Mother Grace again. His bones were trembling in his skin and flesh. The dagger clattered to the ground, his grip loose like he'd been struck on the head. He could hear the breathing of the Wild Moon Wolf, the faint ring of bells as its sides moved with its exhales and inhales.

Focus on anything else, he snapped at himself. *The Three Mothers. Isn't it odd that Nox calls them the Mothers Three? I haven't heard anyone else call them that. Nox is strange.*

And then, unbidden: *I wish she was here.*

That was a terrible thought. A damning, horrible thought. That thought could never appear again. *Think about anything else. Not the Wild Moon Wolf, not Nox. Think about tomorrow. The sun will rise. You will go to Sidero and sign up for the hunt.*

And then it's only five days until the new moon.

Hadrien curled his arms over his head and didn't move until the bells tolled with the rising sun. He peeked between his arms. The soft pink of the sunrise showed that the Wild Moon Wolf had vanished. His skin shuddered. The beast had laid there all night, watching him.

He had the uneasy feeling it would remember him when the next full moon rose.

His lost bow in hand again, Hadrien staggered back to the campsite, his steps dragging with the realization that he'd have to explain to the Arch Shadow how he had *let* Nox escape.

This was his grandest failure.

He was going to be stripped of his title, kicked out, left to rot—

Nox was standing at the crest of the hill.

Hadrien stumbled to a stop, his jaw going slack. Then he stormed up to her. "You," he snarled, "you left. You said you wouldn't."

"I *said* I would be here in the morning." She didn't look away from him. "It is morning, and I am here."

"I needed you last night."

Nox blinked. "You… needed me."

"I—" His face flooded with heat. Embarrassed heat. A true Heir wouldn't need anyone. "I meant that I hunted the Wild Moon Wolf last night. It was a full moon, and I was so close, I could have killed it."

"Why didn't you?"

He opened his mouth to reply, but his voice faltered. *I was too scared.* "It ran. The sunrise, it was near."

Nox didn't look convinced. "We should leave for Sidero. It's not far."

A glance towards the horses showed that Nox had already tacked up her fire-eyed mare, but Ikarus wasn't tacked up. Hadrien found himself saying, "Give me a few minutes, then we'll leave."

As he buckled Ikarus' tack on, his lack of sleep made itself apparent in fumbling fingers. Hadrien swore quietly and shook his head. *Wake up.* Out of sight of Nox, he dug out his flask and downed a sip. The bite of cognac was enough to jar him into the present for now.

But as the day wore on and the sun stretched towards midday, his eyes slipped shut again and again.

"Hey!" Nox barked.

Hadrien jolted upright.

"You're falling asleep," the former Heir said with a scathing bite in her voice. "How long were you out hunting the Wild Moon Wolf? You should have never tried to hunt her without me."

Tired as he was, Hadrien's mind latched onto one thing: *her.* "Her? The Wild Moon Wolf is female?"

"A right old bitch is what she is."

"How do you know this?" Hadrien halted Ikarus and rubbed at his face. His breath tasted sour; he tried to wash it down with a mouthful of cognac, but it didn't help. "I've studied the reports of the Wild Moon Wolf, and no one has ever said anything like that."

"You could call it a close call."

He considered Nox, the way she was scowling against the sun's light. "So you've come across the Wild Moon Wolf before."

Nox, not responding, played with the reins.

Huh. "You failed to trap her." *Nox Vis, the great Heir of the Shadow herself, has her own failures. Are we not so different?*

"Let's keep going." Nox urged her mare on.

"No."

She glanced over her shoulder. "No?"

"You're going to tell me what you know first."

A shake of her head. "We need to sign up."

She's right.

Hadrien turned his gaze to the road that wound up the large hill to the city of Sidero. Assembled on the slope of a hill, it rose in layers like one of those decadent cakes Xenna liked on her birthday. White marble shone at the top, a pristine ornament to crown the russet-tiled roofs and cream-stuccoed walls below: the palace of Sidero itself.

That was where they were headed.

When Nox sent her mare into a canter, Hadrien followed, his thoughts still treading a path around his sleepless night hunting the Wild Moon Wolf. He'd see her again, and he wouldn't fail then.

Chapter Eight
Nox

I HADN'T BEEN in Sidero in more moons than I could remember.

It was an expansive, layered city. I'd heard the Heir mumble something about a cake when we crossed under the gates, and he wasn't wrong. The city of Sidero was akin to a cake. If cake was inedible and made of stone and stucco and marble.

Pushing aside thoughts of delicious vanilla cake studded with strawberries, I guided Embra around a cart full of rolled rugs. The markets in Sidero sprawled across multiple levels, never quite contained to one area, from what I remembered. It was a good city to get lost in. I cast a glance over my shoulder at the Heir. Or to lose someone in.

The further we rode, winding up narrow streets and past shops and houses alike, Sidero drained of color. The markets dwindled. Statues began to appear, always three at a time: the Mothers Three and their respective iconography.

"Nox," the Heir called, "wait up."

I halted Embra at the side of a fountain in a small square. While I waited on the Heir, I examined the fountain. A man with the antlers of a stag tipping out a never-empty urn, from which the water flowed. A god of old.

What would it have been like to walk the lands of Khtonyx when those gods did?

Lupakaria laughed, a rasp of breath in my ear. *It is not near as beautiful as you picture, o dreamer. It was beauty; it was death. My kin, felled; my kin, apotheosized.*

I looked away from the statue of the old god, and my eyes fixed upon the doorway to a cathedral for the Mothers Three. Gods and deities and the endless distinctions between.

"You need to slow down," the Heir said, Ikarus' hooves clattering to a stop near me. "It's easy to get lost here—*Hey,* were you trying to lose me in the streets?"

I couldn't lie. "Yes."

"That's rude." He frowned, but there was something sloppy about his frown. I'd seen him drinking from his flask all morning long, here was the result. But he didn't sound angry or even aggrieved. Just hurt. "You can't lose me."

Mothers Three, I wish I—

YES, A WISH.

Shut up, Lupakaria.

I will if you make one wish. A tiny wish. You could wish for a storm! Or a piece of cake, one with sweet cream and strawberries piled high.

I'm not making any wishes right now.

You're no fun.

And you're a dead wolf goddess I am stuck with.

Lupakaria huffed.

The Heir was looking at me with his brow creased. "What are you doing?"

"Thinking," I replied in a rush.

"About?"

"Cake."

The Heir went, *Hmm.* He clicked his tongue at Ikarus, and the gelding pushed off into a long walk. The red ribbon braided into his tail flashed with each stride, a bright warning to avoid him.

I kept Embra a good distance behind Ikarus the remainder of the way to the palace grounds. A discordant screech reached my ears. The Heir sent Ikarus into a trot, climbing the slope; they disappeared over the top. Embra and I reached the flat level a moment later.

The grounds leading up to the palace.

My breath slipped out.

I had never been up here.

A wide path led straight to the palace itself, a marble monolith bordered by columns and painted with starscapes, the heavens themselves. Vivid grass flourished on either side of the path, broken by gentle walkways and a flowing stream. Olive trees and citrus trees bloomed, their branches heavy with their bounty.

"This is…" the Heir trailed off, his eyes following a bejeweled bird. "What is that?"

It spread its long tail feathers, displaying a multitude of hues and a pattern like eyes.

A peacock, Lupakaria told me. *You can blame my sister for those. She grew tired of the Hundred-Eyed Guard and turned him into the first one. Now his hundred eyes are in the plumage.*

"It's a peacock," I told the Heir and left off the rest.

The peacock screeched—again.

"It sounds hideous."

"It looks pretty."

A soldier approached, dressed in leathers dyed the imperial blue of Atassia. "Shadows," he said, "the registration for the Wild Moon Hunt is at the western end of the plaza. I am happy to escort you there."

I had the feeling he wanted to keep us, dirty from travel, away from the rest of the palace grounds. The Heir dismounted and led Ikarus after the soldier. I did the same, mostly to get a better look at the peacock. It eyed me with suspicion and then screamed; I hurried away.

At the western end of the plaza, there was a table covered by a grand gold-and-blue cloth. A pair of soldiers stood behind it, flanking a woman with a quill and scroll. Other hopeful hunters milled about, some strapped down with more weapons than I could count, others dressed like they were going to talk the Wild Moon Wolf to death.

I hung back while the Heir moved forward to sign us up for the official, emperor-approved Wild Moon Hunt. There were familiar faces in this crowd. People I'd crossed and cheated when I was the Heir out on hunts. I kept my hood up and my head down.

There was one face in particular I had glimpsed.

Artem of Revskia, the Heir to the Bear, the inheritor of a Guild burnt and destroyed. He stood at the table, speaking with the scribe. I hadn't needed to see his face to know it was him. His brown hair was cut short, the telltale designs shaved into it. He wore the same jacket I remembered: azure velvet with silver buttons.

Artem turned, and his eyes settled on the current Heir of the Shadow. Artem said something with a sly curve to his mouth before walking away. He was joined by a man I did not recognize, a tall, broad-shouldered blonde man. He wasn't from here. Too pale in skin tone to have benefitted long from the bountiful sunshine of Atassia, and that aside, he had heavy furs around his shoulders. Maybe a Bear, maybe one that had survived the annihilation of the Guild.

But still… what's Artem doing here? The Bears were mercenaries, not hunters of legend and lore like the Shadows. I scratched at Embra's shoulder, pretended to be preoccupied with her tack as Artem and the man strode past. I angled my head, caught a glimpse of the ring that confirmed this indeed was Artem: a silver bear's head with chips of amber for eyes.

So Artem was here, and he would be competition in the hunt.

The Heir of the Shadow returned, Ikarus trailing behind him. "We can leave now. We're registered; you're under a false name. There's no full moon until next month, when the hunt officially starts, but—" He dropped his tone, and in that lower, quieter register, his voice was like honey. "—there's no reason we can't set up traps now."

It was laughable.

"You think a trap will stop her?" I lowered my voice into a whisper, spun my words into a secret. "You know what will? A certain weapon."

The Heir's eyes lit up. "I knew you knew more. Tell me, where can we find this?"

I shrugged.

He dragged his teeth over his bottom lip, gazing off at the palace. "Domhan Arbre," he said finally. "We'll take an Ianis Frame to Brumais and visit the libraries of Domhan Arbre."

My luck was turning.

At Domhan Arbre, I would find the cursed, and I would deliver the amulet to them as the Exalted Queen had requested. Then I could slip from the Heir's sight and return to Isla Tower to bargain with the faeries.

Or you could wish, Lupakaria purred.

You're more dangerous than them.

It is all a matter of perspective, little wolf.

I blinked, brought myself out of my conversation with the dead goddess, and realized the Heir had started down the long path we'd come up. I followed, and as I walked, I began to plan.

Until the Heir stopped outside a bakery, his expression pensive. He tied Ikarus' reins to a post and motioned at me.

Was he serious?

I tethered Embra far from Ikarus and stepped into the shop after the Heir.

"You mentioned cake," he said, looking more animated than I'd seen him all day, "and I decided I wanted some." His eyes turned brilliant and bright as he looked upon the cakes and pastries and desserts in the glass cases. Meandering closer, slowly, as if the desserts would flee if his steps were too loud, he added, "I've heard the lemon cakes here are something of legend."

"I'm partial to this one." I gestured to the round case with a full, beautifully decorated vanilla and strawberry cake in it. Swoops of pale pink icing went round the sides like waves, and slices of strawberry lined the bottom edge like guards with shields. Strawberries were piled on top, some covered in dripping chocolate.

The baker, smiling, said, "We're famous for our orange cake." He pushed forward a short, single-layer cake with a spiraling pattern of orange slices on top. "You two appear to be travelers, am I right? We also have a variety of muffins and scones that will keep for a few days on the road."

My mouth watered. "Heir, we have time for tea and cake."

"For certain." He didn't sound like he would disagree for anything. To the baker, he said, "I'll have a slice of the lemon cake and a small slice of the orange cake."

There was a chocolate cake that looked and smelled divine, but I had been thinking about the vanilla and strawberry one longer, thanks to Lupakaria. I pointed to it. "A slice of that, please."

"And a pot of black tea for the table. Cream and honey, too. Thank you." The Heir paid, and the baker handed him back a few coins in change. He thanked the baker again.

I picked a table where I could see the door and keep my back to a wall. The Heir hesitated before sitting across from me. He folded a napkin carefully on his lap. I dropped mine in my lap and sized up the other people in the bakery. No one looked like a threat.

A boy brought over a tray with the tea and cake slices upon it. The Heir murmured a polite thanks and waited until the boy was gone to pour himself a cup of tea with far more honey than I expected.

I moved aside a small vase of marigolds so I could reach the teapot better. I added cream and honey to my cup of tea, but it was far too hot for me to drink comfortably yet. I speared a strawberry off my plate and ate it. Strawberries were unmatched by other berries, I decided. When paired with a mild vanilla cake and sweet cream, there was nothing better.

In my peripheral vision, I saw the Heir scoop up a forkful of orange cake. I stilled. His attention was solely on the dessert; he didn't even seem to remember I was there. He put the cake in his mouth, the fork turned over and resting against his lower lip. His eyes closed, his face relaxed. What a strange way to eat.

I dropped my gaze back to my cake and absently crafted my next bite. My thoughts were on him, though. He looked so different when he wasn't frowning or furrowing his brow. Every time he did that, I wanted to reach over and smooth out his forehead with a gentle stroke of my thumb. Just so his expression wouldn't freeze like that forever.

He removed the fork and tried the lemon cake. His fork rested again on his lower lip as he savored the flavors of the dessert. The tines dragged slowly across his lip, pulling it down slightly, catching on the curve. For someone who frowned so much, he had an appealing face.

The Mothers Three save me, was I really thinking that? He was the Heir of the Shadow. He was the boy who had replaced me. The boy who was my competition. He was as off-limits as could be.

The Heir's eyes dashed up, as if he felt my thoughts, and locked with mine. His lips parted, and he said, "Stop looking at me like that."

The words held so much bite and venom that I nearly

flinched. I forced nonchalance onto my face and shrugged. "Like what?"

"Like you…" A flush reddened his cheeks. "Like you're *looking* at me."

That explained absolutely nothing. I stared at him, eyes narrowed. "Don't flatter yourself."

He dropped his gaze to the table, his mouth pressed into a flat line. "Sorry," he mumbled. "I told Xenna I'd be… cordial."

How strange, I thought and couldn't tell if the thought belonged to me or Lupakaria. I didn't reply to the Heir. Of course he loathed me and found me repulsive. I was the former Heir who had reportedly tried to kill his precious Arch Shadow. That would make it all the easier to not think about his lips ever again.

I dug back into my slice of cake, but even the sweetness of strawberries didn't cut the bitter taste on my tongue.

CHAPTER NINE
HADRIEN

IT DIDN'T TAKE LONG to find Sidero's main Ianis Frame.

Unlike the one in his quarters, which resembled a large painting frame, this one was made of marble and arched like a normal gateway. The air between the pillars of the arch shimmered a thousand different colors, a rainbow trapped on earth. This Ianis Frame was large enough for the horses to walk through, too.

But the woman controlling the Ianis Frame shook her head when Hadrien asked how much it was for the horses to travel to Brumais. "No horses allowed in Brumais, 'cept theirs."

He didn't remember that from his previous time in Brumais, but he hadn't had a horse to take with him then. "Passage for two people, then," he said, "and point me in the direction of the nearest reputable stable."

"That'll be the one Fiona manages." The woman handed over two tickets after Hadrien paid. "Best hurry. I'm taking lunch soon."

Hadrien stashed the tickets in his pocket and jerked

his chin at Nox. "The horses are staying. Come on, we don't have long."

The former Heir said nothing in protest, simply followed him to the stable. Fiona accepted the two horses and said the full payment would be due when they returned.

It was a higher rate per day than Hadrien would've liked, but a quick glance showed him the stalls were in good condition and clean. The horses under Fiona's care were all brushed and combed. The rate seemed well worth it.

With a warning about Ikarus' temper, Hadrien left him with Fiona. Nox handed over her mare's reins.

Back at the Ianis Frame, Hadrien showed the woman the two tickets, and then the space in the archway filled with the forests of Brumais. His heart surged. He glanced at Nox, hesitated, and gripped the girl's arm.

Nox's eyes narrowed, and the weight of her glare was heavy on his shoulders, even when Hadrien turned his gaze back to the Ianis Frame. He kept his grip on the former Heir and stepped forward, and Nox was forced to step forward with him. Into the Ianis Frame, into the liminal world, into the space between worlds.

It was a rush of breath and wind and storm.

It was flying and falling and feathers on his skin.

It was waves over his head and sky below his feet.

Hadrien stumbled out of the Ianis Frame and collapsed.

Through his blurring, dimming eyesight, he saw Nox standing over him, flourishing magnolias framing her head. The last thought Hadrien had was, *Nox better kill me fast.*

Hadrien woke and wished he was dead.

It was as if someone had taken up pounding drums in his head. His bones, his very bones, ached when he tried to sit up. He was on his back under a towering magnolia, his head resting on what was likely his knapsack. Huge, ivory-hued blossoms floated before his eyes among the dark leaves of the magnolia. A bumblebee buzzed past, heavy with golden pollen.

Then Nox came into view, hood pushed back. Her brow held a slight furrow, and that was what sent a spike of cold panic into his veins. "You're awake," the former Heir said.

"You didn't kill me," Hadrien croaked.

"Now why would I have done that?" She sat back, barely in view. "You're more use to me alive than dead."

Groaning, he pushed himself up. The little movement rendered him breathless, set his head to spinning. He slumped back against the trunk, let his eyes slip shut, and mumbled, "What happened to me?"

"This healer here says some people forget to close their eyes when they step through Ianis Frames. You saw what is beyond our world, and your mind is rebelling against what it has seen."

If I were to perish now, I would not be remiss. Dragging his eyes open, he peered at the healer. "How long does this last? I feel like my head was used as a drum by wild faeries."

The healer shrugged. "I'm a student still." That explained why she looked so fresh-faced. "I studied the

Ianis Frame Effect last week. I have an exam on it next week."

His eyes burned. He closed them again, swearing to himself. "Where are we?"

"You're in Cristal," the healer-student replied. That was the correct town, the one with the global Ianis Frame. "You came through the Ianis Frame about an hour ago and immediately passed out. I saw it happen."

"Need to reach… Lumieres."

"It's not far, don't worry. You'll be able to take your friend to your home soon."

Friend. Home. Hadrien wanted to lurch up and throttle the student for saying those words. Nox was not his friend. Home was an unknown for him.

"I've given your friend some biscuits. They might make you feel better sooner." With a small scuffing sound, the student stood. "I have to get back to class now, but welcome home, Hadrien."

He wanted to scream.

The student's steps faded, and then Nox said, "So you're from Brumais. You don't look it."

"You say that like people can't move," he ground out. His own voice was resounding in his skull like thunder. "I'm of Atassish descent, born in Brumais. Family moved back to Atassia when I was young." He cracked one eye open, and because Nox had brought the topic up, he challenged, "You?"

Nox didn't reply. She stared at the ground, her jaw working. Finally, she admitted, "I don't know." She considered her hand, the sun-bronzed olive skin. "I look Atassish, don't I? Truly, who holds weight to this? Only bloodlines and crowns." Her gaze returned to Hadrien.

"But you, this explains why you have that map of Brumais in the drawing room." Cobalt-blue eyes skimmed across the trees. "I can see why. It's beautiful."

And that seemed so genuine that Hadrien shut his eyes to hide the sudden tears. By the Three Mothers, what had that Ianis Frame done to him?

It didn't matter.

It was temporary.

They needed to get moving.

Hadrien dug his fingers into the ground, tried to shove himself up. His arm shook. Buckled. He spat out a curse.

"You should take it easy," Nox said. Her hand hovered over his shoulder, a slight weight that didn't quite land; Hadrien rolled his shoulder, the hand moved. "But if you insist…"

Hadrien tried again to stand. This time, he made it as far as rocking onto his feet before he had to lean against the trunk of the magnolia. His chest was tight, constricted. He rubbed at his sternum, jangling his Shadow medallion. A breath rasped in.

He could do this.

Sunlight flooded his eyes. "Let's move on."

Nox didn't protest, but the weight of her gaze was on him. He wanted to whirl and snap at the former Heir. He wanted to claw out his eyes and rip these images of countless worlds out of his mind. He wanted to burn down everything around him.

Hadrien made it two steps before his ears filled with a chorus in languages sidereal and unknown. His vision disappeared, replaced by spinning stars and thunderstorm beings and half-flesh, half-bone canines bearing lightning bolts.

He howled, all the pain and anguish shredding his voice.

Nox startled back, eyes flying wide. "Heir," she shouted, "focus!"

Hadrien swung his head towards Nox. The air fuzzed and blurred around her form, astral horns swooped up from her head, weightless drakonoid wings unfurled behind her back. White-blue phantom flames sprung up along her frame, heatless but filled with a quiet roar. In her hands, she held a massive heart, gilded and still beating.

Nox offered up the heart.

Hadrien reached out, and his hand passed right through the heart and collided with something solid below. Something wrapped around his fingers, and he was jolted forward into an unyielding mass, and the chorus and the visions fell away, leaving him face-to-face with the former Heir. Nox was clutching his hand in a crushing grip, chin jutted up and eyes challenging.

"Whatever is going on in your head," Nox growled, "you need to quell it."

He snatched his hand out of her grip. He stayed where he was, so close that his chest, rising and falling with his hard breaths, brushed against her. "You," he replied, trying to act like his head wasn't spinning so fast he thought he might fall over, "need to remember your place."

"My place?" Nox looked like she was going to snarl. Then she grinned, flashing that chipped canine tooth.

"Unless you're talking about my place being above you, then you can take your opinion and shove it up your—"

Hadrien slammed his palms into her shoulders and shoved her back. Nox laughed, rolling out her neck. Her fists came up, and she bounced on the balls of her feet.

"You want to fight, pretty boy?"

The last fight he'd picked with Nox had decidedly not gone in his favor. He didn't care. He raised his own fists and drew one leg back, settling into a ready stance.

Nox was still grinning when she threw the first punch.

Hadrien, dazed and dizzy as he was, didn't manage to dodge. Her knuckles cracked against his cheek. Both of them swore, though Nox did so much more gleefully.

"Cease!"

Hands grabbed Hadrien and hauled him away from Nox, and someone else held Nox back. Nox shrugged them off with a snarl, never once looking away from Hadrien. Hadrien struggled against the hands on his shoulders, distantly realizing he had recognized the voice that spoke the Brumesian.

"Stop this at once and leave Cristal."

Hadrien tore his gaze away from Nox's to look at the guards. Horror cooled his temper. Being thrown in jail would cause more trouble than he needed. "We were leaving," he replied in Brumesian, slipping back into the tongue of his homeland with no hesitation.

"See to it that you do." The guard paused. "I know you, don't I?"

"Once upon a time."

Nox's eyes darted between Hadrien and the guard. "What are you saying?" she hissed, her Atassish words out of place and hard compared to the mellifluous Brumesian tongue.

Hadrien cut his hand at her, a signal to be silent. He tried to place the guard's name, tried to dredge up more than the memory of him as a young boy with a propensity for flinging mud at windows. "We won't cause any more trouble," he promised. "We're on our way now."

He snatched up Nox's hand and pulled her away from the guards. The former Heir curled her lip. Hadrien widened his eyes pointedly. She stopped fighting and trundled along.

Out of earshot of the guards, Hadrien muttered in Atassish, "They would've tossed us in jail. Best to leave now."

"You know one of them," she replied, her tone sharp, almost accusing.

"Used to. I knew him when he was a boy."

Nox was silent for a handful of minutes, and then she asked, "Is your plan to walk all the way to Loom—what was it?"

"Lumieres, and yes." Like a stone plummeting through a lake, Hadrien realized he was holding Nox's hand still. He dropped it. "It won't take us long to walk there." He cast a glance up at the sky; it would be evening soon. "Look for a cave or something. We're better off stopping earlier rather than later. The woods are not safe at night."

"Then let's turn around and stay in Cristal."

He shook his head. "Not an option."

Nox snorted. "Afraid that guard may remember you?"

"Afraid that I'll slit your throat for irritating me." A grimace split his face immediately. That had been a downright stupid thing to say. "I—I'm sorry."

"Are you apologizing because you didn't mean to say that, or because you didn't mean to say that aloud?" Nox didn't seem to care; she hadn't faltered in walking. But she wasn't even glancing at him.

There was no good answer.

He was silent too long, for she scoffed and muttered, "That's what I thought."

It was an hour before Nox said, "There's a cave." Her finger pointed deeper into the woods.

Not too far from the road. Should be safe. Hadrien stepped off the road and into the forest. Nox was a few strides behind, her steps nearly inaudible.

The shadows of the trees swallowed both of them up. Stray leaves crunched underfoot. Hadrien walked ahead of Nox, his eyes set on the dark opening of the cave. He would send Astre Noir in to clear it out, and then they could settle down for the night.

A branch snapped further into the forest. "Deer," Nox murmured.

He rubbed at his shoulder and continued. When a twig cracked behind them, he didn't glance in the direction. "Deer again?"

Nox didn't reply.

The silence stretched too long. He turned, ready to snap at the former Heir. But Nox was gone, and standing between the trunks of two large oaks was Varen. Hadrien's breath was a shard of ice in his throat.

Varen opened his jaws and screamed.

Hadrien ran.

The thundering hooves of the elk sounded behind him. In a matter of strides, Varen had caught up to him, and he was thrown to the ground. Hadrien scrambled.

Varen planted a hoof on his back; a bone cracked deep within. Blinding pain lashed his vision. He couldn't reach his knives, couldn't reach his bow, couldn't do anything.

Varen tipped his head near Hadrien's, and from the corner of his eye, the Heir saw the stark white bone of the beast's skull. Varen's jaws parted, teeth glistening, and he uttered a soft, keening cry into Hadrien's ear.

This time, Hadrien heard it as the cry Rogus had made when the claws of the Chimera pierced his stomach.

Hadrien gasped into the leaves, and Varen nudged at his neck with the cold point of a nasal bone. He keened again, sounding like Xenna crying late at night when she thought no one could hear her. Varen's weight shifted; another bone broke, and now it was Hadrien who screamed.

When Varen screamed again, he screamed like Hadrien.

Hadrien's fingers clawed at the dirt, at the leaves, at the fallen twigs. There was nothing to help him. He dug his fingers in and *pulled,* straining to move himself even an inch. Varen's hoof didn't budge from his back.

His nerves were numbing under the pressure. He couldn't even feel the broken bones. Didn't feel it when Varen leaned more weight onto that leg and something in his spine splintered.

Varen ran the tip of his skull along the back of Hadrien's head, hot breath spilling across his hair. The ragged edges of the bone caught on his hair with whispers. Varen exhaled, and Hadrien heard an echo of Nox howling in pain. He'd never heard that.

That wasn't his memory.

A whistle sounded, and Varen staggered back, his weight leaving Hadrien. He tried to scramble to his feet; pain struck him down into a curled-up ball, arms wrapped around himself. In his blurry vision, he saw Varen with his great fan of antlers, galloping away, oil-slick, oil-dark ichor dripping.

And between him and the retreating Varen was Nox.

"What was that?" Nox demanded, keeping her sword at the ready and not looking away from where Varen had fled. "Heir, what in the name of the Mothers was that?"

Hadrien couldn't catch his breath. His ragged gasps turned into hiccups that jarred his ribs and the broken bone. Then he cried—from pain, from fury, from grief renewed.

Nox grabbed ahold of his shoulders and shook him. "Heir!" Then she pinched his upper arm until he yelped. "What was that?"

"V-Varen," he managed.

"Varen?"

"He's a god, an immortal, I don't know." He sniffled, felt sorely pathetic for the tears streaking his face and the dirt and leaves on his bedraggled clothes. How glad he was that the Arch Shadow couldn't see him now. "He haunts the woods here. He plucks memories from your head and mimics the sounds."

Nox's face drained of color. "That was—I heard Rogus." She bit down on her lip, a muscle ticking in her jaw. Her eyes shone with unspilt tears. She gripped Hadrien's arm and said, "We're getting to that cave. Come on."

"Something's broken."

"Then I'll carry you if I have to." She sheathed her sword and jogged over to a fallen branch. She snapped off a few loose twigs and brought it back. "Here."

Without warning, Nox hauled Hadrien to his feet. Caught between an inhale and an exhale, his cry of pain faltered. Nox closed Hadrien's hand around the branch before wedging her shoulders under as support.

"Suppose it's good you're taller," Nox grunted out.

Hadrien could scarcely breathe. He leaned heavily on Nox and the branch, unable to focus his vision. A rib was broken, maybe two, and something was damaged in his his spine. Half his body felt like it belonged to someone else. The moment his weight shifted to step forward, his leg buckled like a slender stick.

Nox kept him upright with a curse. "I can either carry you or drag you."

He wasn't sure which would hurt more. One was certainly more embarrassing than the other. Why was he even thinking of that now? Embarrassment wouldn't matter if Varen came back and slaughtered the both of them. But could Nox even carry him?

"Drag me," Hadrien said through gritted teeth. "There's a blanket in my pack."

Nox muttered something inaudible and eased the knapsack off his back. As she laid out the blanket, Hadrien awoke Astre Noir. The wolf, he thought, would be able to help.

He tried to lower himself to the blanket.

His vision blackened instead.

He came to with Nox and Astre Noir peering at him, their heads ringed by the orange brush of the sunset through the canopy. Under his fingers was the cloth of the blanket. At least he was on it now.

Nox motioned to Astre, and the wolf took up one corner of the blanket, Nox the other. Hadrien put his gloved hand between his teeth. When Nox and Astre pulled together, the blanket slid over the leaf-strewn ground. Every little bump and jar made Hadrien clamp his teeth around his hand, stifling his pained sounds.

After what seemed like an eternity, they stopped. Astre bounded off, and Hadrien turned his head enough to see the wolf dart into the cave. Nox stood nearby, hands on hips, panting. She blew out a long breath, pushed back a strand of hair from her face.

Astre barked. Only once. No trouble.

The wolf returned, and Nox sighed before gripping the corner of the blanket again. Hadrien screwed his eyes shut as the blanket jostled over small rocks. At last, it stopped.

He opened his eyes to the darkness of the cave. Astre Noir sat at the entrance, ears on high alert. Nox was busy unpacking supplies, but when Hadrien made a pitiful croak, she turned.

"I'll get you a healer in the morning," she said. "You can't travel anywhere with your leg like that, never mind what other damage Varen did. I'd go now but… I don't trust that he's gone."

Hadrien shut his eyes, wondering if he would die in this cave. It was deserved, since that was how Rogus had met his end—and that was Hadrien's fault.

Chapter Ten
Nox

The Heir was screaming.

Endlessly, in my thoughts.

I sat against the cave wall, watching him pass between fitful sleep and pained consciousness. Sometimes, when he was awake, his eyes landed on me, and he looked like he could see through all my defenses.

The Heir had arguably had the worst day possible between the Ianis Frame Effect and Varen. Oh, and my fist. There was a sizable bruise blossoming on his face from that.

I glanced at the cave entrance, where the night flooded in. Astre Noir was long gone, and I wouldn't wake the Heir to summon the Ink again. There was no sign of that massive elk that had attacked him earlier.

Varen.

To Lupakaria, I asked, *What is Varen? Is he a god like you?*

He is not a god, Lupakaria replied, *and he is not from this world.*

How do you know? You aren't immortal.

I am not. My kin are not. He is of another ilk. Pray you never see his kind. Like him, they are not from here. Worlds are far vaster than you or even I will ever know. Your Heir over there glimpsed that knowledge today, and look at what's become of him.

I scowled and flicked my nail against the jawbone in reprimand. *He's not my Heir.*

Lupakaria merely hummed in response, the sound grating against my bones. She said no more on Varen. If *I* hadn't heard Varen's cries, heard the voices I knew within them, I would have thought the Heir was simply imagining that an angry elk was screaming at him. Another byproduct of the Ianis Frame Effect.

But it wasn't.

Silently, I rose and crept to the mouth of the cave. My eyes scanned the woods, the deep shadows within the trees. No sign of Varen or any other living being, immortal and vengeful or otherwise.

A shiver danced across my frame. I returned to my spot and wrapped my arms around myself, my eyes on the Heir as he mumbled in his restless sleep. Was he hearing Varen again? I was.

Varen had taken the sounds from the Heir's memories. Xenna, crying. Rogus, screaming. That meant… the Heir had heard them make those sounds. That meant they had *made* those sounds at some point.

I knew with heart-stopping certainty that the Heir had been there when Rogus died. What had they been hunting that could have killed Rogus? Rogus, who was better than the majority of the Shadows. A beast would've had to take him by surprise. If the Heir was there with him, how could something have surprised him? The Heir should've been watching his back.

The Heir hadn't.

And Rogus was dead.

In my mind, I heard Varen's keening rendition of Rogus' voice again.

Rogus had not died swiftly.

I couldn't even manage a tear. I rubbed at my dry eyes, then folded my hands over my eyes. How long ago had he died? The Heir and Xenna—*Xenna.* What had caused her to cry in that way that Varen had mimicked? Had the Arch Shadow hurt her in some way?

Drawing my legs up, I pressed my forehead into my knees. Behind my closed eyes, I saw Varen standing over the Heir again, pinning him with a single hoof. He had looked like a regular elk. Then I had noticed the strangeness. The sheer size. The rack of antlers so big it was a wonder he could hold his head up. The fact that his skull was visible, not a trace of fur or flesh or even eyes in his skull, just bone.

Mothers Three damn it.

A small sob drew my head up. A chill swept down my back. The Heir was silent and still; it hadn't been him.

Varen.

My heart racing, I skidded across the cave to the Heir and draped my cloak over him to hide him. He murmured something, and I clamped my hand over his mouth. His lips moved against my palm, then his eyes flew wide. He locked gazes with me, horror blanching his face.

Then he began to thrash, even as pain contorted his features. I bore down on him, digging my knees into him and pressing him flat. He stopped struggling, his pulse ticking frenetically. His eyes were shining with tears but full of fury.

I laid my finger on my lips, then slowly lifted my hand.

He drew in a breath, and I slammed my hand down again. His teeth scraped against my palm. An unsuccessful attempt. I was about to pinch his nose shut when he clamped his teeth down on my palm. Successfully this time.

My teeth snapped together. I yanked my hand back, hissing at the blood, and shoved a corner of the cloak into his mouth. I ducked my head close and snarled into his ear, "I will let Varen feast upon your bones."

His hair tickled my mouth as he tried to look at me. His voice trembled when he said lowly, "I thought you wouldn't try to kill me."

"I wasn't. Varen is near."

"So you put your hand on my mouth."

"It was either that or a boot." I realized how close our faces were. I reared back, his words from the bakery whirling back to the front of my mind. "Stay down, stay silent."

Keeping myself between the Heir and the cave entrance, I slid my sword out of its sheath and waited. I could hear something, presumably Varen, outside. Then there was silence, deep, hair-raising silence.

Was Varen gone?

A rock clattered.

My heart fled my body, and I could do nothing but watch as Varen's crowned head appeared in the cave opening. Silhouetted by the night sky, in the faint wash of the moons, the skull was a bare impression of white and gaping eye sockets. His antlers scraped the top of the cave; he lowered his head and shuffled further in.

Varen let out a long, lilting cry, his head snaking from side to side.

He was trying to locate us.

The Heir could do nothing if Varen tried to attack again. I edged back until I pressed against the Heir, kept Eclipse at the ready, and prayed to the Mothers Three that Varen would leave.

I felt the Heir tense a heartbeat before he spasmed in pain. His boot scuffed against the rocky wall, and the sound was akin to thunder.

Varen's head swung towards us, slow as dripping honey.

He advanced one long step at a time—until his antlers caught on the ceiling again. He tried to duck lower, but there was only so low a beast his size could go. His skull leered at us. He stretched his neck out further and further, and I could hear the vertebrae pop and crack. His breath washed over me.

How does he breathe? I wondered, fixating on that instead of the skull looming over my head. *I assume there are normal lungs in that chest somewhere. But breathing, that seems beyond his capabilities—*My thoughts stumbled to a stop; Varen was so very close.

The Heir's hand tightened on my knee. I had no idea when it had gotten there or why it was. His fingers dug in like claws. Tremors wracked his hand. I lowered my hand to his and tried to still it.

A squeak of pain eeked out between his teeth.

Varen's bellowing breath halted.

In the silence, I could hear the ichor leaking from the

wound I'd dealt the beast. I could hear the Heir trembling against me, his body lost in the throes of pain. I could hear my pulse, an ocean of sound in my ears.

Out in the woods, some traveler called for a dog.

Varen moved faster than possible for such a large frame. He was out of the cave within two heartbeats. Hooves pounded the forest floor.

Then the screaming began.

I loosed a breath that had sat tight in my chest. Shifting away from the Heir, I asked in a low tone, "What happened?"

He raised his hand from where it had covered his forearm. A rancid stench drifted into the air; my stomach turned. There was a blistering, rotting wound on his forearm that had not been there earlier.

"The ichor," he managed. "It did this."

I pushed myself up. "Stay here. I'll be back."

"It's night still. Where—Nox, you can't leave." He tried to sit up, but it left him breathless and pale and sweating. He couldn't stop me.

With Eclipse at my hip, I strode to the cave entrance. I glanced back at the Heir. He looked so vulnerable, curled beneath my cloak with his arm outstretched.

The gleam that marked his eyes found my gaze and held it. He drew in a breath, enough to whisper in a barely lucid tone, "You were in great pain."

I felt frozen. Carefully, trying to hide how my voice was strangled, I replied, "You weren't there for that." *You weren't there when the Arch Shadow ripped me open with my own sword.*

"Varen told me."

Curse that skull-faced elk.

I said nothing in reply and left the Heir in the cave.

My head high, I stalked through the woods. Night dampened the sounds of the woods waking and living. Leaves and undergrowth rustled against animals slinking through the shadows; Varen likely didn't deign to hunt such small prey that he couldn't torment with memories.

Through the dark and quiet, I hurried.

Was Varen nearby? He could be lurking behind any tree, waiting for the chance to pluck voices from my mind. But the road should be near, since we hadn't walked far into the woods before reaching the cave.

My next inhale pulled with it the tang of blood.

My steps slowed.

In the faint light from the moons, I saw what had become of the traveler Varen had found. Splintered bones and splatters of blood were all that remained. I stared at the remains for a minute. That could have happened to the Heir, to me.

After a glance around for Varen, I pushed into a jog, slipping out from the woods and onto the road. The road seemed safer. But now my thoughts were consumed by worries.

What if I didn't make it to Cristal?

Was there even a healer there who could help?

I kicked off the road harder, tried to pound my thoughts into the ground through my steps. Cristal was closer than I remembered; lights glimmered in the distance. Relief flowed into my muscles. I shoved myself into a sprint.

But I couldn't stop the thought of, *Should I leave?*

Three more strides. *He'd never catch up to me.* I passed

the first home in Cristal. *He'll probably die in that cave.* My steps faltered. *Or Varen will shred him.*

The Heir's voice whispered again, *You were in great pain.*

In the middle of Cristal, I stopped, panting.

With a huff, I strode to the building that the student-healer had come from earlier in the day. My knuckles collided with the door in a resounding drum. I waited, dragging in gulps of air and trying not to think of what the Heir had said. What he had learned when he heard Varen yank that pain from my memory.

I knocked again, harder and louder. Then beat my hand against the door until someone opened it with a startled yelp.

Oh thank the Mothers Three, it was the same student from earlier.

"You again?"

"Yes, listen, we ran into Varen—"

The student dashed off.

I stared dumbly at where she had stood.

Barely a minute had gone by before the student was back, tailed by a yawning healer. Both burst past me, headed towards a young boy approaching with a trio of horses. I had the sinking suspicion the people of Cristal were used to travelers suffering damage at the hooves of Varen.

On horseback, we hurried back to the cave. At the edge of the woods, the healers hung lanterns off the sides of their saddles, blue-green witchfire within lighting our way. My head on a swivel, I checked for signs of Varen. I had purposely guided them away from the remains of the traveler, but I was sure that we were not far from the cave.

And there it was.

I sent my horse into a trot, springing past the healers. Outside of the cave, I swung out of the saddle and approached the cave. I couldn't see if the Heir was still inside. I hesitated. I could still leave. The healers were here, they would take care of him; his blood would not be on my hands.

"Nox?"

By the Mothers Three, did the Heir sound so pitiful. And scared.

I walked in and knelt next to him. "I brought the healers."

The strange light of the lanterns filled the cave, sweeping over the Heir and showing how terrible he looked. His face was wan and slick with sweat.

The healers began conversing in Brumesian, and I stepped back to let them work. The Heir, thankfully, was given something to render him unconscious. I stood in the cave entrance and kept an eye out for Varen.

Sunrise was staining the sky a delicate shade of pink when the healers left. They took one of the horses, leaving two behind after I swore to return them soon, and told me to let the Heir rest for another hour before traveling again.

I watched them ride into the trees before I pivoted on my heel and faced the cave. The Heir was awake, peering at the world with bleary eyes. *Should I walk over to him?* I took a few steps in his direction, then stopped, then realized how awkward I looked in the middle of the cave. I closed the distance between us.

"How are you feeling?" I ventured. I didn't know how we stood now, now that he had heard my pain and I'd heard his—and Rogus' and Xenna's. "Did they heal everything?"

The Heir trailed his fingers over his arm, where the wound had been. "Not even a scar." He twisted at his hips. "No pain."

"They said for you to rest an hour."

"We have to get moving." He shifted to his knees, a hand braced on the ground.

I darted forward and planted my hands on his shoulders. "No, you are going to rest for an hour, and then we'll leave. One hour won't cost us the hunt."

The Heir tipped his head back to level a glare at me. "Get your hands off me."

So that was where we stood.

I stepped back, shrugging. "Don't forget that I saved your life, Heir."

"I have the inkling you will never let me forget, *former* Heir."

It was better this way, I told myself.

Chapter Eleven
Hadrien

He saw Varen in his nightmares.

He woke from one of these nightmares, echoes of screams vibrating through his skull. He clutched at his head. Varen's skull, it was behind his eyes, it was there in the shadows, he was here to flay flesh from bones and scream like him as he ripped Hadrien apart.

Hadrien's breath broke into a choked sob.

Curling over his knees, he clamped his teeth onto his hand and let loose a shout. It would've woken Nox, had she not already been awake. Hadrien hated this. Hated that the former Heir of the Shadow was here to see him shudder and shake and shatter apart.

Nox didn't say a word, but he felt the weight of her keen cobalt gaze.

His shoulders wracked with trembling, he dug in his knapsack for his jacket. He shrugged it on and fished the flask out. That was what he had sought.

With cognac burning in his throat, he rubbed at his temples. They were so close to Lumieres, but so was the new moon. He'd seen the moons earlier: a thin claw of the waning blue moon, less than half of the silver moon, and a golden moon heading towards its half-stage.

His scars itched, and he tossed back more cognac.

The bed on the other side of the room creaked as Nox shifted her weight. Feet met the floor with a soft sound, and joints cracked. Out of the corner of his eye, Hadrien could see the form of Nox standing and stretching out her arms.

"It's too early to leave," Hadrien mumbled.

"Neither of us can sleep," Nox pointed out, "so we might as well leave." She straightened the blankets on her bed. "Besides, it smells like rosewater here, and I can't sleep with that."

He had to admit the rosewater scent was a little off-putting. "You didn't complain when the innkeeper offered you a cup of rose-hip tea."

"That's tea. That's different." She padded over to the window. She braced her arms against the frame and peered out; moonlight of different shades glinted off her outline. "I don't… trust this."

In the back of his mind, Hadrien heard Varen again. He screwed his eyes shut and downed a long gulp. The cognac couldn't fuzz his thoughts—dull his fear—soon enough. Then he muttered, "Don't trust what?"

"These inns on the side of the roads between towns." Nox tapped her fingernail on the glass. Once. Twice. Thrice. Then she turned, eyes glowing like miniature twin moons.

Hadrien blinked. "Your eyes…"

She blinked as well, a flash of darkness cutting

through the small moons and dimming them. "What about them?"

There was nothing strange now about her eyes. "Nothing. Just a trick of the light." *Thanks to my overactive, fanciful mind. No one's eyes glow like a cat's. Not even Nox's, despite how strange she is.* "Go back to bed."

Nox sat on her bed, hands clasped, elbows resting on her knees. Hadrien rolled his eyes towards the former Heir. Why was she sitting like that? Like she was waiting for something?

"What?" he groused.

Her knee bounced up and down, making something in the bed rattle. "You were there when Rogus died."

His thoughts stalled.

He should have seen this coming now that Varen wasn't a near threat. The former Heir had heard every sound Varen had drawn out from Hadrien's memories. He opened his mouth to reply—and found a choked exhale waiting.

Nox's knee stopped bouncing. Then started again, more aggressive this time. "You were." The words were sharp like steel, quick like lightning. "I heard. Varen pulled that sound—*his scream*—from your memory." She stood and grabbed Hadrien's chin, jerked his head up. "How," Nox asked in a tone so low the dead could hear it, "did he die?"

His inhale shook his shoulders. Tears skidded past Nox's hand. Revulsion and slick disgust snaked through his gut. Hadrien ripped his chin out of her grip and forced a scowl onto his face. "Don't fucking touch me," he spat.

"Tell me."

"You want to know?" Hadrien shot to his feet, glared down at her. "Three months ago, the Arch Shadow sent us to hunt the Chimera of Chalybos." He saw her eyes widen, knew that Nox knew the dangers of that beast. "I was still inexperienced. Rogus put himself between the Chimera and me. Took the death blow that was meant for me. I *tried* to recover his body."

Nox turned her face away, but the moonlight caught on the tears coursing down her cheeks. She said nothing.

His whole body was shaking. Visibly. Three Mothers take him, he was going to fall apart right in front of the former Heir. He had dealt with this, hadn't he? He had grieved for Rogus, someone he had called friend, and he had shoved the remaining grief so deep down that it shouldn't bother him anymore.

Right?

But now, standing before Nox and speaking of him, Hadrien felt as though he had staggered back into the House of Shadows without the Chimera's heads and without Rogus.

Nox swiped her hand across her face. "Three months." At her sides, her hands flexed wide, clenched into fists. "Three months he has been dead, and no one managed to retrieve *any* of him for burial rites."

Hadrien's silence was the reply.

Nox was still, the stillness of a predator before a strike. Then she exploded. She hurled her boot at the wall. Before it had even impacted, she was grabbing a candle—fire and all—and dashing it against the floor.

With a curse, he leapt back. "Nox!"

The former Heir, shoulders heaving with her furious

breaths, stared at Hadrien as she brought her heel down upon the flickering wick. Smoke curled up. "You," Nox said, "are going to help me find his bones."

"I will. Now stop destroying the room."

In her eyes, tears still glimmered. Then in a breaking voice, she whispered, "I loved him."

Something akin to regret weighed on him. But then he thought, what would the Arch Shadow say? What would she do in the face of her rival's weakness? She would strike.

In a voice he barely recognized as his own, it was so short and cold, he said, "You doomed him."

Nox dragged in an audible breath. Light glinted off her canines as she bared her teeth, looking ready to lunge.

"We're leaving," he said. "Tack up the horses."

Without further pause, she grabbed her knapsack and slipped into the washroom. In the time it took Hadrien to wipe any traces of tears from his face, Nox had reemerged, dressed for travel. She eyed Hadrien for a moment and then left.

Without Nox there, the room seemed awfully quiet and the shadows oh so dark.

Hadrien could still hear Varen.

He collapsed onto the bed again, hiding his face in his hands, fingers digging into his head. The points of pressure did nothing to ground him. His head was full of screams and antlers and a great weight bearing down upon him.

A floorboard creaked.

His head shot up.

Nox stood in the doorway, light silhouetting her form.

One hand poised on the doorframe, the other curled around her jawbone amulet. She didn't speak. She turned on her heel and walked away.

How long was she there? What did she see—what did she think? His eyes felt strained and scorched. The thought of rising and following her, it was more than his frame could bear. But he gritted his teeth and shouldered himself up.

He was the Heir of the Shadow, and he had a job to do.

Nox didn't speak the entire day.

Hadrien didn't start up a conversation.

The hours dragged on. The dappled sun beat down upon their backs. The horses trod steadily down the road through the trees.

Every stride brought them closer to Cipres—and from there, Lumieres and Domhan Arbre.

But as afternoon turned into evening, Hadrien began to glance over his shoulder. His eyes darted from tree to tree, shadow to shadow. Varen could be hiding anywhere.

Pulse ticking faster and faster in his ears, Hadrien urged his horse into a sweeping canter. The small town of Cipres crept into sight, hidden amongst the grand oaks and elms. Hedges encircled it like shields, and the road led into the mouth of a tunnel, comprised of the dark green leaves and soft purple blooms of mountain laurels.

Varen would never follow him here.

Hadrien rode under the arcing branches of the tunnel; blossoms rained down upon him, a sweet perfume engulfed him. Butterflies and bumblebees flitted through the falling petals, drunk on nectar and pollen.

Then he was through the tunnel of petals and in the town of Cipres. He could hear the water from the nearby fork of the river, see the tall cypresses that waved in the breeze. These were different than the ones in Atassia, more wild, more vivacious. And these here were certainly not associated with death in old tales like they were in Atassia.

Nox slowed her horse next to Hadrien. Her eyes flashed towards him, then lingered. "You have petals in your hair," she said.

"So do you," Hadrien replied.

He glanced at Nox, something meant to only be quick enough to see the petals, but then he couldn't look away. The setting sun gleamed along the edges of the petals caught in the windblown onyx locks. A hint of flush from exertion and sun gave life to her cheeks. Her eyes were bright, despite the sleepless night. Nox looked like a wild thing.

He wished he'd held back the sharp words yesterday.

Nox was the first to turn her face away. "Where's the inn?"

He had no idea. "That way," he said confidently.

He was wrong.

The inn, in fact, was situated not far from the river, cloaked in the shade of trees, flanked by gardens of mushrooms. Nox stared at the rows of various fungi for a minute, her head tilted like a confused cat's.

"They grow well here," was all Hadrien said. "Lumieres has a chef from Atassia, who cooks this simple and elegant dish of pasta. I haven't had it in a while, I remember it from my childhood, but I think it was a peppered cream sauce over chicken, spinach, and mushrooms. With pasta, of course."

Nox worked her jaw. Her stomach rumbled faintly. "I could eat that now."

"We'll eat here." He hoped for pasta.

The inn failed him on two accounts: the room and the food. While the inn had enough stalls for both horses, the last room only had a single bed. The innkeeper smiled and gestured to Nox and Hadrien and said a sentence in lilting Brumesian that made him force a polite nod.

The moment they were in the room, Nox whirled to Hadrien. "What did she say?"

"Nothing of importance," he lied and brushed past the former Heir. He set his knapsack down and leveled a glare at the single bed in the room.

"Uh-uh-uh, not so fast." Nox was in his eyesight again, her eyes alight. She had found prey to toy with; he could see it plain as day. "Your ears turned red when she spoke. That's not nothing, little Shadow."

"Don't call me that."

"Don't call you princeling, don't call you little Shadow, why you leave very little for me to call you." Her smile could cut glass. That chipped canine was on full display, her grin as wild as the wind. "Come now, what did the innkeeper say?"

His breath gusted out. "You won't rest, will you?"

"Nope," Nox replied, her words light with glee.

What did I do to deserve this? he wondered, and the deepest depths of his mind replied, *You failed at everything,* and Hadrien said aloud, "The innkeeper congratulated us on being such a pretty couple."

Nox's eyebrows climbed so high it was a wonder they didn't fly away.

"I don't know what gave her that idea." Hadrien splayed out his gloved fingers. "No ring. We weren't even standing that close to each other. She can't read people, that's all." He strode to the bed and started constructing a barricade of pillows down the middle. "It's a touch pathetic, really. How can you run an inn and not read people well?"

Nox didn't reply.

The silence stretched on so long that he glanced away from the bed and to her. Surprise jolted through him. There were tears gathering in her eyes.

Hadrien fidgeted with the cuff of his gloves. "I'm going to see about food." And he darted out of the room.

By the Three Mothers, I don't understand her. He zipped down the stairs, his hand gliding along the banister. *She's angry one minute, full of mischief the next, and now almost in tears. What is it? Is it Rogus?* He stopped in his tracks. *Oh. It's grief.*

He should have realized that *before* he fled the room. His face flushed hot, shame dragging at his bones. That was a misstep.

Good thing I'm not here to be friends with Nox.

Hadrien shrugged off the shame and entered the dining room of the inn. The mouthwatering scent of fresh rosemary bread filled the room. But he was fated for disappointment—the bread had turned out burnt, and the cook stormed out with enough curses to scald water.

Muttering a curse of his own, Hadrien left the inn and found a bakery further into town. He hesitated only a moment before buying food for Nox as well. With the basket in hand, he returned to the inn and stood outside the door.

He should open it.

Nox might have fled in his absence.

He should really open the door.

Chapter Twelve
Nox

I could hear the Heir standing outside the door. I could also *smell* the food he had. There was the warm, buttery scent of toasted bread, cheese and chives, and then something sweet.

The Heir opened the door.

He said nothing as he laid out the items in the basket. The small table in the room, the one I sat at, was soon covered by food. How much had he gotten?

"This is for you," the Heir said and gestured to a wrapped sandwich. "And these." He indicated first a lemon and poppyseed muffin, then a croissant with chocolate drizzled on top. "I assumed you like chocolate. You seemed to want that chocolate cake in the Sidero bakery."

I eyed the food. "What's the trick?"

"Trick?"

"Is there poison?" Poison might be worth it to try that croissant.

The Heir sputtered. "Why would I poison you?"

I shrugged, unwrapped the sandwich, and bit into it. The chive-studded cheese was gently melted, the baguette bread warm, toasted, and buttered. I paused a moment. "Hmm. No poison yet."

"Why again, would I poison you?"

"Many reasons. You seem to think you can take down the Wild Moon Wolf on your own." *Good luck with that.* "You're the current Heir. Why not take out the old one and make the Arch Shadow proud?"

The Heir blinked. "I…"

"This is a good sandwich. Where'd you get it?"

"The bakery." He finally sat down and took a bite of his own sandwich. It looked different than mine, and I wanted to try it.

Around a mouthful of food, I mumbled, "Should get these tomorrow before we leave Cypress."

"Cipres."

"Cypress, that's what I said."

"Your pronunciation is all wrong."

"I don't speak Brumesian."

"That's for sure."

I held out my sandwich. "Try this."

The Heir's brow furrowed. "What? Why?"

"Because I want to try that one you've got, and I figured it's only fair."

With a little shrug, he cut off a small triangle of his sandwich, from the opposite end he'd been eating, and held it out. I accepted the sample and offered him a similar triangle of mine. Where mine was only sharp orange cheese with chives—did the Heir actually know that this was my favorite type of cheese?—his had a soft, creamy cheese, offset by slices of sour green apple, a sweet fig spread, and roasted turkey. It was delicious, and I was mildly jealous.

"That's good," the Heir said. "I might get that tomorrow."

"Yours is good, too."

I ate the rest of my sandwich in silence. Spinning the lemon and poppyseed muffin around with my fingertips, I said, "Rogus used to laugh whenever people would assume we were together. We loved each other dearly, but we never were."

"Why not?"

I considered not answering. "He wanted a different sort of life. I never felt a spark for him, but I cared about him. We never wavered as friends. He would have found a nice girl to settle down with, and I would've been happy for him." *He'll never have that life now.*

The Heir stared down at the table and the remainder of his sandwich.

"How did you know Rogus?"

"Xenna befriended me when I joined. She introduced me to Rogus. He just… He was always trying to do better and help others." His mouth twisted, and he said quietly, viciously, "It should have been me."

Maybe it should have been.

His gaze, so furious and so full of loathing, seethed at the floor. But there was something about the inward curl of his shoulders that said his anger was not directed outward. This boy, this boy with the scars and the warpaint around his eyes, suddenly looked so lonely and vulnerable.

I would tear him apart.

"It should have been," I said flatly. "Rogus was a

better person than you could ever be. You should be dead, not him."

The Heir's expression crumpled like wet paper.

There was no blaze of triumph.

Guilt slunk slick through my insides. I couldn't draw my words back. Maybe it was for the better, maybe I—

The Heir's jaw set. Maybe I had lit the spark to the kindling.

The Heir rolled his shoulders back, raised his chin. "I'm the one who's here, not him."

It was true, and I hated him for it.

I bit into the croissant with all my burning, building anger. The pastry was demolished—I barely even noticed how delectable it was, flaky, soft pastry and smooth chocolate inside—before I said, "If it weren't for him, you wouldn't be here."

The Heir opened and closed his mouth soundlessly a few times, an extraordinarily tall fish out of water. He shoved his chair back and stomped away from the table.

I laughed, but no humor warmed the sound.

"He was better than you," I called after his retreating back. "Don't you forget that!"

The door shut, and I was alone in the room, the echoes of my words hanging in the still air.

My gaze flitted over the remainder of the food on the table. He had brought this back for me, too. A twinge of regret pulled at my heart. But I kicked it aside. I was who the Arch Shadow had made me.

The Heir deserved every harsh word I threw his way; he was responsible for Rogus' death. I drummed my fingers on the tabletop, eyes narrowed at the door. An idea was blooming.

Not only could I lead the Heir on a wild golden goose chase across all of Khtonyx in the name of hunting the Wild Moon Wolf, I could make his life miserable until he quit and forfeited his title. Retribution for Rogus.

I slunk out of the room and shortened the stirrups on his saddle. The Heir wasn't in the room when I returned. Night draped over the town; I peered out of the window at the street.

Where is he?

Lupakaria stirred in my mind, unfurling and stretching. *What do you care?*

I don't have the money to pay for this room, that's what. I flicked my nail against the jawbone. *Stop acting like there's more to it. As of right now, I need him for that endless Shadow money.*

Yet you know the truth.

And he *doesn't. He won't. Not if I can help it.* I leaned my shoulder against the wall and gazed out of the window, watching someone stumble towards the inn. *And I certainly can help it.*

Lupakaria chuckled.

I had already identified the stumbling figure as the Heir, but nothing could have prepared me for the wave of alcohol that dripped from him when he walked—*staggered* —into the room. He glanced at me, no hint of recognition in his eyes.

He's quite drunk, Lupakaria observed. *Get rid of him.* Glee sank into the dead goddess' voice. *I can help. Just wish!*

Shush. We can't kill him yet. I crossed my arms. "Heir, this is not pinnacle Heir behavior."

"I don't care what you think." He pressed his back against the wall opposite me and slowly slid to the floor, legs sprawled out. A half-empty bottle of amber alcohol was clutched in his fingers. He'd lost his gloves some-where. "You can say all the cruel things you want." Blue-grey eyes locked on mine, and suddenly the Heir did not seem so drunk. "You're just like her."

I went rigid and snarled, "You know nothing."

The Heir laughed, far too similar to how I had laughed earlier. He tipped the bottle against his lips and drank. And *drank.* I could not understand how he wasn't coughing. A thin line of whatever he was drinking—cognac, brandy, whiskey, something else—slipped past his lips, rolled down the length of his throat in a gleam.

Deciding to ignore him the rest of the night, I stepped over him into the washroom and shut the door.

You're just like her.

Sitting on the edge of the tub, I watched the bath fill with hot water and floral-smelling bubbles. The Heir's words circled in my head. I splayed my hand across my abdomen. He didn't know anything; his words weren't true.

I undressed and sank into the waters. Without the Jaws of Lupakaria around my neck—the jawbone was tucked safely among my discarded clothes—I couldn't hear Lupakaria. I rested my head back, shut my eyes, and sighed. A rare moment that it was just me and my own thoughts.

The Heir knocked on the door.

I opened one eye. "What?"

"I need to wash my hair."

"Well, you can wait." I scrubbed my fingers through my own hair, frowned at a mountain laurel petal I pulled free.

"It's bothering me."

"That's not my problem."

He grumbled something, a low string of words barely audible through the door. The handle turned. For the love of all unholy, I had not locked it.

I met the Heir's gaze as soon as he stepped in. "I'm bathing, in case you didn't notice."

The Heir paused in his tracks. Slowly, a deep flush colored his face, already flushed from the alcohol. His hand clapped over his eyes. "I didn't realize."

How he did not realize that is beyond me. "Just leave. I'll be done soon."

"I have mead in my hair."

This boy. "And whose fault is that?"

"Some drunk woman at the tavern down the road. It's sticky, and I smell bad."

"That's for certain." I waved my hand at him, droplets of water flinging against him. "Get out. I'll be a few minutes."

Loathe as I was to end my bath, I did. The Heir paced outside the washroom until I left, and then he darted in. From what I'd seen, his hair did look decidedly tangled. I couldn't quite blame him for wanting to wash the mead out as soon as possible.

He'll be fine, I told myself as I settled the Jaws of Lupakaria around my neck again.

Lupakaria asked, *Who?*

I want to sleep, be quiet. I picked the side of the bed farthest from the washroom and slid under the blankets. A pillow rested on my shoulder; I shoved it back into the barricade the Heir had built. It really was the silliest thing I'd ever seen.

I tried to sleep, but I was still awake when the Heir's weight made the bed dip. Suddenly, every single noise was thunderingly loud. I was highly aware of where my hands were. I folded them atop my chest, felt my heart beating against my ribcage.

The Heir's breathing evened out, sleeping the easy sleep of the drunk. I envied him. My mind was churning. Where were the other hunters? Likely in Atassia, since the Wild Moon Wolf had not yet been spotted anywhere else. How long could I keep this up?

The Heir shifted in his sleep, and his hand dangled over the pillow barricade. I frowned. I breathed on his fingertips; his hand flexed and relaxed. It was so strange to see his hands. He always had those gloves on. Why? Was his touch poisonous?

Holding my breath, I brushed my fingertip against his palm, skimmed it down to the pad of his forefinger. Nope. Nothing. But his hand was covered in small scars, thin lines that crossed back and forth and back and forth. Some were tinged with purple. Recent scars.

I rubbed my fingers against each other. Still nothing, not a deadly touch. Did he wear those gloves to hide the scars? But they were such little scars. He was a Shadow, scars were to be expected. But perhaps these were from clumsiness or poor knife skills.

Beyond his scarred hand was his wrist. The outline of a vein arced faintly over the fine bones in the joint. A curl of ink swept from his thumb up to the rest of the tattoo. I pushed myself up onto my elbows and studied the tattoos covering his forearm—at least, what I could see, for it appeared to continue on the underside of his forearm, too.

Flowers.

Huge, sweeping magnolia blooms, towering foxglove and wolfsbane, delicate candle larkspur, thistle, and aster, all done in black ink with realistic, intricate shading. Thorn-studded vines twisted through the flowers.

There was no sign of a wolf. This was not his Ink; this was not Astre Noir. Which meant it was indeed simply a tattoo. I rose up further. How far up his arm did the tattoos extend? My eyes followed the flowers up his forearm, past his elbow, up his arm to his shoulder. His shoulder.

His bare shoulder.

My gaze snagged on the line of his shoulder blade under his skin. There was no shirt. The Heir was on his stomach, his back exposed to the night. *I shouldn't look.* But I did. I glanced over his back until the blankets wrapped halfway down.

I laid down on my back and stared intently at the ceiling. Even with my eyes open, I saw flashes of him. His back was scarred with thick, uneven scars. No scar marred the Ink across his shoulders: the starry expanse and the wolf leaping among the stars.

When I closed my eyes, all I could see was him.

Intriguing, Lupakaria mused.

I was going to strangle a dead goddess. *Let me sleep.*

You aren't exactly trying to sleep, she pointed out. *You're thinking about him.*

I am not—I am.

I knew it. A pause, a heartbeat. *He's awake.*

I stiffened. He had been asleep a few hours.

"Nox?" the Heir mumbled.

Letting my head loll to the side, I pretended to be asleep.

The Heir grumbled something indistinguishable and then, "I need to talk with you." He poked my shoulder with very little precision, more of a sluggish nudge. *"Nox."*

I didn't know if I should keep pretending to sleep or not.

"Nox," he murmured, and Mothers Three, had I been right. In the dark of night, his voice, quiet and low, was thick like honey and deep as oceans, like he was afraid if he spoke too loud someone would overhear. He said my name like it was a secret he wanted to keep.

I couldn't think of anything else. I wanted to hear my name fall from his lips again in that indulgent, decadent voice.

It's so late, I told myself, *you're not thinking clearly, you just found out about Rogus, the Arch Shadow is in your life again, nothing is right, and* he *replaced you.*

The Heir shoved me, and I startled. "Good, you're awake."

The spell broken, I sat up and faced him. "What do you want? I was—" I faltered.

"Asleep? Yes, irrelevant." The Heir was certainly still tipsy, that was clear from how he leaned towards me over the pillow barricade. Possibly *very* tipsy. Either he hadn't noticed yet that his shirt was off or he didn't care; the pillows covered all but the tops of his shoulders and the lines of his collarbones. "You," he said, "wear that jawbone everywhere."

"That's what you poked me for?"

"You said it was yours." He reached out and touched

one of the fangs. "It can't be because—" That fingertip brushed my chin. "—you have yours. Right here."

I considered running out of the room. A tipsy, coming down from being drunk Heir who was suddenly prone to touching me and being close to me was not something I had anticipated.

Leaning back, I replied, "You should go back to sleep."

"Hmm." The Heir blinked. Very slowly. In a sudden flurry of movement, he retrieved his shirt from somewhere and dragged it on. He then rested his head on the pillows, his eyes on me. "Tell me."

"About?"

"The jawbone."

He'll think this was a dream. I lowered my voice and said, "Have you heard of Lupakaria?"

A little shake of his head.

"Legend has it that Lupakaria was an ancient goddess, who took the form of a wolf and wandered the wilds. If someone found her and offered up something—"

Cheese, the goddess herself interjected, audible to only me. *I really liked when people brought me cheese.*

"—she desired, Lupakaria would grant a single wish. But there is rumor in old accounts that they would go mad, claim to hear whispers at all hours. All the accounts agree on this: Lupakaria, when asking for their wish, would say, 'Wish, o dreamer.'"

I do like that turn of phrase.

"I found the Jaws of Lupakaria, a remnant of her own form, in the mountains north of Sanguinos, and I ripped the heart out of the thief who wore them." I lowered my voice further, into a raspy whisper, and continued, "I was meant to deliver the Jaws to the Arch Shadow, but I made a wish like all the wanderers before me, and now, the Arch Shadow doesn't remember this. She tried to kill me for other reasons. And let me tell you, o dreamer, there is more than you will ever know."

"That's made up," the Heir mumbled into a pillow.

If that was what he wanted to believe.

Lupakaria told me stories of travelers and dreamers and wanderers, and I spoke of them in a low voice until the Heir was far into sleep. Then I, too, finally fell asleep, my thoughts whirling with inked flowers and ancient gods.

I was warm on one side, cold on the other.

Confused, I cracked my eyes open. I hadn't been asleep very long, and the room was still dark. There was time to sleep yet still.

I nestled my head into the pillow, shifting my hand to tuck under my head. But my hand was under something. Or rather, my arm was. I raised my head and tried to take stock of the situation.

Oh. I was sleeping on my back, and the reason one side was warm and my arm was trapped was simple. The Heir. He had kicked and pushed aside the pillow barricade until he was draped across me. He was currently using my sternum as a pillow, which did not seem very comfortable. The Jaws, fortunately, were not under his face—that would be *highly* uncomfortable; those were hanging off my opposite side.

This was unexpected.

The Heir murmured something in his sleep. He still smelled a little like cognac, but there was the sweet scent of orange blossom soap intertwined with it. His eyes flickered open, focused on me. Then his eyes closed again, and he *curled* closer to me.

I didn't know what to do.

In the end, I drifted back into sleep, the Heir right next to me.

Chapter Thirteen
Hadrien

I didn't dream of Varen.

His eyes opened slowly, as he savored the thought and the soft, warm morning light. But the sunlight stretching across the floor hadn't hit the bed yet. He had gone to sleep on the side furthest from the window, yes? So why, oh why, was he on the opposite side of the bed now?

Hadrien raised his head, all the cognac from last night making itself known in a splitting headache. The headache was the least of his worries, he realized. Sometime during the night, he had ended up sleeping atop Nox.

Oh, Three Mothers end me.

Teeth gritted, he tried to extract himself without waking her. If he moved his arm and rocked his weight to the side—oh. Nox was awake. Cobalt eyes were already watching him through a haze of long eyelashes. Hadrien froze, hovering over the former Heir's chest.

Nox wrinkled her nose. "Please drink some mint tea."

Face hot with shame, Hadrien scrambled away as fast

as he could. He caught a whiff of cognac from his own skin. He had bathed last night, hadn't he? A quick rake of his fingers through his hair, they came away damp. So he had.

He untangled his legs from the blankets and set his bare feet upon the floor. Placing his palms on the edge of the bed, he tipped his head back, arching his spine, until he heard the pops of vertebrae. Whew. That was better.

Now to get ready to leave.

His gaze dropped to his knees. His bare knees. His thighs, so brilliantly pale even with his olive skin, were on display until the hem of his nightshirt midway up.

Where were his pants?

"Nox?" His voice was so high a dog must've heard it two miles away.

Nox grunted something.

"Why do I have no pants?"

"Well," she said and stood. Her expression was serious and still—then that crooked smile broke across it. "You were rather foxed last night."

Hadrien sputtered and managed no full word.

"You even climbed into bed fully nude."

He was going to melt through the floor. "I—I —what?"

"You did. You also walked into the washroom while I was in the bath."

"I'm—"

"Don't worry, I left." Nox waved a hand up and down at him. "I didn't see any of that, only your Ink and those flowers along your arm."

His mind raced, took stock of where his scars were. There were the ones at his wrist and crook of his elbow, but the tattoos obscured those. How much of his back had been exposed? The scars there would raise questions. The brief thought that Nox had seen more caused him to cover his eyes and hiss a curse between his teeth.

"I'll have you know," Nox said, "you were a pestilence."

How was former Heir so blasé? His face heated further. But it made sense. Nox seemed to have a different range of life experiences than he did. Of course seeing a little of his shoulders wasn't cause for a reaction.

His eyes landed on his pants, crumpled in a heap outside the washroom. His glorious, wayward pants.

Hadrien, holding his shirt down with one hand, snatched up the pants and retreated into the washroom. The quick movement sent his head spinning; he leaned against the wall and drew in deep, slow breaths.

He was all too aware of his drunken foolishness when he stepped out. Bits and pieces of the night were filtering back to him like a broken dream. Feeling too hot and stripping off his clothes. Pestering Nox.

I will never drink again. He shrugged his jacket on, tucked his flask into a pocket. *That much again, that is.* His gaze darted to the former Heir; Nox was buckling on her vest. *I certainly need* some *to drink with her around.*

He slung his knapsack over his shoulder. "Ready?"

Nox arched a thick eyebrow. "Not before breakfast. I have no interest in seeing you take ill while we ride to Lumieres." She held a hand out, fingers motioning for something. "What do you like?"

"Rainy days—"

"From the bakery." She rolled her eyes in an impressive display and asked, slower, "What do you like from the bakery? You'll have to give me money, too."

I am so slow this morning, he thought and rubbed his temples. "A croissant. Make that two. I'll want one later." He fished out a small purse from his knapsack. "Here. The bakery is only a bit down the street, take the first left, it's on the right then."

"I'll be back."

Nox exited the room, and Hadrien wondered if she indeed would be back. It was Brumais. Nox could disappear from the Arch Shadow here.

Instead of following her, which he should have done, Hadrien ducked back into the washroom to clean up more. He ran a brush through his hair, tamed it back in its usual style. In the mirror, he still looked tired, even with fresh warpaint.

Hadrien braced his hands against the washbasin and squeezed his eyes shut. The tears that slipped out, he blamed on the pounding headache.

Or maybe, he thought, raising his head to watch the tears track down his face, *it's because I was nearly killed by Varen.*

It had been a rough few days, admittedly.

The door opened; he startled. He listened to the quiet steps, the slight drag in each stride. It was… Nox. She had returned. She hadn't taken the chance to run. And— Hadrien inhaled, smelled the sweet scent of freshly baked pastries—she had brought croissants with her.

So, do I not have to worry about her running again? She did *return in the morning that last full moon, like she had said she would.* His stomach dropped out. *Nox could have left last night, and I wouldn't have roused at all.*

His gaze tracked the former Heir as she laid out a few pastries on the table. *She's still here.* Hadrien decided not to apply any more significance to the thought and eat a croissant instead.

The croissant helped.

Still, when he was seated on the Brumesian horse an hour later, guiding him away from the inn, his head spun. He closed his eyes briefly. This last day of travel to Lumieres could not go by fast enough.

"I have a question," Nox said, riding a safe distance from him. "You've been the Heir since my unfortunately not permanent demise—what's the recent Guild news?"

Hadrien frowned. "Why do you care?"

"I don't. I'm merely curious."

"The… uh, the Viper Guild is in shambles. The Heir —what was her name?—she's gone. There's a new one, a man. I think he's in his mid-twenties."

Nox dropped her gelding back to let Hadrien go through the exit tunnel first. Her voice carried up: "Riona died?"

"Should be dead." He twisted back to see the former Heir of the Shadow's face and instantly regretted it; nausea crept up. He faced front again, dragged in a long, slow breath, full of the perfume from the mountain laurel blossoms. "Riona's name was placed on the Mallina List by Sergio himself."

"They were married."

"Marriage doesn't stop names from going on the List." *I don't think he ever loved her, though, if he was so willing to place her name on a kill list at the top for her fellow assassins to vie for.* "No one's claimed the prize yet. I think Riona fled Mallina and went to Revskia or Skogia."

Nox scoffed. "Knowing her, no one will find her." Hooves struck the road in a trot, and then Nox settled her gelding into a walk alongside Hadrien. "You didn't know Riona like I did. She killed her older sister to seize the title of the Heir for herself. No target ever escaped her; every name and prize at the top of the Mallina List was hers." A pause. "I suppose it's good that she's in hiding. If she was set on this hunt for the Wild Moon Wolf, she would win, no matter how inept her partner was."

Hadrien smoothed his palm across his horse's shoulder. The strawberry roan coat was soft—and where were his gloves? Trying to quell his rising panic, he shifted his knapsack around and searched. His sternum ached, his pulse was too fast in his veins.

"Lose something, little Heir?"

His eyes locked on Nox.

"Your hands are quite scarred." She considered the gloves she held in one hand. "I can see why you wear these."

"Give them back."

"Ask nicely."

He worked his jaw, then said, "Please."

Nox stretched her arm out, the gloves offered. Hadrien snatched them up and tugged them on, covering the scars on his hands. He fiddled with the reins, his teeth pinching his lip. Nox could tell the Arch Shadow about this. She could speak of how *panicked* Hadrien became without his gloves.

She turned her gaze to the road and forest ahead. "You were the one who signed us up for the hunt. Did you recognize any other names or people there?"

"No," he replied, but he wasn't certain. "Did you?"

Only the sound of hooves plodding along the road.

"Nox?" A glance at the former Heir showed she was holding the jawbone around her neck with one hand, her eyes fixed on the road ahead. "You know one of the others hunters." Hadrien sat straighter in the saddle, told himself, *I am the Heir of the Shadow, and I am unquestionable,* and ordered, "Tell me."

"He's not a concern," she replied flatly. "He's just a mercenary, about a year or two older than we are. I knew him… before. Don't worry. He won't get the Wild Moon Wolf."

A mercenary? I suppose that makes sense. This Wild Moon Hunt is supposed to have a great reward. His anxiety climbed, trapped his breath in an iron grip. *Once the new month starts, we only have fifteen days to win. That's not much time. By all the relics and holy bones, I hope that this weapon Nox mentioned is easy to find.*

"Enough talking," Hadrien snapped, his wild worry sharpening his words, "let's move."

* * *

When Hadrien laid eyes upon the city of his soul, his breath swept out, and with it, all the tension in his body. Lumieres was a sight to see—perhaps not as impressive as the Floating City that was the capital, but this city was far more dear to him.

There were no built structures in Lumieres, and save for the size of the trees and the trodden dirt paths winding between them, you could mistake Lumieres for the rest of the forest. The trees themselves were the buildings. Golden light seeped out from the doorways and windows set into the trees. Above it all rose a towering maple with magic glittering along the branches, the World Tree itself, Domhan Arbre.

Nox breathed out a soft curse of wonder. "Is that…"

He grinned. "Domhan Arbre." Everything was forgotten in the majesty of its view. "The largest tree in the entire world. All the libraries of Lumieres are housed within, and that is where we'll find that weapon you mentioned."

Nox, frozen, gazed longer upon Domhan Arbre in silence.

I wish I could stay here forever, Hadrien thought. He winced. Such a thought undermined everything he had been working towards in the Shadow Guild. He couldn't be the Heir of the Shadow—set to lead the Guild one day—and live in Brumais. He couldn't have it all.

"We'll stay at The Roasted Chestnut," Hadrien said and urged his gelding forward. "It's the inn closest to Domhan Arbre. Then we'll go to the libraries. There's enough time to start on research before nightfall."

"Two beds this time."

A flush hit his cheeks so fast it was like whiplash. Glad that Nox wasn't able to see his face, he pressed his horse into a trot. A matching set of hoofbeats followed.

"I decided," Nox said when they slowed at the chestnut tree that was the inn, "that I'm going to call this pretty gelding Ettore." She dismounted and patted the shoulder of the newly named Ettore. Like Hadrien's temporary steed, Ettore was a strawberry roan, fine in stature.

Hadrien slid out of the saddle and considered the two horses. "They're siblings," he decided. "They have a similar face." Both were smaller than Ikarus and Embra. "More of ponies, huh."

"Perfect for me," she replied and tossed him a sly grin. "You, not so much. I saw your legs today; they were halfway to the ground. You're too tall for these little ponies, as you call them."

A thousand different responses flashed through his mind. He settled on: "At least I can get things off shelves."

Nox made an offended noise. "For that, I'm calling your horse Tiny." She pointed at each of the horses in turn. "Ettore and Tiny. Mine has the socks, yours has the star."

Hadrien found himself about to laugh; he covered it up by clearing his throat. Nox shouldn't make him laugh. "Get your pack and wait in the inn, I'll take the horses to the stables."

Not staying to see if the former Heir did as he said, Hadrien hooked his fingers through the reins of the horses. One on either side, he walked them to the stables behind the inn.

The stables, like all other residences of Lumieres, were formed from trees. A row of perfectly sized stalls, each set in individual trees. A few curious horses peeked out, ears pricked at the newcomers. A trio of stablehands jogged up and took the horses from Hadrien.

He watched them go.

Then he turned and strode back to the inn. Nox was leaning against the trunk next to the arched door, arms crossed loosely and one leg bent to rest on the bark. Her gaze was cast off in the distance, focused on something that Hadrien couldn't see.

"Nox."

She startled. "Ha—*hey* there, Heir."

He blinked. "If that was meant to be a joke, it was rather terrible." He grabbed hold of the handle and pushed the door open. "Why didn't you go in?"

"I don't speak Brumesian."

Thank the Three Mothers that the inn had a room with two beds. He did not ever need to repeat last night. Though he could still remember how warm Nox had felt in the night. Those were the thoughts that would land him in trouble. *Curse this body. Tamp it down. Remember Renata, that girl in Arezza. This is all just the want of comfort after a terror, after Varen. Find your comfort in a bottle of brandy, not in the closeness of Nox. She's the former Heir, after all.*

Maybe when he got back, he would say yes to that girl with the kind eyes. Maybe he'd kiss her under the light of the three moons.

"Heir," Nox said, jarring him from his thoughts, "you ready to go?"

Hadrien threw his knapsack onto a chair and motioned to the bed. "Weapons. Domhan Arbre allows no weapons into the libraries." He cast off his bow, his quiver, his daggers, and his knives. "Put yours out. I'll be counting."

And he did.

He counted each weapon that the former Heir shed.

Nox stepped back and nodded shortly. "There."

Hadrien closed the distance between them, and keeping his eyes locked with Nox's, knelt at her feet. He skimmed his fingers up the outside of her boots, and Nox shifted her weight slightly. At her knees, he dipped his fingers into the inside of the boots, ran them around in a slow arc until his fingertips caught on the hilt of a knife in both boots.

He smiled and slipped the knives free. "Liar."

He rose, towering over Nox, and shook his head. "I know these tricks." He tossed the two knives onto the bed. "Don't try them on me." *Hold your ground,* he told himself. "Now, are you ready?"

Silence stretched out, and the space between them didn't grow. Nox didn't drop his gaze. The air turned charged, rife with tension that only needed a spark to boil into an inferno.

The corner of her scarred mouth twitched up.

Then Nox pivoted on the heels of her boots and sauntered to the door. "Lead the way, Heir."

With one last glance at the weapons, scattered across the beds, Hadrien locked the door behind himself and followed Nox out.

Chapter Fourteen
Nox

Domhan Arbre was breathtaking.

The entirety of Lumieres was wondrous, but this colossal maple was truly something else. I could not stop myself from tipping my head back to marvel at the sheer size. I could have never imagined a tree this massive. It was a god tree, a deity tree, a tree beyond mortal scope.

The Heir started up the stairs carved into the side of the maple. I ran my fingers over the bark as we wound our way up to the doors set into the tree. The Heir caught my eye for a heartbeat, then he was looking away.

The doors to Domhan Arbre swung open without a touch.

I thought about the amulet in my pocket.

"Nox," the Heir said, his eyes ablaze with a mix of pride and wonder, "welcome to Domhan Arbre."

He crossed the threshold, and I followed him in. The doors closed behind us. My senses were dazzled. The air smelled of a hundred million books, old and ancient and eternal. I couldn't process what my own eyes were seeing.

"How is this possible?" I breathed.

"Magic," the Heir replied.

As insurmountable as the maple appeared from the outside, the inside was even more expansive. A network of stairs and balconies and walkways sprawled across the interior. The entirety was bathed in amber light from floating glass globes with miniature suns within.

Spiraling staircases curved up through the interior, some covered in trailing vines, others in blooming flowers. Stairs wove down, too, to a garden below with benches.

The books. The shelves. Every wall of the maple was studded with shelves that were filled to the brim. Small trees—actual, regular-sized trees growing within Domhan Arbre—were dotted throughout the hundred or more levels; shelves were built into these, too.

My breath whooshed out. "Where do we even start?"

"May I help you?"

That wasn't the Heir.

I glanced around. Where was that voice coming from?

But the Heir was looking down, a pleasant expression on his face. "We're only looking right now. Tomorrow is when we'll need more help."

I barely heard his words.

There was a dragon before me.

A small dragon, to be sure, and I had slain larger ones, but it was a *friendly* dragon. Its luminous violet eyes peered up at us behind a pair of wire-rimmed spectacles perched on its snout. Short feathers ran down the length of its spine, the same autumn leaf color as the glistening scales. Unlike other dragons I had seen, this one had two pairs of feathered wings like a bird's.

"Nox," the Heir said, "this is a library dragon."

"My name is Aveline, and I can help you find what it is you're looking for," the dragon chirped.

I could never kill a dragon again.

Painfully aware of where the leather on my armour had come from, I said, "I can see that." The Heir's eyes were on me, the weight of them digging into my bones. "Do you know of the Wild Moon Wolf?"

Aveline nodded. "You may follow me. It is on the forty-fifth floor."

"How did you—"

"I am two thousand years old, Nox," the dragon replied, trotting towards the stairs, "and I know much."

I missed this place, Lupakaria said softly.

Oh, of course, you've been here. I couldn't picture her walking these stairs, though. But she had never shown me what her other forms looked like, what her god form was, only her wolf form. It was hard to imagine a wolf pacing the stairs, flipping through an ancient tome with large paws.

By the fifteenth floor we'd scaled, my thighs were burning. Ten floors later, Aveline was waiting while the Heir and I collapsed on benches, panting. I swiped sweat off the back of my neck and wiped it on my pants. No one had told me the libraries would involve so many stairs.

"Is there a particular text you're in search of?" Aveline inquired. "I can fetch a number of tomes for you if you're seeking information."

The Heir groaned. "I love this place, but I wish there were magic stairs."

And I'll have to go to the very top before we leave. I shut my eyes. "I don't know what text. Anything on the Wild Moon Wolf."

"I'll return shortly."

As the little dragon's claws pattered off, I laid down on the bench and stared into the seemingly never-ending heights of Domhan Arbre. It felt like I had rested only a minute before Aveline was approaching again.

"You have traveled far," she said, "and I think it may be more beneficial if you return tomorrow to learn. I have sent a select collection of texts down to the garden for you to peruse at your leisure."

The Heir covered a yawn. "I'm sorry. Thank you for finding those, Aveline. I think we had best return at a later time." He paused, then said quietly, "We ran into Varen on our way through the forest."

Aveline's wings fluttered. "For you to be alive still… Something protects you."

The Heir laughed shortly, humorlessly. "Trust me, it's the opposite."

Out of sight of them both, I surreptitiously touched the Jaws of Lupakaria. Just a light brush of my fingertips against the bone, my nails dipping into the silver-filled etchings.

Aveline promised to keep the texts available for us and to help us when we next stopped by the libraries. The Heir stood after a minute; he seemed twitchy, anxious, rubbing at his forearm like it was bothering him.

"What's with you?" I finally asked, sitting up.

"Nothing," he answered.

Ah, too fast, little Heir, I thought. But I was tired. I was slipping up—I'd almost said his name earlier. I didn't give chase to his lies. "Let's go back."

It was a good decision.

The Heir was yawning and looking faintly sick when we entered our room at The Roasted Chestnut. I started putting away my weapons and told him to go bathe before he fell over. He didn't put up an argument, and that made me stare after him until the washroom door closed.

What's with him? I wondered, my hands stilling on a pair of knives. *It was his idea to go to the libraries immediately, but he seems so tired. Maybe he needs a long night of sleep. I know I do. Neither of us have slept well since, well, since before we even met each other.*

The rush of water filling the tub drew my eye to the shut door again. I considered an idea for a heartbeat, then rifled through his knapsack until I found a coin-purse. With quiet steps, I slipped out of the room.

Are you running? Lupakaria stretched out her limbs in my mind. *This is not a good time to run, little wolf. You had many other chances that you did not take.*

I'm not. My gaze fixed on the sign for a bakery a few trees down. Night had fallen, but lights were still on in the windows.

Ah.

I used the Heir's money to pay for a basket full of croissants, lemon-glazed madeleines, sandwiches, and a jar of fresh assorted berries. As I walked back to the inn, I popped a few blackberries into my mouth and savored the burst of tart and sweet.

At the door to the room, I hesitated. Would he think I had tried to run? No, I hadn't been gone that long.

I stepped back in. A glance at the washroom: door still closed, the faint sound of moving water within. A glance out the window, craning my head back to see the outline of the moons: silver, just past the waning half; golden, closer to a new moon than the silver moon was; and the absent blue moon.

So there was a new moon in the sky tonight.

I ran my fingers along the fine links of my moons necklace. Set on different lengths of chain, the three disks mirrored the actuality of the moons. I tucked the necklace back under my shirt, hiding it. It settled against the medallion I still wore. My thumb brushed the surface, felt the design of the wolf's head in the silver.

The Wolf Guild was long gone, I reminded myself, and the Shadow Guild was what had risen in its stead.

I rapped my knuckles on the door to the washroom. "Heir, there's food on the table."

The Heir didn't reply.

My pulse kicked faster. I knocked harder. "Heir."

Water sloshed. Then: "Sorry. Dozed off."

"Don't drown," I replied.

Pulse calming, I exhaled and went to eat a sandwich. I had gotten two like the one the Heir had bought in Cipres yesterday. That was *only* yesterday. Days of travel always stretched on for eons.

The door creaked, steam pooled out, and the Heir, head ducked, came out. He said nothing and climbed into his own bed, his back facing me.

By the time I bathed and was in my bed, it was near midnight. The Heir had eaten while I was in the washroom—the other sandwich was gone, as was a croissant. At least he had eaten, even if he wasn't talking to me. Why, I didn't know.

I fluffed my pillow and rested my head on it.

The sharp, hissed inhale seemed like it was from my imagination.

But I wasn't asleep yet, and Lupakaria whispered, *It's real.*

I raised my head, searching through the room. The sound, the pained sound, had been close enough to be in the room. I hadn't fallen asleep; I would have heard if someone broke into the room.

The Heir.

I was out of bed in a heartbeat, lighting a candle and crossing the room to his bed. "Heir," I said and shoved the foot of his bed, "wake up."

His shoulders curled tighter. "Go away."

"Are you sick?" *Or suffering from too much drink?* That would explain why he'd been nauseous today and seemed to be in pain now. "You can't be. You need to be on your feet soon."

I lifted the candle higher, and light spilled across his form. His body, tight and tense under a blanket, shaking every few heartbeats. *He must be really sick.* My eyes roamed up to his head, his hair dark from the bath still, his hands clutched at his jawline. *Strange to not be wrapping his arms around his stomach if he's sick.*

Look closer, o dreamer.

What did Lupakaria see that I didn't?

And then I saw it: the blossoms of scarlet blood upon the pillowcase.

"Hadrien," I breathed out.

His shoulders stiffened. "Go away," he said again. "You don't want to see this."

I swallowed hard, grabbed his shoulder, and rolled

him. My thoughts faltered to a standstill. Even my breath stopped.

Something was terribly wrong with him.

Thorny vines spiraled in and out of his eyes, the hooks snagging and slicing the skin around his eyes. His hands bore fresh scratches from the thorns already.

I forced out a breath. "I can't say I've seen this before." I considered him. "This is why you wear the warpaint, isn't it? It conceals the scars and the scratches." Setting the candle down on a small nightstand, next to his gloves, I added, "Same for the gloves. That's why you panicked when you couldn't find them."

"Don't tell anyone," he whispered, and beyond the blood, tears glimmered in his eyes. They slipped free, one by one, and mingled with the blood and warpaint to smear dirty tracks across his face. *"Please."*

I looked away at that broken word.

Hadrien turned away from me again, shoulders hunched.

I stepped away, returning with a damp washcloth. "Clean your hands and your face." I waited, then tapped his shoulder with his gloves. "Here's your gloves."

He was still. Then, like a fern unfurling in the sun, he grabbed the gloves and slid them on. "Thank you."

Folding the dirty washcloth in my hands, I asked, "How long will this last?"

"Until the new moon is done." His voice wavered. "And then it will start on the next new moon, and the next, and the next."

Seems you aren't the only who has trouble with moons, Lupakaria murmured, her voice silky and full of secrets.

Lupakaria, hush.

No one can hear me but you.

"Every new moon, you have this?"

"The dark garden."

Dark garden. Was that a cruel twist of fate, or was it inspired by the tattoos on his arm? "How did this happen?"

"Don't cross witches," he said through his gritted teeth. "I was cursed. I almost clawed my eyes out the first time. It can be broken, supposedly."

Of course, he's cursed. Why wouldn't he be? "By the breath of fresh spring upon a windless day?" I guessed, keeping my voice light, trying to mask the horror chilling in my blood. "Or is it the evergreen true love's kiss?"

He laughed without humor. "Something more impossible than those."

Thank the Mothers Three I don't have to break this. "Do you need anything now?"

"I should bathe. It's… easier to wash away the blood that way."

I threw back the blanket covering him. "Come on. I'll help you get there." He rolled to the edge of the bed, his head down, and I pulled his arm over my shoulders. "Take it slow. I've got you, Hadrien, I've got you."

My words hit my ears too late; I grimaced. I needed to stop saying his name. He was the Heir of the Shadow. He was not just some boy, some hunter. He was not Hadrien, not to me.

In the washroom, the Heir perched on the edge of the tub, his face turned away. The water began to pour into the tub, steam curling up. The Heir leaned down, trailed his fingers through the rising waters. A drop of blood plinked into the water, vanished in the swirl.

"Can this kill you?" I asked.

"No, but I can."

It took me a second to puzzle through what he meant. "You have a job to do," I told him. "If that's something you've tried or are thinking of trying, you're not doing that while I'm around."

He touched his wrist, his thumb moving back and forth. Then he snatched his hand away and reached for the hem of his nightshirt.

"Call for me," I said and left the washroom.

I shut the door and stood there, motionless, not seeing the wall across from me. Thorns. Thorns in his eyes. Spiraling and twisting endlessly. How could he bear it each time?

What had he done to be cursed like that?

Wish, and I will tell you, Lupakaria offered. *I will read his blood like ink.*

I didn't refuse immediately.

You want to know.

I do.

Then utter the words you know so well.

I opened my mouth and whispered, "Lupakaria, I— No. Nothing. I'll find out on my own."

Your loss, little wolf.

I glanced at the blood on the Heir's bed; a shudder rolled through me. I didn't know him. For all I knew, the Heir had done something brutal and terrible, and the dark garden was a punishment curse.

The same Heir who had rescued a maned wolf pup from vultures.

No, it didn't add up.

The curse had come from something else.

I tried to distract myself for an hour, pacing the length of the room. But it was so quiet with Hadrien—no, *the Heir*—in the washroom.

I knocked on the door. "Are you alive in there?"

A beat of silence. "Open the door."

"But you're—"

"I know. Open it. I—I need you here."

Did you hear that, little wolf?

Shut up, *Lupa.*

Fury split my head. *My name is Lupakaria of the Wishes and you will—*

I knew that would infuriate her. I lifted the Jaws over my head and set them on my bed. *Negotiate with silence for the time, Lupakaria,* I thought and cracked the door to the washroom open. The heat of steam washed over me, bringing with it the scent of peach blossoms and blood.

"Where do you want me?" I asked through the gap.

"Sit in here."

I slipped through and closed the door behind me, enclosing us in steam and quiet. The Heir had his arms stacked atop the side of the tub, his head turned sideways on them. With the angle of his head, I saw only his tangled waves of wet hair, gilded by candlelight.

To the wall, he whispered, "I don't want to do this alone again."

His voice shaking, he added, "I still hear Varen."

I lowered myself to the floor near the foot of the tub and leaned back against the wall. "What do you want me to do?"

"Talk to me?"

So I did.

I told him stories of my days when I was the Heir.

The hunts I'd been on, the places I'd seen, the beasts, beautiful and monstrous alike, I'd encountered. Tales of mischief Xenna, Rogus, and I had gotten up to in our years, both with and without the influence of alcohol.

"You're telling me that you and Xenna and Rogus are responsible for burning down the Iron Vintage vineyards?" He moved his arm, water dripping and the golden glow of the candle glistening off his skin. His fingers swept across his face, then dipped bloodied into the bath. "I remember hearing about that fire."

"That was us," I said and grinned. Rogus had been so distraught, and I'd plied him with whiskey until he was laughing with us. "That was the last time I ever saw Rogus touch fire, too." My smile faded. "I wish I could've spoken with him one more time."

Safe words to say without the Jaws of Lupakaria at my throat.

I missed him.

But in a way, I had lost him six months ago when the Arch Shadow left me for dead. In a way, I had already grieved for him, when I grieved for the life I'd lost. Missing him now was a distant, old ache.

"He seemed sad that day," the Heir said, his voice so quiet it was nearly inaudible. "I asked him about it, and he said that the dreams had come back."

I drew my knee up, rested my hand atop it. "Rogus used to dream of the beasts we'd slain clawing their way through the dirt and decay to kill us in our sleep."

"Then… why did he seem sad?"

"I would stay awake with him on those nights." My fingers drummed along my knee. "He probably was remembering that." A cruel thought twined through my mind. *I'm glad he's dead. The Arch Shadow can't hurt him anymore.* It was nothing I could attribute to Lupakaria; the thought was wholly my own.

After a long beat, the Heir said, "I'm sorry I couldn't save him."

In the near dark, with him in pain, I could say it. "It's for the best. The Arch Shadow would've hurt him."

"No—"

"You don't know her like I do." I raised my head and found his eyes behind the thorns. "Tell me, does the Arch Shadow know of this dark garden, or have you hidden it from everyone?"

His silence and him turning away was the answer.

"I don't know what she's told you. But she is willing to give me the title of Heir back if I win. She has and will sacrifice lives."

"It's…" The Heir trailed off, then he breathed out, "Oh."

"One of us is meant to die, Hadrien."

And it will not be me.

Chapter Fifteen
Hadrien

How HAD he been so oblivious to the reality?

Yes, it was partners for the Wild Moon Hunt, and yes, two people could receive the reward from the Emperor. But there was only one title of the Heir of the Shadow.

Hadrien didn't imagine that Nox would just let him walk back to the House of Shadows with the head and heart of the Wild Moon Wolf; he would have to kill the former Heir or let her die.

Or maybe the Wild Moon Wolf would kill Nox and save him the trouble.

"Leave," he told Nox. "I'm getting out."

She padded out.

Hadrien toweled off, dressed, and tried to ignore the pain. To an extent, he felt numb. The realization that within a month he could be dead, that shouldn't rattle him like this. He'd never fully embraced the idea of a long life, so why did the thought of a soon death affect him?

He supposed it was because it wouldn't be his choice.

Feeling utterly foolish for that, Hadrien laid on his back in the bed and stared past the thorns to the ceiling.

"I need to sleep," Nox said. "Will you be fine?"

What a stupid question. "No," he spat out.

She climbed into her bed and turned her back to him.

Regret slunk through Hadrien. That had been uncalled for; Nox had been helping him. "I mean… not right now. I'm not fine right now. Maybe one day I will be."

The bed creaked, and then he saw cobalt eyes staring at him. Nox didn't respond immediately, maybe searching for something to say. Finally, she replied, "That day will come."

"One of us will be dead this time next month." Hadrien scoffed. "At least I only have two more dark gardens to suffer."

"Excuse me for trying to be optimistic." Nox's hand curled around the jawbone amulet, back on her neck again, resting on her sternum. "You should try it some-time. Who knows, maybe you'll break your little curse and won't have that to darken your days."

Even if he did understand how to break his curse, it wouldn't change the fact that Mother Death was coming soon for one of them. Maybe even both.

His thoughts ran rampant.

As night slipped into day and pain settled its teeth soundly into his bones, he saw Varen looming over him, his antlers the branching shadows on the ceiling. Hadrien's body wouldn't let him scream. Varen's breath washed over his face, rank with the stench of rotting teeth. He couldn't move as the dead elk leaned down and gnawed a hole into his chest until Varen reached his beating heart.

Nox stood over him then, barely visible past Varen's form. With a frown, she waved her hand over Hadrien's face. "What are you looking at? There's nothing there."

The paralysis loosened its grip; he floundered for air. Shoving himself up, shuddering at the blood rolling down his cheeks, he muttered, "Nothing." He turned his face away from Nox. "What time is it?"

"Close to midday."

Hadrien sighed. "Just put me out of my misery."

"Don't tempt me." Nox skimmed her fingers along the jawbone amulet. "Do you need something?"

He should eat. But his stomach was tied up in knots. He shook his head. "I need time to go by faster."

"Can't help you there." She paused—an awkward pause, her head tilted like she was listening. But Hadrien could hear nothing. Then she said, "Unless you told me more about this curse."

Why does she want to know? It's not as if she'll be in my life long. "Go to the library," he ordered. "Start researching how we can trap and kill the Wild Moon Wolf."

"I have a better idea."

Listening to her stride away, Hadrien scuffed his knuckles over his sternum. There were no marks, no bruises, no gaping wounds, but by the Three Mothers, had that felt real. A waking dream, he supposed. He hoped he wouldn't have more of those.

Nox dragged a chair over, and then a glass thunked down on the nightstand. "There's water for you. And I am going to read you fairytales. You seem like the type of person who enjoys fairytales."

"You can't read all day," he protested, but he didn't mean it. Anything to distract him from the pain, he would welcome.

"I can, and I will." Nox cleared her throat and began to read aloud in a steady, clear voice.

And Hadrien thought that maybe in a different life, he could've been friends with Nox.

But that was not this life.

When the dark garden faded away, Hadrien sobbed.

He staggered to the washroom, startling Nox into sitting up taller. The washroom was dark and cold, but he could make out his haggard reflection in the mirror. Sweat and dried blood stained the collar of his shirt; rivulets of blood, sweat, and tears had run down the shirt.

"Are you fine?"

In the mirror, he met the cobalt eyes of Nox. "I'm fine now." He wet a washcloth and scrubbed at his face, stripping away the mess from the dark garden. "You should get some sleep. We'll return to Domhan Arbre in the morning."

Nox nodded and said nothing more.

He couldn't blame her. The former Heir's voice had turned hoarse, the skin under her eyes had turned dark like a bruise, and yet she had kept reading from the book of fairytales.

It had not been lost on Hadrien that every fairytale Nox read dealt with the breaking of a curse. One did ring familiar, but it was only fiction. And surely Calixta, the sorceress in Borrasca who'd told him more about the curse based off what Hadrien had remembered, would've said if that fairytale was a viable example.

But that fairytale had ended in the cursed dying.

That didn't bode well for Hadrien.

It lingered in his thoughts all night, even as he tossed and turned between bouts of fitful sleep. After the dark garden, he should've slept more. An impossible task when he had two more rounds of the dark garden approaching. Two more new moons before the first full moon, before the Wild Moon Hunt even began.

If only he could make the next ten days pass in a heartbeat like stepping through an Ianis Frame.

The light of morning came too soon, but Hadrien forced himself out of bed and through the motions of cleaning and dressing for the day. Nox grumbled faintly.

Neither of them spoke through a quick breakfast of leftover pastries and fresh tea. Nox clung to her teacup like it would save her from exhaustion. Given that it was black tea from Qarthanda, the caffeine—and honey Nox added—in it very likely could.

After a day suffering the dark garden, stepping out into the sunshine of Lumieres was a blessing from the Three Mothers. Hadrien tilted his head back, eyes shut, and let the sun's warmth sink into his bones.

Nox waited without a word.

Truly, there was nothing so relaxing as a strong ray of sunlight, one to ease aches and tensions away.

When Hadrien opened his eyes again, he saw why Nox was waiting so quietly—the former Heir had her face turned up to the sun, too. Her expression was soft with content, her usual scowl faded away.

Her eyes slid open, settling on Hadrien like she'd felt the weight of his gaze. "Time for reading lots and lots of books?"

Why did this suddenly seem so undoable? The thought dogged at his heels as he climbed the steps to Domhan Arbre again. Even with the help of Aveline and Nox—and just *how* helpful was Nox going to be?

"You're making that face," Nox said, peering around at the expansive interior of the libraries, "the one that says you are thinking too hard and are straining your little mind."

"I am not," he protested. There were no nearby mirrors to check, but he made an exaggerated smile. "See? I'm smiling."

"That's not a smile, that's a grimace."

Aveline landing in front of them halted any more conversation. The dragon had a new set of spectacles today, rimmed in gilded bone and strung on beaded thread. "Hello again, Nox and Hadrien, welcome to Domhan Arbre. Are you still searching for information on the Wild Moon Wolf?"

"We are."

"The texts I collected two days ago are now located in the garden for your reading. Since you are here so early, I can accompany you to translate or provide further explanation upon anything. Should I not be able to offer a suitable answer, I will send for Fleur."

"Thank you."

The dragon soared on feathered wings to the garden below, leaving Hadrien and Nox to descend the stairs. Nox's head swiveled around as she looked at more of

Domhan Arbre. Then she halted so suddenly Hadrien collided with her back.

"Nox!" he snapped.

She twisted around, mouth parting to reply. With a shake of her head and not a word, Nox continued down the stairs.

Hadrien glanced around but saw nothing that would've made her stop like that. *What a strange girl,* he thought, and then all thoughts were replaced by a sense of wonder at the garden. It was a riot of every flower he could imagine, plus ones he'd never seen before, clustered around a blooming magnolia that looked like it had stood since the beginning of time and would stand until the end of time.

Aveline was carrying a stack of books over to where Nox lounged on a bench in the dappled shade of the magnolia. The former Heir smiled—actually *smiled*—at the dragon and then leaned forward, and her lips moved in words Hadrien couldn't decipher. The dragon paused, head cocked, and nodded.

Nox watched the dragon fly off. Her eyes locked on Hadrien. "Are you going to stand there all day, or are you going to read?" She kicked her legs up on the bench, knees drawn up, and indicated the books at the other end of the bench. "Pick one, start reading."

Why is Nox acting like she's the current Heir, not me? Giving me orders. Hadrien strode forward and grabbed the first book. "Look for any mention of that weapon," he instructed, trying to grab hold of some semblance of authority, "as well as any methods used to trap eclipse-born beasts like the Wild Moon Wolf."

"E... eclipse-born?"

Hadrien, pausing in flipping through the pages, slowly brought his gaze to her. "Eclipse-born. The Wild Moon Wolf was born during an eclipse. Or created. Or whatever brought that beast onto the lands of Khtonyx." He scoffed. "Surely you would've heard about this, considering your blade is named Eclipse."

"It's a phenomenon," Nox replied, snatching up a book and opening it, "a rare one. I thought it was a good name for a sword."

"Regardless, I'm sure there's something on beasts like the Wild Moon Wolf." He divided up the remaining books and handed half to Nox. "You take those."

She frowned. "One of these is in Brumesian."

"Ask Aveline to help you."

"No, trade with me. Give me one in either Atassish or Vox Terrae." She shook the book at him until he switched it out for one of his. "Now, let me read."

Hadrien took his books and retreated to the bench on the other side of the magnolia. In the quiet of the garden, he heard the whisper of pages turning as Nox read. With a sigh, he began to read as well.

After he had skimmed sixty pages in search of similar situations, Aveline reappeared, bearing a scroll in her talons. The dragon carried the scroll to Nox; Hadrien furrowed his brow. What was Nox looking into? Then her words rang in his head—*you're making that face*—and he tried to smooth out his expression.

"Aveline," he called.

The dragon trotted over. "Yes?"

Now he wasn't so sure he wanted to ask. He lowered his voice. "Is there a section on curses?"

"Of course. However, due to the nature of some of

the tomes, we do not allow them down here. You can find them at the top of Domhan Arbre, and I am happy to assist you with further locating."

"That is fine. I'll look later. Thank you."

Aveline laid in a patch of sunlight from a miniature sun, and Hadrien returned to reading. He had to finish these before he could look at the books on curses. It was only fair. The curse was personal, the Wild Moon Wolf was for the Guild. Guild business came first.

But his focus wandered.

Finally, Nox said, "Whatever it is that is distracting you, alleviate it. You are distracting *me* with your endless shifting and sighing. I cannot understand what I am reading."

He practically leapt from the bench. Aveline raised her head, a stray petal clinging to her feathers, and followed Hadrien out of the garden.

"There is a lift," she said, "only for reaching the top floor. It is slow."

As long as he didn't have to climb all those stairs.

The lift was a simple hammock constructed of blossom-studded vines. Hadrien eyed it, dread locking his muscles. The vines ascended up, up, up.

Aveline promised it was safe.

He kept his eyes shut the whole time, until his boots were alighting on the solid platform at the top of Domhan Arbre. His legs shook as he shifted his weight forward, left the lift behind. With a quiet shiver of vines on bark, the lift descended, empty.

"It will return when it's needed," Aveline said. Gliding across the platform to the shelves, all secured behind iron-set glass, she added, "Now, here are the tomes on curses. Some are bound by curses, so only a librarian like myself can handle the books. What are you seeking?"

He rubbed at his neck. "Curses dealing with thorns, new moons, and 'punishment for not being true to myself.' That last part is exactly what the witches said."

The dragon's eyes glowed white. A heartbeat later, Aveline scurried over to the shelves. She slipped on some sort of glove, made of links of metal, then slid the glass back and plucked a book off the shelf. The pages rippled, settled.

Aveline carried the book over to Hadrien but didn't offer it. Eyes dashing across a series of pages, she said, "There is not much on the particulars you mentioned. A knight many years ago was cursed when he began under the employment of a queen, who outlawed all of his order save for him. From then on, every new moon, he had thorns upon his hands, until he revoked the lies he told himself and rejoined his order. The knight's curse never returned."

Decidedly unhelpful.

Hadrien sighed. "Is that all?" *But where am I not being true to myself? Is it the Shadow Guild? Maybe it's linked to Rogus.*

A scuff of a boot made him turn around. "Nox?"

Her eyes were wide. The former Heir stood at the edge of the platform, stock still. She tore her gaze away from his and looked at something in her hand. Then she whispered, "It's you."

His skin went cold for reasons Hadrien could not explain. "What do you mean? What's me?" But she kept staring. "Nox. What?"

"I came up here to find you, to tell you about the Wild Moon Wolf. But now, I have something else I need to tell you." She approached on quiet steps and held out her hand, palm upturned, fingers cupped around something. "This is for you."

It was a circular amulet. Pure silver with a rose etched into the surface. There was nothing special about it. It wasn't even very remarkable.

He frowned. "That's not mine."

"It's meant for you. The Exalted Queen of the Isle gave it to me and bade me to bring it to the cursed at the top of Domhan Arbre." Nox looked around. "It's only you here."

"The Exalted Queen? As in… a faerie?"

She nodded.

Feeling as if he'd break if he moved too fast, he lifted the amulet from her palm. Hadrien almost dropped it; it was *heavy*. Holding the amulet firmer, he turned it over. The back was silver with no designs upon it, unlike the front. He ran his thumb over the surface, around the edge —His nail caught on a latch.

His mouth went dry. He opened the amulet—locket, more of—and a length of silk ribbon unspooled endlessly. Nox leapt back.

Hadrien touched his finger to it. Smooth as oil, the silk was the grey of tarnished iron and about as wide as his thumbnail. There didn't seem to be an end to it. "It's just silk."

Nox worked her jaw back and forth, the joint clicking. "I didn't know that was in there."

It's strange but nothing noteworthy. He shoved the amulet into his jacket pocket, where it clinked against his flask.

"Now, what did you find out about the Wild Moon Wolf?"

"I'll show you in the garden."

Wondering what Nox could have found, Hadrien started for the lift. He sat down and waited for it to begin the descent. It didn't move, and Nox cleared her throat.

"Scoot over."

"No, it can't hold both of us."

From where she was reading a book, Aveline called, "Yes, it can."

Nox gave him a triumphant look. "See? Now, scoot over."

This was a terrible idea.

He shifted over a few inches, and Nox squeezed in next to him. Her shoulder, her side, her hip, her entire thigh was pressed against him. Hadrien stiffened, his awareness of his body heightening and sharpening to a fine point. He tried not to breathe.

The lift descended so slowly, it was agonizing.

Nox slung one leg over the other, her body leaning ever so slightly away. "Breathe a little," she said. "It would be a shame if you passed out and fell."

Thanks for that fear. He looped his arm around a vine. "I'm fine." He shut his eyes and exhaled, more forcefully than he intended.

"You don't sound fine."

"You're *right* next to me."

"I have nothing to stab you with." But the heat and weight from her body shifted away a little more. "Is that better?"

He didn't dare open his eyes. "Yes."

"We're almost to the garden."

Hadrien managed a noise that sounded pitiful even to his own ears. *Distract yourself,* he thought, but he couldn't think of anything to focus on. *The amulet, the silk. What are those about?*

"Almost there," Nox said. "And I've found something you'll want to see."

Chapter Sixteen
Nox

As the garden drew closer, I inspected the Heir. He was who the Exalted Queen had sent me to find and deliver the amulet to, and now, I could return to Isla Tower and strike my bargain. But why? Why was Hadrien —the boy cursed with the dark garden, the boy who had replaced me as the Heir of the Shadow—why was *he* the one?

The lift stopped; my boots rested on the ground.

I tapped the Heir. "Come on."

His breath swept out, and Hadrien scrambled out of the hammock-lift. I followed less frantically and led him to where I had left the books I was reading. A soft whisper of feathers and wind announced Aveline's arrival; she had brought with her another dragon, this one hued like a field of spring flowers. Fleur, probably.

The Heir thumped down on the bench and ran his hands over his face. Given his sharp hiss of breath, he had aggravated one of his cuts from the thorns. "Tell me what you learned."

I grabbed the book and opened it to the section. "There are others."

"Wild Moon Wolves?"

"No, just eclipse-born creatures like the Wild Moon Wolf."

When I said nothing more, the Heir cracked open one eye past his fingers. A blue-grey iris glared at me. "That's it? That was the oh so important information you found?"

"So far." I shrugged. "I can't read these texts very fast. You were fidgeting and distracting me."

The Heir heaved a sigh and lowered his hands. "Aveline," he said, his voice bearing with it all the rasp of exhaustion, "can you look for information related to these others?"

Their eyes glowed white. Fleur blinked, her eyes returning to their usual sky blue color, and began to carefully turn the pages of one book. She murmured to Aveline in Brumesian, and the bespectacled dragon nodded.

"Fleur found this. Faerie children born under the dark of an eclipse are rumored to be burdened with a curse from their first breath until their last. The curse fates them for the form of a monster during full moons. They differ from other mortals cursed with lunar monster forms as they are susceptible to the Fetters of Aisling and iron only in that form. There is no known remedy."

"Aisling?" I asked.

"The place where mortals blessed with Inks go at thirteen to learn about their Ink."

Oh. I glanced at the Heir. "So you've been there?"

He nodded once, his gaze on Aveline. "What else is there?"

"The Fetters of Aisling haven't been seen in years. The last recorded sighting was with the fair ones. They took the Fetters back to keep hunters from trapping their fellow faeries with them."

The Heir looked faintly ill.

I remembered our fight at the House of Shadows. He knew what lay under the pelts of some beasts, or so he had claimed. The Arch Shadow never told us. Most of the Shadows didn't know.

I had found out in a way that lingered in my nightmares. He must have, too.

Fleur said something that made the Heir turn his face away.

In a grave tone, Aveline said, "We know that you are the Heirs of the Shadow, current and former. While we know that we cannot stop you from hunting your quarry, nor can we stop the hunt that the Emperor of Atassia has decreed, we ask that you leave the Wild Moon Wolf to live."

The Heir's mouth flattened. "We can't. The Arch Shadow has set us on the task. Whoever brings her the head and heart of the beast will be her Heir."

"Whoever doesn't is already dead," I said.

He gave me a sharp look. "We don't know that." But his voice was defeated. Did he think he would lose? The first full moon was still over a week away. Was he giving up now?

Aveline's feathers fluffed up. "We ask that you leave now."

The Heir massaged his temples. "Someone else will be here," he told them, "and they too will seek information on how to slay the Wild Moon Wolf. I cannot promise to let her live, but I can promise to not let her suffer at my hand."

The two librarian dragons then looked to me, and Lupakaria laughed in my head. *They are awaiting your response, little wolf. You can wish for them to forget that you never said a word here.*

I inhaled, brushed my fingertips against the Jaws. *Lupakaria, I wish for Aveline and Fleur here in Domhan Arbre now to disregard that I say nothing and to return to helping us.*

I felt nothing.

The dragons both nodded, and Aveline was the one who said, "I suppose then that we will return to helping."

Lupakaria stretched in my mind, head tilting up, tail curling. *I feel so alive! Come, let us devour cheese and the bones of our enemies.*

I knew she would call upon payment later.

However severe that payment would be, that remained liable to change given her capricious nature.

The Heir glanced at me, then at the librarian dragons, his brow furrowed deeply. But all he said was, "I'm going to read more. Fleur, Aveline, please bring any mentions of a specific weapon to me. Nox mentioned that there was one."

Not words I was keen on hearing.

Playing at nonchalance, I settled onto the bench and began pretending to read. If I went over these books, then unless the Heir asked the dragons, he'd never know if I found anything. I bypassed mention of the Fetters of Aisling—blessed by the holy under a full moon—and kept turning pages.

The Heir closed the book, squishing my fingers.

I yanked them free and looked up at him. "What?"

He thrust a journal into my face. "Explain this."

My eyes crossed trying to focus. I reared my head back and studied the sketch within the pages for a second. "It's the Wild Moon Wolf. Whoever did this had a chance to study her."

The Heir's finger jabbed at the signature under the sketch. "You did this."

"No, I—" I faltered. That was my name. That was my signature. "Where did you find this?" *How did this get here? I thought it had been lost in the storm last year.*

"So you *did* draw this. You have been *that* close to the Wild Moon Wolf long enough to make this. You know that the Wild Moon Wolf is she. You claim there is a certain weapon that will harm her. What else do you know?"

I opened my mouth to reply and had no voice.

Aveline swooped up and landed before us, drawing the Heir's attention. "There is no specific weapon in any records, save for iron. Weapons of iron, that is all."

The Heir turned narrowed eyes on me. "You said there was a certain weapon."

"Yes." A certain, uncontrollable glee filled me—definitely Lupakaria's influence. "*Iron* weapons."

He leaned close and whispered in a harsh hiss, "What else are you lying about?"

The glee faded as fast as it had come. "I *didn't* lie," I snapped. "I said a truth, you decided we should come here to research. It's not my fault you decided that."

His breath shot out. "We wasted time."

"What time?" I rose from the bench, jutted my chin

up at him. "The first full moon isn't tomorrow or even the day after. We haven't wasted time; we've learned about the Fetters of Aisling."

He scowled—and I had to fight a laugh. His face was not made for scowling. His gaze darted to the dragons. "Aveline, Fleur, thank you. I think that's all. Nox, we're leaving."

"Wait," Aveline called.

The Heir paused.

"We found something that perhaps means nothing but does not bode well. The Emperor of Atassia declared this the Wild Moon Hunt. It is strange that he would name it something so close to the—" Her voice lowered to a whisper, as if to keep something—or *someone*—from overhearing. "Wild Hunt. He is asking for their attention, and by taking part in it, you are helping."

Oh, Lupakaria whispered, and cold fear bit into my body.

If *Lupakaria* was scared of the Wild Hunt…

"Why does that matter?" the Heir demanded. "The Wild Hunt is just a story told to scare children. The Shadows jest about it."

"They are real. They are immortal. They are… beyond the deities, even. They are astral and sidereal and not of any world. So far, the hunts you Shadows have carried out have been too small to capture their attention, but now, this Wild Moon Hunt is bound to draw their eye."

"I don't understand."

Fleur murmured something, and Aveline said, "If the hunt is pleasing, the quarry challenging, they will bless the lands. The Emperor of Atassia certainly wishes for this."

In a thin voice, the Heir asked, "And if they aren't pleased?"

Fleur said one word in Brumesian; the Heir's face blanched.

"Ruin," Aveline breathed.

"How long do we have? How can we stop them from coming here?"

"The first full moon of the hunt is likely to remain under their attention. The second will draw their eye. They will descend on the third and engage in the hunt." Aveline's eyes darted to the top of Domhan Arbre, and she said in a rush, "Don't speak their name, don't think of them in their named host. You have met a reject of their host already; you know of their power."

The Heir's knee buckled, he stumbled. His lips moved in a soundless word: *Varen*.

Nox, Lupakaria said, her voice sharp and cutting, *you must not allow them to come here again. They cannot linger on this realm. Last they did, they hunted my fellow gods for moons.*

I'll stop the hunt, I promised.

Rubbing his temples, the Heir ventured, "I take it there is no way to stop them."

"It is unknown. They seek the hunt."

"Perfect," he sighed out. "Just perfect."

"We have a journal from a god that bears mention of them. Would you like to read it?"

Before the Heir could reply, I said, "I would."

The Heir glowered, but Aveline flitted off to retrieve the journal. Muttering to himself, the Heir looked toward the stairs—but he didn't leave. When Aveline returned with the journal, I took it and opened the pages to where a faded green ribbon and a square of paper with formal writing rested.

Within my mind, Lupakaria uncoiled and looked through my eyes to the jagged handwriting upon the page. She said nothing, but her unease was palpable.

The extra paper—an excerpt?—said:

"She the sidereal harbinger is the end. With unfettered eyes, She beckons the Wild Hunt to plains near and far in the fêted dance of life and death." —Passage from Of Despised Ryodin, a long-destroyed text by the thanatonaut Mara from the reign of Revered Empress Myca.

"She the sidereal harbinger is the end. She who drinks deep of pain and decay, crushing the writhing, withering worms of the world below Her trod. The highest authority of the astral undying hunters, those whose hearts no longer pulse with mortal threads—the darkest depth, the brightest of teeth in the night. She shall descend again. When the prey is nigh and the wind sings, She will call forth from beyond, and you shall heed Her call.

Dread not.

For Ryodin is no devil from below, no fallen god, but a daemon, ecto and supernal in form, so virtuous, so wicked. She is an end and a beginning, one among multitudes. She is saint, She is sinner, She is divine, She is myth. With unfettered eyes, She beckons the Wild Hunt to plains near and far in the fêted dance of life and death.

In Her wake, unworthy fade, and worthy thrive."

—from *Of Despised Ryodin*

Chapter Seventeen
Marsillio's Journal

They arrive with the full moon's shine.

One among us knows of the riders that gallop down from the stars themselves, storm and fire sweeping before them. The thunderous clamor of their six-legged steeds, hooves flashing flint-spark. The heteroclitic chill in the high swelter of summer's end.

At their head rides a ghoul, white and ghastly in form, a pennant of death-black hair streaming behind, bones rigid behind thin skin, clad in plated quicksilver. And in her grip is a spear, bristling with the hairs of a long-forgotten prey, bearing a weighty point of moonlight-lustrous metal, iridescent as the stars above. Her steed beats its eight hooves upon the ground, summer-crackle grass igniting at the touch. Smoke bellows out from its defleshed skull, and it watches us with orbs of curling flame.

There are no words enough to describe the feelings evoked at their sight.

In a tongue that is not of Khtonyx and yet I knew it, the leader of the host asks what our lauded prey is.

No one knows.

She is disappointed. She tells us that we, then, will be her prey.

"Ryodin," one of my kin whispers, and his fear is sour upon my breath. If I had known then what I know now, I would have been scared, too.

He is the first to die, caught by the long and lean skull-faced hounds that spring from Ryodin's sides. They rend him asunder before our eyes. Ryodin, through his cries and screams, looks on. I cannot speak of her appearance in truth, for there is nothing so undoing as witnessing her with your own eyes.

It is only when there is silence that Ryodin raises her empty hand. Shrouded by a gauzy veil, the teeth lining her helmet grin at us. Ryodin lowers her hand, and I watch as my kin are cut down around me.

It is a week later, and I still do not have knowledge of all the gods felled that day. The known names number in the hundreds. Basilin is among the dead. I shall never see him again.

The thanatonauts, for they are dauntless and deathless, retrieve the bodies after each night, once Ryodin and her Wild Hunt have returned to the skies, leaving in their wake burned lands and bodies. The bodies, my kin and those of the mortals and the faeries, too, lack teeth.

After a few nights, a thanatonaut reports that Ryodin has armoured her steed in rigid lines of small bones. These are undoubtedly the teeth of the fallen.

The sun proves to be our only solace. When fair golden effulgence spills across the lands, Ryodin and her ilk stay away, presumably preparing for the night's coming hunt in which we are the prey. Night following night, the Wild Hunt chases those of Khtonyx, and the wavering song of owls has been replaced by howls.

Two nights ago, we learned of one among the Wild Hunt by the name of Varen. Varen, at first look before moonlight strikes him, resembles an elk. Akin to the hounds and hawks who hunt at Ryodin's beck and call, Varen's skull has been stripped of flesh—or perhaps there never was flesh to begin—and within the sockets burn twin flames. Or rather, burned.

The flames were doused out by a god before Varen struck her down. Without the fire, he appears to be blind and unable to descry those fleeing if they are taciturn. He has since taken to imitating the cries of ones held dear from our memories; this is lure enough.

Do not heed his calls. Recall that they are dead, beyond your saving now.

A faerie warrior discerned, mere moments from his fatal end, that Ryodin has not yet bade her lieutenants to amalgamate with those on the hunt. Ryodin herself has not dirtied her spear. What puissance she and her lieutenants hold behind their skull-helms is beyond our measure, surely.

I fear Ryodin will linger upon Khtonyx until not a living soul remains. Already, my kin are crafting what they believe will be an escape Ryodin cannot follow through. I do not trust that another world is safe from Ryodin; she shall come eventually with her horrid host.

The end comes for me, even now. I hear their hooves in the streets. There is nowhere so hidden that Ryodin and her ilk shall not uncover me, only the endless dark of death.

I leave this as a warning. Do not attract the attention of the Wild Hunt, for they bring only death.

—Marsillio

CHAPTER EIGHTEEN
NOX

I raised my gaze from the journal, closing it absently. I understood most of it. The terror, the death, the inevitable end. But: "What's a thanatonaut?"

Aveline replied, "In the days of past, there were those who sought to study and learn all of death's fields. They were not necromancers as we still have today, far and few between those are. Thanatonauts were something else, something capable of, after a point of knowledge, unlocking the gates to death."

I cocked my head to the side, my expression as puzzled as the Heir's. "What does that mean?"

"They could die, and in their state of death, venture into death-realms and visit death-gods."

I knew one of them, Lupakaria said, *a death-god. His followers were thanatonauts. Pleasant people, always carrying around snacks.*

"After a time," Aveline continued, "the chosen tether, someone near and dear to the thanatonaut, would pull the thanatonaut back from death. Alive again, they would record what they had seen and then delve back into death again and again and again. They discovered and outlined many painless, quick ways to die for their purposes. For that reason, extant thanatonaut texts, of which there are only two, are forbidden from the eyes of any but us librarians."

I didn't want to see those. I handed the journal back to the dragon. "In the journal, that Ryo—"

"Careful. She listens." Aveline tucked the book into a sling under her wing and folded her wing over it before saying, "Yes, should this come to pass, she is the one who will ride at the head."

Next to me, the Heir mumbled a small curse. With a shake of his head, he started for the stairs again. "Much as I do not like this new knowledge, thank you for the help." His eyes locked on me, and he tipped his head at the exit.

He definitely had something to say, and it wasn't about the Wild Hunt.

I thanked the dragons as well and followed the Heir out of Domhan Arbre, wondering what his plan was now. He was silent, his steps quick and forceful. He wasn't headed towards The Roasted Chestnut though.

"Heir," I said, jogging to catch up. Curse his long legs. "Where are you going?"

"Why did they not get a promise from you?" he demanded, his gaze focused on an elm tree in the distance.

Lupakaria's glee filtered through my mind a second before the wolf goddess grabbed ahold of my jaws and voice and said, "Because the little wolf made a wish, and I am nothing if not a generous goddess."

The Heir's eyes shot towards me. "Lupakaria."

"Yes. Tell me, o dreamer, do you have a wish?"

"No." The word was short, curt.

"Aww, I am disappointed. I thought you of all people would have a wish." Lupakaria reached out with my hand and tried to caress his cheek, but the Heir jerked his head out of range. "I could remove all those scars you try to hide."

The Heir stopped, his sternum rising and falling with his tense breathing like an enraged bull. "How do you know about those? Does Nox know?"

"She does now."

Lupakaria stalked in a circle around the Heir. "I know much about you, Hadrien, much that Nox does not know. I could spill it all, speak your secrets forth, and she would hear."

His eyes flashed, anger sparking in them. "What did you do to her?"

"The little wolf is fine, simply sequestered out of control of her own body and mind."

"That seems cruel. You're a parasite."

"I am no parasite; I am a blessing. She agreed to it when she took my Jaws and placed them around her neck."

His hand lashed out, closed around my wrist, pulled me to a stop. "Why do you keep calling her 'the little wolf?'"

Lupakaria smiled with my mouth. "Wish for it, o dreamer."

Around my wrist, his fingers tightened; my pulse drummed against his fingertips. The Heir replied, "How about a bargain? I tell you a secret, you tell me why."

I would hear it. *Lupakaria, give me my body back. You can't distract yourself from the astral hunters forever.* She would know what I meant. *Let go.*

"Whisper away."

The Heir bent his head close. His lips brushed against my ear as he murmured, "I used to look up at the stars and wish something would happen in my life. Something exciting, the stuff of stories and legends. Now that it has, I want nothing more than for it to be done."

Lupakaria gazed at him sidelong. Then she hooked my fingers around the links of my necklaces and pulled them into the light. She held aloft the medallion I'd worn for years, long enough for the tarnished silver to wear away at the edges. "There once was a Wolf Guild."

The Heir stepped back, his eyes darting from the medallion to my face. He was piecing it together. "Before she was the Heir of the Shadow, Nox was the Heir of the Wolf. Wasn't she?"

Lupakaria chose that moment to relinquish control, and I jolted away, shoving my necklaces back under my shirt. "She shouldn't have done that." I raked a hand through my hair. There was a jittery feeling racing through my veins. I shook out my hands, blew out a breath.

"How often… Has she done that before?"

I nodded but didn't meet the Heir's eyes.

There was a long, long beat of silence. "I used to live there," the Heir admitted, pointing to a house set within an elm, and the façade of the Heir of the Shadow faded away, and it was just Hadrien standing before me. "There's a beech tree out in the forest behind it. I was bit by a werewolf there." His hand touched his collarbone in a movement he didn't seem aware of. "No one could explain why I didn't contract lycanthropy, but here I am now, not a werewolf."

Hadrien then indicated another house-tree. "That's where the first girl I had my heart set on lived." Color rose in his cheeks, and lower, he added, "I'm not sure why I told you that. I didn't want you to know anything about my life here… but now, I don't know. I shouldn't tell you anything; you know more than you ever say." He swung his gaze to me, pinned me down with his blue-grey eyes. "How much of that is because of Lupakaria whispering to you?"

My hands crept up to hold the jawbone on their own accord—or of Lupakaria's? And I felt so far from my body, from my bones, as I whispered, "I don't know."

His eyes not leaving mine, Hadrien considered me for a minute. "We should go to Aisling next. There's no possibility the other hunters will have learned of the Fetters. We can get them and trap the Wild Moon Wolf by the first full moon. We can't let that particular host of hunters come here."

But the Fetters of Aisling might still be with the faeries. I opened my mouth to say so, but Hadrien was already looking away, and the words were held fast in my throat. It seemed Lupakaria was not done with me yet.

What was that for? I demanded, rubbing at my throat with one hand, as if I could free the words Lupakaria had trapped.

Do you truly seek an end so fast?

She was right. I caught up to Hadrien, and I didn't say a word about the faeries.

CHAPTER NINETEEN
HADRIEN

IT WAS time to leave Lumieres.

Hadrien let his gaze linger over the trees he'd grown up around. His heart ached to stay, to not leave only a few days after returning. There hadn't been enough time to walk the paths, visit the gardens, eat the food from his childhood, and simply *revel* in being in Brumais again.

Pretty as the sun-drenched hills and valleys of Atassia were, the dappled, flower-shrouded forests of Brumais were his home.

He gave one last look at Domhan Arbre before urging his gelding after Nox and Ettore. "The plan," he said, slowing Tiny and keeping him in check, "is to return to Atassia and proceed to Aisling. We should be able to go to Aisling since I have an Ink. You…" It dawned on him. "…might not be able to go." *I need to decide where to leave Nox safely and securely while I'm gone if that is the case. Can she stay with Siena? I dislike the idea of her being around Siena.*

With a sharp shake of his head—his neck cracked in a painful way—he added, "I'll figure that out soon. It will take us longer to reach Cristal with Varen in the night-time forests." A flash of hot fear sliced through him; he shut his eyes against the memories of Varen that played in his mind. Varen was only a *reject* from the Wild Hunt. What horrors would the real, true Wild Hunt bring?

To focus himself, he reiterated the plan: "First, Cristal. Then Sidero. Aisling. Get the Fetters. Then we ready for the full moon."

Nox had been quiet ever since the incident with Lupakaria. She said nothing now. Didn't even glance at him.

Nox remained silent through the day of travel and the night at Cipres *and* through the next morning.

Maybe it was the silence. Maybe it was the fact that Hadrien didn't know when he'd be back in Brumais. Maybe it was simply the sheer impulse to see one last beautiful thing.

But he turned Tiny off the road and onto a faint trail. He twisted in the saddle and gestured for Nox to follow. There was no danger of encountering Varen in these woods with the sun shining golden and warm.

Birdsong soared around them as they followed the trail through the trees and undergrowth. The trees grew thicker and taller, cloaking their path in shadow—and then sunlight dazzled against his eyes.

Tiny picked his way out of the forest and onto the shore of Fontaine de Eternite. The Lake of Eternity, a brilliant expanse of blue-green waters. It wasn't a very large lake, but it was remarkable. A gentle noise filled the air: more singing birds, the lap of waves, and the tumble of the river that fed into the lake.

Hadrien slid out of the saddle, dropped the gelding's

reins, and walked down the languid slope to the shore. Sand crunched under his boots. At the lake's edge, he lowered himself to the ground and crossed his legs. The sun melted over his body, and he loosed a sigh that came from deep within his chest.

Footsteps approached, barely audible.

"What is this?" Nox asked, her voice rough from disuse.

"Fontaine de Eternite," Hadrien replied, keeping his eyes on the lake as she sat beside him. "In the trade tongue, it is the Lake of Eternity. There's rumors that the waters here extend life." His shoulders lifted in a small shrug. "I don't think they actually do, but I've always loved this spot."

"I can see why." She trailed her fingers through the sand. "Why did you bring me here?"

He didn't know why; he said the first thing that came to mind, "I needed a moment of peace. Once we're back in Atassia, it will be… not peaceful."

"The dark garden is soon."

Hadrien closed his eyes, as if he could ward it off.

Nox bumped her hand against his. "Here." With surprising gentleness, she uncurled his fingers, and something warm and metal settled into his palm. "I think you need this more than me, Hadrien."

His eyes opened to find a necklace there. It was silver with three disks suspended on three different lengths of chain connected to one clasp. The disks each held a different shape in three colors: silver, gold, and blue.

"Oh."

"It shows the moon phases. Blue for Azura. Silver for Argento. Gold for Minimus Sol."

Looking at it, Hadrien could see that he'd suffer the dark garden before they reached Atassia again. His stomach knotted.

"You can keep it."

He should thank her. This was an invaluable tool. A gift. For when he couldn't see the moons to track their progress. The dark garden would never catch him by surprise again.

"Thank you," he whispered.

Nox stood, brushed off her palms, and without a word, padded away. She stretched out along the shore a short distance away, her head pillowed on her hands. *She's like a cat sprawled out and sunning,* Hadrien thought and breathed out a quiet laugh. His attention went back to the moons necklace Nox had given him. He fastened it around his neck.

Next to it, his Shadow medallion now resembled the dark circle of a new moon. Strange. With all the talk of eclipses lately, the shiny, not-yet-tarnished silver around the circle of onyx made the whole medallion call to mind the image of an eclipse.

Hadrien unclasped his Shadow medallion. Rubbing his thumb over the surface, he considered it. Was there a deeper meaning here that the Arch Shadow had intended? Other Guilds had different metals on their medallions. The Lion Guild had gold and their lion seal. The Hawk Guild, bronze and a hawk. The Shadow Guild's was silver and the flat, smooth onyx circle.

Perhaps the Arch Shadow had designed it to remind others of the Guild she had razed to the ground to build the Shadow Guild upon. The Wolf Guild, the Guild Nox had been the Heir of, the Guild none of the Shadows ever spoke of.

For the first time, Hadrien wondered how many Shadows had begun their Guild careers as Wolves. How long ago had the change occurred? He'd have to ask Nox, but if she had been the Heir of the Wolf, it couldn't have been more than ten years ago. Unless she was older than she looked.

Shadows, Wolves, Guilds, it was all a mess.

At least he wouldn't have to attend a Guild Gathering again until after the Wild Moon Hunt was over. He'd wanted to rake his eyes out at the last one just for some excitement, just for a change of pace from the droning voices of Guild leaders discussing topics like tariffs and murders.

A heartbeat later, Hadrien remembered that Xenna had given him a box before he had left. There had been so much going on, sleepless nights and walking nightmares and long days. He had forgotten.

The box turned out to contain a feather charm.

He stared at it for a long while, blinking. There was a note curled inside the box with Xenna's swooping, flowing handwriting. *For Ikarus' bridle,* it read.

He set the box away since Ikarus wasn't nearby to attach the charm to his bridle. Kicking his legs out, Hadrien leaned back on his elbows and basked in the sun.

He must've dozed off, for the next thing he knew, Nox was prodding his shoulder with the tip of a boot. "Wake up, little Heir."

"I'm awake," he grumbled, his voice sounding like he had eaten sand all day. "You can quit poking me."

"But what if it amuses me?"

"You can also stop then."

Nox stopped. "I brushed the horses while you napped."

Shoving himself to his feet, Hadrien groaned at his sore body. He stretched out his limbs, one by one, wishing there was time to take a longer break. Then he turned his back on the lake, made a silent vow to return one day soon, and walked away.

Nox didn't speak again on the road, but now the silence was more akin to quiet. But when night drew closer and they were deep in the woods, the same woods that Varen hunted in, Hadrien wished for anything but silence. His skin crawled at every rasp of his breath.

Varen was going to hunt him again, Varen would scream and scream, and his own screams would join and then become not his own but still *his*—

"There's lights up on the left," Nox said, bursting the silence.

Shuddering, Hadrien fixed his gaze on the lights. An inn, a farmhouse, a murderer-filled home, he didn't care. Anything was better than riding on this road in the deepening dark.

The lights and the building came into clearer view: a small inn, flanked by a ramshackle barn and a garden that had seen better days. The barn, Hadrien saw with his stomach sinking and anxiety twisting through him, was full.

Nox noticed this, too. She hopped out of the saddle, her boots hitting the road with a muffled sound, and strode to the door. The knock of her knuckles against the wood rang out; Hadrien adjusted his reins, glancing around for any signs of Varen.

The door creaked open, and the elderly man there shook his head.

Nox turned away, fury written on her face. Her scowl was monstrous. "No rooms. There's another inn a mile up the road."

Hadrien sent Tiny into a canter, trying to ignore how frantic his pulse was. The gelding sensed it, though, and chomped at the bit. A few strides later, he threw his head down and bucked; Hadrien was nearly unseated.

Swearing viciously and breathing hard, Hadrien slowed the gelding into a walk. He could not go on like this. Switching the reins to one hand, he hurriedly yanked his flask out and downed a few gulps. Let the burn of alcohol smooth his nerves.

"Hadrien?"

The voice was soft and low, and he couldn't figure out why sometimes Nox called him by his name and other times by his title.

"Maybe we should stop and camp in a tree for the night."

His entire body went cold and hot, all at once.

"Or not." Nox patted Ettore on the shoulder. "I'll ride ahead and get us a room. You follow—slower, since Tiny is skittish right now."

Just a week ago, he wouldn't have agreed.

But now, he nodded.

Nox rode off at a trot, and Hadrien let Tiny walk after.

When he next saw her, Nox was waiting outside the inn, her horse nowhere to be seen. But she didn't look haggard like she'd fled Varen or lost Ettore. It must be safe, then. Hadrien guided Tiny towards Nox, and the girl met him halfway.

Nox held the reins below the gelding's chin. "I'll take care of him."

Was she being... *nice?* Why was she being nice?

Hadrien slipped from the saddle, his legs shaky from the long day of travel and the jittery adrenaline in his veins. "You got a room?"

Nox placed a key in his palm in response.

Relief swept through Hadrien, so strong his knees nearly buckled. He stumbled into the inn and up the stairs to the room. He didn't even care that there was one bed within. These four walls would protect him from Varen.

By the time Nox entered the room, he had already washed off the grime of the day and was in bed. Nox's steps paused, then started again, quieter, and disappeared into the washroom. The door eased shut.

Hadrien drifted in and out of a light sleep. The bed dipped under weight, and his eyes flew open. It was only Nox, settling under the blanket next to him. He let his eyes shut again, stifled a yawn.

A cold hand touched his shoulder and pushed lightly. "Your legs are on my side of the bed," Nox grumbled in a tone that didn't sound very upset at all. "Unless you want to wake all curled up on me like you did before, I suggest you move."

He grabbed an extra pillow and stuffed it between them.

Nox laughed, a sound of pure delight and mirth that Hadrien didn't think he'd heard before. "Pillows didn't stop you last time. Face it, you crave my warmth." Her eyes, speckled with lantern-light and starlight, appeared over the pillow. "You're the one who was in this bed first, and you didn't put down the pillows. Tell me why."

A flush heated his face. The truth lurked behind his eyes. It was embarrassing. He looked away from Nox and whispered, "You keep the nightmares away."

After a beat of quiet, she inquired, "Varen?"

He could only manage a nod.

Nox slipped out of the bed. Hadrien propped himself up to watch her pad around the room. She loosened the ties on the curtains and arranged the fabric so that no sliver of night sky was visible through the windows.

"Varen can't reach you here," she said, "but I understand feeling like he can." Sitting on the edge of the bed, she stared at the far wall and added, "I don't want the title."

It took Hadrien a second to realize what she meant. "You don't want to be the Heir of the Shadow again."

"She tried to kill me, Hadrien. Whether or not you believe that, it's the truth, and I can only utter the truth." Her fingers drifted up to the jawbone amulet. "Lupakaria will tell you that the Arch Shadow struck first."

"Then why are you still in the Wild Moon Hunt?"

"Where else can I go? The Arch Shadow found me once before; she'd find me again. One of us joining Mother Death is the only way for a peaceful life." Nox quirked her mouth up. "I suppose, though, if I am dead, truly dead, then I can't have a peaceful life, and I doubt she would live the rest of her days in quiet. It is her death that I seek."

Hadrien should probably kill Nox for saying that.

"You're likely wondering why I don't just let you win

this." Lying down, she tucked her hands behind her head. A long breath swept past her lips. "Many reasons. I've been close to Mother Death's door, she has looked upon me and waited for that last breath to slip away. I don't want to die. I want to be free of the Arch Shadow for good."

I don't see a way for her to get what she wants, and for me to get what I want. What do I even want? Keeping the title? Spending the rest of my able days hunting beasts of legend? Do… do I still want that? His stomach turned; he saw the blood on his hands, a memory, clear as if it had happened recently. Varen hadn't reached this memory. Maybe because it was a memory in silent hues, broken only by his own ragged gasping when he realized what he had done.

There had been a beast similar to the Wild Moon Wolf that he had hunted, months ago, when he was a new initiate to the Shadow Guild. A bird, hued in feathers made of rubies, each one delicate and impossible. He had hunted it through the moonlight-soaked night, pinned it down before dawn, his knees weighing its wings down. His tired fingers were fumbling with his dagger. Then he cut the bird's throat and sat back, closing his eyes against the rising sun.

When he had opened his eyes, there had been a dead human below him. He remembered horror rushing cold through him. The human had been halfway through the transformation back; the ruby-feathered wings were still there, but the face… the face belonged to a human.

He had sawn the wings off and never spoken of what had happened. Tried to forget it even occurred. None of the other Shadows ever mentioned anything similar—not until Nox had uttered the words in fury.

"Hadrien? You look like you've seen a ghost."

"Thinking about the dark garden," he lied. "We should both get some sleep."

Nox curled onto her side and murmured, "Goodnight, Hadrien."

"Goodnight, Nox." But he didn't sleep for a long time, his gaze on the ceiling and his thoughts running wild. He wasn't thinking about the dark garden at all.

Chapter Twenty
Nox

I was prepared for the sight of the dark garden this time.

Hadrien kept himself secluded in the washroom when the thorns first sprouted, but he didn't shut and lock the door. I read to him, alternating between leaning against the doorframe and sitting crookedly in a plush chair. The hours passed, my voice became hoarse and quiet, and I ate far too many pastries after midnight.

With the dark garden gone for now, he washed away the blood, tended to the cuts. I left a plate of croissants and a glass of water on the nightstand for him.

How did we get here? I wondered, stretching out on my own bed. *I suppose that a week of long travel and nightmares and saving each other will... ease animosity. It will all be over soon, though. One more new moon. Then the full moons aren't far off.*

The morning brought the end of our time in Brumais.

I led Ettore and Tiny to the healers' building and left them with one of the healers. Before I walked away, I scratched Ettore's cheek and told him what an excellent steed he had been. Embra was my favorite, but I was fond of this little strawberry roan now. If I could've, I would've taken him back to Atassia. But I didn't have a villa, even a small one, and two horses would be hard to keep up with without one.

Maybe one day.

I frowned. Did I want that?

It was an idyllic image, a small villa situated atop a hill with stables bordered by an olive grove on one side, a citrus grove on the other. Gardens fit for an alchemist, full of flourishing flowers and herbs. I could picture walking out of the house and over to the stables, a trio of bright-eyed horses nickering at me, a soft breeze rustling the trees, and waiting for me by a sparkling fountain was a man, his scarred hand raised to shade his eyes from the sun.

I blinked. That was never going to happen. I'd known him a week; I would not know him a month longer, let alone enough years to see the striking man he was going to become. He already was striking—and what traitorous thoughts were these.

I can make that dream come true, Lupakaria whispered, smug. *I knew you thought of him. Give me a wish, and that will all happen.*

But there would be a catch. There always was a catch. Besides, wishing for a life with someone who had no say in it, that was something the Arch Shadow would do. If that dream of the villa happened, with the boy with the blue-grey eyes, it would not be through one of Lupakaria's wishes.

Leave him out of your wishes, I replied. *I've told you I don't like the wishes that involve other people. Makes my skin crawl. It's what* she *would do, if she'd gotten ahold of your bones.*

I remind you that you did wish for her to forget about me and my jaws that you wear.

That was different. I rubbed at my neck. *It's the Arch Shadow. It's Skota. She's done worse. Do you really want to spend your days fulfilling her wishes?*

Lupakaria was silent. Then, grudgingly, she muttered, *I want another one of those chocolate pastries you had last night.* And even more grudgingly, she added, *I'd rather have you than her, though if I were answering her wishes, I wouldn't find it in me to care what the wishes did.*

I know. You're only so good or evil or grey as your bearer. You don't have your own body anymore to carry out your own desires.

I could, if you wished it.

That seemed like a terrible idea. Lupakaria walking the lands of Khtonyx once more, her mind filled with the knowledge she'd learned through passive listening over the many years. She would either save the world or tear it asunder.

I caught the eye of Hadrien up ahead and tipped my head at a bakery. He nodded, and I ducked in. *How about a pastry instead?* I asked Lupakaria.

Sufficient.

I paid for two pastries, one for me, one for Hadrien. Lupakaria was chatty today; she started talking about dragons and her fellow gods of old. I caught something about a portal and another world before I returned to Hadrien.

"This is for you," I said and offered him the wrapped croissant with chocolate and almonds. I kept the one full of chocolate and hazelnuts for myself, since that was the one Lupakaria had loved.

Hadrien looked between the pastry in his hand and the Ianis Frame waiting for us nearby. The color leeched from his face.

It was clear what was going on in his head. "Are you sure you want to go through an Ianis Frame again?" I asked, and the distant echo of his howl from the Ianis Frame Effect vibrated through my mind.

His head shook, barely perceptible, and then he replied, "We don't have the time to take a ship, even if we can find one powered by magic. There's no other way than the Ianis Frame." He stowed the croissant in his pack. "I'll eat that after."

I put my croissant in my knapsack as well. We approached the Ianis Frame, a frame like a garden gate, decorative leaves and blooms made from metal adorning it. Morning glory vines with massive purple flowers spiraled over the metal frame.

There was no charge for passage back to Atassia. The pair of women at the Ianis Frame wished us safe travels.

Hadrien stared at the city of Sidero visible through the metal and vines for a minute. A butterfly swept past his cheek, wings batting his skin. He didn't even blink.

Closing his eyes, he stepped through.

And for a second, I was on a whole other continent than he was.

What are you going to do? Lupakaria challenged.
Follow him.

I entered the Ianis Frame, eyes shut tight against the galaxies that whirled against my eyelids. A fraction of a heartbeat later, I stepped out into Sidero. I exhaled slowly, flexing my fingers. I seemed fine.

Hadrien, on the other hand, was crouched down, his head braced against his arms. No one was talking to him or even checking on him. He didn't look particularly strong or tall at the moment, just haunted.

I knelt down next to him, let my fingers alight on his shoulder. "Hadrien." His head lifted a hair. "You need to rise. You don't want any of the other hunters seeing you like this."

He shoved to his feet so fast that he bashed my face; my hands flew to cover my nose, white-hot pain stabbing tears into my eyes. "Shit! Sorry, Nox."

"It's fine," I mumbled. "Been broken before." I tested it gingerly. Something had cracked loudly when his shoulder collided with my nose, but it didn't hurt near the way it had when it had been broken. No blood either, so it was superficial. Probably. "Ow. I'll survive it."

His eyes darted around the faces of passersby. "We should move in case any of the other hunters are still in the city. I don't want them asking or wondering why we used an Ianis Frame." He struck off down the street. "It's this way to Fiona's stables, right?"

I fell into step next to him. "Why are we getting the horses if Aisling is through an Ianis Frame?"

Hadrien faltered in his strides. "Uh. Habit."

"Do you even know yet if I can go to Aisling?"

He stopped and turned with a monumental sigh. "I'll go ask. Wait here."

I stepped out of the flow of people and into the narrow alley between two buildings. My eyes tracked Hadrien as he walked back the way we'd come. Then I saw an azure jacket in the shadow of a shop, and the figure within in watching Hadrien, too.

I slipped over to Artem's side and said, "Hello again."

To his credit, Artem barely blinked. "I heard you were dead."

"As you can see, I am very much alive." I needed his attention off Hadrien. In one smooth motion, I slid the ring off his finger and onto mine. I raised my hand to admire the bear's head. "You're just asking for someone to recognize you with this on."

Artem swiveled to face me fully, his back now to Hadrien. "Give that back," he said, but he was smiling, his amber eyes bright. "You're not very sneaky, you know that?"

In answer, I wiggled my fingers at him.

He held my hand, his touch light and warm. His fingers skimmed along my skin as he eased the ring off my finger. He held my gaze, replacing the ring without pause. A shiver traced a languid path down my back as memories swept to the forefront of my mind: wandering hands and hot breath and chapped lips.

He cocked his head to the side, considering me with a smile that spoke of untold secrets. "Since you're not dead, why is that boy still holding the Heir of the Shadow title?"

"Many reasons."

Artem laughed and rolled his eyes. "I've always hated that reply of yours. It's like you can't bring yourself to lie, but you also don't want to tell the truth. You were always such a nuisance at Guild Gatherings." A shadow darkened his eyes. "Can't say I miss the boring discussions." The shadow lifted, his smile curved up higher. "I may be persuaded to miss the *other* discussions."

I ignored that last part for now. "Does everyone still think you're dead?"

His smile was a sharp thing. "Not after I slay the Wild Moon Wolf, they won't."

"Not if I kill it first," Hadrien said, his face appearing over Artem's shoulder.

They were both so tall.

I felt so short.

Artem pivoted enough to bring Hadrien into his line of sight and still keep me in view without yielding a step. "So you're in the Wild Moon Hunt, Heir?"

"I'm a Shadow. Should it be a wonder that I have joined the most prestigious hunt in Atassia?"

"No, only that this hunt requires pairs." Artem's keen eyes raked over me and then Hadrien. "You two make an interesting pair."

"We're not—" Hadrien started, but Artem held up a hand.

"Don't treat me like a fool, Heir. I'm too smart for that. Now, I must be going. Gunnar has likely found his way to the nearest tavern, and we have a few things left to finalize before the first full moon, when we'll be capturing and killing the Wild Moon Wolf, not you." His gaze locked on me. "Nox, if you want to pick up where we left off... I'm staying at the Southern Heart Inn."

When Artem was far out of sight and hearing range, Hadrien gave me a look with raised eyebrows. "You and Artem?"

"Somewhat," I answered, distracted by what Artem had pressed into my palm in a sleight of hand. I pocketed the key before Hadrien could notice. "We were both Heirs at the same time. I'd sneak off with him after Guild Gatherings and practice kissing."

Hadrien's face was reddening, his eyes averting from mine, and I plowed on for the sole intent of seeing his face turn crimson. "Well, at *first*, it was just for practice. Turns out, two Heirs bored of Guild business much prefer to pass the small talk time after meetings by engaging their tongues in a different way."

"Did you know he was here?"

I admitted that I did.

"And did you not think to mention that one of our competitors is someone you've slept with?"

Oh. Hadrien was mad.

But his words stung, and I reacted as I always had.

"You're one of my competitors, too—or have you forgotten?" I stepped forward, jerked my chin up, and glared into his eyes. His furious, blue-grey eyes. "Exactly why are you so suddenly up in arms about this?"

"Because Artem was right here, talking to you like you were old friends."

"We *are!*"

He scoffed.

I grabbed his jacket collar and yanked him down. "Be very clear about what you are saying right now."

His eyes narrowed, his nostrils flared. "I think you're going to visit Artem and give him tips on hunting the Wild Moon Wolf." Gloved fingers wrapped around my wrist. "Now, let go of me."

I lifted my fingers off his collar, one by one, and then whispered, just to see his reaction and because what he believed was a lie that grated against my bones, "I didn't sleep with him."

"Does it matter if you did or didn't?"

"To me, yes." I stepped back. "I don't expect you to understand."

Something wounded flashed across his face like a lightning strike. "Don't act like you know me."

This was not a conversation for the street. I only shook my head. "I know you are a liar. That tells me all I need to know about you." I turned on my heel and walked away.

Hadrien didn't chase after me.

I was out of the city before I looked back. My stomach dropped. No sign of Hadrien. I shouldn't have stormed off. He shouldn't have provoked me. I should have stayed in the city. He should have come after me.

Damn it. I rubbed at my wrist, ran my finger around my ouroboros tattoo. Around and around and around my skin the ouroboros went, endlessly chasing and catching its prey. *Lupakaria, did I go wrong?*

Perhaps.

I don't know what to do. Hadrien was supposed to tell me if I would be able to go through the Ianis Frame to Aisling. I sat down in the grass outside the city, gazing out over the hills of the Atassish countryside. The beauty was lost on me. *I should find him.*

But I didn't move.

People walked by, a few sparing a glance at me but most continuing on their way without noticing me. I toyed with the key Artem had given me. I wouldn't go see him—whether to talk or kiss. Anything between Artem and me was done and had been done.

Not that I wasn't tempted.

Passing the coming night with lazy kisses would be a welcome distraction from the Wild Moon Hunt. But distraction was the problem—or only part of it, if I was honest with myself.

The memories of Artem were still there, but the spark for me wasn't. Maybe time and care would nurture it back. It seemed unlikely, given that I was undoubtedly interested in the last person I should ever be interested in.

It was so foolish.

But I couldn't get him out of my head. His outward appearance had lured me in early on, then his voice had ensnared me, and then his rare smiles had trapped me completely. He was the absolute worst person my heart could have decided to throw itself before.

It is not easy, Lupakaria said quietly, and I could hear old grief in her voice. *I would wish away my own love if I could.*

Who do you love?

I fell in love twice. The first was with a human man long ago. We raised a child together until he took ill and I could not save him. I gave up my daughter. I don't know what happened to her. The second time, I fell in love with a faerie man who crafted poetry. He was kind and gentle, and he was brave in his own quiet way. I was slain and bound to these bones before I could ever profess my love. The wolf goddess drifted into silence.

I brushed my fingers over the Jaws, hoping it was some sort of comfort to her. Even a god who could grant wishes couldn't have all she wanted. I was a fool to think I could have anything I wanted.

Standing, I brushed off my clothes and started back into the city. I made my way to where I had last seen

Hadrien, but he wasn't there. I went to Fiona's stables, and both Embra and Ikarus were there. Wherever Hadrien had gone, he hadn't taken his horse.

I patted Embra's neck while I tried to think. There were multiple inns within the city. I could check all of them, but most innkeepers wouldn't give up the names of current residents. It was likely I'd miss him.

My steps led me away from the stables, through the streets. With twilight nearing, I found myself back at the Ianis Frame. I stared hard at it for a moment, knowing already what I would hear.

I asked anyways. "My companion, the boy about this much taller than me, did he go through here again?"

A short nod.

"To where?"

"Aisling."

I turned away without another word. Hadrien had abandoned me. I had no money, no place to go, and no idea of when he'd return.

My fingers drew out the key of their own volition.

I set my sights on the Southern Heart Inn and Artem.

Chapter Twenty-One
Hadrien

He shouldn't have left Nox in Sidero.

But he hadn't been thinking clearly.

Hadrien had only see Artem talking to the former Heir, smiling at her, leaning close, and he'd known. He would have to do this on his own. Nox was liable to tell Artem everything.

Nox never said she loved Artem, he thought, *but she did love Rogus. If Rogus were alive and a competitor in this hunt, would Nox tell him everything? Would she tell Xenna everything if she was here?* Hadrien knelt and fixed a buckle on his boot. *Maybe she won't tell Artem anything at all.*

His gaze raised from his boot to the packed-dirt trail leading away from the Ianis Frame at his back. *I couldn't have brought Nox with me into Aisling anyways.* Before him sprawled the forested hill of Aisling, a massive hill that was more akin to a gentle mountain. Silver mist cloaked the ground, swirling around the trunks of the ancient, immortal trees.

Hadrien breathed out a small word of wonder.

He had been young when he had last seen Aisling. He wasn't even at Aisling yet, and from his faint memories, the buildings themselves were breathtaking, even more so than the forest.

Shouldering his pack, he started on the path.

Mist swept around his boots, matching the cloud-blanketed sky above. The air held tiny droplets, and the sky promised rain to come. Hadrien walked faster, knowing that he had an hour's walk ahead of him before he climbed to the top of the mountain.

Last time he had been on this path, he hadn't been in a Guild. Hadn't even known what Guild he would want to join. Now he was the Heir to a Guild—and doubts he never imagined he would have crowded his thoughts. How quickly paths could change. How quickly *wants* could change.

No, he told himself, *you are the Heir. This is your path.*

A raindrop smacked against his head.

Hadrien jogged into the cover of the trees—and stopped dead.

The sunlight filtering through the clouds, weak as it was, was enough to send shadows stretching across the forest floor. Jagged, branching shadows like antlers.

A shudder shook his frame.

Varen is not here, he told himself.

But the shadows lingered in the forest, and the rain drummed down. The forest was thick and deep, and though it was not the Brumesian forest, the moss-adorned oaks could hide Varen. Hadrien would face Varen alone; Nox—*no one* was here to watch his back.

With a deep breath, he plunged into the forest.

He was alone.

No one was seated upon the stone benches scattered along the trail. Movement snapped his breath away. But it was only a pointy-eared fox skimming along the trail ahead; it melted into the twisting roots of the trees.

Under his boots, the path changed from dirt to pale pebbles that shifted and crunched. He passed the outdoor meeting area for the Inksworn, a weathered stone alcove set into the mountainside, moss draping over the stones. When he was young, an acolyte had waited for him here, but now no one was.

Maybe they had sensed that Hadrien already had an activated Ink, and so no one was sent to guide him through the forest.

Or Varen *was* here, and he had killed them all.

Don't think about that, he scolded himself and focused on his boots moving across the path. *The Moonsworn does not allow danger in her realm, and Aisling is her realm. Even if there was any sort of danger, Astre Noir would protect you.*

He still startled when thunder cracked somewhere in the sky. The path climbed ever higher. As the slope of the mountain steepened, a wall appeared to his left, shrouded in moss and ivy, a protection against rain washing dirt over the path. The raindrops fell from the trees, faster and faster.

Pausing in the semi-shelter of a shrine to the Moon-sworn, Hadrien tugged a cloak out of his knapsack. The cloak went over him and the pack, the hood pulled low over his face. Clutching the edges of the cloak close, Hadrien dashed back into the rain.

His legs began to ache.

Finally—the stairs.

He had to slow his strides now, place his boots down

carefully on the stones. There were only a dozen stairs, and then the path resumed in a mud-slick, root-strewn dirt trail. Mud clogged his boots, sucked at each step.

Thunder snarled again. Hadrien huffed out a sigh. As long as he didn't get struck by lightning, the storm wouldn't hurt.

Through the trees, he saw a flash of terracotta tiles along rooftops. *Aisling.* The fatigue in his body faded away, and he forgot about how the rain had soaked his bones. The last of the forest fell behind with a series of trees covered in green moss, russet mushrooms, and dark ivy.

The trail slipped into a road of cobblestones, worn smooth by countless years and countless wanderers. Golden glows ahead marked lights, the collection of buildings at the end of the road. Hadrien's breath came easier.

Aisling, for reasons he didn't understand, held the same architecture style as Atassia. Cream-colored stucco had been smoothed across the sides of the buildings and the wall that enclosed the area. Parts of the stucco had fallen away long ago, revealing the bricks below. The roofs were all lined in curved tiles of terracotta, softened by lichen and moss.

Hadrien stepped onto the porch in the front court-yard, his gaze darting around. This felt like a dream. The herringbone-patterned tiles on the porch drew his eyes straight to the wooden door awaiting him.

He didn't approach the door quite yet.

Wondering if he could find another entrance, he investigated the verandas flanking the courtyard. One veranda was a wing of the building and had windows but breaking a window seemed irreverent. The other dropped into a mist-silvered olive grove before the ground fell away to the forest below.

He slunk around the olive trees, but none of the branches quite reached the wall. And if he missed and slipped, he'd break his face on the wall. Nox would laugh.

Through the door then.

The wood was old, faded grey, tinged with moss, and bordered by lanterns on either side. It wasn't a particularly grand door, but it was a notable door. He seized the curl of metal and pulled the door open by the handle.

Lightning flashed in the sky behind him as he crossed the threshold, throwing his shadow across the tiled floor. In his shadow, antlers feathered out from his head.

Hadrien yelped and whirled.

Only the rain greeted him.

Pulse skittering in his veins, breath a shaky beast in his chest, he shut the door on the storm and stood alone in the foyer. Warmth and light cascaded over him, eased the tension out of his shoulders. There was safety in here.

"Hello, Hadrien."

He did not yelp again. He held a startled noise in his throat and forced it down. "Hello."

"You already have your Ink," the acolyte said, somehow knowing. "You have returned for something else. I will send for an Inksworn to assist you."

Hadrien, when the acolyte had floated away, closed his eyes and sighed. Yes, he was safe here. Yes, Varen was not lurking in the forests outside. Yes, he only had one more dark garden to endure this month. But he was so tired.

I really should have not left Nox in Sidero. At least she brings some companionship. But... that last conversation—argument, truly

—she *was the one who stomped off like she could shake the deities from the heavens.*

Hadrien opened his eyes again at the sound of approaching footsteps. For a wild, delirious heartbeat, he thought he would see Nox walk in. It would have been impossible.

The man that walked through the door was draped in ebony silk, as dark and sheer black as his hair and short beard. Light wrinkles feathered out from the corners of his eyes, betraying how much he smiled. His irises were a steely blue, set off by the steely grey speckled throughout his hair and beard.

He smiled at Hadrien, a kind, welcoming smile.

"May I help you, Hadrien?" he asked, in a voice so deep it could dredge oceans. "I understand that you have come here to seek a legend. My name is Ettore, and I am here to assist."

How funny that his name is what Nox named her gelding in Brumais. "I am looking for the Fetters of Aisling." Hadrien wondered if he would have lines from his smile if he should live to have grey in his hair. He doubted it. Probably lines from his frown instead.

"I know of those." Ettore swept his hand at the doorway he had walked through. "I do not know much, but Kartha will know more. We will walk to the hothouse."

Hadrien fell into step beside him. "The hothouse?"

"Kartha prefers to spend her days in the hothouse among the gardens." Ettore pushed open a door, and rain-shimmering sunlight dazzled before them. "This way to the gardens."

When he had been here before, Hadrien had only

been in the building that housed the Bath of Ink. These gardens, sprawling before him, were more beautiful than anything he'd seen. Paths of crushed granite swirled among the sculptures and fountains. The small stones varied in shades of blue, from the palest sky to a deep cobalt shot through with black and silver that reminded him of Nox's eyes.

Wait.

Why was he thinking about Nox's eyes?

I'm concerned about what she might be telling Artem, that's all. Focus on what Ettore is talking about. He looked at a sculpture as they passed it, a pair of lovers caught up in an embrace. Before his eyes, he pictured Nox and Artem in the same pose. He quickly averted his eyes, blinking rapidly to rid himself of the image.

"Over there," Ettore said, "are the first olive trees to grow here. The Moonsworn herself planted them. They have never taken ill in all the years."

Look at those trees, Hadrien; don't think of Nox. He fixed his eyes on them and tried to concentrate on how the trunks were riddled with twists and nooks, centuries upon centuries of growth influenced by the weather. There was such beauty in the art of the branches and the song of the hollow bamboo wind chimes and—

And that was the Wild Moon Wolf in broad daylight.

Hadrien halted in his tracks, his hands flying to the bow across his back.

"That is one of the Luxian wolves," Ettore said, his words lit with a smile. He whistled, and the antlered wolf swung her huge head towards them.

Relief dropped Hadrien's shoulders. The wolf had only two eyes, not three; she had antlers like a stag and not horns like a ram; no bells tolled with her strides as she approached at a languid walk. Her rain-darkened coat gleamed in the faint sunlight. A second, smaller but broader, Luxian wolf trotted up and nuzzled the first in what was clearly a display of affection. The wolves stopped before them, towering over even Ettore.

Ettore indicated the first. "Luna, the oldest one here. And that is Auric. They're a pair and have been as long as anyone can remember."

"Are they immortal?"

"No one knows. The ones upon these grounds have been here since the beginning. They have shown signs of aging, but none have passed on."

Hadrien held himself very still as Auric sniffed at the top of his head. The breath swept strands of his hair astray and tickled. Slowly, Hadrien raised his hand and stroked his palm across the massive shoulder. And then he wished that Nox was here to see this, and by the relics, what was wrong with him?

The Luxian wolves settled on the thick grass off the path, their heads nestled close. Ettore walked on, and Hadrien followed, trying to center his thoughts on the Fetters of Aisling and not the former Heir of the Shadow.

Ettore opened the door to the hothouse, a multi-roomed enclosure of glass and metal with diamonds of rain sparkling along its peaked roof. Heat washed out. Hadrien shed his cloak and jacket before stepping in.

Inside was a riot of bright colors and nectar.

He recognized some of the flowers: hibiscuses with huge petals, delicate orchids with their graceful arches, and more, all flowers that flourished in climates decidedly different than Aisling's. A few of the windows were decorated with stained glass that sent color stretching across the tiled path between the rows of flowers.

"Kartha?" Ettore called. "I've brought Hadrien here to speak with you about the Fetters of Aisling."

Kartha appeared around the corner, holding a pair of garden shears in her hand. Like Ettore, she had grey in her hair; these Inksworn lived long lives. Her eyes were still bright and keen behind her spectacles. Tattoos extended up her arms, full of color vivid on her dark skin. An Ink?

Catching Hadrien's eye, Kartha smiled and brushed her fingertips against a hibiscus bud. The bud unfurled, and the trumpet-shaped petals spilled out.

That was a beautiful, magical Ink.

"Hadrien." Kartha clasped her hands together, and that alone told him he was not going to like her next words. "The Fetters of Aisling are not here."

"What?" he burst out.

"They're not here. The Fetters have not been seen in many years, not since the Exalted Queen retrieved them." Kartha raked a suddenly critical eye over Hadrien. "Heir of the Shadow, for what beast do you require the Fetters?"

His mouth went dry.

If they knew so much else, how did they not know this? Did they want him to say it aloud? He was in deep trouble. The Arch Shadow had said some would try to stop him, for they considered the Wild Moon Wolf sacred; were the Inksworn some of those people?

Ettore was now also looking at him with an intense gaze, and Hadrien dropped his eyes to the ground. He closed one hand over the other and rubbed his thumb back and forth, his knuckles tight.

"I—" he started. "I need to kill the Wild Moon Wolf so I can keep the title, and if I don't, Nox will kill me because only one of us can live." The words rushed out of him in a single breath, and he panted shallowly, fear coursing like acid through him. At their silence, he hurried to add, "Please don't—don't kick me out. I truly need help."

Kartha's expression was anything but welcoming, as was Ettore's. "The Wild Moon Wolf is sacred. Not a beast to be hunted and stuffed as a trophy." She exchanged a glance with Ettore. "You should leave now, Hadrien. Do what the Emperor of Atassia will not and abandon this endeavor of hunting the Wild Moon Wolf. Face what comes your way."

He was going to be sick.

Hadrien fled the hothouse and the grounds of Aisling.

CHAPTER TWENTY-TWO
Nox

ARTEM WOKE me in the morning with a kick to the bed. "Hadrien is at the door, asking for you."

I groaned and rolled to the edge of the bed, sitting up with a yawn. The Heir of the Shadow had been gone for a few days. It was the last day of the month. The Wild Moon Hunt officially started tomorrow.

Yesterday had been a new moon.

I knew what that had meant for the Heir.

Artem considered me, his face unreadable. "It's lucky timing, him returning the day before the hunt begins." Then a sly smile turned up his mouth. "Unlucky for you, not knowing any more than when you came here."

I ran a hand through my hair. "As if we've talked much."

"As if you did anything but sleep and eat cheese and desserts." He stepped closer and tucked a strand of my hair behind my ear, giving me a familiar smile, the one he used to wear when he caught my eye at Guild Gatherings.

He tipped up my chin with his fingertips. "I really thought you were here for other reasons."

If only I had been.

Artem sat on his bed. His knees bumped into mine. "Nox."

"Artem," I replied in the same pointed tone.

"Are you going to tell me what happened?" Out of the corner of my eye, I saw Gunnar appear in the doorway, and Artem shooed him away. "No one will say how you died—or not fully died—not even Azzarda in the Fox Guild, and all of us Heirs and former Heirs know she knows everything."

"The Arch Shadow decided I was no longer useful to her and stabbed me. Seven times. With my own sword." I forced a shrug. "She left me for dead in the catacombs, I crawled out, and surprise, I lived."

"Is that true?"

It wasn't Artem who had asked that. I rested my head in my hands. "Heir. You've returned."

His steps dragged closer, and he dropped down onto the bed next to Artem. "What you said. Is that true?"

My knee bounced. "I think I've told you it before."

"Considering I spent the last few days with a broken leg—"

I snapped my head up. "How did that happen?" Where had he been?

His eyes darted to Artem, who merely offered an innocent smile in response. "I'll tell you later. Tell me the truth."

It was easier to show him. Artem would see the truth too, but it was mostly for Hadrien. I pulled up the hem of my shirt enough to expose part of the scars slashing across my torso.

Artem whistled out a breath.

Hadrien stood. "Nox, get your pack. We're leaving." He glanced at Artem. "Artem, ah, I don't wish you luck in the hunt."

"The same to you."

My joints stiff and protesting, I grabbed my knapsack and disappeared into the washroom. The moment the door closed, Hadrien and Artem began speaking in low tones. I pressed my ear to the door. What were they talking about?

I couldn't make out anything.

You could wish for it, Lupakaria murmured.

Could be nothing, I replied.

Abandoning the effort, I cleaned myself up and dressed for travel. Hadrien would likely want to take the horses and move on from Sidero, now that he had the Fetters of Aisling. The thought made me want to curl into a ball for hours, but that wasn't an option.

I yanked open the door, startling the two of them. "Ready?"

Hadrien, still limping, headed for the exit, and I lingered long enough to say, "Thanks, Artem. For everything."

His smile didn't reach his eyes. "Take care, Nox."

Catching up to Hadrien, I wondered if I should have said anything else. I waved at Gunnar in the hallway, who gave me a perplexed look in return. He, I had found out, was from Skogia and part of a group that sought high value items. The head and heart of the Wild Moon Wolf were, indeed, high value items.

Hadrien glanced down at me. "It feels like an eternity since I've seen you."

"That sounds like you missed me."

"Definitely not." He paused, leaning against a wall with a wince. "Damn it," he breathed out, "this leg. That healer had no idea what she was doing. Whatever she gave me, it was not Grace Breath."

Light tipped across his face, and I saw the new scratches from the dark garden. *Oh, he must have come here as soon as he was able.* "What happened?"

"I'll tell you outside."

"Very well."

I want to know, Lupakaria said. *I also want a blueberry muffin again.*

We can get one. I tugged on Hadrien's sleeve. "Have you eaten? The bakery should be open. I've been going there for breakfast."

"Uh-huh. With Artem?"

Is he… jealous? "No. Artem and Gunnar were busy planning their hunt strategy and preparing their weapons."

"Did you tell Artem anything *we* learned?" His tone was sharp enough to cut.

That's it. He's worried I gave away our secret. "I didn't. Ask him. We hardly spoke."

He snorted, derisive. "Too busy tangling tongues."

I grabbed Hadrien's sleeve again, this time pulling him to a stop. "What is with you? It is none of your business what I was and wasn't doing with Artem beyond the Wild Moon Hunt."

"He is a competitor."

"This? Again?" I rolled my eyes. "Really, Hadrien?"

He made a frustrated motion with his hands, a huff gusting out. He stormed down the street, his limp becoming more and more pronounced. It only took ten strides before he was leaning against a carefully cultivated tree on the side of the street. His head twisted back, and his glare landed on me.

I approached him like he was a wounded animal. "What happened to you?"

Hadrien's glare smoldered for a moment longer, and then he sighed, the fire in his eyes fading. "I went to Chalybos."

"Chalybos. Why? There's nothing in that town, aside from some truly horrendous orange cakes."

He straightened up, wincing. "I went back to the cave, the Chimera's cave."

Tension froze my body.

"It was gone, and I slipped in. I wasn't fast enough. The Chimera returned and threw me against the side of the cave. Astre Noir held it off long enough for me to drag myself away."

He could have died, and I would have never known. "Why were you there? It was foolish to go on your own, and you should know that after——"

Hadrien closed his eyes. "I brought Rogus' bones back."

My jaw clicked shut. He had risked his life to retrieve Rogus' bones. I didn't think about it; I threw my arms around him and held him tight.

After a surprised noise, Hadrien patted my shoulder. "You can let go now, Nox."

"No," I said and squeezed him, partly to confirm he

was real, partly because I was certain it would annoy him. "You smell like rosemary."

"Thanks, I suppose." With every word, his voice vibrated low in his bones, and I felt it everywhere I was in contact with his body. "You, uh, you smell like chocolate and butter."

"I ate a muffin in the middle of the night."

Hadrien squirmed. "This has officially lasted too long." His gloved fingers pushed at my arms. "Let go." When I finally stepped back, his brow was furrowed, and he murmured, "You are very strange." The corner of his mouth twitched. "One could even say obnoxious."

He has a point there, Lupakaria sniped.

But I was too distracted by how Hadrien was smiling.

Hadrien seemed more at ease now, though his features tensed in pain when he tried to take a step. "Ow. I've arranged for Xenna to meet us at the cathedral to the Three Mothers in Ferros in two days' time. If we leave Sidero within a few hours, we'll have enough time. And there's still enough time before the first full moon to get everything we need for the hunt."

My stomach dropped out. He didn't have the Fetters of Aisling. "First things first, you need a better healer."

"That's unfortunately true."

He tried to hide his limp the whole way to the closest healer's shop. He didn't ask for help, and I didn't offer, mainly because my way of helping was carrying his pack and the small box of Rogus' bones. I didn't want to think about how all that was left of him fit in this box. What had happened to the rest.

So I focused instead on Hadrien.

The healer fixed what was making him limp: a small fracture in his femur bone. There was also residual bruising along his back and side. It must have ached when I hugged him.

I wondered how badly he had been injured before the first healer. Varen had crushed his spine. The Chimera of Chalybos could have easily done the same or worse.

Outside of the healer's shop, I asked him.

Hadrien chewed on his lower lip. "The healer in Chalybos said my broken ribs punctured my lungs. The leg, obviously, was broken." There was a long pause, but I could tell he had more to say. "I lied earlier. The Chimera didn't hit me just once. It ignored Astre in favor of attacking me. My bow was broken, and I couldn't move my hand to draw a dagger. I only managed to escape when the Chimera went out to hunt some travelers."

He was very close to death. I felt a twinge of remorse for snapping at him earlier. "Sounds like you need food." *Was he trying to get himself killed for a lack of care?*

"I do."

"You also need to explain what happened in Aisling."

"I will."

And he did, seated across from me at a small table tucked into the corner of a quiet bakery. I sipped my cup of black tea and ate two muffins, one with a swirl of cinnamon through it and one studded with blueberries. Three muffins sat untouched in front of Hadrien: blueberry, lemon and poppyseed, and plain, boring, honey-drizzled and butter-smeared wheat.

"So," I said, setting down my empty cup. "Let me consider this for a moment. Eat, drink, feast upon the muffins." While he started to do that, I mused to Lupakaria, *Hadrien was kicked out of Aisling, which doesn't seem like it should be possible, and the Fetters of Aisling are with the Exalted Queen.*

Horribly convenient for you, little wolf.

I know. I don't trust it. I glanced at Hadrien; he was chewing a mouthful of buttered and honeyed wheat muffin. His eyes were closed, his expression relaxed. Surely that wasn't better than a blueberry muffin. *Do you think there is more than what Hadrien said?*

No. Now get something with chocolate in it.

I slipped up to the front and bought a small slice of chocolate cake with a raspberry syrup below the icing. Possibly not the best idea to eat before a day of travel, but Lupakaria wanted chocolate, and so Lupakaria would get chocolate.

Hadrien opened one eye when I returned with the plate. There were no more muffins in front of him, and his teacup was empty, too. "Isn't it too early for cake?"

In answer, I snatched the unused fork from in front of him and speared a bit of cake on it. I offered the fork to him. "It's never too early for cake."

His face said he disagreed, but he took the fork anyways. The instant he tasted the cake, his expression lit up. "I see your point."

Stop talking and eat the cake, Lupakaria ordered, pounding her paws on phantasmal ground.

For once, I followed what the wolf goddess said. Then, after the cake was gone—I let Hadrien steal what he probably thought were sneaky bites—I ventured, "How was the dark garden? That was the third one, right, so you're done with it until next month."

Hadrien shrugged, his fork still in his mouth, upside-down so that the tines curved over his full lower lip.

Around the fork, he mumbled, "Fine, I guess." His eyes darted up, met mine for a heartbeat, and dashed away. "No one read fairytales to me that were specifically about curses."

It was my turn to shrug. "I didn't think you'd be gone that long."

"I wouldn't have, if not for, you know. Chalybos. Chimera."

Quietly, I admitted, "I didn't think you'd leave at all."

"Nox." He tapped the blunt handle of his fork on the table. "You wouldn't have been able to go through the Ianis Frame to Aisling anyways. Did it matter if I left then or found you again before leaving?"

"Yes." The word was just a breath.

Hadrien laid his fork down, silent.

I picked at the threads on my napkin.

Finally, he said, "I'm sorry."

My head snapped up before I could curb my reaction.

"I—I was mad," Hadrien said to the table. His eyes flicked up for a second, a beam of sunlight cutting through the dark of the warpaint to illuminate his blue-grey irises. "I didn't fully consider the dangers for you. That there are still those who want you, as Nox Vis, dead."

It wasn't forgivable, and I didn't want to say that. So I replied, "I acknowledge that."

One eyebrow rose, and a furrow appeared on his brow. "You... acknowledge that."

I nodded. "I won't say something I don't mean."

His jaw dropped slightly. A hint of a flush crept into his cheeks. "You don't?"

"I told you. I don't lie."

"When? At Domhan Arbre—about the weapons?" He leaned forward, speaking low and fast. "I hardly count that as a moment of you declaring that you don't lie. What, is it some kind of moral code? How can you have that when you were first the Heir of the Wolf and then the Heir of the Shadow?"

"I did tell you."

"Tell me the sky is pink. Right now."

I offered him a lackluster scowl. "Of course it isn't."

Squinting at me, he said, "I suppose time will tell about your lies."

"No lies," I muttered, too low for him to hear.

His chair scraped back, and he stood, unfurling to his full, absurd height. "If you're done with your muffins and cake, it's time to go."

I tried to quell the panic rising, a trapped bird in my chest. *Lupakaria, I have no plan.*

You could wish for one.

Following Hadrien out of the bakery, I wrapped both hands around the jawbone, Lupakaria's remnant, and let the teeth dig into my palms, tried to ground my racing pulse in the dim flicker of pain. *I am going to die before the hunt is over.*

The hunt dies when you die.

Mother Death would hold me then. Death meant a few simple things: no hunt to win, no title to seize, no competitors to outsmart, and no Arch Shadow to torment me.

Chapter Twenty-Three
Hadrien

Nox was quiet.

She had been, ever since they had left Sidero, stuffed full of muffins and cake. Nox held Embra's reins with one hand, the other lightly resting upon the Jaws of Lupakaria. Hadrien couldn't tell what was on her mind. He supposed that was for the best.

His gaze dragged over the road sweeping up to the city of Ferros. He could still remember the day not long ago that he had ridden into the city and knocked on the door to the House of Shadows. Then there was the day he'd been granted the title of the Heir. That was the same day he had been told about Nox Vis and what the former Heir had done.

It was strange how quick life changed. That thought seemed to be recurring in his mind as of late, turning about like the moons sweeping through phases.

"Does the Arch Shadow know we're here today?"

Hadrien wasn't sure. "No."

"You don't sound sure."

"I'm not." He checked Ikarus' reins, held the gelding back from snapping at a passing traveler. "Ikarus, would you ever behave?"

Nox muttered something. Louder, she added, "The Arch Shadow might be there."

"Why?"

"Why does she ever do anything?"

That wasn't much of an answer, and the queasy warmth of fear scaled higher in Hadrien as they neared the city. The feeling only increased with every step he took through the streets towards the cathedral. Then a deep, resounding toll vibrated through the stones underfoot.

Hadrien startled back, swearing.

"It's the cathedral bells," Nox said, her voice tight, betraying some hidden emotion. "Unlike the Wild Moon Wolf, the Arch Shadow does not have bells that toll with her every step."

While the bells were still signaling noon, he entered the cathedral. Nox stopped at the threshold, biting her lip, staring at the box she held. She'd follow, he was sure of it.

When only his steps rang out on the smooth tiles, Hadrien turned, brow furrowed. "What is it? Nox, come on."

"I-I can't." Tears rolled down her face. "Please. Take this. Have Xenna meet me outside the city walls. She'll know the spot."

Nox was gone before Hadrien could form a thought, never mind stammer out a response.

What in the name of all that is holy was that? He waited a few minutes, but she didn't return. Carrying the box of

Rogus' bones in careful hands, Hadrien walked further into the cathedral.

The cathedral, like most to the Three Mothers, was split into three sections, one for each Mother. Each section was its own nave, connected by pointed archways at the sides and the walkway near the entrance that Hadrien was turning on. The tiles underfoot changed into the color schemes for each Mother. He made sure his boots were following the squares of berry-red and white tiles, the ones for Death.

He hesitated before the entrance to the nave for Mother Death. Dark-stained wood swept over the archway, lined with tarnished silver filigree. At the far end of the nave, twin torches flickered around a statue of Mother Death, twice the height of any mortal. Behind the veil of lace, her silver skull grinned.

Xenna stood in the firelight, staring up at the face of Mother Death, her hands clasped behind her back. At Hadrien's approaching steps, she turned, and her glittering eyes went to the empty space beside him. "Where's Nox?"

"She said she couldn't." Hadrien stopped and handed the box of bones to the veiled priest who slunk up wordlessly. His eyes went to the statue looming over them. "I don't know what that means exactly."

But Xenna nodded, the torches reflecting in her eyes. "I do."

"Nox said to meet her outside the city walls. That you would know what spot she means."

"I know where." Xenna lowered her head, and the priest made the sign of the Three Mothers over her hair.

"May the Three Mothers bless you, guard you, and keep you," she murmured to the priest.

Hadrien bent his knee and dipped his head to bring it low enough for the priest. He repeated the same words Xenna had uttered. As he raised his head again, he glimpsed a gleam of scarred-white eyes behind the veil. The priest was blind or near-blind, but their movements were sure.

In silence, the priest opened the box and laid Rogus' bones out, one by one. There were so few. The Chimera had broken and ground to dust too many. Astre Noir had been able to only identify these as his.

The bones, arranged in rows on the tiles before the feet of Mother Death, formed a measly approximation of who Rogus had been. Hadrien stared at them, bleached-white and stark against the red tile below. The priest anointed each bone with a drop of oil, water, and blood from vessels two other priests had brought over.

These other two priests were in different colored robes and adornments, a priest for each Mother. One in grey and iron for Mother Fair, one in gold and laurels for Mother Grace, one in red and thorns for Mother Death. The priests clasped hands and prayed over the bones.

Xenna closed her eyes and murmured a soft prayer of her own.

Hadrien didn't know what to do. But he shut his eyes and thought fervently, *If you can hear me, I am sorry, Rogus. I should be the one on the ground now, not you. I hope you are at rest.*

The three priests gathered the bones and placed them in an iron-clad box. The priests for Mother Fair and Mother Grace faded away, and the remaining priest bore the box away. Hadrien and Xenna stood in silence,

Hadrien's eyes burning dry and Xenna's eyes gleaming with tears.

When the priest returned, it was with an urn of ashes.

Xenna blew out a shaky breath and accepted the urn. "Thank you."

Hadrien couldn't remember how to speak. Rogus was bone and ash because of him. It was his fault that all that remained of Rogus' mortal body was contained in the pottery of a single urn.

"Nox will be at the lightning-struck orange tree," Xenna said, her voice thick with unshed grief. "Rogus loved that spot, how it overlooked the lake and the forest. If you couldn't find him in the city and he wasn't out on a hunt, he would be there."

Hadrien had no right to say anything now.

Xenna was correct; the short form of Nox was under the orange tree, leaning against the blackened bark. Hadrien wondered when it had been struck by lightning, why it hadn't died or failed to flourish; glossy leaves and burgeoning oranges filled the branches. Bees drifted by, landing on nearby flowers, filling the air with a soft buzz under the distant hush of waves.

It was a beautiful spot, a fitting resting place for Rogus.

Nox embraced Xenna, tucking her chin over the arch of her friend's shoulder. Tears glimmered in her eyes, and Hadrien saw himself reflected in them. He moved away, not wanting to intrude upon the two who had known Rogus far longer. Who hadn't been responsible for his death.

Xenna scattered the first handful of ashes, letting the breeze carry them away. Nox took the urn next and held it squarely between her hands, her gaze directed into the depths. Wordlessly, she offered it to Hadrien. He was still for a moment—surely Nox wasn't offering the urn to him—but she gave him a pointed look, made soft by the tears.

Hadrien dipped his gloved hand in and withdrew ashes to cast out. Nox then tossed out her own handful of ashes, her eyes lingering on the wind carrying the ash away. Handful by handful, they emptied the urn of ashes.

Nox touched her fingers to the bark of the tree and whispered, "Goodbye, my friend. May the Mothers Three keep you."

Her head bowed, Nox stood in silence for a minute. With one last pat upon the trunk, she turned away from the view that Rogus had once loved, the place where Rogus would rest until the world ended.

Hadrien fished his flask out, took a sip, and pressed it into her hand. Nox stared at it for a heartbeat; her mouth flickered up. In a swift motion, she knocked back a gulp, hissed at the burn, and returned the flask.

With a cough, Nox muttered, "Thanks."

Xenna slung an arm around Nox, then Hadrien, and said, "Thank you, Hadrien, for going back there. Rogus deserved a proper burial." She glanced between the two of them. "Do you need to leave Ferros now, or can you stay for a night?"

As tempting as it was to stay for a night, he shook his head. "We need to move on to Argentaria. The first full moon is soon and—" He hesitated. "We learned something. This hunt has to be as quiet and as quick as possible, otherwise Atassia may draw the attention of something that we don't want looking here."

"Foreboding."

Nox poked Xenna in the side. "You could come."

Hadrien looked over and tried to catch Nox's eye. He didn't want Xenna to get hurt. And if the Wild Hunt descended, those he tentatively considered friends were bound to be hurt.

But Xenna was already saying, "No, the Arch Shadow has me setting out to hunt some of those white-coated, golden-antlered harts in Brumais. I'll be gone for a few weeks." Letting go of Hadrien, she scuffed her knuckles over Nox's hair. "I'll be back by the time you're done with this hunt."

They parted ways outside of Ferros. Xenna headed north on her horse, aiming for the city Hadrien and Nox had so recently come from: Sidero. Hadrien and Nox turned their horses west and settled onto the road that would eventually lead to Argentaria.

"What's in Argentaria?" Nox asked, her voice rough. A sidelong glance confirmed that her cobalt eyes were bright with tears, her jaw held tight. She was trying so hard to stamp down the grief.

"The Exalted Queen is nearby," Hadrien replied, choosing to not comment on Nox's grief-stricken expression. But he extended his flask again without a word.

She took a long sip, so long that Hadrien feared she'd emptied the flask. "Faeries," she murmured. "That's what we'll see there."

"Just don't make any bargains with them."

"What exactly is your plan, little Heir?"

"For the faeries?" He shrugged. "Watch what I say."

Nox shook her head. "For the Wild Moon Wolf. Once you have the Fetters, how do you think you're going to trap her? She's not going to simply walk into the Fetters if you ask nicely."

"She's usually in the forest between Ferros and Ferrugo. I'll find her and bait her into a trap there."

"All within one night?"

A firm nod. "I'll see if I can find her on the upcoming full moon. I've seen her around Ferros before, so maybe she'll be lurking around the southern wilds. That would be a stroke of luck."

Nox stared down at the flask. Suddenly, she asked, "What girl is it that you have a liking for?"

"What?"

"You mentioned it in passing."

Hadrien motioned for the flask. "Give me that back." After a deep gulp, with cognac burning his mouth still, he muttered, "She lives in Arezza."

"How convenient. We're passing through there."

"Means nothing." Putting every ounce of authority from his title into his voice, he said, "We are stopping in Arezza, for I have someone to see there."

"This girl?"

"No."

"Not yet, you mean." Her expression curved into something sly and knowing. "Time is running out, little Heir. You heard Aveline and Fleur: soon the host of hunters from beyond this world will turn their eyes to us." Her own eyes alighted on the road ahead. "Abandon the Wild Moon Hunt and live while you can, is what I heard."

Of course that was what Nox had interpreted the dragons' words as. "That's not it, at all. One way or another, the Wild Moon Hunt needs to be done so that those sidereal hunters do not descend."

Hadrien let silence slip over him, a thought blooming. "Maybe the Wild Moon Wolf needs to leave the continent long enough for the hunters to forget about her."

Nox scoffed. "Unlikely."

And it was.

Only the Wild Moon Wolf's head and heart, sawn and severed from her body, would render the Wild Moon Hunt complete and Khtonyx safe from the eyes of the Wild Hunt once more.

In Arezza, Hadrien left Nox on her own at an inn for a meal under the pretense that he was going for supplies. He kept Ikarus near Embra outside the inn, to keep up the illusion that he was nearby. Checking over his shoulder in case Nox was tailing him, he slunk away to the outskirts of town.

A farmhouse awaited him at the end of a winding path.

His shoulders slumped at the sight, and he knocked on the door in a three-beat pattern. A sigh rolled past his lips. He darted a glance at the path—no sign of Nox. But he didn't have long.

The door opened, and Hadrien ducked through.

"I heard about the hunt the Emperor is putting on," Siena said, locking the door. She leaned against the doorframe and crossed her arms. "So Skota has sent you on the hunt."

Hadrien didn't need to nod.

Her eyes sharpening, Siena asked, "Where is your hunt partner?"

"At the inn. She didn't follow me. I made sure of it." Unbidden, a smile tugged at his mouth. "Desserts distract her well enough." The patter of paws announced Zira's arrival, and he dropped to one knee to greet the maned wolf. "Hi, you." If Zira was here… "Is Xenna here, too?"

But even as he was asking it, he knew it was impossible, since Xenna had been leaving for Brumais.

"Not today. Have you made up your mind yet?"

Could he really do this? Was it worth the risk of failure?

It seemed to take all his strength for him to nod.

"I assume that is a decision I will like."

Again, he nodded.

"It will take me a few weeks to gather who and what I need. Continue as you are and don't let Skota know."

Hadrien turned his face towards Zira and scuffed his fingers through the russet fur. "Nox Vis is my hunt partner," he admitted.

Siena's intake of breath was audible. Then she laughed. "Of course. I should have known Skota would track her down again."

"You knew she was alive?"

"Hadrien, *I* dragged Nox out of those catacombs myself."

Hadrien stood and finally voiced the question that had been lingering in his mind. "Why did the Wolf Guild fall?"

Siena sighed first, then she shook her head, gaze distant. The weight of memories dragging at her words, she told him, "Skota and I never saw eye to eye. She thought I was too cautious, that I was holding back the Wolf Guild from grandeur.

"She sent her Heir and other Wolves out without proper training. Including my son, Lucco—her nephew; I was once married to her late brother." A gleam of tears misted her eyes. Siena blinked them away, and Hadrien wondered how much loss she had borne the weight of in her years.

"Skota loved that boy as if he were her own son and thought the world of him; he could do no wrong. Nox, on the other hand, was every fault and flaw, despite being the Heir. So, when Nox returned from a mission without Lucco, Skota believed Nox was to blame."

The Arch Shadow did the same to me, Hadrien realized. *Are Nox and I so different?*

Siena's expression was a complicated one that Hadrien doubted he could ever truly understand even if he viewed it every day. Part grief, part rue, part acceptance. "Nox could have never saved Lucco that day. No child can pull a half-grown teenager up from a cliff. Nox was only a child." She said the last part like she was reminding herself.

And I could not have saved Rogus. Hadrien waited, knowing there was more, trying not to let his thoughts play across his face. Because, by the Three Mothers, did this lead to more questions.

"Nox's age—she was so young, so little—didn't matter to Skota. Skota only saw her failure and the things she did to, as Skota put it, make her life difficult." Siena traced her fingers along the doorframe. "I pushed back, and one day, I pushed back too much. Skota destroyed the Wolf Guild."

Siena held her hand out. "Here, give me your Shadow medallion."

Hadrien dropped it into her hand.

Rubbing her thumb across the surface, Siena said, "I was the Moonstalker. Not the leader of the Wolf Guild, no, but that was what I was known as. Skota eclipsed me, eclipsed the Wolf Guild, and hid us all away behind shadows. So she made her symbol an eclipse. The Wolf Guild was killed and buried without ceremony."

But he knew better—Siena had a plan and a desire to seize back what once had been hers.

She held his gaze. "Don't tell Nox about this."

"Why not?" He felt his brow furrowing and tried to smooth it out. "Surely she would help."

"That's exactly the problem. Nox would help."

He didn't see the same problem Siena evidently did. "Nox is…" Then he trailed off, not sure if he wanted to say the characteristics that flashed through his mind. Not all were flattering. "Nox," he finished.

"Keep her out of this, Hadrien, do you understand me?"

He didn't understand why, but he nodded anyways. And when he returned to the inn and found Nox surrounded by empty teacups and crumbs, he didn't tell her that Siena was near the town.

He did tell her, though, that he had arranged to see that girl after the first full moon.

Nox only offered him the last bite of a muffin in response.

CHAPTER TWENTY-FOUR
NOX

HADRIEN KNEW SOMETHING, I could tell.

He was fidgeting constantly, shifting his weight and tucking his hair behind his ears. Mostly, he held his left hand, curled into a loose fist, in his right, the middle finger of his right hand tracing circles across the back of his left hand. Sometimes the circles were languid and expansive; other times, the circles were quick and small.

I wondered if he even knew he did that.

We secured a room at Argentaria's inn, the single inn in the small town. While we unpacked, he fidgeted. I wanted to reach over and grab his hands to make him stop.

Finally, I threw a dirty shirt at his head. "Stop that."

"What?" He plucked the shirt off himself and wrinkled his nose. "What is this for? I don't want your dirty shirt."

"You've been fidgeting for the past hour, and it is infuriating." I grabbed the shirt back and tossed it into the pile that needed washing. "If you're so restless, you can make yourself useful and wash these clothes."

He shook his head, his eyes clearing. "Nox, you can wash your own. The tub's in there, or you can go to the lake."

"Lake."

"Then go."

He's not coming with me? I gathered up my dirty clothes and walked slowly to the door, waiting for him to realize.

But he didn't.

I let the door shut behind me and shrugged. *Guess he's not worried about me running away anymore.*

He is preoccupied, Lupakaria pointed out.

I know. I stole a glance back at the room door, still firmly shut, no sign of Hadrien following me. *I don't know what he's thinking about.*

Ask him. Or— Lupakaria's voice sharpened with glee. *—torture him until he talks!*

Flicking my nail against the jawbone, I replied, *That will surely make him hate me more than he already does.*

Hate you more? Silence filled my head, my own thoughts crept back in, and then Lupakaria said, *The only thing that boy hates is himself—and his family.*

I had picked up on the first but not the second. That was information Lupakaria had gleaned from her interaction with Hadrien. *You shouldn't tell me what you learned about him.*

Oh, but you desire to know, little wolf.

I couldn't tell her otherwise, and so I was quiet all the way to the edge of the lake. The moons provided enough light for me to see as I pushed a flat rock to where the water lapped at the sand. I dunked my clothes in the lake and scrubbed at the dirt and sweat until the clothes were mostly clean.

After arranging the clothes on nearby branches to dry, I rested back on my hands in the dry sand and watched the moonlight play over the waves. For a few minutes, it was just me and the sound of the water moving under a gentle breeze. Then a boot brushed against sand, and Hadrien was lowering himself to sit next to me.

"It's pretty," he said quietly, his voice slipping out like honey.

I remembered the last time we had sat at a lake's edge. "Do you like the Lake of Eternity in Brumais better?"

"Brumais is the place that has my heart. So, yes, I like the Lake of Eternity better." He trailed his fingers through the sand between us. "You?"

What was meant to be a quick glance at him stalled into a longer stare. The glimmers of moonlight and starlight were reflected in his eyes, tiny pinpricks of dazzling light. He held my gaze for a handful of heart-beats that were at once the span of a breath and the length of an eternity. He looked back to the lake, and I forced myself to do the same.

I never did answer his question.

"Is that someone swimming out there?" Hadrien pointed, and I followed his finger to the moonlight gleaming off the wet head of someone. "Isn't that dangerous with the faeries?"

"The faeries are at the other end of the lake," I replied.

"Hmm."

The swimmer struck out towards the shore, not far

from us, but clearly not noticing us. It was a man, broad and scarred, running a hand over his short hair as he stood in the hip-deep water. The dark lines of tattoos flowed over his forearms.

I recognized those. Why was Artem here?

I eyed Hadrien, but he was looking at the stars above and didn't seem to have recognized Artem. Granted, Hadrien probably didn't know that Artem's Ink was twin daggers upon his forearms. Few people knew that, as Artem covered his Ink with his signature azure jacket. With the distance and shine of moonlight, Artem's face was hard to see.

I ignored Artem and asked Hadrien, "Do you not have dirty clothes?"

"I took care of those already."

Right, we'd been in different locations. "How's the leg?"

"Better. How's the…" He trailed off, seeming lost.

I could fill in the missing words—any manner of the ways things had turned wrong recently. I shrugged. "Depends."

Hadrien lapsed into silence. Over his shoulder, moonlight flashed off Artem as he waded out of the lake. I averted my attention to safer subjects. Hadrien was staring at the shore now, his gaze unfocused, a frown playing over his features.

What is going on in his head? I mused. *So restless all day and now this.*

Wish for it, and I will tell you, Lupakaria murmured.

Sometimes, I wanted to take the Jaws off and never put them back on again. *Lupakaria, I promise you cheese if you be quiet the rest of the night unless I speak to you first.*

"Are your clothes dry yet?" Hadrien pushed himself to his feet, his back to the part of the shore where Artem had exited the lake. "I want plenty of rest before tomorrow."

Before we went to Isla Tower. I strained my fingers towards the hem of the closest shirt. Still damp. "I'll be back in the room when my clothes are dry."

Blue-grey eyes stared down at me. "Will you?"

I knocked my knuckles gently into the side of his knee and looked back out over the lake. He seemed to take that as a promise; his steps moved away, faded. I wondered if he was going back to the room or elsewhere.

But my thoughts flitted back to Artem—he wasn't following us, else he would have been farther from the town, but why was he here at the same time as us? Were other hunters here, seeking the Wild Moon Wolf?

I should track him down and interrogate him. Find out why he was here. Instead, I stayed there on the sand, drawing absent shapes in the grains with my fingertips.

Once my clothes were dry, I swept them into my arms and trekked back to the inn. Hadrien wasn't in his bed when I pushed open the door. I dropped my clothes in a bundle on an empty chair and glanced at the washroom: door open, space empty.

Where was Hadrien? And why were people appearing and disappearing on me tonight? Shaking my head at the frustration of unanswered questions, I began folding my clothes while I waited.

I didn't have to wait long.

Hadrien slunk into the room, his steps quiet and careful enough that I instantly knew he had been up to something. The way he blinked when he saw me was another telltale indication. "Nox, you're back."

"Where were you?"

Out came his flask, and he tipped back a mouthful. I had no idea when he was refilling that thing. "I found Artem."

Good that I didn't go in search of him.

"Gunnar is dead already. He was recognized by a team of bounty hunters. Apparently, there was quite a sizable bounty on his head back in Skogia. Artem is on his own but still in the hunt."

"Why is he here?"

"Outrunning the bounty hunters in case they're after him, too. He has already moved on from Argentaria; I saw to it." Hadrien shook his flask and frowned at the hollow noise.

"Did he ask why we were here?"

"I told him we planned to search the surrounding countryside for the Wild Moon Wolf." From his knapsack, he withdrew a bottle of cognac and popped the cork out. His focus on refilling his flask, he added, "I figured a half-truth was better than a full-out lie. Artem knows as well as I do that the Wild Moon Wolf is normally in the forests near Ferros, but there's always the chance."

I stuffed my clothes into my knapsack. Then I challenged, "And do you think he believed that?"

"Does it matter? As long as he doesn't follow us tomorrow. Two of us can outhunt one of him."

A laugh broke out of me. "Artem is not someone to underestimate."

Hadrien scoffed. "I'd like to see you do better."

"Me? I wouldn't have even found him and notified

him that we were here!" Never mind that I had considered it. I closed the space between us and jutted my chin up, held his gaze. "If he is there tomorrow, that is your fault."

"You—you're a rotten little wolf!"

I couldn't help it; I laughed.

Everything else forgotten, I gasped out between laughs, "That's the best you can do?"

His face flamed. Hadrien sputtered something and then managed, "Lupakaria calls you a little wolf. It was all I could think of." Backing away from me, he added, "I'm sure I could think of something else, given enough time."

"Given enough time," I repeated. "I suppose it's good you're not the Heir to that Guild of jesters, isn't it?"

Hadrien just sent a glower my way.

The morning brought about the kind of eye-heavy exhaustion that came only from a restless night of sleep. I grumbled my way through readying for a trip to Isla Tower; a cup of strong tea softened the drag of exhaustion.

When he thought I wasn't looking, Hadrien tipped a bit of cognac into his tea, which rather seemed like a poor choice to me. That would merely serve to muddle the flavor of the tea.

Leaving our belongings at the inn room, we saddled our horses and rode for the far end of the lake. Through the trees, I caught glimpses of the island and the tower upon it. When we drew even with the island, we halted the horses and led them on foot.

A safe distance from the mischief of the dock and any far-wandering faeries, I secured Embra's reins to a sturdy branch. Hadrien left Ikarus nearby but not close enough to bite or kick Embra.

I motioned for him to follow and strode through the trees. Aside from the leaves crunching underfoot, the forest was silent. Not even a whisper of noise slipped off the island. Any and all revelries to occur on the island would begin with the sunset.

The thought brought me to pause.

I sank into a crouch at the edge of the trees, my hand resting on the nearest trunk. The Exalted Queen would be asleep right now; it was long after sunrise.

"Hadrien," I said, "we need to wait until night."

"Then why did we come out here already?" Grumbling, Hadrien thumped down on the leaf-strewn sand, knees bent up. "You should've told me earlier."

"I remembered now." Standing, I brushed my hands together. "We should find some nicer clothes. There will be a revelry."

Hadrien looked down at the hunting attire he wore. "But this is clean. And practical."

"And faeries like a little flair."

"So you have a plan?"

I didn't. "You seem to forget I was the Heir before you. How much do you like wearing a doublet?"

"Very little." Hadrien fished out his flask and drank from it before swirling it—the contents swished—and staring into the dark interior. "Very, very little." He took another gulp, closed it with a smack of his hand, and stored it back in his jacket. "There's a tailor in the town who owes the Arch Shadow a favor; we'll get the clothes there."

Tipping his head back, he ran his gaze up and down me. "You're going to wear a dress?"

"Just for today."

"Huh."

What did that mean? "What are you getting at?"

"You don't seem like the dress-wearing type of girl."

I shrugged. "Who I am, Hadrien, is not stagnant like a brackish pond."

His hand twitched like it was about to move for his flask again. "How did you figure that out with being the Heir on so many hunts? Doesn't seem like the time for trying different attires."

"Time. Whimsy. Dares."

The hand slipped slowly into his jacket and withdrew the flask. Absently, his gaze fixed on the island, he knocked back a sip. "I won't wear a doublet."

"That's fine." Did he expect me to stand there and argue about it? "But you need to wear something with more shine and shimmer than you have on right now."

He was beginning to feel the effects of his drinking, I realized, when he replied in loose syllables, "Nothing with silk. Too slippery."

"A nice tunic and pants will do just fine."

"Let's go. The tailors will need time."

I walked ahead of him back to the horses and reached for Ikarus' reins, thinking to hand them over to Hadrien. The gelding's ears shot back; his head snaked down. Blunt teeth thudded against my thigh, pain burst like a bubble, and I leapt back before he could open his jaws and bite further.

I shook my finger at him, called him a rude boy, and retreated to Embra. My thigh smarted when I climbed into the saddle. I collected the reins and guided Embra through the trees, ducking low on her neck to avoid branches.

When the trees thinned out, I waited for Hadrien. A few minutes later, he appeared, leading Ikarus on foot. He stretched up and pulled himself into the saddle. With a nod at me, he sent Ikarus into a trot towards the town.

In Argentaria, Hadrien strode directly for the tailor's shop. His steps were slightly muddled. *I'll steal his flask,* I decided. *Soon as he's trying on clothes and his jacket is unattended, I'll take that flask and empty it, then replace it. He won't have time to go back to the inn for the bottle. If he gets drunk, he could fall prey to the whims of the faeries. It would be amusing but—*

It would *be amusing,* Lupakaria declared, *and there's no negatives. I want to see him lost in the revels of a faerie ring.*

Lupakaria.

Try to tell me you don't want that, too.

There was no sense in arguing with that.

I pulled open the door to the shop and couldn't find Hadrien anywhere. *Of course. Well, he can't have gone far.*

I ventured into the forest of clothes, careful not to brush against any of the fine silks and velvets; some of the fabrics looked like I could snag them with only a wayward glance.

Keeping one eye out for Hadrien, I skimmed my gaze over a display featuring a dress that I didn't mind the look of. It began as dark blue, nearly black, at the hem and lightened to sky blue at the shoulders. The skirt was flowing and loose, sure to whirl around my legs in a spin or breeze.

In contrast, the bodice was close and fitted, leading into long and slim sleeves. The sleeves ended in triangular points that slipped over the middle finger of each hand. Silver thread spanned the entirety, forming stars and moons and constellations.

It was almost perfect.

The neckline dipped low, and I tried to picture how revealing that would be on me. I wondered if Hadrien would follow the line with his eyes.

I should find him.

Hadrien was lingering near shelves filled with socks, which was not what we needed. It didn't take me long to find what was keeping him there, not with the furtive glances he was casting over: a girl around our age was perched atop a box nearby, a tailor kneeling before her. The girl was encased in an expanse of scarlet velvet, pearls studded along the skintight bodice. Mirrors around her showed the front and sides of the dress; flames arced up the flared skirt, golden and white threads tipped with shimmers of mica.

Sidling up to Hadrien, I whispered, "See something you like?"

He startled, then turned a mild glare on me. Without a word, he stomped over to the counter and waited, fiddling with a display of buttons. I ambled over and watched him spin around the display to examine all the buttons closely, as if he was planning to take up something involving lots of buttons.

A tailor came over, a pleasant smile on her face.

Hadrien held up his medallion, impassive, acting as the Heir of the Shadow again.

Expression falling, lips pressed tight, the tailor nodded. "What would you like?"

"A dress and a jacket," the Heir said shortly.

"Two masks," I added.

The Heir shot me a furrowed look, but I didn't explain. I wanted a mask simply for flair and fun. Maybe that was Lupakaria's doing, maybe that was mine, but I wholeheartedly agreed with the idea either way.

The tailor gestured to the rows of masks on a nearby wall. "Choose whichever you'd like. If you do not have a preference on dress or jacket, I will select them myself."

I pointed back towards the starry blue dress. "That one for me. Please."

The tailor nodded and looked to the Heir, who, in turn, shrugged and said, "Nothing in orange, that's all. Something fancy."

The tailor vanished among the clothing, and I focused on the masks. It was an easy choice, and I stretched up to pluck it free. I set the mask on the counter. A glance over my shoulder showed me that the Heir was still looking at the masks.

I ran a finger along the silver ram's horns spiraling out from my mask. The rest was painted black, paired with black ribbons to tie it on my head. It would work.

The tailor returned before the Heir was done looking at masks. "If you'll follow me, I have selected a few options and set them in a room for you." She glanced at me. "Bring your mask since you've picked it out already."

I did as the tailor said, highly aware that the Heir was following a few steps behind. Both to my relief and dismay, we had separate rooms. I'd have to sneak the flask out of the Heir's jacket later.

"I'll wait for you in the main room," the tailor said and left us at the doors.

The Heir slipped into one, and I started for the other. But then he was turning around and saying, "That's my room, your dress is in the other."

I pivoted on my heel and went into the room he had exited. The dress awaited me, a sea of blue fabric. It truly was pretty.

I used to have dresses like that, Lupakaria said, nostalgia coloring her tone. *They were beautiful.*

You're a cheese-eating mongrel. Why am I surprised that you liked dresses? The thought of Lupakaria in anything but her wolf form was strange, like a half-forgotten dream.

Lupakaria hummed, and I ducked behind a screen to change out of my clothes and into the dress. It slipped over my head like a wave, and I smoothed the skirt over my legs. With the style of the neckline, the Jaws rested directly on my collarbones and sternum.

The skirts were certainly too long.

I shoved my mask over my face and walked out. The skirts swept against my legs with each step, soft and sensuous on my skin. I felt like someone else as I stepped atop the box, faced with a triple reflection of myself. Letting my gaze settle somewhere beyond the mirrors, I waited for the tailor.

The tailor approached soon after, and as she was checking the fit, I felt the heat of eyes on me. I flicked my gaze up; in the mirror, blue-grey eyes dashed away. My mouth fought a smile. I saw the Heir whirling away in the reflection.

The tailor placed pins along the hems of the skirts, shortening them, and pinned the dress in a bit more above the hips. She stepped back and surveyed me with the eye of someone looking for flaws—in the dress's fit, not me.

The Heir crept into my line of sight, still wearing his regular attire. How disappointing. His jacket, however, was new, the deep purple of midnight. Silver threading emblazoned flowers upon it, stretching up from the hem and sleeve cuffs. Had the tailor seen his flower tattoos and purposely selected that jacket?

"You're done," the tailor told me. "Leave the dress in the room. Don't remove the pins. I'll alter the dress after I see to the jacket's fitting."

I stepped off the box, and the Heir swooped up. Now was my chance. I could slip into his room and take the flask from his discarded jacket.

But I heard the tailor behind me: "The fit is perfect."

The Heir's boots sounded against the floor, and I bit back my sigh and went into my room instead. I carefully lifted the dress over my head, hissing when a pin poked me in the side. I donned my clothes again. Time to find the Heir.

The Heir was waiting at the door leading out of the shop. A mask hung at his belt, but I couldn't get a good look at it. His flask was somewhere secure in his jacket.

His eyes met mine, and his expression softened like ice melting, and there was Hadrien again. "Do you want to get pastries while we wait? The tailor said it'll be an hour."

Food would do him some good. "Lead the way."

As night fell and stars glittered in the sky and the moons promised tomorrow night would feature a full moon, we approached the lake once more.

Across the waters, lights glimmered silver and gold on the island. The dock was festooned with drapes of greenery and small lights. A single boat of silver filigree bobbed in the water.

"We should leave our packs on this side," Hadrien decided, breaking the silence that cloaked the shore.

"I'm going to change. Don't look."

I ducked behind a wide tree to shield me while I changed into the dress. Thank the Mothers Three I didn't need help with fastening the dress. I settled my mask over my face, the ties secured and laying atop my hair.

I heard Hadrien cursing a moment before I returned. He was glaring at the mask he held in one hand. His flask was in the other, and he took a long sip, his throat working as he swallowed, before he asked, "Can you tie this on?"

I motioned for him to give me the mask. He handed me it and swept his hair up with one hand, revealing the pale length of his neck. I smoothed down his jacket collar first.

"It was crooked," I told him. "Can't have the Heir himself looking poor."

His eyes flitted down to mine, then lower; I raised the mask towards his face, and his eyes closed. I lifted his hand to hold the mask in place and slipped around to his back. Balancing on my tiptoes, I carefully tied the mask's ribbons behind his head. Hadrien shivered, even though I hadn't touched him at all.

"There." I stepped away, adjusting my own mask.

Hadrien let his hair down, hiding the ties, and turned. His mask was silver and feathered, and he tipped the small beak up to drink from his flask.

"Give me that," I said and held my hand out.

"Why?"

"I want a drink." *And I don't want you getting more muddled before we see the faeries, not unless it's on my terms.*

With a shrug, he pressed the flask into my hand. Steeling myself, I brought it to my lips and tilted my head back. Liquid fire raced into my mouth. I forced myself to down the burning alcohol. Damn, how much was in this flask? I had intended to empty it, but my stomach was already twisting after three gulps. I gave up and thrust the flask back at Hadrien.

He tucked it away in his jacket.

Hadrien snatched up an oar and waited for me settle in before shoving the boat off the dock and hopping in. As it had when I approached the island before, the boat glided seamlessly over the waters without a falter.

Seated across from me, Hadrien glanced over me, then mumbled, "Your… dress looks nice."

He was not very good at compliments, was he? "Thank you," I replied. "I like that jacket."

He tugged at the cuffs of the sleeves, gaze downcast. "It's very fancy." His fingers traced the curls of a flower stem climbing the sleeve. "I don't know how they make things like this, the embroidery." Blue-grey eyes dashed to me. "Yours is the night sky. Fitting."

The shore scraped against the boat. Hadrien sprang out—more of, scrambled out—and dragged it further up the shore. Water gleamed on his boots, and droplets studded the knees of his pants. He peered around the shore and the lush undergrowth before the trees, his eyes sharp as glass.

After a beat of hesitation, he offered his hand to me in a moment of gallantry, and I accepted it. His fingers curled around mine, strong and warm. I climbed out of the boat to stand before him on the shore. His eyes met mine through our masks. Maybe it was merely my imagination, but his hand lingered on mine.

Hadrien reached towards my face, and I went still as a deer pinned by torchlight. His fingertips caught on the snarl of my mask. Then his fingers tripped up the snout and across the furrowed brow to the curl of a horn, skimmed along the horn. Eyes glittering bright behind his mask, his head cocked to the side, the picture of an inquisitive bird.

Then he blinked. He jerked his hand back like he had been burned and strode off into the forest.

This won't end well, I thought but followed him.

Go, Lupakaria said, *I will protect you from ill fate.*

The forest was still and quiet, but far off, I heard the lilting sound of flutes. Hadrien's head turned in the direction of the music. But I was the one who angled to it, drawn like a moth to a flame. It was the direction we needed to go, after all.

Hadrien grabbed my shoulder. "Where are you going?"

"To the music," I replied, feeling far from my bones—and entirely in control. The Exalted Queen had given me safe passage last time I'd been here. The lure of the flutes meant nothing to me. But if I was going to wear this dress, I was going to attend the revel for a bit.

A final revelry before the hunt.

Hadrien opened his mouth to reply.

I tensed, the skin over my spine crawling under the weight of eyes. Fun didn't entail being ensorcelled by a faerie. Only Hadrien was vulnerable here. I widened my eyes pointedly at him before turning to face the faerie. I would handle this.

Gold streaked the faerie's pouting mouth. "Who are you?"

"Lost," I answered.

The faerie smiled, a slow, lazy smile. "You are lost no more." With a heavily ringed, extra-jointed hand, the faerie motioned for us to follow.

His eyes dim, dazed, lost in the pull of song, Hadrien walked after the faerie first. A thought flickered through my head: *Should I stop him?* It was gone in a heartbeat. I fell into step beside him. One night wouldn't hurt.

I eyed the faerie's rings. I could slide a few off those long, taloned fingers without the faerie noticing. Any curses would be worth the coin. *But if I'm dead before the month is over, coin doesn't matter.*

The song of revelry grew louder and louder, each beat more enchanting than the last, until it thundered in my veins and vibrated through my bones.

The faerie began to sway, then to dance, skipping and leaping, pulled forward by the music. My boot kicked into a red-capped mushroom, and my gaze slid to Hadrien. I seized his hand and pulled him into the ring.

Revelry was safer than him wandering the isle alone.

A faerie passed an eggshell full of wine into my hand, and I tipped it against Hadrien's mouth. The music had already entranced him; he drank without question. Then a lion-legged faerie took his hands and drew him into the circle of dancers.

I downed my own faerie wine, and with an ice-cold burn slipping down my throat, I slipped into the circle after Hadrien.

Then I began to dance.

Spinning, whirling, twirling. Heart beating, pounding, drumming. Feet tripping, hands scraping, blood stinging, singing. Laughing, smiling, sweating.

At one point, the moons shining high overhead, I was hand in hand with a boy in a feathered mask. The boy's smile was stained with berry juice, his laugh as infectious as the faerie wine heating my veins. We swept up together, closer than the dance dictated, close enough for his breath to meet mine. I led him into the next steps, wilder than any of the faeries around us. He didn't falter, and the smile below his mask was as wicked as mine.

When the song ended, the boy gave a bow with a breathless laugh. I watched him reach into a pocket in his jacket and withdraw a silver flask. He drank from the flask, a drop of amber liquid beading on his lower lip and rolling down the smooth line of his throat.

I staggered back a step.

The boy returned to the dancing, softer and calmer now, and I backed away to the edge of the mushroom ring. My feet ached within my boots. I sat down, my tailbone colliding with a root hard. The music swept over my head. Every pulse made my bruised sides and trembling legs hurt.

I blew out a sigh and leaned back until my spine was aligned with the earth and my head was pillowed upon soft moss. I shut my eyes against my blurring vision—the faerie wine and the cognac I'd taken earlier from Hadrien were meeting in a violent way.

I slept, and in my sleep, I was aware of the revelry continuing around me, feathers tickling my cheek under my mask.

Early sunrise's warmth crept over me. The revelry was fading. I stirred, scowling against the pounding headache. My hand was closed around something cold. I peered at it through the dim.

My thoughts collided into a single, resounding, *Shit.*

Clutched in my hand was Hadrien's flask.

Oh, how I love visiting the faeries, Lupakaria said.

CHAPTER TWENTY-FIVE
HADRIEN

THE BLOODY LIGHT of dawn speared through his eyelids.

Hadrien slapped his hand over his eyes, his palm skidding across the smooth surface of something. His hand fumbled around the edges. What was it?

He grabbed the edge and ripped it away from his face. For wild, heart-racing moment, it stuck. A flash of fear shot through his mind with an image of his skin tearing away. Then the object lifted, pain snapping against the back of his head.

It was a mask. Feathered and silver, vaguely avian in design. The ribbons dangling from either side were ragged. Oh. He'd broken the ties when he pulled it away so fast.

Around him was a thick, luscious forest. At his feet were shattered eggshells. This was the strangest place he had woken up. His mouth was dry, his head pounding—he had certainly been drinking a lot. His body ached with every little movement, as if he'd spent all night...

Dancing.

In flitters, the night returned to his memory.

The faerie had led him and Nox to a ring of mushrooms, where the revelry was beginning in a roar of music and lights. Nox… Nox had grabbed his hand, hadn't she? And she'd pulled Hadrien forward, across the mushrooms, even as he had been distantly, through a haze of music and longing, thinking that it was a bad idea.

After that, there had been no thoughts of hesitation in his head. Nox had worn a grin like the faeries, her crooked smile visible beneath the snarl of her mask, when she pressed an eggshell of faerie wine to his lips. He had danced after, and Nox had only appeared in flashes and glimpses until Hadrien was pressed against her, his sweat-slick fingers intertwined with hers, so close his breath was hers.

His face flushed now, as he remembered.

Where *was* Nox? He glanced around the immediate spread of trees but saw no living being. Surely she was nearby.

Swearing under his breath, Hadrien pushed himself to a sitting position. All his aches protested loudly. He stretched out his arms, one by one, joints popping.

"There you are."

A yelp escaped him.

Nox snorted. She looked none the worse for the night, her mask still on, her dress still as lovely as ever. "Enjoy the revel?"

A flash of memory, of her body against his. "I can't remember," he lied and looked away. *Make a distraction,* he told himself. He wished for a drink. He reached into his jacket for his flask—but his hand closed on empty cloth.

Patting his jacket pockets, he asked, "Have you seen my flask?"

She handed him the flask. Hadrien sloshed the contents around, then tucked it back into his jacket. He rocked to his feet, instantly stumbling as his head spun. Nox caught him, hands flying to his shoulders to steady him.

Hadrien remembered again the dance. He shrugged out of her grip and muttered, "I'm fine." His fingers flexed into fists, skin sliding on gritty skin. "Where are my gloves?"

Those, too, Nox handed over.

Why had she had his belongings?

"Now," Hadrien said, casting aside that thought and fitting his gloves firmly on, "let's find the Exalted Queen and get the Fetters of Aisling. We have until sunset to prepare for the hunt."

Nox struck off into the forest without a word. Hadrien blinked. His brow furrowed. That had seemed so abrupt. But with the utter silence of the forest descending on him and the full sunrise approaching, he could see why she might want to leave as fast as possible.

Hadrien hurried after, his head down to avoid the glare of the rising sun. Whatever drinks he had combined last night had been a terrible idea; the forest floor dipped and wove under his feet. He paused, shut his eyes tight.

A leaf crackled, and Nox said, "You could wait here if you wanted to."

"Uh-uh," he managed. "I do that, then you leave me stranded with the faeries."

She scoffed. "I wouldn't."

Then an arm slipped around his back, and Nox's

warmth was at his side. "You're so tall," she grunted. "Why are you so tall? *How* are you so tall?"

"I need to sit down again." That was all Hadrien could say before his knees buckled and he was on the ground. A fern waved over his face, and Nox peered down at him. "What did I drink?"

"Faerie wine and about half that flask of yours," Nox replied. She poked his leg with a boot tip. "You ate no faerie food, only a few mortal blackberries."

"Why are you not on the ground, too?"

"I drank less and slept more."

Hadrien wished he could close his eyes and open them when the hunt was over. He was so tired, his bones ached, and the first full moon was tonight. Maybe it was the alcohol still lingering in his body, but if Mother Death walked up to him right then, he would gladly go to her cold embrace.

Nox nudged him again. "You need to stand up. Time is wasting."

Grumbling, Hadrien sat up. Everything was spinning and tumbling around him. "How can the faeries drink that every revel?" Standing again with Nox's help, he frowned. "Can faeries even suffer hangovers?"

"Who knows?" With a pat on his shoulder, Nox asked, "Now, are you fine on your own?"

Inexplicably, that question was an undoing. He turned his face away from Nox, ignoring how her expression was wrinkling with worry. "I don't know what's wrong with me. I felt fine yesterday."

Or had he? All he could recall right now was a sense of sorrow and despair, weighing down on his bones and very being. It yawned before him, unending. Eyes shut, he fumbled for his flask, but a hand on his wrist stopped him.

"Have you considered that you're drinking to dull the pain but you're just making it sharper when the alcohol wears off?" The hand left his wrist and slipped the flask out. The remaining liquid sloshed inside. "I've watched you. Every time you are uncomfortable, you reach for this flask and take a sip. You want to know why I think you're still cursed with the dark garden?" He opened his mouth to refuse, but Nox continued, "I think it's because you drown everything in drink."

He had nothing to respond with. He croaked out, "Did Lupakaria tell you all that?"

In silence, Nox considered him. Finally, the former Heir said, "I don't need Lupakaria to tell me what I can see."

Was he truly so pathetic? Hadrien wondered if the Arch Shadow could see those things too, what that meant for his future as the Heir. At his sides, his fingers tightened, curled up. *Find the anger, hold onto that like it is breath,* he ordered himself.

He exhaled slowly, and when he inhaled, he willed every speck of his body to stand tall. "We should continue to the Exalted Queen." His voice barely wavered, but it was cold, so cold it was unrecognizable to him.

Nox blinked at his tone. "Hadrien, I—" Her features shuttered, hardened. "No. You're right. We should continue."

The silence that hung between them as they trekked through the forest was cluttered with unspoken words. As the dawn brightened further, birds began to trill in the trees, welcoming the sun with their song. And then the Isla Tower itself came into sight.

Nox didn't pause before shoving her way into the tower. Inside, Hadrien cast his gaze up, up, up, into the heart of the spiraling staircase. The snap of Nox's boots against the steps rang out in the space.

Slowly, trailing his fingers along the ridges of the horn railing, Hadrien followed Nox up the staircase. Tiny nautiluses were set into the staircase, glossed over with some sort of cold, impossibly smooth surface. This all was impossible, he thought.

"Is this real?" he murmured.

"Unfortunately," Nox replied.

In the face of Isla Tower, all was forgotten. His headache and tired, worn bones, Nox's words and the cutting truth in them, the unerring fact that the full moon was tonight. The wonder of Isla Tower swept all those thoughts from his mind.

But the stairs came to an end eventually.

Nox sighed, her gaze fixed on an open door. "Time for you to meet the Exalted Queen of the Isle."

Hadrien stepped in first, his eyes sweeping across the room, expecting radiant decor and a sprawling throne of flowering vines. He found only a faerie, crowned by sunrise's glow and her own gilded antlers.

The faerie smiled upon seeing Hadrien, and her eyes were like eternal skies and forgotten seas. "You may have your bargain now," she said, "seeing as you wear the amulet."

Nox sputtered out a curse. "*I* wanted the bargain, *I* delivered that amulet for you."

She shoved forward, clipped Hadrien's shoulder so

hard he stumbled, and then, with a furious glint in her eyes, Nox seized hold of the amulet. His eyes flew wide; his breath slipped out to tell her to stop—the chain snapped against the back of his neck, a brilliant sting.

Nox hurled the amulet at the feet of the Exalted Queen and spat, "Have your *damned* amulet back."

The Exalted Queen simply lowered her gaze to the broken, shattered amulet at her feet. Hadrien wasn't even sure how Nox had managed to break the silver, but it was beyond repair now, and the ribbon within had come unfurling out, a shimmery, endless snake, an ouroboros.

Nox stormed from the room, her boots pounding against the stairs.

"I'm sorry," Hadrien said. "She's… usually like that. May I ask a question instead of a bargain?" Remembering how faeries were, he hurried to add, "And that wasn't my question."

"You may."

He had to ask this carefully. "What is the location of the Fetters of Aisling right now?"

"Here." The Exalted Queen gestured down.

Hadrien looked to the ground, and he wondered if he was still drunk. The Exalted Queen had indicated the grey ribbon that had been within the amulet. Impossible. A ribbon couldn't hold anything, not a mouse, much less the Wild Moon Wolf.

He scooped up the ribbon carefully, his palm dipping under its astonishing weight, and coiled it into his pocket. If this ribbon was the Fetters of Aisling, how could he ever trap the Wild Moon Wolf? If it had been a length of chain, he could wind it around her muzzle, then hook it around each front leg and stake the chain to the ground, hold the moon monster down that way.

But a ribbon.

A fucking ribbon.

A ribbon to the beast was a feather to a sword, a raindrop to a desert, an ember to an abyss.

The Exalted Queen turned away, and so did Hadrien, his heart clenching around the dragging despair. But as he reached the doorway, the faerie said in a carrying voice, "Speak with the bones my changeling bears."

The words tumbled over each other in his mind as Hadrien descended the stairs, his steps far lighter than Nox's had been. Where was the trick? Faeries were known for tricks. But every word had seemed careful, deliberately chosen, and he could find no hidden meaning—and no actual truth within the words.

Nox, washed in sunlight, was waiting outside the tower. Hadrien approached, unsure of the girl's temper at the moment. The horned, snarling wolf mask on her face hid her expression; she swung her head towards him, cobalt eyes glimmering behind the mask, and it was like being pinned by a real wolf's gaze.

"Useless waste of time," Hadrien groused, throwing all his exhaustion into the words. *By the Three Mothers, please let Nox believe this. Let her believe I failed to get the Fetters of Aisling.* "Let's get off this isle as fast as possible. We'll trap the Wild Moon Wolf through mortal means alone."

"What?" The word burst out in a harsh breath. Nox ripped her mask from her face, and her snarl was no softer than the mask's. "The Fetters weren't here?"

"No." He brushed past her and plunged into the

forest. No steps followed. Over his shoulder, he shouted, "Nox! Come on!"

With a grumble, Nox followed.

Weaving through the quiet forest, Hadrien tried to sweep his thoughts in order. He had the Fetters of Aisling in his pocket. The Fetters were just a ribbon, a very long and heavy ribbon, but a ribbon nonetheless. The Exalted Queen had told him of some bones to speak with.

His eyes darted to Nox, tromping ahead of him now. No. It couldn't be.

But what bones other than those of Lupakaria were around to hold a conversation with?

That would mean Nox was a changeling, though. A child born of faeries and exchanged for a child born of humans. It was doubtful. There were rules to faeries; Nox broke those rules.

There was one way to find out.

At the shore where they'd left the boat, Hadrien called, "Nox."

She shot a glance back over her shoulder, her hands clasping the delicate arches of the boat. "What?"

It was now or never. "Are you a changeling?"

Nox went as still as a frozen lake. Then a rough laugh burst out of her. "Why do you ask that?" Body angling away, she reached for the Jaws of Lupakaria.

"Don't touch those," he ordered. Closing the distance between them in a few long strides, he captured her hands and held them pinned in one of his. With the other, he grabbed ahold of the jawbone of the dead wolf goddess. "Answer the question. Are you, Nox Vis, a changeling?"

Against his gloved palm, the bone hummed.

Fury bloomed black in Nox's eyes. "Yes."

Releasing her hands, Hadrien stumbled back. "But you—you've lied."

"You haven't been listening closely enough, then." She trailed a finger along the length of the jawbone, her gaze cast at the lake. "What do you want to know?" All heat and bite and anger had faded from her words, and the weight of the truth curled her shoulders forward.

"Does the Arch Shadow know?"

"No."

"Who knows?"

"You. Lupakaria. My father, wherever the bastard is." Her mouth twisted into a scowl. "The Exalted Queen."

And there was something so broken about the way Nox said it that Hadrien knew. "She told you today, didn't she?"

"Lupakaria told me today." Nox shook her head, seemed to shake herself into motion again; she settled into the boat. "What else?" she challenged.

Hadrien shoved the boat off the shore and leapt in. Water dripped off his boots. He set the boat on a course for the opposite shore before asking, "Are you a full-blooded faerie?"

Her lip curled, as if the thought was repulsive. "No. If you seek a bargain, look elsewhere."

He wanted to know more, but her face had closed off. He let it drop, focused his attention on the boat slicing through the water. His questions didn't need answering anyways, not for the Wild Moon Hunt.

Two hours before sunset, Hadrien walked out from the town of Argentaria again, his weapons slung and strapped over his form. He was armed with the Fetters of Aisling wrapped around his forearm, hidden below his sleeve and vambrace.

At his side, Nox was coiling a length of rope again and again between her hands. She had been quiet since leaving the isle, since the truth about her very being had been ushered into the light. Hadrien hadn't much wanted to talk, but that had left him alone with his sinking thoughts and his increasingly drying mouth and the lure of the cognac lingering in his flask.

But every time he reached for it, he heard Nox's words ringing in his head again. That had squelched any desire for drink firmly until the next craving.

Now, his hands felt unsteady, and there was a faint pounding in his head, like he had a hangover, even though he'd had not a drop since the night before. He could—and would—push down the pain, he told himself. Grit his teeth through it and hunt down this wolf of moon and night.

He barely knew where to start.

It was true. The Wild Moon Wolf could pick anywhere to appear tonight. Maybe he should've tried to tail Artem. Maybe he should've brought more than some various muffins to bait the trap with.

Nox had given the muffins a questioning look earlier until Hadrien had explained that he'd read a myth in which a monster was drawn by the scent of warm, honey-drizzled orange cakes. She had shrugged and admitted it was a decent idea.

The muffins seemed silly now.

Hadrien picked a hill that overlooked a valley, spotted with copses of trees. A decent distance from the nearest villa, it was still within sight of the lights of Argentaria. He checked for places to scramble out of the Wild Moon Wolf's reach. There weren't many. Trees were too delicate. The jumble of rocks down the hill would have to work.

The sun dipped lower.

His pulse ticked faster.

"Go scout for tracks," Hadrien told Nox. "Return here by night. I've seen the Wild Moon Wolf hide in rivers before. Don't underestimate her."

She started to turn.

"Nox," he said quickly, "be careful."

She slipped away without a word.

Hadrien trekked down to the valley and began to set his trap. It was simple and not at all perfect and very unlikely to work. The Arch Shadow, if she saw it, would certainly regret ever naming him the Heir. *Any other Shadow could have done this better,* he thought bitterly. *But it's me here.*

He set down the basket of muffins on a flat stretch of ground. The breeze would, Three Mothers willing, carry the scent of the pastries up the valley and lure the Wild Moon Wolf in under the starlight. Then Hadrien would risk life and limb to tether the monster down with the Fetters of Aisling.

After that, he would dispatch the beast with as little pain as possible. For both himself and her.

Returning to the hilltop, Hadrien awaited nightfall.

The sun slipped behind the horizon, and the sky darkened with evening, turning a beautiful shade of deep violet. Hadrien frowned, peered down into the valley sprawling before him. No sign of Nox.

The stars began to sparkle. The moons climbed higher, the full moon drowning the valley in cobalt light, struck through with hints of gold and silver. And yet, Nox had not reappeared.

Hadrien toyed with the iron-encased relic in his pocket. Too much coin had gone into the purchase of this little splinter of saint-bone and blessed iron. But all he could remember was how the Wild Moon Wolf hadn't crossed into the small temple. Maybe, just maybe, he could keep himself from getting killed with this holy relic.

Where is Nox? A bell tolled across the hills; his body chilled. Drawing in a long, measured breath, he unfolded his legs, rose, and readied his new bow.

Only one of us can win the title, he reminded himself. *I would have to get rid of her somehow anyways. Better if she's not here to begin with.*

Focusing hard on keeping his breathing even and deep, he listened to the bells drift closer. He squinted. Across the way, was that the gleam of the golden eyes?

The bells fell silent.

Hadrien waited.

And waited.

And waited.

Midnight came and went. He feared that the Wild Moon Wolf was uninterested in the muffins. His hand cramped around his bow. Flexing his fingers out, he chewed on his lip. Night was slipping fast from his grasp; he had to act now.

Hadrien descended into the valley, pulse tap-tap-tapping in his ears. The bells remained silent. The Wild

Moon Wolf remained where she was. He reached the spot where he had left the basket.

Exhaling a shaky breath—this was surely a fool's idea—he nicked the side of his hand. A drop of scarlet rolled slowly out. Blood to bait the beast.

Not even a heartbeat after the blood had disappeared into the dirt, did the ground tremble under heavy paws. The sound of bells wavered through the night.

The beast was approaching.

Between one breath and the next, the Wild Moon Wolf landed in front of Hadrien, shadows dripping off her coat. A breath huffed out into the air.

There was no time to ready his weapons.

No time to run.

No time to think.

In a single leap, the Wild Moon Wolf knocked Hadrien over like he weighed nothing. His back hit the ground, his breath left his lungs in a whoosh. The three golden eyes of the Wild Moon Wolf stared down at him as he gasped and fought for air.

A snarl rippled out, the vibrations traveling through the paw that pinned Hadrien. His own bones felt the snarl. As the beast above him lowered her massive muzzle and sniffed at his throat, he strained for the Fetters of Aisling. *Almost—almost—there!* His fingers closed around the end of the ribbon; he inched it out, his jaw trembling.

The monstrous wolf was investigating the blood on his hand now. Shadows from the heavy coat dripped and slid across him like oil on water. The tongue darted out, a blood-black, slick appendage, and raked along the crimson line. He shuddered, disgust twisting his stomach.

The Wild Moon Wolf shoved his hand aside, tearing

his fingers from the Fetters. A sob jarred out. His eyes screwed shut. He was going to die here. Just like when Varen had pinned him in the forest of Brumais, he was helpless and fated for death.

But at least he could look Mother Death in the face.

Hadrien forced his eyes open.

The Wild Moon Wolf was simply staring down at him again. An ear swiveled back, listening to the sounds of night; moonlight glinted off a silver ring near the top of the ear. Hadrien's thoughts stuttered. The moon-monster raised her head.

Hadrien settled his palms into the ground and pushed up as hard as he could. The paw raised enough for his ribs to bow out and air to rush into his lungs; then the paw flexed, talons pricking through his armour into his skin, and his back met the ground again.

The Wild Moon Wolf kept him pressed down even as the golden gaze was turned elsewhere, lip curling back to reveal the glimmer of teeth.

Sunrise stained the sky behind the Wild Moon Wolf's horned head. Under the faint toll of bells that marked the beast's sides rising and falling with her breathing, Hadrien heard a sharp whistle. Muscles bunched; the beast went to leap away; the arrow slammed into her side.

With a scream that rent the sky, she fled.

Hadrien sat up so fast his head spun.

Someone had shot the Wild Moon Wolf.

His gaze snapped to the hills cresting the valley. It had come from that direction. No flicker of light or blur of movement. Who had fired the arrow?

He made a heartbeat-quick decision.

He snatched up his bow and ran after the Wild Moon

Wolf. His legs shook with every stride, his heart still racing from the encounter. He kept low and raced through the cover of trees. He prayed the archer didn't shoot him, too.

Divots and scrapes in the ground led him on the path the Wild Moon Wolf had taken. Hadrien knew he had no chance of catching up, but he pressed on all the same. The sunrise lightened his surroundings, and with a start, he realized he was at the shore of the lake again.

His steps faltered. Why had the Wild Moon Wolf come here?

He slowed to a jog, his heaving breaths painful against tightening muscles. He pressed a hand to his side, breathed out deeply. Realizing he should've summoned Astre Noir sooner, he brought the Ink into being and beckoned her to follow the scraps of trail. The trail was staggered here, slower, dragging strides from the Wild Moon Wolf.

And then the trail disappeared.

"Shit," Hadrien whispered.

He crouched by the last mark and scanned the ground. Among the fallen leaves and vibrant grass, there was a splash of red blood. Good.

Hadrien followed drips and drops of blood, his bow exchanged for a dagger in the close quarters, his Ink bristling at his side. The ground sloped down, turned to sand underfoot. On the shore of the lake, he paused. His eyes skimmed over the shore. There was nowhere for the Wild Moon Wolf to hide, except in the waters of the lake itself.

Slowly, he approached the lake's edge, palming his

dagger. Sunlight bounced off the lapping waves. Nothing stirred below the surface.

The hiss of movement on sand snapped his attention to the edge of the forest. Astre Noir snarled. A girl stumbled out and into Hadrien, head ducked, arms wrapped close to her body. Hadrien dropped his dagger and clutched Nox close.

"Hadrien," Nox said, sounding so small and scared. Then she coughed hard; blood splattered against his armour and hers.

His hands trembled as he swept his arm under her shoulders, holding up the deadweight of the girl. "Where are you hurt?" he rushed out, but he found the answer a heartbeat later: an arrow jutted from Nox's side, the end broken off and splintered. "Oh no," Hadrien breathed out, "Nox."

Cobalt eyes in a blood-speckled face fluttered open and fixed on his. "All you had to do," Nox rasped, "was ask."

Chapter Twenty-Six
Nox

Pain was all I knew.

Shattering, blinding pain.

It ended worse than it began. It had started as a sharp prick, like a thorn, and then it was a cutting, ripping pain to end.

I wanted to bite off the hand of whoever was taking the arrow out so poorly. I wrenched my eyes open, teeth bared. Hands held me down, my back against a soft surface.

"Quit it," Hadrien snapped, his face haggard. Dried blood had rusted across his cheek. His warpaint had smeared and run in tracks down his face. "Stay still."

Someone else murmured a response, and I rolled my eyes toward them. A healer. They were staunching the wound with careful hands. I looked back to Hadrien, searched his face. He held my gaze for a heartbeat before turning his face away, expression closing off.

I stared at the ceiling until the healer had finished

cleaning and closing the wound. Slowly, cognizant of how sudden movement could undo the healing, I sat up. The healer produced a small vial of Grace Breath; it tasted of raspberries this time. Hadrien paid the healer, and steps faded away. A door closed, a lock slid shut.

"We're at the inn," he told me. Taking a seat, he watched his hands flex. Quietly, he said, "You're the Wild Moon Wolf."

I groaned.

Lupakaria sang out, *He knows!*

"Is that why you picked your mask for the faeries?"

That was his question? I nodded.

"Is… That's why Lupakaria calls you 'little wolf.'" It wasn't a question.

Is he wondering how he didn't piece it together sooner? "Partly. I was also the Heir of the Wolf, as you know."

Hadrien blew out a breath and sat back, his frame slumping against the chair. "You're the Wild Moon Wolf," he said again.

"Saying it more won't make you understand it further." I worked my tongue against the roof of my mouth. My mouth was so dry, it might as well have been the deserts of Kryzia. "Is there water and food?"

He tipped his chin toward the table, loaded down with cups and plates. "The tea should still be hot. There are some leftover muffins from this morning, also some soup and bread from lunch. I've already eaten."

So it was the afternoon, at the very least. I slung myself off the bed and staggered to the empty chair. My elbows hit the table with twin thumps; a cup rattled. I snatched up the nearest full cup of tea and downed it in a few gulps, scalding my throat in the process.

I grabbed a bowl of soup and dunked a piece of warm bread into it. The soup was some sort of tomato soup with rich notes of garlic and basil. I devoured half of the soup and a few thick slices of bread before pausing for breath.

"Hungry?" Hadrien asked.

"Famished." I swirled my spoon in the soup, watching the basil leaves dip below the surface. I tore off more bread and slathered it with garlic-infused butter. "The full moons make me hungry."

"No wonder. You're… You take on a massive form."

Around the mouthful, I mumbled, "Is that an insult?"

His expression soured. "You licked my hand."

"It was bloody." I wasn't particularly proud of that moment; cruel instinct had taken over.

"How do you even become that?"

I shrugged and focused on the food. "Why don't you tell me? You're the one who read all about my kin in the libraries of Domhan Arbre."

"Every full moon, huh?"

My nod was small. "Every full moon since I turned eighteen."

"Tell me your story."

That was a tall order, though maybe not as tall as Hadrien. "Born to a human father and faerie mother, given away as a changeling, sold to the Arch Shadow as her ward and later Heir. Seeing as I was born during an eclipse, I had the ill fortunate of being cursed with the form of the Wild Moon Wolf—and it is cursed, not blessed by the Moonsworn like some would say. I will always be trying to outrun my own shadow."

The weight of his gaze lingered on me. "You can't win this, can you?"

I huffed out a laugh that I didn't feel. He was right. All I was doing here was trying to keep anyone from winning this hunt by killing me. I avoided responding by filling my mouth with soup.

Hadrien helped himself to a chocolate-studded muffin, eating it in small bites, his brow furrowed with thought. Finally, he said, "You have to die for the host of eternal hunters, you know which ones I mean, to not destroy Khtonyx."

My jaw tightened. Knowing it was one thing. Hearing it fall from his lips was another. Considering that I had only ten days left to live at most—that made the food taste like ash.

His fingers traced absent circles atop the back of his left hand. Hadrien gazed at the table, his eyes unfocused. "You're a changeling. Somewhere, there is the child you were swapped for. That's—that's unimportant right now." Bloodshot eyes fixed on me. "Does Lupakaria know how to end the hunt?"

Reflexively, I touched the Jaws. "Lupakaria," I said aloud, and in my mind, she stirred. "Do you know another way to end the hunt?"

She stretched, unfurling her spine with rhythmic pops. *Of course there is, little wolf. You need only utter the words you know so well.*

I worked my jaw back and forth, abandoning my connection to the jawbone of the dead goddess. It was a wish. It was always a wish with her. She would ask for a high price, surely she would. Lupakaria would get her wish through me getting mine.

"Well?"

At his prompt, I replied, "Lupakaria says there is a way. I have to wish for it, and the cost… I don't want to know how great the cost would be for something like that."

"Something that is essentially your life."

I pushed back from the table and considered the tired boy before me. "Why do you care?"

"I don't," Hadrien shot back, too fast, too sharp.

"Then you should have just left me on the shore with that arrow in my side. I would've died soon enough."

Crossing his arms over his chest, he responded, "I need the head and heart of the Wild Moon Wolf to show as proof. I can't deliver *your* head and heart to the Arch Shadow." His jaw clicked audibly as his mouth closed. Color leeched from his face; he scrambled out of his chair and into the washroom. I heard him retch.

I suppose he thought about what that might have been like, had he sawn my head off. Cut my heart from my chest. I shifted in my chair, discomfort curling slick through me. It wasn't an image I wanted to linger on.

All these days since the Wild Moon Hunt had been announced, I had thought only of eluding the hunters for three full moons until the imperial hunt was over. Then the library dragons had brought up the looming danger of Ryodin and the Wild Hunt. I could no longer simply evade the hunters for three full moons.

I hadn't made a plan.

Now reality was staring me in the face.

I had until the next full moon to make my decision. I could make it sooner, but it wouldn't matter, for the next full moon would bring about the transformation.

Hadrien stumbled out of the washroom, his face gleaming with water. He had washed off his warpaint and the dirt and blood. With a sigh, he flopped down on his bed, head tilted back, arms flung out to either side. His throat bobbed as he swallowed.

I forced down another spoonful of soup. "Did you find who shot that arrow?" Hunters would descend upon the area as soon as word got out.

"Haven't had time," he muttered to the ceiling. "Whoever it was might think you're dead. Or… that the Wild Moon Wolf is dead. It was an iron arrow."

A fact I knew very well.

"But—" He sat up with a grunt. "—I doubt it was chosen specifically. I know, iron greatly hurts faeries. A lot of hunters still use it for regular hunting. Cheaper than steel in these towns." His jaws strained against a yawn. "Likely whoever shot you was a normal hunter with little knowledge of what they were shooting exactly."

Unless it was Artem. He was in the area. He would have shot me without hesitation, but he also would have pursued me until he had brought me down.

"I want to speak with Lupakaria."

I blinked. Cocked my head to the side. Let out a disbelieving breath of a laugh. "Why?"

"The Exalted Queen of the Isle told me to speak with the bones her changeling bears. You're her changeling. You carry around the jawbone of a dead goddess. That bone can speak."

It seemed foolish to me. Lupakaria would bend his mind to her desires.

Do you really believe I will do such tricksy things, little wolf? Lupakaria said, but her voice held a sharp lilt, a hint of the danger that pulsed below her words. *I thought we were beyond that, given our shared love for cheese.*

"No," I told him. "She's dangerous."

"And you don't think I can handle myself." Chin lifting, eyes narrowing, Hadrien dropped his voice in pitch, hardened it. It was the Heir of the Shadow who said, "I've spoken with Lupakaria before. I can do it again."

I didn't think.

I grabbed the jawbone, shut my eyes, and started to wish. *Lupakaria, I wish for—* My hand was wrenched away from the Jaws, unyielding fingers wrapped around my wrist. The Heir loomed over me, his brow set in fury.

"Don't finish that wish," he snapped. "Hand over the Jaws of Lupakaria."

"You'll have to kill me."

His free hand twitched. "Is that so?"

For someone who had thrown up at the thought of taking my severed head as proof of the Wild Moon Wolf's demise, he sure seemed capable of killing me for the Jaws now.

"Nox," Hadrien said, his voice low, "do as I say."

"I cannot." His grip tightened; I winced. "The Jaws of Lupakaria only can pass on to a new bearer by the death of the former."

One by one, his fingers lifted from my wrist. Hadrien, crossing the room to sit on his bed, said, "Then let Lupakaria speak through you."

"Take note, I don't think this is a good idea." But this time, I closed my eyes and let control slip from my grasp; Lupakaria seized it in her snapping jaws. She peered through my eyes, said through my voice, "Hello again, Hadrien."

"Lupakaria." His voice was measured. "Tell me why the Exalted Queen wanted me to speak with you."

Lupakaria dragged my body up and over to him. Hadrien watched, wariness glinting in his blue-grey gaze. Then my hand was feathering over his cheek, tipping his chin aside. His eyes slipped shut. Through Lupakaria's heightened hearing, I heard his heartbeat quickening.

"You," Lupakaria murmured, turning his face side to side, "resemble a face I have not seen for many a year. One of my ilk had a face like yours, one suited for paintings and poetry. As for why the Exalted Queen sought our meeting, that is beyond my knowing."

"But you're a god."

"I am of the wishes, not knowledge." Lupakaria walked back to the table and plucked up a muffin. She bit into it with no regard for crumbs—or that I wasn't hungry. "As is the way of faeries, her words were likely a play to trick you."

Hadrien furrowed his brow. "So it's unimportant."

Lupakaria gave a languid shrug. "Sometimes things arise and have no importance ever. However, without Nox here to stop me, I can now tell you something to keep you alive because I find you less annoying than others. That little piece of bone you carried last night wasn't enough. If Nox so desires to, she can rip you apart in her moon form."

I seethed inside my own mind, unable to stop the conversation.

"What can?"

"The Fetters of Aisling. You already knew that. But know this, should you use those on Nox, you can never return from it."

"What do you mean?"

And because Lupakaria was Lupakaria, that was when she chose to drop control back to me. I shook my head and snarled, chocolate from the muffin thick in my throat. I washed it down with cold tea.

"Nox," Hadrien said, "what did she mean?"

"As if I know," I groused and scowled into the cup. I threw myself down on my bed, turned my back to him. "I'm going to sleep."

After a minute, his voice split the silence. "I'm sorry you could not enter the cathedral for Rogus' final rites."

Tears burned behind my closed eyes. I offered no reply.

<hr>

I slipped in and out of sleep all day, wasting away one of my numbered final days. Hadrien was quiet most of the day, a lone figure perched by the window with his head bent over a book. I heard him talking to someone once, and through a haze of eyelashes, I thought I recognized Artem. But that was nonsense—Artem had left Argentaria already.

None of my fitful dozes were restful, not until evening, when I at last felt myself drifting toward a deep sleep. Dreams began to flit through my mind, lace-veiled wolves with bared, grinning ribs and a rabble of knucklebones stripped clean of flesh. The wolves leapt at me, jostled me, nipped at my hands with blunt teeth. Jaws closed around my shoulder, digging into the dip at my collarbone, and—

Hadrien was shaking me awake, his hand gripping my

shoulder tight enough to bruise. "We have to leave. *Now.* Get up, Nox."

This was a dream, I thought, but I kicked the blankets away anyways. "What's going on?" I mumbled, rubbing at my eyes. They ached.

"Other hunters in the hunt are here. They must have heard the wolf—you—were sighted. They'll trap you if you're in the area. Until I figure out what I'm doing, we need to move north." He breathed out a quick, hissing exhale. "I don't know. Maybe it would be best to leave Atassia entirely and let you be seen under the full moon on another continent. It will all only serve to prolong the hunt, though, and then Ryo—the host of eternal hunters will come down."

He had spoken far too fast for my tired mind to keep up. I packed and stumbled out of the room after him. It was a few hours after midnight, I discovered, and the town was quiet, save for a few boisterous taverns.

Hadrien had the horses tacked up and waiting, held by a yawning, sleepy-eyed stablehand. He exchanged a few words with the stablehand, and coin flashed as it was passed to the stablehand.

As we rode away from Argentaria, keeping off the roads, letting the horses' hoofbeats be muffled by dirt, I cast a glance at Hadrien. His eyes were wild, starlight reflected in their depths. He looked over his shoulder like he was running from something.

Did he even see the other hunters? I wondered.

While you slept, Lupakaria replied, *I observed him. He sees Varen everywhere. The shadows of trees are his antlers. The darkness under the bed is his empty eyes. The howl of wind is screams torn from memories. When Hadrien sleeps, he is haunted by Varen.*

Any levity was gone from the dead wolf goddess' voice, and she was somber as stone. *He is falling apart, Nox. Should the hunters from other planes arrive and set upon the world with fire and storm, it will break him. They will cause ruination.*

My death was a sure way to stop that.

I just didn't know if I could surrender.

Chapter Twenty-Seven
Hadrien

His mind was slipping.

He could tell.

Maybe it was the poor sleep, the incessant stress and travel, the looming full moons. But something was near breaking, and he didn't know how he would recover if it shattered.

He stared long and hard at the door, his fist raised. Had he knocked? He couldn't remember. The noontime sun bounced off the segment of the doorknob that had been rubbed shiny from touch; he squinted against it.

The door eased open, and someone said his name.

Hadrien startled.

The door slammed shut.

He turned, brow furrowing, and said, "Nox?"

"It's me. What are you doing here?"

"You're supposed to be at the inn." The situation crashed into him; his eyes widened. Nox had followed him to Siena's farmhouse outside of Arezza. Siena did not want to see Nox. "Why did you come here?"

"You were being sneaky. Poorly, I might add." Nox shrugged. "I followed. Lupakaria encouraged it."

He couldn't exactly blame her; he would've likely done the same. But Nox was now striding closer and peering through a window into the farmhouse. Her head tipped to the side, and his stomach sunk in dread.

"Hey, why is your maned wolf in there?"

"No," Hadrien replied, drawing the word out until Nox was staring at him. "That's a different maned wolf."

Her eyebrows rose. "I've only ever seen one, and that one is yours." Slipping around him, she knocked on the door before he could protest. "Let's see who lives here that you were coming to see. Oh! Is it that girl?"

Heat washed his cheeks. "No—it is not!"

"Secret lover? Secret family? Secret... Hmm, can't think of anything else."

The door opened suddenly, and Siena stood on the threshold with her arms crossed. "Hadrien, I explicitly told you to not let Nox know."

"She followed me!"

Nox, for her part, only blinked. "I did not have secret Guild on my list."

Siena heaved a sigh. "Get inside, both of you, and shut that door." As soon as they had done so, she added, "Nox, the Three Mothers know I love you, but you should not have come here."

"Nice to see you, too."

With a shake of her head, Siena pulled Nox into a tight embrace and smoothed back her hair. Hadrien, petting Zira, pretended not to see the shine of tears in Siena's eyes. Or how Nox trembled when she stepped back, had to take a moment to clear her throat and straighten the cuffs of her sleeves, to gather herself again.

"Come on," Siena said, brusque but somehow still soft. "I've just made tea." Over her shoulder, as she walked farther into the house, she added, "Did you get a room at the inn? You might as well stay here. I have extra rooms upstairs."

"That'd be better," Hadrien replied. "Thanks. We'll bring the horses and our packs over later." Sitting down at the sturdy table in the kitchen, he wrapped his hands around the cup of tea Siena offered to him. "Thank you." The heat warmed his palms—then went beyond warm to uncomfortably hot, but he held on. Anything to distract him from his sudden want to open his flask.

Zira rested her head on Hadrien's lap and released a sigh. He set his tea down and scratched behind the maned wolf's massive ears.

"Here," Siena said and handed a cup of tea to Nox. She indicated a basket with a flick of her fingers. "There's blueberry muffins in that basket."

Nox reached for the basket faster than Hadrien could blink. A muffin landed squarely in front of him, nimble fingers nudging it closer to him until he took it up in one hand. He nibbled at the edge of the muffin, noting in his peripheral vision Nox devouring a muffin in a few quick bites. Zira stalked around the table and snapped up any crumbs.

Sighing, Siena settled in a seat. "Now, Nox, I assume you have an idea of what is going on. As to why the current Heir of the Shadow is here, meeting with me in some semblance of secrecy."

"You want the Guild back, yes?" Half the words were muffled by muffin.

Still, Siena nodded once. "Skota has had her merry reign for long enough. I should have stopped her long ago." Grief darkened her expression, turned her mouth down. "There are too many who perished on Skota's orders, even if her hands never got dirty."

Nox drank a long sip of tea. The cup clinked when she set it down at last. She tilted her head up to look at Siena but said nothing.

Am I supposed to say something now? Hadrien wondered and remained silent, chewing a blueberry.

"I have people within the House of Shadows—Wolves, those who stayed after the fall only because they had nowhere else to go, or those who stayed at my behest like Xenna. These Wolves will aid in the usurping. I will take the title from Skota, become the Moonstalker once more, and lead a new Wolf Guild. Hadrien is to be my Heir."

A flicker of stillness flitted over Nox; her eyes cut over to Hadrien. "And what if I say that I would like to be the Heir of the Wolf once more?" Not looking away from him, Nox dipped her hand down her shirt and withdrew her Wolf medallion. "I am the one with the medallion still."

Does Nox really want to be the Heir of the Wolf again? She had said she didn't want to be the Heir of the Shadow. Hadrien supposed that under Siena, the Guild would be a better place, one that didn't... He didn't know what exactly.

He couldn't say what the Arch Shadow did, couldn't pinpoint why his stomach twisted at the thought of returning there. He only knew it did, knew that being away from the House of Shadows had eased something within him, and now at the prospect of going back soon, he felt ill.

Or maybe that was simply his hunger for a drink.

He massaged his temples, forgetting where he was. What was he even doing this for? He was the Heir of the Shadow. The Arch Shadow wouldn't live forever. He could outlive her or arrange an accident—and by the Three Mothers, he would end up like Nox. Except no one would be there to save him.

You have to remember, he told himself, *Nox has the scars from the Arch Shadow's attempt on her life. A woman who does that is not fit to lead a Guild.*

But she gave you a place to stay, a voice argued back in his head. His own voice, just sharper and colder. *A meaning in your pitiful life. A title.*

His fingers tipped harder against his temples. *Yes, but she also acted like it was my fault that Rogus died. She knew the dangers of the Chimera, yet she sent us to kill it anyways.*

She gave you a second chance—and more. Far more than you ever deserved.

I already gave Siena my answer. I'll stand with her. What does it matter? I'll be the Heir either way. The Heir of the Shadow or the Heir of the Wolf.

Is that how you repay the kindness and generosity of the Arch Shadow? She who gave you more than you deserved. Remember, you deserve so very little. If Siena's plan fails, the Arch Shadow will kill you, as she should, as you will deserve.

Someone tapped on his shoulder, and Hadrien jerked out of his thoughts. "What?"

"You crushed the muffin." Nox curled his fingers open, one by one, showing the muddled mess of crumb and squashed blueberry within his fist. "Siena went upstairs to get the rooms ready. What's going on in your head?"

"Nothing."

"Tell Lupakaria if you won't tell me. It's clear you have a veritable storm of thoughts in your head. But clean your hands first."

He washed off his hands, mostly because the blueberry juice was sticky. When he returned to Nox, she glanced over his hands and then nodded, satisfied.

The jawbone was offered, still strung around her neck. Nox turned her head away, tendons standing out under her jawline, offering a sort of privacy. Hadrien hesitated, then laid his fingertips on the cool, smooth surface of the bone. He noticed for the first time the silver filigree that swept through carvings along the bone.

Hello, Lupakaria said, sounding bored. *You have brought to me a dilemma and no cheese.*

Sorry. I... I can't puzzle out how I feel about this. Siena. The Arch Shadow. Being the Heir.

Tell me.

Hadrien told her, through memories and thoughts and feelings.

Lupakaria was silent for a minute that stretched into an eternity. Hadrien was distantly aware of Nox next to him, the quiet breathing of her. Nox shifted her weight, a joint popping like a crackle of lightning. But she did not interrupt or move away.

Then the dead goddess said, *Hadrien, I am old, older than I know. I have seen much. I have seen this before. Mortals like Skota, mortals like you, the spider and the moth, the weaver and the webs. You don't know it, you never know it, not until you are looking above at your listless body. You are a rabbit with its foot in a trap that eased shut so slowly that you never noticed. You are a bird, born within the cage, raised within, until the cage is all you know, and you believe there is nothing beyond it, so when the door is opened, you stay within the lines you have known.*

He shut his eyes, as if that would stave off the reckoning.

Lupakaria only continued, *You would not be here now, entertaining Siena's plans and keeping her location a secret from Skota as you have for months, unless you knew your decision. You know what you want to do, Hadrien, you simply have to be brave enough to do it.*

How odd that a dead wolf goddess would be able to provide clarity. But then again, Lupakaria was of the wishes. She knew what someone wanted before they ever said or even admitted it to themself.

Now, go. I must compel Nox to find cheese.

Hadrien lifted his fingers from the Jaws of Lupakaria, and Nox said, "I assume she helped because she is now declaring that I must find cheese for her." Her lips twisted. "Though, she would want cheese either way."

"She helped," he replied, hoarse. Then, quieter, he added, "Thanks."

A small shrug. "It's—" Nox shrugged again. "Going to find cheese now."

Staring after her, watching her leave the room, Hadrien realized Nox had been about to lie. The faerie blood had prevented it. He thought over the conversation again, let his mind fill in the next words: *It's nothing.* If Nox hadn't been able to say it, that meant it ·was *something.*

He put a hand to his face, suddenly warm.

The floor didn't seem so unsteady underfoot anymore.

When Nox slunk back into the kitchen with a wedge of chive-infused cheese, tailed by Siena, Hadrien told them he was going to get the horses. Siena gave Nox a pointed look. Nox stuffed the rest of the cheese in her mouth, brushing her palms against each other and moving toward him.

Outside of the farmhouse, she offered him a slice of cheese, some other type. Hadrien wasn't sure where it had come from, but he accepted it anyway. Nox then offered a small tidbit of cheese to Zira.

Her boots scuffing against a stray pebble, Nox inquired, "When do you meet that girl?"

Strange. Inside his gloves, his hands felt too hot. Blooming with sweat. *Only nerves,* he told himself and cleared his throat. "Tonight."

Nox eyed him. "Is that what you're wearing?"

"What?" Hadrien looked down at himself: dusty and dirty hunting gear. "I... I was going to." A spike of uncertainty heated his veins; his brow furrowed. "Do you think it looks bad?"

"No," she replied, fast enough that had it been anyone else saying it, he would've suspected that she was lying. But this was Nox, incapable of lies.

"But?" he prompted. "You wouldn't have mentioned it unless you had a reason."

The silence either meant Lupakaria was talking or Nox wasn't sure how to phrase her thoughts. Eventually, she said, "You could wear that jacket you wore to the isle instead."

Hadrien plucked at the sleeve of his hunting jacket, dark brown and admittedly scuffed. The other jacket was far more suited for meeting someone. "That's a good idea."

Nox shrugged. It wasn't until they were at the stables that she spoke again. "How did you meet Siena?"

"Through Xenna. It wasn't long after I was appointed as the Heir. Xenna tested me first, asking these questions that seemed so strange, yet kind, at the time, and I guess I answered the way she was looking for. Then I met with Siena."

Leading Embra out of the stall, one eye narrowed at Ikarus, Nox asked in a careful, almost hesitant tone, "Did Siena tell you about her son?"

"She did." Hadrien kept Ikarus a good distance from Nox and her mare as they all walked toward the inn. "I… I didn't know how young you were when you were in the Guild."

"Sold, like a little chicken. A regular chicken, not even a prize chicken."

In all that had happened, he had forgotten that Nox had told him that her father—her human father—had sold her to the Arch Shadow. A child, then a ward and the Heir of the Arch Shadow. A thought struck him, and he blurted out, "Did the Arch Shadow have a different name?"

"Huh?"

"In the Wolf Guild."

"She was just the Shadow back then."

Faltering in his steps, Hadrien shook his head. "You mean to tell me that she named an entire Guild after herself?"

Nox tied Embra's reins to a post outside the inn. Her

hands braced against the post, fingers tapping rhythmically. "She did," Nox said at last with a sigh. "She did indeed."

There was something else, wasn't there? Or maybe Hadrien was imagining things. He mulled it over as he followed Nox to the room at the inn, collecting their packs within a few minutes. The Arch Shadow had named the Guild built from the remains of the Wolf Guild after herself.

"If I named a Guild," Nox said, breaking his thoughts, "I wouldn't name it after myself."

"What would you name it?"

"I have no idea, which is exactly why I won't name a Guild."

Despite everything, a smile tugged at his mouth. He hid his smile by checking Ikarus' tack and sweeping his palm over the gelding's back.

"Hadrien," Nox said, "someone is waving at you."

Sweat prickled cold at his neck. Who would be here, waving at him? He craned his neck over his shoulder; relief crashed over him. It wasn't an enemy. It was only Renata, offering him a flash of a smile, her eyes crinkling at the corners. His smile in response felt wooden.

Nox peeked under Ikarus' neck. "Is that her?"

"It is."

She only went, *Hmm,* and disappeared from sight, reappearing a moment later atop Embra's back. With no perceptible movements, Nox guided her mare around Ikarus. Her eyes were fixed on Renata as she waved again, shot Nox a puzzled look, and walked away.

With a quick glance at Hadrien and not a word, Nox

urged Embra into a trot away from the center of town. Zira barked and loped after the girl. Confusion furrowing his brow, Hadrien could only follow them.

Chapter Twenty-Eight
Nox

Sprawled on my bed at Siena's farmhouse, the warm weight of Zira pressing against my side, I paged through a book I had taken from the small library downstairs. Siena was busy concocting her plans to overthrow the Arch Shadow, contacting people or drawing up a map of the city or something; she had shooed me out of the room and told me in stern tones to not bother her. I was, in her words, to stay far from her plans.

It was fine.

I wanted the Arch Shadow gone from my life. That didn't mean I had to help take her down. It was probably best if I didn't. I had enough to think about with the Wild Moon Hunt.

There was a soft knock on the doorframe, and I glanced up. Hadrien stood in the open doorway, his hand twisted behind his back. My pulse kicked faster; I rocked back onto my heels. The Jaws bumped against my sternum.

"Hadrien," I said, level, unsure of why he was here.

"Were you looking for Zira?" I jerked my chin towards the maned wolf. "She's here."

"What are you reading?" he asked, his voice as quiet as his knock. The warpaint was wiped clean off his face, his scars left to line his eyes in plain sight. His eyes sparkled in the late sunlight streaming through the windows.

I suddenly forget everything I had read ever. "Um." My eyes darted to the pages opened before me. "History. Right. This is a book on the history of the gladiator rings that are still active in Ostitha today."

He padded closer and without asking, sat on the edge of the bed, propping his heels on the frame. His long legs bent up, he rested back on his hands. For a heartbeat, he met my eyes, and then he was looking down at the book between us.

If I leaned forward, I could kiss him.

I blinked.

That was a thought I should not be having. Hadrien was complicated, and he confounded me. I had a feeling he even confounded himself at times. He was someone to stay away from, certainly not someone my thoughts should be dancing around. Wondering if his lips would be soft against mine, if they would give under my teeth, those were dangerous things to wonder.

Pity for me, I liked danger.

I shifted my weight, keeping my face turned down to hide the heat. "So, what did you come here for?" I buried my hands in Zira's scruff. "Surely it wasn't to ask me what I was reading." In my mind, I imagined him saying, *It was for this,* and closing the space between us to kiss me.

What he said was, "I wanted to know if you had any thoughts on how to end the hunt."

Any wayward thoughts vanished. My body went cold, and I suppressed a shudder. "No." The word was quiet, a feather-brush of breath. "I don't have any thoughts on how to prevent my own death."

On the blankets, his fingers moved in circles. "I didn't have any either. I'm sorry."

He rose and left before I could say another word.

He is strange at times, Lupakaria mused. Then her tone sharpened with mirth. *And you are* smitten! *You little love-struck wolf.*

I— I sighed. *It might just be a fleeting flutter. I don't know yet.* And that was the truth. I wouldn't know until time had passed, until these feelings—inopportune as they were—had either lasted or faded away. They very well might fade.

It would be for the best if they did fade because at the end of the day, Hadrien was still the Heir of the Shadow, still my competitor in this hunt for my own life.

I laid back on the bed and exhaled a curse.

Zira promptly laid her head on my stomach.

The Jaws settled higher on my sternum, the knobby ends of the mandible resting on the arteries in my neck. In her days of gods and monsters, in her wolf form, Lupakaria could have bitten a human's head clean off in a single, solid snap of her jaws. My pulse tripped harder against the jawbone.

Lupakaria, I said, hesitating.

Yes, o dreamer mine?

My skin crawled. She hadn't used that in a while. This was Lupakaria of the Wishes, not the Lupakaria who took glee in mischief. The two were one and the same. It was all too easy to forget.

Never mind.

I would figure it out on my own.

Displacing Zira, I shifted around to lay on my stomach again. The maned wolf scooted close to my side and pillowed her head on her paws like she was going to read the book with me. I paged through the book of history, not paying much attention to the words.

My mind was elsewhere. Lupakaria was silent, a shadow of a presence lingering along the walls of my mind. I knew she was listening to my thoughts, though, the scattered flickers of images and remnants of feelings slipping around. Not a single scrap escaped her notice.

Golden sunlight dipped into the deep scarlet light of a sunset. It skimmed the book, cast it in a bloody glow. Evening had arrived fast, faster than I thought it would.

Hadrien would be leaving soon, if he hadn't already.

With one finger, I closed the book, not bothering to mark the page. Zira leapt off the bed and loped down the hall. My jaw was slung tight; I wrenched it into a yawn, accompanied by a click and pop.

Not sure of what I wanted to find out, I rose and stretched slowly. Then, on light feet, I crossed the hall to his room. The door was closed. I could hear a shuffle inside.

He was still here.

Heartbeat tapping faster, I raised my hand, fingers curled into a loose fist, and knocked twice upon the door. Nerves jittering, I played with the cuff of my sleeves. Did I want him to answer the door, or did I not? I wanted both and neither. Should I act like I had accidentally bumped into his door? No, I had knocked twice, that was too deliberate.

Why was this what was undoing me?

Hadrien called out for me to enter.

My hand refused to move. I steeled myself and reached for the handle. I eased the door open, and then I couldn't breathe.

Hadrien, stood in front of a mirror, was smoothing his gloved palms over the flower-embroidered, deep purple jacket from the isle. I had seen him in this jacket before, of course, but he'd slicked his hair back. The ends curled against his neck, still dark with water. He'd been more careful with the warpaint around his eyes, but it was there, contrasting to the rest of his tidy appearance.

I wanted to see him disheveled.

My gaze flicked to the inked flowers winding up his arm, barely visible as he rubbed nervously at his sleeve. I desperately wanted to touch his tattoos. Run my fingers from his palm along the inside of his forearm, pause at his pulse point and find out if his heart was hammering like mine.

But.

But Hadrien wasn't interested in me. He was going to meet that girl, the one with the foxfire hair and the quick smile. I could never match up.

So I just told him, "That jacket's proving useful." And I felt like my heart was dying.

"I'm nervous." He turned back to the mirror, his eyes running over his reflection. He slipped his flask out and downed a gulp. To the mirror, he said, "It's strange being nervous."

I found no reassuring words to utter.

His eyes found mine in the reflection. "It doesn't feel real."

"What do you mean?"

"This. Feels like I'm wearing someone else's life." He held the flask out to me, an unspoken offering in the tilt of his head.

I took a drink from it; the cognac raced like red fire all the way down. It was a heady sensation, a bolt of daring that shot straight to my heart. Ill-advised as it was, I had another sip, and in my head, Lupakaria whispered to me.

Hadrien extended his hand for the flask. "Don't drink all of that, Nox." But he didn't say it in a cruel way, he said it with a surprised breath of a laugh. "You're supposed to share."

Handing it back, I wondered what he would say if I asked him to stay.

He heaved a sigh. "Is it embarrassing?"

"What?"

"This," he said, which explained nothing.

"Be more specific."

He mumbled his response, and I strained to hear, finding myself leaning closer. His words weren't much of a surprise; he had a reserved, isolated air about him, the kind that didn't lend to letting people close very often, if at all.

I saw a chance to steal the one thing I could never deserve. I took another step towards him, and he faced me, his brow furrowed, his anxiety evident in the flickering of his eyes, the way he thumbed the cap on his flask.

"You can practice with me," I offered. "I'll show you how it's done."

"But I'm not... interested."

I shrugged, hid the sting under a veil of nonchalance. "Then it means nothing, doesn't it?" I stepped closer, rose up on my toes, and cupped his face. "You've danced with a partner before, right?"

He nodded, his soft skin slipping against my palm. His head was inclined down towards me enough that I could reach without too much strain. *Perfect,* I thought, even as an anguish so great it could fell a mountain shot through me.

"Kissing is just like a dance." I leaned in and brushed my lips over the corner of his mouth. "There's a leader and a follower." I kissed the other corner of his mouth. "It's a give." I kissed him firmly now, threading my fingers through his hair to pull him close. I tilted my head, guided his lips to move against and with mine. When I felt returned pressure, I drew back to breathe out, "And take."

His head moved a fraction, seeking my mouth. I laid my finger on his lips, felt the heat of his breath. He opened his eyes, a slow flutter of lashes like waking from a dream. His pupils were dilated, his cheeks flushed, and his hair, oh, his hair. I had mussed his hair quite well. He was looking at me like he wanted to keep kissing me.

"You learn fast," I told him, shattering the expression on his face. I smiled tightly. "I'm sure Renata will appreciate that." I stepped back, put distance between us, tried to ignore how cold I felt without the heat of his body. "I'll be in my room. Don't worry, I won't leave."

In my room, I leaned against the wall, feeling so far from my body, so unanchored. Liquid agony welled up in my eyes. I refused to let the tears fall; I dashed them away with a flick of my fingers.

I pried the top off the flask I'd stolen from Hadrien's jacket. The bite of cognac drifted up. I'd told him not long ago that he hid behind the haze of alcohol. Now I was going to do the same and numb this turmoil within me.

I chased the first sip with another and then another, panting from the searing burn. For a dizzying, stomach-flipping second, I thought the cognac was going to rocket back up. I pressed my head into the wall, squeezed my eyes shut. It stayed down.

Little wolf, Lupakaria said. *Nox.*

Be quiet, I snarled back. *I don't want your pity.*

Of course, she didn't listen. *I do not pity you. I find you a fool. You could make all this anguish vanish with a few words, and yet you do not.*

I eyed the flask. If Hadrien had the Jaws, would he wish away what troubled him and drove him to drink and numb himself every day? Was I a fool to not do so? I had such power at my fingertips, and like Lupakaria had said, all it would take was a few words.

My fingers trailed across the teeth of the jawbone on their own accord. A hum traveled through the bones, rooted into my veins and blood. My bones vibrated, trapped within the cage of my body, just as I was. Everything was ill-fitting.

I shuddered, jarred myself loose.

Trying to shake off the feeling of being untethered to this form, I raised my hand from the Jaws. My fingertips were blackened. Breath in my throat, I touched one; it was frigid. Were they about to fall off?

I flexed my fingers. Like ice melting, the color swept back into my fingertips.

Lupakaria, I said haltingly. *What in the name of the Mothers Three was that?*

What are you talking about? You've been staring at your hand the past few minutes. There is nothing strange occurring, aside from you acting like your hand is the strangest thing you've seen. It truly isn't. It's a normal hand. Maybe your fingers are a touch too long, but that's all.

I formed a fist, watching the skin stretch over my knuckles. The joints pressed white against the stretched skin. I relaxed my hand.

Whatever had happened, I didn't think I would make a wish tonight. Maybe I wouldn't make a wish ever again.

With a flick of my wrist, I set the contents of the flask to sloshing inside. I took the flask with me to the washroom and drank while I lounged in a hot, bubble-filled bath. My ouroboros tattoo flashed each time I raised the flask. I dripped water onto it; the drops rolled around the edges before falling back into the bath.

When the hot edge had faded from the bath, I traded it for my bed, curling up below the blankets in only a shirt. I tucked my legs up to my chest. Then scowled. This felt odd. I clambered out of bed, tugged on pants, and climbed back in. Better.

I tipped the flask against my mouth and let a little cognac seep in. It had long lost its burn. I hadn't forgotten *why* I was drinking; it just didn't seem to matter as much anymore. That was the magic of the drink: dull thoughts that couldn't cut.

Some time later, I really wasn't sure how much time had passed, I was skimming my palms along the length of the Jaws. Lupakaria was grumbling faintly in my head. "O dreamer mine," I mumbled.

Go to sleep, little wolf. There will be time later to make mistakes.

There was no compulsion in the words, but my eyes slipped shut.

A door hit the frame hard enough to rattle me out of the strange half-sleep I'd fallen into. I squinted at the door to my room; a dim light seeped under the door, swimming from one side to the other. Footsteps shuffled in the hall.

I untangled myself with slow movements from the blankets. My hand hit something hard, a hollow *clang.* For a head-spinning heartbeat, I thought it was a skull.

I extracted it from the mess of blankets. A silver flask, Hadrien's flask, empty.

Oh. I'd drank it all.

That had certainly been a mistake, I realized, stumbling toward the door. Mistakes were all I seemed to make. I paused at my door to rub my eyes, try to shake some sober into myself. Nope, didn't work.

Still quite drunk, I opened the door.

Chapter Twenty-Nine
Hadrien

Nox had been on his mind all night.

He pressed his back hard to the door, hand seeking out the flask in his jacket. His fingers closed on empty air. Where was it?

He had been passing it back and forth with Nox earlier, watching how her eyes darkened with the burn of the cognac. She had been so close, so damningly close in a way that she should never be again, that Hadrien shouldn't want again.

Shrugging out of his jacket, he tossed it aside without regard for where it landed. His thoughts circled the moment earlier with Nox. Practice, she had called it. If that was only practice…

He shook his head viciously. *Forget about her.*

An impossible task, when there was a knock against the door. He hesitated. That could only be her. Was it a good idea to see her now?

Caution wasn't in his nature tonight. He blew out a breath, smoothed his hair back, and opened the door.

"Nox?" Surely she had noticed how low his voice dipped on her name. With a rough clearing of his throat, he added, "Nox, what are you doing here?"

"You woke me," she replied, but her voice was soft, her words suffused with cognac. *So that's who my flask has been with after all.*

"Sorry about that." Distracted from his thoughts by how she swayed, he moved forward and laid his hand on her shoulder. "You need to go sleep this off. Come on." He guided her across the hall, and Nox didn't protest, not even when he pushed her to her bed in a clumsy attempt at assisting her. "I'll see you in the morning."

He turned away; Nox caught his wrist in a surprisingly strong grip. Hadrien glanced back, found the glint of eyes on him. He pried the fingers off his wrist, one by one, and told her again to sleep.

This time, she didn't stop him before he left.

Hadrien closed the door softly, his mind awhirl. Why had Nox decided to drink so much she was—as she would say—thoroughly foxed? She had seemed fine when he had left earlier. Perhaps, he thought, Nox remembered something troubling and then proceeded to drink the contents of his stolen flask. Likely something related to her past with the Arch Shadow.

Whatever it was, the Three Mothers willing, Nox would be sober in the morning. Sober and ready to escape the hunt for her very head and heart.

That alone was a good enough reason to drink away lucidity.

Hadrien stood in the hallway for a long moment, his gaze absently snagged on the floor. Within a few short days, the second full moon would rise and bring with it the attention of the Wild Hunt. Then only five days later, the third and final full moon of the month would sweep into the sky, and the Wild Hunt would rain down upon Khtonyx.

His fingers twined around the Fetters of Aisling.

Should you use those on Nox, Lupakaria had said, *you can never return from it.*

If using the Fetters of Aisling on the Wild Moon Wolf —on Nox—meant harming his eternal soul, Hadrien wasn't so sure he cared.

It was terrible, wasn't it?

But he withdrew the ribbon that could trap the moon monster and considered it. So fragile, so plain, so deceptive. With one fell blow, he could win the Wild Moon Hunt, keep the Wild Hunt from destroying Khtonyx, and remove his strongest competition for the title of the Heir of the Wolf.

Because Siena, with his help, would succeed in usurping the Arch Shadow and dismantling the House of Shadows. There would be no Heir of the Shadow title before month's end. Best if Hadrien secured his path to the Heir of the Wolf mantle through the hunt.

Siena would have to forgive him for the unavoidable death of Nox.

Nox Vis had long been believed dead anyways; Hadrien was simply ushering her to the state of actual death. Picking up where the Arch Shadow had failed.

Funny.

The Arch Shadow had failed at something.

Hadrien wound the Fetters of Aisling around his wrist, slid his sleeve down to hide the innocuous ribbon, and went into his room. He only had a few days to prepare, to lay the trap that would bring down the Wild Moon Wolf.

Until then, he would do whatever it took to keep Nox unaware. Lupakaria wouldn't be able to sniff out his plans unless he touched the bones, likely. The dead goddess would be his greatest danger; Lupakaria saw too much.

Hadrien sharpened his knives and didn't let himself think about anything except how before the next full moon was up, he would be the Heir and Khtonyx would be safe.

Morning's light speared through his eyelids.

Hadrien, stifling a groan, rolled himself to the edge of the bed. Stiff, joints creaking and protesting, he sat up and stared around the room. Every weapon he had sharpened and honed during the night was packed away. Around his wrist was a single ribbon, the Fetters of Aisling.

He donned his hunting gear. In the mirror, he watched his hands, pale and scarred, encircle his eyes with the dark warpaint. How many days was it now until the full moon? He did a quick count. Two days away.

The Fetters of Aisling hidden under his sleeve and vambrace, he walked into the kitchen. Zira, by the boots of a certain former Heir, raised her head. Nox, seated at the table and hunched over a cup of tea, looked up, too. Dark circles swooped under her eyes.

"Morning," Nox mumbled, her voice rough. "How was your evening with what's-her-name?"

Hadrien shrugged. In a clipped tone, he replied,

"Fine." He didn't need to tell Nox how much *she* had been on his mind instead. He poured himself a cup of tea, selected a lemon and poppyseed muffin, and sat across from Nox. Holding her gaze, he said, "I got rid of the Fetters."

"You did *what?*" She winced, as if her own voice had been too loud. Rubbing at her temple, she added, quieter, "What did you do?"

"I got rid of the Fetters," he repeated. Recalling the trickery Nox had used on him at the House of Shadows, he let his gaze drop to the table and dragged up the memory of her mouth; a flush heated his face, and he felt a thrill at his success. Let her believe he was truly feeling that way. "I won't use them against you."

Lies, it was all lies.

But she seemed to not catch the lie. "That's…" She took a long sip of tea, eyes shutting. "Why?"

"We'll figure out some other way to end the hunt and keep you alive." The words tasted like bitter iron upon his tongue. His stomach twisted. "Between the two of us, we can think of something. Maybe it's as simple as hiding you during full moons."

Another long sip of tea. Nox then sighed. "I don't know what will work. People have seen me as the Wild Moon Wolf nearly every full moon. I can't disappear without people searching for me; someone will eventually find me. I'll be a legend they seek for the story alone."

Hadrien didn't have a lie for that.

When he was starting on a plate of fresh fruit, Nox interrupted his thoughts with, "Why did you join the Shadow Guild?" She popped a blackberry in her mouth, tossed one to Zira, and added, "You didn't join the Guild until after I was, well, gone."

Mid-bite, he froze. *Speak, Hadrien.* He forced down the wedge of strawberry and mumbled, "It was time."

"And?" Her fingers flitted toward him. "You're certainly not twelve, like most people are when they join a Guild."

Despite his plans to kill the girl sitting across from him, he laughed. "No, I definitely wasn't twelve. I was…" He longed to tell someone, and what better person than the one who would be dead and unable to speak of it soon? "I was exiled from my family. I had nowhere to go. Ferros and the Shadow Guild were the closest."

"Surely you know what I'll ask now."

His exhale was a puff of joyless humor. "Yeah, I do. Why was I exiled?" The truth felt like thorns as it tore from him, slow and painful. "My eldest brother inherited the family name and fortune upon our father's death at the hands of a Viper. Actually, at the hands of the new Heir of the Viper. It was before he became the Heir.

"But long story rendered short, my brother did not like me very much, and I was told to leave the villa and never return. So I did."

Nox ate another blackberry, eyes narrowed in thought.

If my family knew now how I had shook with fear before the Wild Moon Wolf, I would be exiled all over again. His face burned with shame. "I won't be trying to get my family name back. They're as good as dead to me, and I'm as good as dead to them."

"They don't know what they lost."

The words made his heart skip a beat. "No," he

replied, his voice faint, "they know exactly what they did: a failure."

Nox stared at him.

His breath was shallow.

Had he said that aloud?

It was true, but it was too true, a truth that he should've left locked in the walls of his mind.

Trying to play it off with a smile and a laugh, he said, "It's meaningless. Now, what did—"

"Do you believe that?"

Hadrien did. "No," he said. "Of course not. That slipped out. Bad jest, that's all. I don't believe that."

Nox leaned back in her chair, one leg languidly drawn up on the seat. "Sometimes, I wish I could lie—Lupakaria, that was not for you, please be quiet—and then I see how you lie to yourself." Her head cocked to the side. "And I no longer wish I could lie."

"Well, thanks." His gloved fingers scraped at the edge of the table. Was he that bad at lying? "It was merely a jest, though."

A scoff burst from Nox's lips. "Unconvincing."

He glowered at her. "Is your curiosity satisfied?"

"Not quite." She shifted her weight, angling closer. Her voice dropped into a whisper that Hadrien strained to catch. "Tell me, would you join the Guild now?"

Would I join the Shadow Guild now? Knowing what I know, what I've seen and experienced? Never. The thoughts were traitorous to everything he had worked towards.

His head shook before he could decide on what he'd say aloud. Then, with a harsh edge snapping into his words, he said, "That's enough about me."

Nox shrugged and sat back. Her knee, visible above

the table, waved from side to side. "It is strange, to have been working alongside the boy who replaced me as my mother's protégé."

His brow furrowed so deeply it almost hurt. "I'm not. I didn't meet the Exalted Queen until a few days ago."

"I assumed," Nox said, "that the Arch Shadow was my mother."

"Your what?" The words were as flat as a pane of glass.

"My mother. I thought my father gave me back to her. I thought that made sense. I thought that was why I was her Heir so young. I didn't know until later about the money exchanged." A laugh, rife with bitter bite, broke out. "I didn't know that I wasn't her child until she tried to kill me. Funny how that happened."

He pointed at her. "So you, Nox, believed that the Arch Shadow was your mother up until… six or so months ago."

Her head bobbed in affirmation.

"I didn't replace you as your mother's protégé; I replaced you as the Arch Shadow's protégé." After a sip of nearly cold tea, Hadrien continued, "I don't even think I 'replaced' you. You were believed dead. You can't replace someone who's dead. You were dead; you couldn't uphold your duties as the Heir. I stepped in to take up the title and be the Heir the Guild needed."

Under her breath, Nox muttered, "I don't think they needed you."

"What was that?"

Raising her voice and her gaze, Nox repeated, "I said I don't think they needed you." Her eyes didn't drop from his, unerring and startlingly in intensity. "The Guild didn't need a new Heir. The Guild needed—and still needs—a new leader."

And Siena would be that leader.

Hadrien held Nox's gaze for a minute, noting every flicker of change in the cobalt irises, the near silver around the pupil. Then he sighed and asked, "Do you enjoy starting arguments?"

"Only with you."

He rolled his eyes. "Stop saying things like that."

"Like what?"

"Like…" He cast about for the words as his mind supplied: *Like I'm something beyond a rival to you.* Heat shot to his face—*This is another of her tricks,* he told himself—and he mumbled, "Stop trying to provoke me." *What can I do to get this infuriating girl out of my head?*

Nox dropped her leg down and sat normally. "Maybe I will, maybe I won't." And then in the light of morning, quite plainly, she said, "I used to feel bad about the prey I'd hunt for the Arch Shadow, even when we were Wolves. I would stay awake at night, seeing the whites of their eyes, hearing their little hearts beating so fast and the sounds they'd make. I told myself it was simply business. Learned to live with it."

Hadrien hadn't.

He knew that what he was going to do would stay with him for all his waking and sleeping moments. That was what alcohol was for: dulling the memories, turning the hand of time quicker until he could fall into his own grave and eternally forget what he had done. What else could he do?

Standing, Nox stretched out her arms until a joint popped. "I'm going to town."

I really don't want to go, but I can't let her out of my sight right now. "I'll come with you."

"Very well."

The morning was already filled with travelers cutting through the center of town on their way to grander things. Nox tracked one lone rider on a bay mare with narrowed eyes; but when Hadrien prompted her, she said nothing.

The rider turned out to be a Shadow, one that approached with a smile that was anything but friendly. His eyes were on Hadrien, didn't so much as flicker toward Nox as she melted away, hood tugged up against keen eyes.

"Heir," the Shadow said, "the Arch Shadow has sent me to find you with new orders."

"How did you find me?" Hadrien demanded, shoulders squared, chin lifted, eyes ablaze, all to cover the fear trembling in his bones. If the Arch Shadow knew he was here, what else did she know?

"Luck," he replied. "The Arch Shadow sent out a group, each on a different road. Your orders, since you didn't ask, are to not let your hunting partner remain alive after the hunt is over."

She wants me to kill Nox. Or at least, ensure that Nox is killed in the hunt. It's no different than what I was planning to do already. The Arch Shadow didn't know that. But his stomach turned at the thought. "Anything else?"

The Shadow walked backward a few steps and spread his arms. "We've joined the hunt, every last one of us. Whoever wins gets—" He pointed at Hadrien like he was raising a glass in the Heir's honor. "—your title." Then with sarcasm soaking his voice, he added, "May luck be with you."

Hadrien waited until the Shadow had strode away—joined by none other than Rook, who had to be his hunting partner—and then he went in search of Nox, his hands clenching and unclenching at his sides.

This hunt had certainly become more complicated.

CHAPTER THIRTY
NOX

HADRIEN'S STERNUM rose and fell with his ragged breaths.

His eyes were wild, whites showing like a wounded animal.

I shrugged. "It doesn't change much."

"What?" The single word exploded out in an exhale.

I turned back to the shelves of books in the store and said, "I suspected the Arch Shadow might do something like this. It isn't a surprise that she has loosed the rest of the Guild to the Wild Moon Hunt. Unfortunate and an annoyance, but not a surprise." I slid out a thick tome, perused the cover—eh, boring—and put it back. "Which Shadows did you see?"

Hadrien hesitated.

"You don't know their names, do you?"

"One was Rook." His boot scuffed against the ground, and he muttered, "I don't know the other."

Truly, a terrible Heir. I cast a glance over my shoulder, letting my gaze linger on him. He was frazzled, fraying at the edges after this turn of events. "You should go back to the farmhouse. You'll give away something if the Sha-dows see you again. Mothers Three on our side, they'll have moved on now that they've told you of this new development."

His head moved in a nod like a broken puppet. His right hand closed around his left wrist, palm pressing against the back of his left hand. His thumb brushed back and forth, back and forth, back and— "What are you looking at?"

"Your hands," I replied bluntly, raising my gaze slowly to his face. His face, reddening with a flush in his cheeks. "You give away your thoughts through them."

"I—I do *not.*" His hands formed fists.

I bit back a laugh.

His face flamed brighter, and he stalked off to the window. I picked my way through the books, searching for *something.* I didn't know exactly what I wanted, only that I wanted a story that would capture my heart in these final few days. Something stirring, something funny, something heartfelt.

Hmm. My gaze lingered on a title. *The Exodus of the Gods.*

Lupakaria stiffened. *Bring that nearer, little wolf.*

I brought the book out. It was a thin book, near the size and shape of a journal. My fingers skimmed along the cover—gilded flowers and acorns surrounded a wolf's head—and opened it. The text inside was like that of a journal, too. Entries and dates, the inner thoughts of someone. It did not promise much humor.

This is not fiction, Lupakaria said softly. *This is truth.* Her voice sharpened. *Buy it, read it.*

I did as she said, packing the book away in my knapsack to read that afternoon at Siena's farmhouse. Or whenever I had a chance.

Hadrien walked at my side in silence on the way back. His head was on a swivel, his eyes darting about for signs of the other Shadows. At the slightest sound, he startled, body tensing so fast I felt my own bones protest.

Did he feel as I had?

Did he feel like prey now?

Once the door to the farmhouse was shut and locked behind us, his shoulders lowered, his breath rolled out in a long sigh. Quietly, so quietly I nearly didn't catch it, he said, "I don't know what to do."

I continued into the kitchen, no solutions at the ready.

Hadrien wandered in later while I was sipping a cup of tea, ignoring everything to do with the hunt, and reading interesting parts of *The Exodus of the Gods* aloud to Zira. He was clutching his right hand, his brow creased.

I raised my cup to my mouth, but the steam brought with it a scent of copper and iron. Blood. Fresh, from an injury. I set the cup down slowly.

"I seem to have…" Hadrien held out his hand, and by the Mothers Three, I had no idea why he'd come to me and not taken care of the wound himself.

I closed the book and took his uninjured hand and led him upstairs. With a pressure on his shoulders, I pressed him down into a chair, laid his injured hand along the surface of the small table. I spun the other chair around and straddled it, leaning over the back to get a good look at the injury.

With careful fingers, I turned his hand this way and that, finding the full extent. "What did you do?" I wasn't sure if I was asking about the fresh wound or the scars laddering up his forearm. The ones he hid.

"I was trying to cut a branch outside. My blade slipped."

"Doesn't look deep." I realized why he'd come to me for help; it was his dominant hand, and wrapping the wounded hand in a bandage would require more coordination than he seemed to possess. "What were you doing, trying to cut a branch?"

Wincing as I pulled the bandage tight, he mumbled, "Siena mentioned something about some dying branches in the orchard."

"There's tools for that, not your hunting knife."

"I realize that *now.*" His face was flushed.

I tied off the bandage, my jaw tight like the knot. Why was this incompetent boy the one who had replaced me? The Arch Shadow had selected someone who failed at everything. It was an insult.

"Don't," I told him through gritted teeth, "get injured again." I grabbed his uninjured wrist, digging my thumb into his pulse point, fingers curling around his forearm like a vise. His gaze connected with mine, his eyes wild and wide. "Do you hear me?"

He dropped my gaze and stood; I didn't release his arm. "Nox, let go."

"Will you try any more foolish things like pruning trees with the wrong tools?"

Wrenching his arm away, he rolled his eyes. "I'm not a fool."

So he says, Lupakaria sniped.

Hadrien retreated a few paces, fiddling with the cuff

of his sleeve. "Thanks for bandaging this. What—what were you reading earlier?"

How bored is he that he is asking? "A journal. Lupakaria says it's real, that one of her god-kind wrote it during their flight from—" I made a motion to the ceiling. "—those hunters." The Wild Hunt, the ones Marsillio had written of in horrid scenes. The ones threatening to descend soon and hunt me.

"Did Lupakaria flee with them that day?"

Grief so strong it was a tidal wave hit me; I blinked rapidly. This grief was not my own. This was Lupakaria's. She fed me the words, and I repeated them to Hadrien, "She stayed here long enough to see others through a gateway to somewhere else. The hunt caught her before she could escape."

You never told me, I said to her.

My demise is not something I am keen to speak of. Do you seek that wish yet?

Is there no other way?

Your death, my dear little wolf.

"What is she saying to you?" Hadrien asked, jarring me out of my internal conversation. "You went quiet."

"That she wants cheese," I replied, for Lupakaria had murmured that in response to his question.

When Hadrien had padded out of the room, called away by a distant bark from Zira, I ventured, *What is the cost of the wish?*

You fear it is the end, do you not?

Yes.

The end will come one day, Nox. Somber weight hung on her words. *I want to know if one of my descendants lives. One of them must have the blood of a god still.*

Sighing through my nose, I started cleaning up the mess. *Why?*

I want to grant them a wish.

She didn't need to explain further. I understood her with stomach-sinking certainty. My wish, should I make it, would not be the last wish. The wish for her descendant would be. One last wish, one so great it would strip her of her extant power and render her dead at long last.

Selfishly, I hoped we would never find her descendant with the powers of a god. That Lupakaria would never use the last of her power. If that came to pass, I would be left with ephemeral bones that would crumble into dust, and I would truly be alone.

***

A howl jerked me out of sleep.

I was up in a heartbeat. *Did the Arch Shadow find us?* A knife in hand, I dashed across the hall. *Are the other Shadows here?* That had been Hadrien I'd heard.

The cold metal of the handle under my hand, I twisted it. It didn't budge. Locked. Shit. Trust Hadrien to lock it. I rocked back and drove my heel into the door. The wood creaked. Again and again, until my leg ached fiercely and the lock had yielded. Siena would have my hide; that wasn't important right now.

Hadrien had fallen silent, his limbs kicking and churning under the blankets. He was trapped in a nightmare. My eyes darted to the windows: shut, closed, intact. No intruders, then.

I sheathed my knife and shook his shoulders. "Hadrien, wake up."

He only thrashed harder.

I didn't pause to think; I scrambled onto the bed and sat on him, hands going to his arms, keeping his hands away from his face, using my weight to hold him down. I jostled him again. *"Hadrien."*

Behind his closed lids, his eyes circled.

From his parted lips came an unholy keen that made my hair stand on end—and I realized what he was seeing in his dreams. Varen.

Hissing out a curse, I let go of his arms to pinch his nose shut, clamp my hand over his mouth. With any luck, I'd wake him before he—what, died? I wasn't entirely sure. I adjusted my grip so I could feel the thrumming pulse in his neck.

His eyes flew open.

Hadrien made a startled sound, sank his teeth into my palm, and twisted under me like an eel. I sprang back.

"You're trying to kill me *now!*" he yelled.

"No—you were—" Anything else I could say was cut off by him driving me down to the bed, one arm pinned under me. He grabbed my other arm, gloved fingers unyielding. He'd held me so differently mere hours ago.

Fury burning in his eyes, any trace of sleep swept away, Hadrien glared down at me. "You were what?" His words were the chill of the winter wind, his gaze the heat of the summer sun.

"I was trying to wake you. You were dreaming of Varen."

His grip loosened a hair. "How do you know?"

"You sounded like him."

Hadrien rocked back. Retreated to the pillows and wrapped his arms around his knees. The fire and fury were gone, replaced by a quiet woundedness. A shudder shook the edges of his frame. He buried his face into his arms.

"I hadn't seen him in my dreams in a few nights," he said into the shelter of his arms. "He was back tonight. Chasing me through the woods, crying this awful sound, and I couldn't get away." Misery choked his voice, muddled it further. "I am tired to the marrow, and I don't understand anything anymore."

"What don't you understand?"

It took me a second to discern what he said in reply in a voice so distraught it was like he was being carved open slowly. Then I understood, and my breath faltered.

I could not handle this. "Oh," I managed.

"But I shouldn't."

"Oh." Was I capable of saying anything else?

He raised his head, looking the most disheveled I'd seen him and still unbearably alluring. "You're everything I should stay away from, and yet I cannot keep myself away." Closing the space between us, he grasped my face in his hands and kissed me. So startled, all I could do was blink.

"Oh," I breathed in a far different way than I had moments ago.

Hadrien sat back, shaking his head. "The Three Mothers know I shouldn't want this."

Words evaded me until Lupakaria mentally nudged me, and I whispered, "I've liked you for a long while now." *He has so much to use against me.*

A little furrow appeared in his brow. "So… that kissing 'practice.'"

The most cowardly thing I'd done. I couldn't look at

him as I admitted, "I thought I would steal the one kiss I would ever get from you."

And maybe I would've gotten another freely given kiss right then, if thorns hadn't started falling from his blue-grey eyes.

His breath sucked in, then shot out in a ragged exhale. Blood joined the thorns dropping from his eyes, liquid rubies landing in his palms. Then, as quickly as it had started, the thorns ceased.

Hadrien lifted his eyes to mine, and with a halting laugh and holding handfuls of thorns and blood, he said, "I think the dark garden is done."

Oh. Like lightning, the ugly thought struck me: *Was he admitting that he liked me only to rid himself of the curse?* And I couldn't even utter a word because anything on my tongue was a half-lie, half-truth, and anything but the truth was worth as much as a full lie.

When he slipped from bed to wash his hands clean, I left the room on feet so light and quiet I was near a ghost.

CHAPTER THIRTY-ONE
HADRIEN

HADRIEN MET his gaze in the mirror.

What had he done?

He was meant to kill Nox, not kiss her.

By the relics and holy bones, he was so damned.

Chapter Thirty-Two
Nox

I avoided Hadrien.

Evening was fast approaching, and soon, it would bring a full moon. My skin was ill-fitting and pinching. I could barely choke down a few bites of stew; it was delicious, I registered distantly, full of rich broth, vegetables, and cuts of beef that melted between my teeth. But my mind was furiously circling.

I was nervous.

My knee bounced in an uneven rhythm, jangling the table.

Why was I nervous?

I stole a glance at Hadrien, eyes dashing over his uneaten bowl of stew to snag on his face, drawn and worn. What was dogging at his heels so? He didn't have the dark garden to worry about anymore, so why did he look like he hadn't slept since we'd last spoken?

He finally plucked up his spoon and dipped it into the bowl of stew. He ate quietly and without conversation.

Siena asking him a question warranted no more than a grunt. Not even Zira whining at him got his attention.

Siena gave me a pointed look.

What? She wants me to talk to Hadrien? As if I can say anything to him right now—he admitted he likes me and then kissed *me on his own initiation, but I think it was all for breaking the dark garden. I can't even ask him without seeming so insecure. Without seeming like I don't think someone would want to kiss me without ulterior motive.*

Still, I cleared my throat and said, "Hadrien."

"Hmm."

"It's a full moon tonight."

"Hmm."

"It's the second full moon."

"Hmm."

I raised my eyebrows at Siena and mouthed, *You try.*

Siena, sighing a small sigh, prodded, "Hadrien."

Silence. A clink of his spoon against the bowl.

Siena's chin tipped from side to side, and I stiffened in my chair. I knew that motion. "Hadrien," she said again, her voice hard and unyielding as an Amaranthic blade. "Actions have to be taken tonight to avoid the coming of the host. The one you yourself told me of."

A muscle ticked in his jaw. Then, setting his spoon down, he replied, curt, "I know."

His chair scraped back. With a tap of his fingers on the table and a click of his tongue—as if he was going to say something but decided against it—he left. I stared at his empty chair as his steps faded.

Siena stood as well, much quieter. "Nox, I find this to be a difficult situation. Skota has set you in a challenge with death the prize for the loser. As long as you and Hadrien do not raise a hand or blade against each other, you will both live through this. Be careful out there tonight. The Wild Moon Wolf is not a beast to under-estimate."

How true that was.

I nodded, not trusting my voice.

After finishing off my bowl of stew, I trudged upstairs to gather a few supplies. I strapped my sword on and tucked knives into my boots. Focusing intently on buck-ling my armour on—in case I was out far from the town when the sun rose—I tried to rein my thoughts in, steer them away from the dangers that awaited me.

But by the Mothers Three, last time I'd been out as the Wild Moon Wolf, I'd been struck by an iron arrow.

I stilled my trembling fingers on my forearm.

I tightened my jaw and walked across the hall. Hadrien's door was shut. For a flicker of a heartbeat, I considered leaving the farmhouse without telling him.

Sighing through my nose, I rapped my knuckles against the frame. "Hadrien," I said into the door. "Come on. It's time to leave."

The door flew open; I startled back a step.

Hadrien gazed at me with wild eyes. At his side, his hands twitched. He looked like he could very easily either punch me or kiss me.

Or maybe my mind was still fixated on last night.

A blink of his eyes, and the frayed edges smoothed out of him. He jerked his head in a nod and brushed past me, the door shutting soundly. Wordless, I followed him out of the farmhouse, Siena sending us off with a wave.

His gaze fixed on the darkening countryside unrolling ahead, Hadrien said, "She really has no idea, does she?"

"About what?"

"You."

There were many things Siena did not know about me. Like the fact that I was staring at Hadrien's back unabashedly, watching his shoulders shift with his strides.

"Does Siena know that you're the Wild Moon Wolf?"

A laugh startled out of me. "No."

"Why not?" He twisted around to look at me, eyes locking to mine instantly; his gaze skirted away just as quick. "It sounded like she was more of a mother to you than the Arch Shadow. At least Siena cares more."

I shrugged. "I didn't want people knowing. The first time it happened, I was scared. I thought it was something wrong, unholy—"

"Well, you *can't* step into holy places."

"And I didn't need you to put that thought back into my head. But, no, Siena doesn't know that I'm the Wild Moon Wolf, and if it goes as I'd like, she won't now." My gaze was surely burning the back of his head. "Only you know."

"Only me?"

"Yes, only you." *What is that lilt in his tone? What does it mean?* "Stop around that bend in the river up ahead. We'll look for a sheltered area to rest in. I don't want to walk all night."

Small stones churning under his boots, Hadrien followed the curve of the river. Starlight flashed across his eyes as he turned back towards me. "It will work." I caught up to him, and he gestured to the large, weather-smoothed rocks. "I can sit there, and if anyone comes by, you can hide in that spot there, where the river once ran."

I ducked into the shallow cave, narrowing my eyes at the height and depth of it. Roots dragged through my hair; sand filtered down in crumbles. Scowling, I tousled my hair clean and retreated.

"Well," he said, "will it work?"

I nodded. My stomach tightened at the looming change. I blew out a breath, sat down hard on a rock—a pinch of pain shot up my spine—and shook out my hands.

Hadrien took a seat near me. "Nervous?" All the hard edges had softened from his tone, leaving behind the low, honey-thick voice that made me sit up taller. He leaned forward, hands clasped loosely between his knees. His eyes glittered in the night. "You shouldn't be."

I ran my tongue over my teeth and looked away.

What was I doing?

Why was I—My skin rippled.

"It's time," I said.

Hadrien tracked me, his gaze heavy, as I walked carefully to the river's edge. The rush of water muffled my turmoil of thoughts. I dipped my fingers into the water, felt it sweep around my fingers, tug on them like it wanted to drag me into its embrace.

Moonlight trickled over me.

I shed my skin like a wave.

Past the blood pounding in my ears, I heard a gasp.

Bells tolled quietly when I turned to face the boy. Through these eyes, I could see every flutter of his pulse, every shift in his frame, every shade of color leeching from his face. *Don't be scared,* I wanted to tell him, for I knew him still.

Hadrien, his arm shaking, held up his hand, palm open and empty. His eyes shone with moonlight. A quiver ran through his jaw.

Don't be afraid, Hadrien.

But I was afraid.

I was struck by how fragile he was. I could break him so easily. He was a feather, I was a hurricane. A single poor movement could have him sprawled across the ground, bleeding, shattered.

His hand connected with my muzzle. I held so still I was practically stone. His palm skimmed along the side of my face, fingers tripping across the fur. I let my eyes shut. His fingers continued on their cautious exploration. I couldn't deny how much I was enjoying this; a bright bloom heated in my chest.

My head tipped to the side, weighed down by his hand on my horn. I shook my head, careful to be gentle, trying to get his grip to loosen. I pried one eye open, the golden glow highlighting his face, turned up as he rubbed his thumb across the ridges of the horn. A mist-laden breeze skidded across my fur, sending shadows dripping onto his gloved hand.

Hadrien met my eye—then hid his face.

I parted my jaws to breathe, catching his scent under the river's fresh smell. Rosemary and oranges, so incredibly *him* and familiar. And a whiff of cognac. My hackles raised.

His grip tightened around the curl of my horn. A vibration rolled through the horn and into the bones of my skull. His breath hissed out between his teeth.

Then with all his weight, he wrenched my head down. I reacted on instinct: an explosion of fur and fang and movement, jerking away from him. Bells pealed out.

But my leg crumpled. I crashed to the ground. Water lapped at my hind paws and tail. Hadrien stood over me, his breath coming quick.

In his hands was a grey silk ribbon, stretching toward me, wrapping around my foreleg and muzzle. Strange. That wouldn't have been enough to stop me.

I rocked up, tried to stand. I crashed down again, a snarl building behind my fettered jaws. Saliva frothed. I fixed my eyes upon Hadrien; his expression was frozen in a war of shock and horror.

Did he know what he had done?

I stretched my jaws—the ribbon slipped—he'd only wound it once around—I fought against the hold, tendons popping and protesting. Growling deep within my chest, bones resounding with the sound, I tore my jaws free of the ribbon.

I didn't think.

My leg still tangled in the ribbon, I leapt at Hadrien. All earlier reservations and worries about hurting him were gone. I slammed my paw into him, talons curling, piercing, pinning him to the shifting riverbank. The heavy tang of blood tinted the air. He squirmed under my paw, eyes bleary, hands scrabbling weakly at my foreleg.

I shoved my muzzle into his face, and jaws cracking open, snarled. Spit and shadow dripped onto his cheek. His eyes screwed shut.

Look at me, I thought in a thunder.

I should bite his head off for what he did. I should rend him asunder. I should—at the very least—take his hand. Or a finger. Biting off a finger was the absolute least I should do in return.

I seized one of his hands between my teeth. Hadrien stared up at me in pale horror. Then he was no longer Hadrien to me and only the Heir of the Shadow, only the boy who had replaced me, tricked me, and tried to trap me.

I crunched down.

Blood spurted hot across my tongue; bone fragments scattered against my teeth. I spat out the finger—a pinky finger. The Heir's scream frayed into a whimper. Crimson flecked his face.

Of all the things we'd done to each other in the past month, this crossed a line we could never return from. Fingers didn't regrow.

But who was I, if not who the Arch Shadow made me?

When cornered, when trapped, I would *bite*.

The Heir thrashed, clutching his blood-coated hand to his chest. Keeping my paw there to hold him down, I ripped away the ribbon—the damned Fetters of Aisling, the ones he'd told me he'd gotten rid of and wouldn't use on me. Fury boiled below my pelt. He was a fucking liar.

I should kill him.

But no.

Let the Wild Hunt have him.

I turned away, hearing him cry over his maimed hand. My thoughts raced like the river. I needed to find somewhere far from him to hide, and then, when the sun rose, I needed to get my things from Siena's farmhouse before the Heir reached her. I didn't know what I'd tell

Siena. The truth could land me in more trouble—white-hot pain shot through my hind leg.

I whipped around and snapped at his arm; the dagger fell away. Iron, sizzling with my blood. The Heir had fallen back, cradling his right arm, blood shining bright where my teeth had left their mark.

I remembered how he had looked when I first met him.

Then I ran, bells tolling with every stride, calling the hunters both earthly and sidereal to me.

CHAPTER THIRTY-THREE
HADRIEN

His arm wrapped tightly in blood-blossomed bandages, Hadrien stared at the window. He couldn't feel any pain past the Grace Breath. But the damage he had seen when he'd staggered to the healer…

Nox had left her mark.

The finger wouldn't regrow no matter how much Grace Breath was used, the healer had said, and the wounds on his sternum and torso and arm would scar. Then the healer had asked what creature he'd run into, and Hadrien had replied with a distant glaze in his eyes that it had been an unholy beast.

Siena paced at the door. Every so often, her gaze would dart to Hadrien's bandaged body and then away, and she would shake her head to herself. She hadn't believed a word he had said.

Hadrien had begun to wonder if Nox had let Lucco fall all those years ago.

Around the fingers—all five—of his left hand, Hadrien tangled the bloodied Fetters of Aisling. He had seen the ribbon work with his own eyes, seen it hold the Wild Moon Wolf. If only he had wrapped it one more time around the fearsome jaws. Then he wouldn't be missing the heart and head of the beast.

He would have *something* to show for his injuries.

"You're sure Nox will risk coming here?"

He nodded once, then said, cold, "She won't leave Embra. If I have to, I'll bait her back with the mare's blood."

A breath hissed in. "I won't have you doing that."

"Need I remind you what she did to me?"

Siena stalked across the room and loomed over Hadrien. "If you hadn't lied to her and betrayed her, she wouldn't have lashed out the way she did."

Not taking his eyes off the window, he replied, "There is only one winner in this, Siena."

"That doesn't mean—" She let out a frustrated noise; Zira, from her spot on the floor, growled in a similar manner. "Three Mothers damn it, Hadrien! Listen to me!"

He felt nothing.

Not even a flicker of shame at Siena's words.

Not remorse at how he'd lied to Nox.

No, nothing at all.

Was this what the Arch Shadow wanted him to be?

He flexed his right hand just to feel a ghost of pain spark up his nerves.

Siena peered out the window, her shoulders held stiff. "Embra is still out there. I don't see any sign of Nox."

"She'll be here."

And his words were premonition, for an hour later, Siena said, "There she is."

Hadrien dashed from the room, his chair clattering to the floor behind him. He burst outside as Nox was reaching for the reins of her mare. Her head snapped toward him, eyes narrowed and lip curled to bare teeth too blunt to tear.

Pain pulsed through his hand. But Hadrien squared his shoulders and strode up to the former Heir. Nox didn't make a move for the saddle. He grabbed her wrist with his good hand and fixed his gaze upon her.

A smirk flickered across her lips. "Something wrong with your right hand?"

It was like a spark among kindling.

He knocked his fist into her smug face. Pain lashed across his knuckles; darkness blurred the edges of his vision; he howled, clutching his injured hand to his chest.

Nox, reeling back, laughed. "You didn't think, did you?" A bright red patch showed on her face where his knuckles had connected. Hadrien formed a tight fist of his left hand, and she snarled, "Don't hit me again. Don't give me another reason to sink my teeth into your throat. Don't believe I will?"

She advanced, grabbed his head by the hair, and tugged him down until their noses collided. Hadrien reared his head back, but her fingers were tangled in his hair in an unyielding way. His pulse flitted through his veins like trapped butterflies.

"I will." The two words were as cold as winter.

Then Nox shoved him away.

Hadrien, his back to the former Heir, gathered up his broken dignity and pieced it back together, smoothing his clothes out. Then, with a measured breath, he turned back to Nox. "Siena is waiting to speak with you."

"Is she now?" Her eyes darted to the farmhouse. "Or is Skota in there?" Sharp as steel, cold as ice, her cobalt eyes returned to Hadrien. "You can lie, after all. Why should I trust that Siena is in the farmhouse?"

It turned out that Nox had no choice.

He had only just noticed the stain of fresh blood darkening her pant leg when she swayed on her feet. With a slurred swear, Nox dropped.

Hadrien poked her with the toe of his boot. "Nox? Are you pretending?" *I did stab her last night. Suppose the blood loss caught up to her.* "Huh."

Siena jogged up. "What did you do?"

"Nothing." As she knelt to lift Nox, he added, "Well, yesterday I stabbed her."

A flat glare was the response.

At Siena's short order, Hadrien grabbed ahold of Nox's dirty boots and helped Siena carry her into the farmhouse. Nox stirred halfway up the stairs. He managed only to draw in a breath before Nox thrashed, threw herself into kicking and bucking.

Stairs snapped at his limbs and neck and head; the wall was suddenly pressed hard against his back, his head was swimming. Hadrien groaned. He dragged his eyes up the slope of the stairs.

Siena was sprawled across the steps, teeth gritted as she pushed herself up on shaking arms. Something scraped along wood; Hadrien yanked his gaze higher; Nox stood at the top of the stairs, face wan, eyes unfocused, blood slicking her palms.

Stomach churning violently, Hadrien scrambled to his feet.

Nox's hands curled into fists. Blood gathered along

her knuckles, dripped once, twice to the floor. "Don't move."

"Nox," he said, and he didn't know if it was a warning or a plea.

"Hadrien!" Siena snapped. She had managed to stand, leaning heavily on the wall. "Don't make this worse." Her voice softening, she said to Nox, "You're injured. You need help."

Nox's jaw, set in a hard line, trembled for the tiniest flicker of a heartbeat. "I can't trust any of you."

Pivoting on her heel, Nox limped down the hall, a hand on the wall to steady herself. Siena glanced back at Hadrien and mouthed, *Go.*

He set one foot onto the stairs to lunge upwards, and then he shook his head. No, there was no way Nox could leave the house without taking the stairs. Climbing out a window and off the roof would only result in more injuries in her current state just as rushing the stairs would likely injure him.

Slowly, step by slow step, he ascended the stairs. He navigated around the drops of blood from Nox's hands and followed the sound of shuffling into the room where she had stayed. Adopting the languid saunter he'd seen Artem use, Hadrien entered the room and leaned against the doorframe, legs crossed neatly.

Nox shot a glare over.

Hadrien said not a word.

She returned to wrapping a bandage around her knee. It was then that he realized she had discarded her boots and pants. She was seated upon the bed, a blanket tucked around her hips, pale and scarred legs sticking out. Heat slung through him. He looked away.

"I wouldn't have this if not for you," Nox grunted. "Keep your eyes away; I'm almost naked."

"I don't want to loo—"

"Oh, spare me. I understand fully that despite whatever base attraction towards me you are feeling, you care naught for me and will cultivate your utter disgust for me until the end of our days."

His face burned with more than whatever it was that had made him avert his gaze from Nox's bare legs. "Maybe you shouldn't have bitten *my finger off.*"

"You betrayed me first."

Hadrien gripped the collar of his shirt. He was two heartbeats away from yanking it down to show Nox the damage done by her talons. The wounds that had healed into scars, even with Grace Breath, scattered across his sternum and torso.

Then there was his arm. He knew when he took the bandages off, his hand would be crossed with thick scars. His forearm, marred by deep scarring from where Nox's fangs had gripped all the way to the bone.

A scuff of a boot drew his attention back to Nox. Dressed again, she was considering him with wary eyes.

Those eyes lingered on the bandages, and for a heartbeat, her expression was wrinkled in a soft, worried way. Then it hardened back into a scowl, and Nox was looking at Hadrien like *he* was the problem.

His nostrils flared. A muscle ticked in his jaw. He pulled the shirt over his head and threw it aside. Nox's eyebrows rose.

"You did this," Hadrien rasped, and then it caught up to him what he had done, and he scrambled for his shirt, donning it so fast he made his head spin. Shoving down the fluster, he said, "Those scars were caused by your claws."

Nox took a long moment to reply, and when she did, it was to say, "The poets would speak of your beauty still."

"Don't—Why do you say things like that?" At her parting lips, he threw his hand out and said, "No, I don't want an answer. You're only going to say 'It's the truth,' and I know—I *fucking* know—you can't speak words you do not believe."

He drew in a long breath, held it for a few beats, long enough to slow his furious pulse, and then exhaled through his nose. "You hurt me."

"You betrayed me. I *trusted* you."

So simple, so plain, so unnerving.

"Well," Hadrien said, shoving his shoulders back, "I need to win."

Nox sighed and thumped down on the bed. She raked her hands through her hair, a leaf fluttering loose. "Why aren't you honest with me?" Soft as a whisper, broken as shattered glass.

He couldn't arrange his thoughts. There was so much he *wanted* to say, so much he couldn't bring himself to say. "Only one of us can make it out of this." *It will not be you.*

"If you keep up that attitude, yes."

He needed to stamp down and smother every traitorous feeling in his body. "I don't want you."

"Stop." She uncoiled.

"I don't—"

"Stop lying." Like lightning, Nox crossed the room and grabbed his chin, forcing Hadrien to meet her gaze.

"You betrayed me. You could have had everything I am. Instead, you will get nothing."

Nox, her grip hard, pushed—until Hadrien yielded a step and then another. Cold swept in where her fingers had been. The door slammed shut a mere hair from his nose. He flinched.

A huff made him look to where Siena slumped in the hall. "You," she said, her voice weary and rough, "did not handle that well." She brushed past him, clipping his shoulder, and knocked on the door. "Nox, it's Siena. Let me in."

And Nox did, opening the door long enough for Siena to slip in and for Hadrien to catch sight of an unguarded exhaustion in her face.

Then there was only the grain of wood in his sight again.

He lost his control.

He slapped his palm against the doorframe. Siena barked something, regret boiled up. Shame hot in his face, Hadrien hurried down the hall. His palm stung, even through his glove. His injured hand and arm ached.

Everything was going wrong. Had gone wrong. Siena knew now that Nox was the Wild Moon Wolf. There was no way Siena would let Hadrien kill her now.

Hadrien swore until he was out of breath.

Outside, the sky was tainted with clouds scuttling in to cover the sun. Hadrien stared at the coming storm for a long breath, a chilly breeze stirring at his hair. He plucked a strand of hair out of his eyes, hunched his shoulders against the surprising chill, and headed towards town.

Soon enough, he was knocking in a three-beat pattern on a door. Steps approached it on the other side, quiet and halting. At a careful repeat of the pattern, the door creaked open.

Angling his shoulders sideways, he slipped through the gap into the darkened room. His boot knocked into something hard. "Ow. Why is this here?"

"It's a wardrobe," Artem replied. "I'm still settling in."

"You should move it."

Artem locked the door. "Why are you here? We agreed that you wouldn't return until the hunt was over because of Nox."

Hadrien wandered through the small space that truly wasn't much of an entry hall. "Nox is incapacitated at the moment." He touched his fingertips to a covered Ianis Frame on the wall. "Are you even capable of using an Ianis Frame?"

"There are workarounds to the tracking. What do you mean, 'incapacitated?'"

"Slightly wounded. She'll live."

"I know you didn't come here to tell me that."

"No." He found Artem's amber gaze in the dim lighting. Outside, thunder snarled, and a heartbeat later, rain began to crash down. "We need to talk about the Shadow Guild."

CHAPTER THIRTY-FOUR
Nox

Hadrien was late.

The storm raged outside, rain lashing the windows, lightning cracking through the shield of death-dark clouds, thunder rumbling my very bones. The glass of the window was cold on my face, far too cold for spring. A slick snake of unease slithered around my stomach.

That journal, had it said the Wild Hunt brought with them the chill of winter?

Siena poked her head in. "Any sign of him?"

"Not yet." My words were clipped. I didn't bother to soften them. "Maybe he'll be struck by lightning and perish out there."

"Nox," Siena admonished. "That's not—"

"Nice? No, I suppose it isn't, but neither is what he did to me."

The sigh Siena heaved was audible over the storm. "I'm going to look for him."

"He's probably in town," I replied, shoving my shoulder into the wall and scowling out the window, "drinking until he can't see straight."

It was when a minute ticked by without a response that I realized Siena had left. "Fool," I muttered. "She'll only get herself killed. And then where will I be?"

Zira planted her paws on the windowsill and peered out. The maned wolf's eyes were fixated on something outside.

"Look at that, Zira."

A lantern's golden light cut through the dark of the storm. On the path below, Siena clutched her hood over her face, holding the lantern close in the shield of her cloak. Wind howled around her. The small flame guttered, light flickering and flashing around her.

Then the storm swallowed up the lantern, and I could see no more.

Siena was not going to return.

I paced, a caged animal.

Stop that, Lupakaria chided, *you'll wear a hole in the floor if you keep it up.*

I don't want to.

I could feel her annoyance like a fly on a horse's flank. *If you don't, I'll take control of you. I seem to recall that there are a few little, delicate wishes you made that I have yet to claim my, shall we say, reward for.*

I stopped and returned my gaze to the storm outside. My eyes ached. I rubbed at one of them, trying in vain to ease the blur that had taken over it.

Well, would you look at that, Lupakaria said.

Disbelief rocked my balance. I pressed a hand to the wall, steadying myself. Maybe a part of me, however deep and shriveled and cruel, had wanted neither Siena nor

Hadrien to return. I couldn't discern the warm feeling that flooded my veins next, as the light strengthened, wavered closer and closer.

Through a gap in the wind and rain, Siena staggered into sight, her cloak swept over the shoulders of a limping Hadrien. *No,* I reminded myself, *he is the Heir.*

The door downstairs banged open; I felt a chill, even upstairs. Zira whirled and ran out of the room. Siena bellowed my name. I couldn't pretend I didn't know they were back. I headed down the stairs, trying to decide on an expression. I settled on a scowl.

I stopped short on the last step.

Well.

The Heir peered up at me through a haze of blood weeping down his face, scarlet trails winding down from somewhere in his hair. Bruises blossomed violet on his jaw; blood clotted his nostrils. He had been beaten —badly.

"What happened?" I asked, checking my tone, dropping it into a cold register. With an inhale, the bite of alcohol coated my tongue. *He drank again. I shouldn't have thought that he'd stop. He drank, he got into a fight at the tavern, and he lost. Pathetic.*

A tear slipped free from his eyes, washed away a little of the blood. "The Fetters were stolen." The cut on his lower lip tore and split. A fresh bead of crimson seeped up. He touched his bloodied, scuffed fingers to his lip. "I was on my way back from town."

So it wasn't a fight. My eyes narrowed, my mind whirled. "Who stopped you?"

Siena shot a look at me that said that was the wrong thing to ask. She was busy working the sodden jacket off the Heir, as he sat awkwardly on the floor, water dripping off him, Zira circling him anxiously.

"Other—" His breath wheezed out. "—hunters."

"Shit," I breathed out.

The Heir laughed, a ragged, broken sound. Hand splayed across his ribs, wet shirt plastered to his torso, he shifted to stand. Siena held his shoulders; the Heir waved her off. "You," he said, eyes fixed on me, "will have to die before the Little Sun is near its zenith."

"Hadrien," Siena snapped.

"Don't be such a coward, then," I told the Heir, speaking a truth—not to his past words, but to others. "Kill me yourself."

With a growl, he lunged forward.

Siena barred his way farther.

A jagged cackle burst out of me, and with it, a stomach-chilling realization dawned: I sounded more and more like Lupakaria with every passing day. "Just try it, little Heir."

"Someone other than me has the Fetters of Aisling now," he spat out, "and they will not fail to trap you and kill you."

I shrugged. "How is that different than what you were trying to do?"

His lips flattened, blood lining the crease between them. It wasn't, and he knew it. He swiped at the corner of his mouth with the back of his hand, reddened knuckles catching on the blood and smearing it. He looked at me like he wished I was dead.

I hated him right then with a gut-twisting fire. *Hated* him. Wanted to drive my fist into his face. Wanted to walk away and never speak to him again. Wanted to kiss his bloodied mouth until mine was bloodied, too.

The Heir clipped my shoulder when he strode past, limping heavily. His steps dragged on the stairs. Siena gave me an indistinguishable look, which I didn't care to decipher, and hurried after him. Zira left, too, and I was alone.

I opened the door, and the storm rushed against me. Staring into the lightning-limned night, I contemplated walking out. The Arch Shadow would eventually find me. Mother Death would come for me, whether at the next full moon or later.

I shut the door and retraced my steps upstairs, passing Siena on the way. I must have stood at the door for longer than I thought, if she was already leaving the Heir. She paused by me, opened her mouth, only to shut it and walk on without saying a word.

I supposed she had no idea how to talk with me now that she knew I was the Wild Moon Wolf.

When I eased past his room, I heard the Heir sobbing through the closed door, a muffled sound. *He is so broken,* I thought. I locked my door when I returned to my room. Rain pattered against the windows. I laid in my bed and wondered if there was a way beyond this hunt.

I couldn't see a way out.

Every path ended in my death.

A chill crept into my bones. It didn't matter if the Arch Shadow was dead at Siena's hand, there would always be someone seeking to hunt not Nox Vis, but the Wild Moon Wolf.

I could run and move every full moon, constantly keeping hunters at bay, never settling anywhere, but eventually, I would slip up. That didn't account for the Wild Hunt and the horrors they would bring in only a few short nights.

Every path ended in my death.

O dreamer mine, you have to only utter the words, Lupakaria intoned, her voice resounding a hundredfold in my skull, sending a deep vibration through my bones. My teeth buzzed against each other.

I lifted the Jaws over my head and set them on the pillow next to me. I laid my head down and stared at the jawbone. The next flash of lightning outlined each fang in sharp edges.

Cold in a way that no amount of sunlight would ever dull, I burrowed under the blankets and tried to sleep. Sleep was far off.

I woke with the words of a dead god in my head.

My hands scrambled at my throat, but no cool bone met my searching skin. No Jaws of Lupakaria. There should have been no voice in my head, none other than mine.

That meant it was another god.

I seized the jawbone and dragged the leather cord over my head. I needed a familiar voice to cut this one out. *Lupakaria!*

Her presence unrolled like a stretch. Then she stiffened, and when she spoke, it was not to me and not in a tone I recognized. *Sytra.*

The other voice replied, *Wish-wolf.*

You have been dead a long time. Even as she uttered the

words, I could feel Lupakaria extending her control over me. What for, I didn't know. I had never felt her so bristled and on edge.

As have you.

The Wild Hunt flayed you apart.

I'll admit, it was not an easy way to go.

Your remnant does not remain. I saw to its destruction myself. Lupakaria bade me, silent, to sit up and creep my hand toward the knife in my discarded boots.

It was foolish of you to do so. Sytra prodded at my skull, a violent jab. *Look at what you have been reduced to, wish-wolf. A bone, to be worn around the neck of a mortal like common jewelry. Seems your pride was left with your pelt.*

My fingers closed on the hilt.

Lupakaria didn't respond to the insults. *For what reason did you find me tonight?*

The Wild Hunt rides near. Ryodin seeks a prey. She will have her prey. She must *have her prey.*

Me.

Lupakaria only replied, *I do not bow to the Wild Hunt.*

They will bring storm and fire and despair! Sytra cried, frenzy lashing their words. *Fury and fire! None will be safe from their hunts! You will—*

Lupakaria seized control of my hand, swept the knife up into my own eye. I howled. I dropped the knife, but the damage was done. Something cold seeped between my fingers.

Oh, quiet, Lupakaria snarled. *You are fine.*

I lifted my shaking hand and saw—with *both* eyes—a strange, slow-oozing black fluid on my fingers. *What is this?*

Did you ingest any of Varen's blood?

I don't know. I remembered the blood sizzling through Hadrien's skin. *Why?*

Varen devoured part of Sytra. Sytra was a god with the power to leap into someone's mind and change the body into theirs. I shattered and burned their remnant and cast the ashes into a chasm so that none could use this power after their death at the Wild Hunt's hands. Sytra reached you, somehow, and was turning you. Slowly.

If I hadn't woken, if I hadn't put the Jaws back on... I didn't want to linger on how Sytra had crawled into my skull, on how some frail scrap of the dead god had clung to Varen or had been borne to the surface by some wayward wind.

Yes, Lupakaria said, her voice losing some of its angry bite, *you would have been lost to Sytra.*

Bitterly, I replied, *That would've solved my current problem with death.*

After a long beat of silence, Lupakaria admitted, *Perhaps it would have.* Then, with a forced cheer, she added, *But Sytra did not like cheese, and I would've never had cheese again, so it would have been quite remiss for me.*

I couldn't bring myself to laugh, though a smile tugged at the corner of my mouth. I tried to stop thoughts of what might have happened. But my mind was whirling.

The Heir had lost the Fetters of Aisling.

The Wild Hunt would descend in four nights.

I was only a handful of days from death.

Padding into the washroom, I rinsed my hands off. In the mirror, I met my gaze. I should prepare for the full moon, somehow. Do something. At the very least, leave Arezza so that the *mortal* hunters would have less of an advantage.

How far could I get without an Ianis Frame before the light of Minimus Sol was shining bright?

The question rolled through my mind again and again as I drank a cup of tea and picked absently at a cinnamon scone. The Heir wandered into the kitchen during the late afternoon, when I was on my third cup of tea. I sized him up out of the corner of my eye. He looked worse than he had last night. No healer had come by.

"Hello to you," I said, letting a lilt slip into my voice. Might as well distract myself by annoying him.

Through his bleary eyes, he glared at me. Sunlight beaming in through the window highlighted his profile in gilded edges, then lit up the bruises.

"You look terrible," I told him.

"Thanks," he grunted. He sat down hard and reached for the teapot. "If you're saying that, then I must truly look terrible." Every word was hoarser than the last, in a rough way that sounded near painful.

I watched him pour himself a cup of tea and add a dollop of honey, then two more. His eyes fluttered shut when he took a long sip, steam curling around his face. When he spoke next, his voice was closer to the low, thick one I had grown used to, smoothed by the hot tea and honey. But his words were cutting.

"You will die at the full moon."

I shrugged, forced nonchalance. "I know this."

The Heir, face twisting with a grimace, stretched for the tureen of soup Siena had made earlier. I could have pushed it closer with my fingertips, but I didn't. A frustrated growl vibrated past his teeth. He sat back with no soup.

"A little help?" he snapped.

I stood and with exaggerated movements, fetched a bowl and spoon for him. I set them down before him; so close, I could see his shoulders shift and tense. The Heir sat rigid as I ladled out soup—roasted tomato with shreds of basil and slices of garlic—into the bowl. Only when I had returned to my seat did he pick up his spoon.

To the soup, he muttered, "Thanks."

I sipped my tea.

He ate quietly, wincing occasionally. Finally, he rested the spoon in the empty bowl and said, "I'm going back to sleep."

The Heir limped out of the room without waiting for a reply, taking his tea with him. I stared at where he had been. I didn't know what to do. I ached to run. But something—*something*—kept me rooted there.

I knew, deep down, what it was.

A foolish desire to kiss that infuriating boy again.

The snap of thunder startled through the night, but that wasn't what had woken me. The hand at my throat had woken me, the weight pinning me down to the bed.

I was fully awake in a heartbeat, my teeth bared.

"Hold still," the Heir ground out.

I twisted my head and sank my teeth into his wrist. My teeth met the resistance of a glove; I bit down harder.

A whine built in his throat. But he didn't let go.

I changed tactic.

I went limp, long enough for him to relax. Pushing my elbows down into the bed, I arched up against him, canted my hips against his. His breathing stuttered, his weight went off balance, and I rolled us. He yelped, one leg slamming down to brace on the floor, precarious on the edge of the bed. I straddled him, not bothering to hold his wrists down.

In the dark, his eyes glittered as he gazed up at me. A dart of lightning illuminated half his face, showed the slack expression, the lack of bruises.

"You must be feeling better," I told him, "if you're trying to kill me again."

"I wasn't—"

"Don't lie to me, Hadrien."

His tongue ran along his teeth, agonizingly slow. I couldn't look away. "I thought I could end the hunt before the... *the* hunters come here."

It was amazing how that did not dim the warmth heating my body.

Lupakaria muttered, *That's because you are truly touched in the head sometimes. Danger is not an aphrodisiac.*

You might be ancient, but I think you're wrong there. I leaned down, throwing myself into the drumming of my pulse. "Did a healer come by?"

That endearing and exasperating furrow appeared between his eyebrows. "What? A healer did—but. Why does that matter?"

I was close enough now to feel the ghost of his chest brush against me as he breathed. "With your permission, I'd like to kiss you." The words were a reverent breath.

"Why?"

"Because you enchant me, and I can't stop thinking about you even when you're trying to kill me."

Please take my remnant off so I do not have to hear your thoughts.

I reared back, swept the Jaws off, and regarded Hadrien. Lightning showed his flushed face—his hesitant nod. "I need to hear you say yes."

"What about… everything?"

"Damn everything else," I whispered.

He awkwardly shifted under me. "I—uh—I'm going to fall off the bed."

"Oh." I scrambled off him.

Hadrien sat up, hands braced on the edge of the bed. *Is he going to leave?* He glanced at me and breathed out a laugh. "I don't know how to do this gracefully."

"Lie down on the bed, Hadrien."

A shudder ran through him; his teeth glinted, biting down on his lip.

Then I was the one biting my lip, looking at him below me, his hair loose and cascaded on the pillow, his hands, bare now. I skimmed my hand up his arm, cradled his head. My fingers twisted in his hair. "I need to hear you say yes," I repeated.

I needed to know that there was more than the dark garden for his confession the other night.

"Kiss me," he said like it was a prayer and a damnation.

I didn't know where to start.

Blistering panic jolted through me. I froze. *Oh, damn it. If I don't move soon, Hadrien is going to have second thoughts and want to leave. I can't—Just do something, Nox!*

I traced the outline of his lips, my thumb brushing over the full sweep, his breath hot on my skin. His lips parted. His brow furrowed still—it seemed he was unsure about what to do here—he bit gently on my thumb. A shiver raced down my spine. I wanted those teeth on my lips.

The storm outside fell away. The waxing golden moon fell away. Everything beyond this room fell away.

I kissed him softly, then drew his lower lip between my teeth and tugged. A noise hummed in his throat. He cut it off, as if embarrassed, and I reassured him with cupping his face and kissing him harder. His teeth teased along my lips. My moan, muffled between our mouths, emboldened him; he pulled me to him, his hand running hard along my back.

It was terrible timing, the absolute worst, but I said into his mouth, "Next full moon, take my heart." *You've already have it.*

Hadrien made a confused noise.

I drew back to see his face. "Neither the Emperor of Atassia nor the Arch Shadow will stop until the Wild Moon Wolf is dead. Until *I* am dead. So you do it. Bring my heart to the Arch Shadow. Win this."

He shook his head. "I can't."

"Hadrien," I said, my voice soft and breaking, "I will die by someone's hand. Let it be by yours."

His fingers wound in my hair and tugged me back to him.

This would end badly.

But in my life, what didn't?

Chapter Thirty-Five
Hadrien

Hadrien woke entangled with Nox.

It was not a position he had ever expected to find himself in, and yet, the unexpected kept finding him. He had been the one to doze off first, his head tilted close to hers.

It was impossible to picture the Nox he had first met with the one before him now, harsh edges softened by sleep, not a hint of a scowl in sight.

There is no way the Arch Shadow ever thought this might happen when she forced us to be partners for the hunt. He smiled at the thought. How fast life could change.

His smile faltered.

How fast life would change in a few nights.

He was a fool to engage in anything with Nox. She would be gone soon. She wanted *Hadrien* to be the one to take her life. He would be left with an aching heart and guilt.

For a minute, he let himself savor the warmth of Nox's body next to his. Then, as quiet as he could, he slipped out of the bed and padded to the door. Nox didn't stir as he opened the door. He eased it shut behind him, and someone cleared their throat.

Hadrien startled. "S-Siena?"

Siena glanced between Hadrien and the room he'd come out of and said, "Well."

"I'm getting breakfast and bringing it up. We're planning the hunt." Half a lie. "Is there tea downstairs yet?"

"I'll put the kettle on." She drew him towards the stairs, her hand light on his shoulder. "Are you and Nox still fighting?"

Did she believe me? "No," he replied and prayed the heat in his face wasn't noticeable.

Siena asked no more questions, thank the Three Mothers, and Hadrien returned upstairs with a platter. Cups of tea were balanced on top along with a selection of scones: blueberry, lavender, and anise.

Nox was awake, the Jaws of Lupakaria around her neck and Zira at her feet, when he walked in. An unguarded expression flashed across her face. With a blink, her normal, hard-mouthed expression fell back into place. "What is this?"

"Tea and scones." Hadrien set the platter down on the small, round table, anxiety nibbling at his fingers. He busied them by fixing up his cup of tea.

"I can see that. Why?"

His thoughts were scattered; the intent gaze Nox was sending his way wasn't helping. "I thought it may be nice," he finally said.

Nox reached for an anise scone. "I suppose I do only have a few nice moments left." She examined the dusting of sugar topping the scone. "I may as well savor them while I can."

A twist pinched at his stomach. He lowered his cup, feeling sick at the thought. Last night had been a mistake, hadn't it? But the Three Mothers willing, this fluttering feeling he got around Nox would fade soon enough. Hopefully before the full moon.

Hadrien cleared his throat. "Do you have a thought for how to live through the hunt?"

Nox brushed the crumbs off her mouth, the scone already gone. After a long sip of tea, she replied, "Do I look like I have an idea?"

"Not really."

"Because I don't. I told you last night my plan for my death." Cocking her head to the side, she added, "Say, what do you think of dragons?"

"I fail to see the correlation."

"There is none." Her teacup clinked against the table. "I don't want to consider anything today. Or tomorrow. Mother Death awaits me at the full moon, and that is that." Something flickered in her eyes; her expression closed off, unreadable. But all she said was, "Thanks for the tea and breakfast."

Hadrien didn't know how to reply. He downed the rest of his tea in one burning gulp and left. Nox didn't call him back. Zira—*his* maned wolf—stayed with the girl.

Not wanting to linger in this discomfort, this skin-crawling uncomfortableness, he headed for the rows of citrus trees not far from the farmhouse. Going into town would have been better for a distraction, but considering how his last venture into the town had gone, it likely wasn't a good idea.

In the crash of sunlight, he wandered through the trees. Bees hummed through the air, sweeping from unfurling flower to flower. A bird sang somewhere in the branches; Hadrien glanced in the direction, trying and failing to find the bird. He wondered how people distinguished birdsong. Maybe he would take that up.

After all, Artem was going to be the Heir.

Even with Siena as the leader and without the burdens of being the Heir, was he still considering leaving the Guild entirely?

He frowned.

Maybe… maybe it would be for the best if he did leave. Thoughts spun through his mind. He could go anywhere, untethered by a title. He hadn't been in the Shadow Guild long; his ties there were few and far between.

It wasn't as if he was very good at hunting legends, seeing as he had failed to slay the Wild Moon Wolf.

Hadrien put his back to the trunk of a citrus tree—was it lemon or orange, he wasn't sure—and leaned against it. A bee buzzed by his face. He let his mind imagine a future outside of the Guild *and* away from his family. He would *not* return to his family if he left the Guild.

What would the Blade of Dreams show him now if he held it?

The Blade had shown him visions of a tree before, a maple that towered in the sky with sprawling branches. A maple quite like Domhan Arbre. It was obvious now, for what other tree held such magnitude? That tree had been in his dreams in his childhood, and it seemed to have lingered years later.

He closed his eyes, face tipped up to the warmth of the sun. Atassia was beautiful, but as he had told Nox, Brumais was his home, the place of his heart. That was where he would go. What he would do there to carve a life for himself, he didn't know yet, but that didn't matter.

With a breath that seemed to carry away weight from his shoulders, he opened his eyes. Sunlight dazzled his vision, and he blinked away the spots. Only to yelp and jerk his head back, smacking it on the tree.

The bee flew off, not knowing the pain it had caused by simply flying too close to his face. Rubbing the back of his head and muttering a curse, Hadrien stalked out of the grove. He tracked Siena down, finding her in the small garden.

"Siena."

She didn't look up from the plant she was tending to. "Hmm?"

"I'm not going to be your Heir."

That captured her full attention. Siena sat back on her heels and peered up at him. "Well, then who is?"

"Artem."

"A boy raised from the dead is not what I foresee as my Heir."

"He's not dead, never was."

Siena stood, brushing her palms together, particles of dirt pattering down. "Does Artem know of this plan?"

Hadrien nodded.

"You seem to think Nox will not want to be the Heir."

"I don't."

Nox's voice had cut out of the shade.

Siena looked over at her, seeming unsurprised that Nox was lurking around. "You don't want to be Heir?"

"No. The Wild Hunt is inevitable."

Hadrien's breath whistled past his teeth. "Don't say their name."

"What? Scared they'll come here?" Nox grinned, a wild glint in her eyes. "Guess what, they already have noticed us." Striding into the sun, she threw her arms out. "Damn the Wild Hunt!"

He hissed, *"Stop."*

Nox instead yelled at the sky, "Come on, Ryodin! Come and kill me, you coward!"

Siena sighed, as if this was not unusual.

Nox stormed off.

Hadrien stared at the sky, his breath in his throat, his hand clutched around the one that had been maimed by Nox. The Wild Hunt wouldn't come down now, would they?

A scrap of cloud drifted by. Heartbeat by heartbeat, his chest loosened, and his breath relaxed. It was safe for now.

"I'll go after her," Siena said.

Hadrien rubbed the mass of scarring where his finger had once been. This, he needed to remember. He couldn't let himself forget what Nox was capable of, what Nox had done. The kisses they'd exchanged last night meant nothing. It would be best to forget those and to fix instead upon the memory of her deathly fangs.

It would be of no matter for long; after all, Nox had told Hadrien to kill her.

He should have known going into town the next day would be a mistake.

The Arch Shadow considered Hadrien from across the table, her eyes piercing and frigid. It was a wonder her eyes could be so cold when they were the color of molten gold. "Why have you not killed the Wild Moon Wolf yet?" Each word was a single, perfectly pronounced utterance.

His stomach twisted, painful.

With a sip from a goblet of wine so dark and heavy it left tears upon the glass, the Arch Shadow said, "I should have never assigned you to this. It is far above your skill. Seeing as it is the third and *final* full moon tomorrow, and there is only failure to account for, even my former Heir has been a disappointment once again."

Hadrien looked to the table, his plate of cheese and grapes no longer seeming appetizing. To avoid replying, he speared a cube of sharp orange cheese and nibbled on it.

The goblet clunked down. The Arch Shadow stood, and two of her Shadows melted out of the edges of the room. Looking down on Hadrien, she said, "Try not to disappoint me tomorrow. I'd hate to see all my time and effort in training you go to waste."

The cheese turned sour in his mouth.

His head in his hands, Hadrien waited in the tavern until the Arch Shadow and the other Shadows were gone. *How did she find me? The Shadow I saw the other day must have reported back to her. At least she didn't ask where Nox was.*

Because Nox had been missing since she challenged the Wild Hunt. Siena hadn't been able to find her, and though she said she was certain Nox was fine, he could tell Siena didn't believe it.

Hadrien ground the heels of his hands into his temples and groaned. If he couldn't find Nox before the full moon, the Wild Moon Wolf would be running wild, and the Wild Hunt would take notice. They would descend, as the dragons at Domhan Arbre had foretold.

He still didn't know if he could kill Nox.

By the relics and holy bones, this hunt would have been far easier if he had never learned that Nox was the Wild Moon Wolf.

As afternoon tipped toward evening and the sun dipped low in the sky, Hadrien strapped on his hunting gear.

He breathed slowly and evenly through his nose, pressed down the swelling, stomach-flipping panic. He tucked a small, iron-bladed dagger into a sheath along his forearm.

The local priest had blessed it and anointed it with oil soaked with the bones of a long dead holy person of some sorts. Hadrien was fuzzy on the details, but so long as the blade was both iron and holy, he was satisfied.

It was a cruel blade.

Maybe it was wrong of him to choose a blade that would cut like fire through the Wild Moon Wolf. But he had to ensure that the job was done.

He would be fast. The pain would be insurmountable. But he would not linger like others might. He would strike for a vital vein, sever it in one swift cut, and hold the head of the beast as the lifeblood flowed.

Hadrien had already sent a letter to Xenna, asking for her return to Atassia. He hadn't explained why. He would, once the deed was done and Khtonyx was safe from the eye of the Wild Hunt. Then Nox's body would be laid to rest as the Three Mothers dictated. Though Nox was an unholy beast, perhaps she could find her final rest in a holy place.

Siena shook her head when Hadrien walked to the door leading out. He met her gaze, saw the despair and disappointment there, and crossed the threshold. No words could ever form an apology for this. Siena did not call after him.

The leaves of the citrus trees rustled as he went by, walking Ikarus in hand. The sun sank ever lower, and across the hills, the moons began to peek over. Hadrien paused at the crest of a hill and gazed out over the darkening countryside.

What if he couldn't find Nox?

No, not Nox.

Better to think only of the Wild Moon Wolf.

Hadrien blew out a breath and climbed into the saddle. Ikarus snorted, shaking his head and jingling the feather charm on his bridle. With a hearty pat on his shoulder, Hadrien said, "Back on the hunt, boy."

It was as it had been before he met Nox and was assigned to this accursed hunt. Riding through the wilds, listening to the sounds of life around him. His eyes roaming over hill and dale, forest and field, seeking the form of his prey.

Golden light blanketed his surroundings; Little Sun had risen in its full glory, flanked by the waning forms of Argento and Azura.

Hadrien let a sigh slip free.

The toll of a bell rolled over the hills.

Ikarus pricked his ears.

Hadrien collected the reins. "It's time."

The bells led him to where the forest spilled into the river. Hadrien left Ikarus at the edge of the forest and ventured into the depths on foot. The Wild Moon Wolf was around here somewhere; he could hear the rasp of breathing, the ring of a bell.

It was strange that the Wild Moon Wolf had stayed near Arezza, the location of the last sighting. Word would have gotten out, drawing more attention to the hunt—and thus, catching the Wild Hunt's gaze.

He faltered.

Had that been the Wild Moon Wolf's intention all along? To actually summon the Wild Hunt to Khtonyx and allow the world to be destroyed for its misdeeds against her?

No, surely not. That was too much, even for—*Don't think her name.*

Hadrien pushed on, shoving aside thoughts of the Wild Hunt. Undergrowth slapped against his boots. There wasn't much time. The longer the Wild Moon Wolf was alive tonight, the sooner Ryodin would lead the charge of the Wild Hunt down.

At the edge of the river, on a stretch of shore cupped by the trees, Hadrien found the Wild Moon Wolf waiting. Waiting for him. The trio of golden, glowing eyes fixed upon him, and the unholy beast rose, near silent.

Hadrien slid out the blessed blade.

The beast's lip curled back, fangs glinting in the moonlight. A flash of hot adrenaline shot through Hadrien. Had the Wild Moon Wolf forgotten what had been said?

Next full moon, take my heart. I will die by someone's hand. Let it be by yours.

Hadrien adjusted his grip on the knife. He drew in a short, sharp breath and moved. Before the Wild Moon Wolf could slip away, he grabbed ahold of the beast and snapped the blade up—only to stop, the point hovering an inch from the thick, shadow-slick fur.

His hand shook.

"I can't do it," he rasped.

The Wild Moon Wolf shouldered him away and stepped back, a bell ringing out with the movement. Hadrien couldn't do it, but the beast had to die tonight.

So caught up in his thoughts was he that he didn't hear the hunters approaching. He whirled, too slow, too late; the Shadow from town grinned at him, thumping a knife hilt into his head. Pain sparked in his skull.

Knees buckling, vision blurring, Hadrien hit the ground. Someone was wresting the dagger from his grip, but his eyes were on the Wild Moon Wolf. Through the remaining wisps of his vision, he saw silken fetters falling over the unholy beast.

Run, Nox, he tried to say, but no words slipped out.

CHAPTER THIRTY-SIX
NOX

LUPAKARIA HAD CONVINCED ME.

If only I had been willing to listen earlier.

Trapped below the insurmountable weight of the Fetters of Aisling, it was all I could do to breathe, let alone escape and carry out her idea.

Thunder rumbled overhead, and I strained my eyes up. The ribbon tightened around my muzzle and legs with the slight movement. Despite the sound of thunder, there was not a cloud in the star-studded night sky.

The Wild Hunt was coming.

I rolled my eyes in the direction where Hadrien was unconscious on the ground. The hunters had moved both of us—I'd had to move myself, while leashed and muzzled—to one of the open fields of grass and wildflowers. It was a beautiful spot in the starlight, a lovely spot to die.

There was faint movement in Hadrien's form; he was waking. He wasn't far from me. If I stretched my paw out, I could snag my talon on the ropes binding his wrists.

I shifted my paw closer and extended one talon. The tip caught on the rope, fumbled off, sank into the leather of his vambrace. I would have winced if I was able to. Hopefully it hadn't pierced through—It certainly had; I smelled fresh blood. I'd apologize to him later, provided we were both alive by sunrise.

I cut the rope without causing further damage to Hadrien. His fingers flexed. The great drum of spectral hooves in the sky sounded again, deep enough to hum against my teeth. One of the hunters made a surprised noise and pointed up.

The air chilled.

My fur stood on end.

With a crack like someone had dropped the world's largest egg, the sky split open.

I wrenched my head up and watched as a fiery red light boiled in a line, cutting apart the constellations. It grew, yawned wider, and from its maw, the Wild Hunt spilled out.

Ryodin rode at front, clad in silver and bone armour. She had a double set of ghostly, chiropteran wings sprouting from her back, which the dead god's journal had not mentioned but were there nonetheless; I questioned if they worked, didn't want to find out. A gauze of veil covered her helm, streaming behind with her pitch-black hair. The wind pressed the veil flat against the ridges of bone and teeth on her skull-shaped helm.

Nearby, Hadrien pushed himself up, his face wan, crimson winding down his wrist, and murmured, "Mother Death."

It's Ryodin, you fool, I wanted to say, *not Mother Death.*

It was now, seeing Ryodin in the flesh and ecto, that I

wondered if someone had fashioned the mortal manifestation of Mother Death after the leader of the Wild Hunt.

That was a silly thought, for what did it matter when the Wild Hunt was barreling down before us?

When the pelt that was draped over the back of Ryodin's ghastly steed belonged to Lupakaria, and if a goddess had not been able to survive the Wild Hunt, then what chance did I, a cursed changeling, have?

The hunters scattered, most screaming. Some stood their ground, fear rolling rank off them. I thrashed against the Fetters of Aisling. If Ryodin reached me while I was still bound, she would kill me without hesitation.

Hadrien staggered back a step. I made a low sound, trying to catch his attention. It worked; he looked to me, his eyes wide. He hesitated. I was going to bite his head off if he didn't take this accursed ribbon off me.

Fortunately for him, Hadrien slipped the knot free from the ribbon and unwound it. Rising to my full height, I shook out my pelt; bells pealed out, shadows splashed against the ground.

Ryodin and her steed alighted on the ground, crackles of ice and ember smoldering across the wildflowers. The steed struck out with one of its many hooves, sparks dancing off. The other Wild Hunt riders landed behind Ryodin in a fanned-out formation, bone-faced hawks and hounds among them.

Ryodin, gripping her massive spear that had felled prey like none other, asked in a tongue I did not know but understood with unfaltering ease, "What is your lauded prey?"

It was me.

Terror buzzed through my limbs.

Through a tense voice, Hadrien got out, "The Wild Moon Wolf."

I wondered, too late, if he could have said something else and the Wild Hunt would have accepted it.

As it was, Ryodin turned her helm in my direction. I felt the weight of her unseen eyes. She hefted her spear. Then, thrill coursing through her words, she shouted, "Let the hunt begin!"

The Wild Hunt roared their approval.

The Mothers Three protect me.

I whirled and ran, leaving behind Hadrien with the Fetters of Aisling between his hands. All I needed was to evade the Wild Hunt until sunrise. Then I could complete Lupakaria's plan.

Behind me, hooves thundered across the ground.

I stole a glance back, saw Hadrien riding alongside the Wild Hunt. Other mortal hunters were there, too, their horses cantering next to the sidereal steeds. The Wild Hunt riders weren't trying to kill them; they were all riding as a pack, focused on bringing me down.

I dug my talons in and ran faster.

I supposed this was what Aveline and Fleur had meant. The Wild Hunt came here only for the delight of the chase and the prey. If they enjoyed it, they would not destroy the lands. If they didn't… horror awaited us.

I *had* to make sure the Wild Hunt enjoyed the chase.

My heart pounding, knowing a single wrong move would land in my death, I led the Wild Hunt across the wilds of southern Atassia. I could hear their joyous shouts and whoops when I leapt over a river and skidded into a forest; they dove among the trees with glee, chasing my tracks.

I could do this.

I kept telling myself it as the hours wore on and my entire body ached. Breathing had turned painful long ago, and the rasps I drew in tasted of blood.

I stole a moment of peace behind the wall of a villa, hidden from sight. My talons were ragged, the pads of my paws shredded. Blood had clotted in a gash from where an arrow had grazed my side. I couldn't remember when it had been fired.

Exhaustion dragged at me when I rocked back to my paws and limped away. A Wild Hunt hound bayed. I gritted my fangs and shoved into a run once more.

Only a few more hours.

It passed in a blur, but every minute felt like an hour. I was face-to-face with Hadrien at one point, Ikarus rearing under him, and he didn't try to make a strike. I had the feeling he was slowing the hunt, leading them on stray paths when he could.

With the Wild Hunt a mile behind me, I rolled down a steep hill. There were trees enough at the base to hide me. I pressed myself flat to the ground, leaves tickling my open wounds.

Morning rose scarlet-bloody across the hills. The vibrations of the Wild Hunt, drawing ever closer, rattled the stray leaves. They would find my tracks soon enough. But all I needed was a few minutes.

In the blink of an eye, I had lost the form of the Wild Moon Wolf. I sucked in a sharp breath, furious pain radiating through me. I scrambled at my pockets, found the vial of Grace Breath, and downed it; it wouldn't heal me fully, not without further care, but it would do enough for now.

With blood-streaked, skin-stitching-back hands, I grabbed the Jaws of Lupakaria. The bone scraped violently against my healing palms.

Wish, o dreamer mine.

I fixed my eyes on two objects near: a twisted coil of olivewood root, loose from the tree it had once been part of, and a mica-strewn, hand-sized chunk of white granite. Beyond, a jagged strike of a fallen branch. Those would do.

Lupakaria, I wish for all who see this root to believe it to be the head of the Wild Moon Wolf, this rock to be as her heart, and the fallen branch there to be her remains. I wish for all who see to believe that the Wild Moon Wolf is dead. I swallowed down blood. *All, save for Hadrien.*

He alone would know.

With bated breath, I waited. What would the cost be?

O dreamer, I will fulfill your wishes. In return, you will seek and find my descendant, the one who lingers in marigolds, and then you will bear my bones to the Living Forest. Return me to my kin, so that I may rest at long last.

Wherever they are, whoever they are, I will find them. I swear it, I will find them and then return you to your kin.

Lupakaria's voice took on a light tone. *And let's find a wheel of cheese, too.*

I huffed out a laugh. *It's a deal, Lupakaria.*

Ryodin approaches. Tread carefully, little wolf. Do not meet the fate I did.

I felt nothing when the wish was completed. But when I fixed my eyes on the root and the rock, I saw flickers of

the illusion. My stomach lurched. I pushed down everything. There was no time for pain.

Holding what would appear to everyone else as the
head of the Wild Moon Wolf in one hand and the heart
in the other, blood streaming down my arms, I staggered
up the hill. At the crest, the rising sun blazing in my eyes,
I shouted, "The Wild Moon Wolf is dead!"

Ryodin stared at me for a heart-stopping minute,
silent. Her steed carried her up the hill on crackling steps.
I swallowed hard, my mouth dry, and tipped my head
back to look upon her. She was horror and wonder.

I prayed she did not take notice of the jawbone I
wore, one from a goddess she had slain.

Ryodin reached down and pressed three cold fingertips to my forehead. "May your hunts be ever fruitful and
your prey ever wild."

My knees shook.

Ryodin guided her steed away, strings of teeth
clinking together, and at a gesture from her, the Wild
Hunt galloped in circles around the mortal hunters.
Faster and faster, they rode, dust and debris kicking up,
wind whistling. The thunder of hooves and paws and
wings was deafening.

The air quieted.

The dust settled.

The Wild Hunt was gone.

I dropped to my knees, the enchanted root and rock
falling from my hands. Mothers Three damn it, I was so
tired. I wanted a cup of hot tea, a bowl full of soup, and
a nap.

A shadow fell over me. "How did you manage that?"

I peered up at Hadrien. "A wish."

His eyes widened. He knelt and touched my shoulder. "I'm sorry."

"For?"

"Betraying you. I never should have."

Everything felt like too little too late. "Maybe we would've been friends, had we met in a different life, one without the Arch Shadow and the Wild Moon Hunt." I searched his face, looking for something, but I didn't know *what* exactly. "Time is all that can heal what I did, what you did, what we both did to each other. Then, maybe, we can start over."

I shoved to my feet, pain shooting up my legs. I gazed down at him, looking up at me. I remembered a peaceful afternoon by a lakeshore in the embrace of a forest. I wanted to touch him one last time, I wanted to punch him one last time, I wanted to kiss him one last time.

Oh, there was so much between us that was sour, that was sweet, that was pain, that was pleasure. I didn't know yet which outweighed the other.

"Maybe one day, Hadrien, I'll see you at a lakeshore under a full moon."

I didn't wait for an answer.

Without another word, I strode away from Hadrien, leaving the root and rock that would fool the world with him. He called my name. I never looked back.

The sun beat down upon my head. Blood was drying stiff on me. But for now, I was free from the Arch Shadow again, and so long as Siena completed her part, I would never see that woman again.

The Wild Hunt had blessed me. I had survived. If a hunt chose my eclipse-form as their chosen target again, mistakenly believing me to be a new iteration of the Wild Moon Wolf, they would never catch me.

I found Embra where I had left her, and I climbed into the saddle, swearing at the pain. Embra flicked an ear back. I scratched my nails back and forth over her shoulder and then urged her into a walk toward the road.

Lupakaria asked, *How soon can we get cheese?*

A flicker of a smile crossed my face, grim. *Soon.*

To go where the gods are, to where my kin fled, you'll need to start with Indikos in Mallina. I once guided my kin through the gateway; I recall glimmers of where to look.

Mallina it is then.

I hear they have good cheese there.

On the road, I turned Embra in the direction of Mallina and listened to her hooves on the cobblestones. The road ahead would be long, the search lengthy and likely dangerous. I had my end of the wish to fulfill, and I would find Lupakaria's extant descendant. Perhaps the blessing of Ryodin would guide my direction.

Surviving these past full moons didn't feel real. But I was alive and unshadowed by the weight of my prior title.

A new hunt was beginning, and I was prey no more.

CHAPTER THIRTY-SEVEN
HADRIEN

HADRIEN STARED at the head and heart of the Wild Moon Wolf, severed and cut from the unholy beast. If he squinted and looked at them through a haze of eyelashes, he saw a twist of root and a rock in their place.

So Nox had brought a wish to Lupakaria after all. What Lupakaria had requested in return, he would never know.

But Nox was gone now.

He had watched Nox walk away. She hadn't looked back once. Where she was going now, Hadrien didn't know. Certainly not to Ferros, not with the Arch Shadow still there.

Maybe one day, Hadrien, she had said. She was right; time was needed between them to heal what had been done, and then perhaps they could meet again without being at each other's throat.

His scars ached, the ones left behind by the Wild Moon Wolf. He stared hard at his right hand, where the glove buckled awkwardly on the empty gap of his bitten-off finger. The scars would soften over time. The memories would remain.

I'll see you at a lakeshore under a full moon. There was only one lake she could mean, the place where he had seen her smile. The Lake of Eternity in Brumais.

He didn't know yet if he would be able to look at Nox one day and not see what had been done. His own mistakes, the deep-seated twist of guilt that slung through him. The Three Mothers alone knew.

Turning away, he whistled for Ikarus. He didn't dare leave the hunting trophies behind, not when he could take them to the Emperor of Atassia as proof. No reason to let the reward go to waste.

From Ikarus' saddlebags, he removed two large sacks and dumped the heart into one. The head seemed too large, but it fit, thanks to the true size of the item it was.

Bile stung the back of his throat; Lupakaria had done well—*too* well—on the illusion. The weight was correct, the feel was correct, the blood soaking through the canvas was correct.

Swallowing back his nausea—these were *not* real, he told himself— Hadrien secured the sacks, one on either side of Ikarus. The gelding snorted, stamped one hoof. Hadrien gave him a pat on his broad neck and promised him an apple later.

Hadrien, careful not to kick the sacks, settled in the saddle. As the Wild Hunt had returned to the skies and stars beyond, only hunters from this world remained. They parted before him, some with praise on their tongues. Others spat at Ikarus' hooves and called Hadrien a thief.

When Hadrien approached the farmhouse alone, Zira

loped out to dance around him, and Siena walked out to meet him, arms crossed, jaw set.

"Did you kill her?" she demanded.

Raising his chin, Hadrien replied, "The Wild Moon Wolf is dead." She would see the proof of the kill upon Ikarus' back, and she would despise him.

Siena held his gaze.

Could Siena know the truth? Nox would have come here, had she wanted Siena to know, right? Hadrien held the truth back, a hard press of words locked behind his sternum.

"Get your things and leave," Siena said, cold. "It is good that you will not be my Heir."

As he gathered up his belongings, shoving them into knapsacks, he wondered if he should tell Siena.

He didn't.

He paused by Siena long enough to say, "The Guild will be better under your lead," and then he rode for Ferros, his maned wolf ranging ahead.

For what he prayed would be the final time, Hadrien opened the door to the House of Shadows. The sacks were slung over his shoulders, the ties pressing heavily into his bones. One corner brushed against the doorframe as he crossed the threshold.

The Arch Shadow awaited him in her office. Hadrien paused at the ajar door, and she called for him to enter.

The brief surprise on her face was worth the horrors he had seen and endured. Then the Arch Shadow sat back, face closed off. "So, you did not disappoint me after all."

His hate boiled. There were no words to acknowledge his success, only that his endeavors had not ended in disappointment this time. All the pain, all the blood, all the loss—it did not matter to her.

"I see only you. Where is Nox?"

"Dead, as you ordered," Hadrien answered, sick. "Nox was in my way."

"Hmm." The Arch Shadow turned her attention back to the ledger before her.

That was it.

That was the entirety of her reaction to hearing that her former Heir, the girl she'd raised and trained, was dead. If Hadrien hadn't already made his decision, that would have been the nail in the coffin.

"You may continue as my Heir."

"No," he replied, and the force of his own voice startled him. *This is for Nox.* "I will not be your Heir any longer. I am leaving the Shadow Guild."

"Then leave." Simple, emotionless. "The Guild is better off without you dragging us down. You are ungrateful, you blame everyone else for your mistakes, and you are more failure than success.

"You contribute so very little to the Guild." The Arch Shadow didn't even glance up, not once. "Remember, you are nothing without what I made you."

His eyes stung, his throat closed, but Hadrien ground out, "I'd rather be nothing." He unclasped his Shadow medallion and slapped it down on the desk with his left hand.

Saying not a word to the Shadows he passed, Hadrien

hurried up the stairs. Most of his things were already with him, but he packed what remained.

Nox's things, he left there. Maybe Nox would return for them. He tucked a small letter into the hidden niche in the bedroom floor among the daggers nestled there—in case.

Hadrien didn't look back upon the House of Shadows.

Xenna brought him news at the start of the new month.

After hugging Hadrien and petting Zira, she looked around the inn room. "Is this where you live now?"

He glanced around, seeing it through fresh eyes. The room was mildly dismal, and he still hadn't straightened the blankets on the bed from where he'd tangled them during his restless sleep. "I'm only staying here until the Emperor sends my reward."

Hadrien had gone to the palace immediately after he left the House of Shadows. He had presented the trophies from the Wild Moon Wolf, and still, he had not been rewarded.

So he lingered in Sidero, breathing out sighs of relief with each new moon without the dark garden. He had kept the moons necklace Nox had given him, but it stayed in his pack, wrapped carefully.

"There's a nearby bakery," he said to Xenna, "let's go there."

"Please."

They situated themselves at a table near a wide window, Zira sprawled at their boots. Hadrien stared out, watching people walk by on the quiet street. Some days, he expected to see Nox striding by.

"She isn't coming back," Xenna said, quiet.

"Am I that obvious?"

A raised eyebrow told him that he was. "Nox told me she wouldn't be back for a while."

He snapped his gaze over. "She found you?"

Xenna nodded. Her eyes flicked up to the boy approaching with a tray. The teakettle was settled on the table, accompanied by cups and scones. "Thanks." She waited until he was gone to start preparing her cup of tea. "Nox came by the House of Wolves."

"House of Wolves. It's official now?"

"Siena is the Moonstalker. Artem—can you believe he's been alive all along?—is the Heir of the Wolf."

He skipped the question about Artem; there was no need to delve into the interactions he'd had with the new Heir of the Wolf under the protection of cloak and shadow. "What happened to Skota?"

"Who?"

"The Arch Shadow."

Xenna grunted in acknowledgement. "Gone. No one knows where. Some Shadows left with her. The rest of us, whether we were allied with Siena before or not, stayed to be the Wolves."

Of course the Arch Shadow wasn't dead.

Death was too easy for her.

Hadrien took a blisteringly hot sip of tea and winced. "Damn, that's hot." He pulled a plate with a lavender scone closer to him. "And Nox?"

"Nox returned long enough to speak with Siena and

gather her things from the Heir's quarters, which, you know, are now Artem's."

Hadrien almost didn't find his voice to ask, "Did she ask about me?"

Xenna's silence was the answer.

He hid his hurt by stuffing his mouth with a bite of scone. A crumb fell onto Zira's snout, and she snapped it up. Hadrien washed his mouthful down with tea. "Do you like the Wolf Guild?"

"It's far better than the Shadow Guild ever was. Siena cares about us all, and she takes the time to ensure that the cruelty trained into some of us is swept away. Rogus…" Her eyes misted over, and she cleared her throat. "He would have liked it."

For a heartbeat, Hadrien wished he could be in the new Guild. But even under a new name, the walls of the house held haunting memories and mistakes for him. His place was not there.

"Oh," Xenna said. "This, by the way, is for you."

Hadrien stared at the letter. *Is it from Nox? By the Three Mothers, you are pathetic, Hadrien. Nox didn't even ask about you; she's moved on already, for certain.* He took the letter, not realizing which hand he'd used.

"What happened there?"

Hadrien tucked his right hand out of sight. "The Wild Moon Wolf bit my finger off." He uttered the words with a bitter taste on his tongue.

"Damn." Xenna picked up her cup of tea with both hands and cradled it. "Oh, why did you send me that letter that said I needed to return to Atassia? I was in Brumais, hunting the white harts. Those gold antlers are so heavy, I have no idea how they can hold up their heads."

Because I was going to hunt your friend like prey and wanted you there for her final rites. Grateful that he could lie, unlike Nox—she was circling his thoughts now, the quick flash of her sharp grin—he said, "Because of Siena's plan. I thought you should be back for that."

A small nod. "Where are you going next?"

"Brumais, as soon I get the reward. I've already secured Ikarus and Zira a pass to enter." He tried to offer Xenna a confident smile, but it wavered, betraying the jittery uncertainty over his future. What if he hated it? What if he really was nothing without the Arch Shadow? What if Varen hunted him again?

He shut his eyes against the memory of the bare-skulled face leering down at him. The Wild Hunt, thank the Three Mothers, hadn't had another elk among their ranks when they came down. But their presence had caused his nightmares of Varen to return in full force. Being among the trees of Brumais might worsen the nightmares.

Nightmares were better than staying here.

"I'll visit," Xenna promised.

Siena apologized for her last words to Hadrien, through the letter Xenna had brought to him. It didn't change anything, though. Hadrien left Atassia and the painful memories there behind for the forests and flowers of Brumais.

Domhan Arbre towered over the rest of the forest,

beckoning to him even in the dark of night. This was what the Blade of Dreams had first shown him, he knew. He had been moving towards this all along.

Though the hour was late, Hadrien climbed the steps up and entered the libraries. His eyes swept over the levels, searching. It had been a small, foolish hope. Nox was not here; she was gone to him.

Aveline landed before him, feathers bristling. "We cannot welcome you here any longer, Hadrien. We have heard word of the hunter who felled the Wild Moon Wolf."

Hadrien knelt, hands held out in supplication, the silken Fetters of Aisling draped across his palms. He did not bow his head, for the library dragon was neither god of old nor deity. He met the dragon's gaze evenly and prayed his truth came through his tone. "The Wild Moon Wolf is not dead. She hides, but she lives still through a wish. I bring you the Fetters back so that they may not be used to ensnare her again."

The dragon plucked the ribbon up. "Remain here."

She flew into the heights of the library. Who or what she consulted, Hadrien did not know. When she alighted again, she dipped her head in a nod. "You spoke the truth. Welcome to Domhan Arbre once more."

Epilogue
Hadrien

It was the night of a full moon, but the hunt was far away.

Hadrien lingered at the shore of the lake, watching the stars and moonlight dance across the waves. It had been months and moons of empty lakeshores. Still, every full moon brought him here again without fail.

Tonight marked a year.

It was foolish, he knew, to hope she would appear in the gloom. When his letters had gone unanswered, and none had arrived for him.

Better to return to the libraries of Domhan Arbre now and let any glimmer of a dream die. There were tomes endless to review with the dragons, and there were texts to write on the truth of the Wild Hunt and the gods of old. Lupakaria and Nox had thwarted Ryodin's wrath once, but they were gone; Khtonyx could not rely on them again.

Warning the world of the Wild Hunt was the only thing that made use of Varen visiting his nightmares and waking moments still. When their paths crossed in the forests at times, Varen watched him with his sightless skull. Hadrien never tried to face him.

Kneeling, thoughts of the Wild Hunt fading for the time being, Hadrien dipped his fingers into the lake. Under the light of Azura, the water drops rolling off his skin glimmered blue and cobalt and indigo. His sigh stirred the surface of the water.

When would he accept that it was over? Nox was not coming back, despite what she had said after the hunt. It was time for him to stop coming here.

Hadrien waited at the lake all night.

As night melted into dawn, he heard the tolling of bells.

ACKNOWLEDGMENTS

Few things in life are solitary acts. Writing, while carried out in stolen moments or the deep of night, is not a solitary act. There's a team behind each story, and I'd like to thank them for their part.

Thank you to Niall Grant for providing an amazing illustration for the cover, one that is beyond what I could imagine and is a perfect blend of the inspirations for this story. You vastly improved upon my hand-drawn map to create the beautiful final version. I could not have asked for a better artist to work with.

Mel, my fellow causer of chaos and to whom every use of "foxed" is dedicated, not only did you provide stellar comments and feedback for multiple drafts, but you also listened to the endless thoughts I had while drafting. When I asked how devastating a scene should be, you didn't hesitate to respond with resounding eagerness. Thank you, and apologies to the readers.

Maegan, my longtime friend, you rooted for Nox and Hadrien in their earliest stages. Casey, Kaite, and Rochelle, thank you for the enthusiasm and support, and to all of The Mighty Pens, I appreciate each of you and the community we've built. Of course, a huge thank you to the amazing Susan Dennard and Kat Brauer, without whom there would be no Mighty Pens.

Sooz, thank you for your mentorship and guidance over the years in the realms of writing and careers (and even video games, though I sank arguably too many hours into *Dragon Age)*. I know my concept of storytelling would not be where it is today without your advice and willingness to share your own writing journey.

Vanessa, I can't even count the number of times over the years we've wandered through bookstores with cups of tea in hand. For the absolute better, you shaped my reading and writing tastes. I owe you a vampire book (and Kerbey Lane waffles).

To the friends, new and old alike, online and offline, thank you for the good times. From coffee chats to late nights gaming to endless music recommendations, it was all memorable. Good friends are worth the world.

To the authors—Sooz, Megan Bontrager, R.M. Gray, M.K. Lobb, Allison Saft, V.E. Schwab, and many more—who share their own writing journeys and offer advice, thank you.

I would be remiss if I did not mention those in academia who had an impact on my writing journey. I had the sheer honor and joy of learning from the listed professors and faculty in a manner of subjects, and while this novel may not relate directly to the contents of their classes, they cultivated my interest in studies. Ultimately, my interest in learning feeds into my storytelling, and so I'd like to thank the following:

- Dr. Carol Blosser
- Dr. Robert Boenig
- Dr. Deborah Carlson
- Dr. Federica Ciccolella

- Dr. Erik Hermans
- Dr. Craig Kallendorf
- Dr. Christoph Konrad
- Mr. Isaac Middelmann
- Mrs. Fran Rader
- Dr. Stephen Riegg
- Dr. David Rosenberg
- Dr. Adam Rosenthal
- Dr. Christina Swan
- Dr. Lowell White

Though WOLF ROTTEN is a largely different story (a different beast, you could say) than my Honors Capstone in university, I want to extend my gratitude to my advising team: Mr. Dustin Kemp, Dr. Adam Rosenthal, and Dr. Lowell White.

To my parents, who supported my habit of buying too many books for far too long, thank you for the unending support, the long chats while I talked about one book or another, and one notable thirteen-hour drive to Colorado to attend a book event.

To my brother, thank you for all the time we spent paused on *Elden Ring* while I wrote the first draft of this book. Too many hours were lost waiting at sites of grace as I typed the next paragraph or two in the story. We did beat the game eventually, and maybe by the time you read this, we'll have completed the DLC.

I always say I'm fueled by tea and music, so thank you to CoffeePeople for the top-tier London Fogs and good vibes. On the music front, my thanks to the artists I listened to during drafting and editing: Bring Me The Horizon, Muse, The Antlers, Thousand Below, Two

Steps From Hell, and more video game OSTs than I can list.

To the horses, the dogs, and the cats that are so much more well-behaved than any of their fictional counterparts, my eternal love and thanks. (Even if the current cats tasked with overseeing writing are closer to goblins than felines. But what's a writer without a pet to hinder the process at times?)

To close us out: you, the reader. Whether you are finding WOLF ROTTEN soon after release or years later, thank you for picking this up and taking a chance on a new story. I hope you found some solace within the pages.

Asteria Gonzalez

Ever fond of history and archaeology, Asteria writes stories that build off her knowledge and embrace the fantastical. After a BA in Classics, she earned her MBA for all things numbers and is working on her MA in Classical Studies. When she is not trekking through fields of Excel spreadsheets, she haunts her local bookstore with a cup of London Fog or entertains her two goblin cats.

Wolf Rotten is her first published novel.

www.ingramcontent.com/pod-product-compliance
Lightning Source LLC
Chambersburg PA
CBHW020901060726
47591CB00004B/1028